Kayla Perrin has been writing since the age of thirteen. She is a *USA TODAY* bestselling author of dozens of mainstream and romance novels and has been recognised for her talent, including having twice won the Romance Writers of America's Top Ten Favourite Books of the Year Award. She has also won the Career Achievement Award for Multicultural Romance from *RT Book Reviews*. Kayla lives with her daughter in Ontario, Canada. Visit her at authorkaylaperrin.com

Rachel Lee was hooked on writing by the age of twelve and practised her craft as she moved from place to place all over the United States. This *New York Times* bestselling author now resides in Florida and has the joy of writing full-time.

Discover more at millsandboon.co.uk

COLD CASE SUSPECT

KAYLA PERRIN

CONARD COUNTY PROTECTOR

RACHEL LEE

MILLS & BOON

First Published in Great Britain 2022
by Mills & Boon, an imprint of HarperCollins*Publishers* Ltd
1 London Bridge Street, London, SE1 9GF

www.harpercollins.co.uk

HarperCollins*Publishers*
1st Floor, Watermarque Building,
Ringsend Road, Dublin 4, Ireland

Cold Case Suspect © 2022 Kayla Perrin
*Conard County Protecto*r © 2022 Susan Civil-Brown

ISBN: 978-0-263-30356-8

0822

MIX
Paper from
responsible sources

FSC™ C007454

This book is produced from independently certified FSC™ paper to ensure responsible forest management.

For more information visit: www.harpercollins.co.uk/green

Printed and Bound in Spain using 100% Renewable electricity at CPI Black Print, Barcelona

COLD CASE SUSPECT

KAYLA PERRIN

Chapter One

Shayla Phillips gripped the steering wheel harder, wondering if the black SUV behind her was actually following her.

You can't escape what you did forever. If you dare to show your face in Sheridan Falls again, you're going to DIE. It's time you pay for what you did!

The email threat she'd received just last week was permanently etched in her mind. She knew that returning home to Sheridan Falls posed a risk. But surely no one would know that she was heading to Sheridan Falls *right now*, would they? She had driven up the east coast from South Florida and was now heading west along the I-90. She was close enough to home that she *could* be being followed, even though that was unlikely. But the black SUV had been behind her for at least ten minutes, and that was making her wary.

Was it someone from her past who had noticed the Florida license plate? Someone who knew that she was heading back home because of her mother's illness? Or was she being exceptionally paranoid, seeing a threat where there wasn't one?

Stop freaking out, she told herself, drawing in a deep,

steadying breath. *Of course you're being paranoid. No one from Sheridan Falls could know where you are right now.*

Returning her gaze to the road in front of her, Shayla saw the sign indicating that she was entering the city limits. The ominous message she'd received via her store's email had her tightening her grip on the steering wheel again. Was she risking her life by returning to the town where she'd grown up? Or was the message—like so many others sent to her over the past nine years—one simply meant to rile her? Make her emotionally suffer for the perceived wrongs she had done?

Shayla couldn't be sure. She only knew that returning to Sheridan Falls was the last thing she wanted to do, but given her mother's grave health diagnosis, she had no choice.

It had been eight and a half years since she'd left, but the familiar landscape was etched into her memory. The sprawling farmers' fields on the left side of the interstate. The thicket of trees on the right. Within ten minutes, she'd be in the center of town.

The memories of the long-ago night that Shayla had hoped to forget came flooding back. How she'd been on the verge of tears when she'd driven up to Lucas Carr's house. How angry Hayley had been at her. Her decision to skip the party because she was in no mood to hang out anymore. Jonathan antsy, irritated at the bickering between her and Hayley, just wanting to get to the party already. Hayley throwing her an angry look over her shoulder as she'd jumped out of the car. Shayla driving off in a huff of steaming tears, both furious and hurt that her friend was still so upset about that stupid dance competition.

And then the next day came the unbelievable news that Hayley and Jonathan were both dead. Their bodies found in a field behind the high school. Two bullets silencing the young teenagers' lives forever.

Tears began to well in Shayla's eyes as they always did when she thought of that horrible day. "Stop. Don't go there. It wasn't your fault."

And it wasn't. She knew that. And yet no one believed her. Not after the news that she had dropped Hayley and Jonathan off at Lucas's place for the party and she herself hadn't attended. To anyone who'd heard the story, it was obvious that Shayla hadn't attended the party because she'd known that Lucas was going to kill Hayley. And why? Because Shayla and Hayley had been fighting over the regional dance competition. As if Shayla cared to lose her best friend over something stupid like that.

That was why she was even more hurt over the fact that Hayley had let the competition come between them. Hayley, consumed with jealousy, had been enraged that she hadn't secured a spot. What was Shayla supposed to do? It wasn't her fault that the judges had scored her higher. It wasn't her fault that Hayley had been nauseous that day. If Hayley had made the regionals and she hadn't, Shayla would have been happy for her. Disappointed over her own failure, yes, but not mad at a friend over something that neither of them could control.

It was absurd that Shayla would want to see her best friend killed over something so trivial, even if Hayley had been irrationally mad at her. But Lucas had had a reputation for being a bad boy, which was why he was living with his aunt and uncle in Sheridan Falls in the first place, and it had been easy for everyone to assume that Lucas had gone to the dramatic lengths of murder to keep Shayla happy.

The rumors didn't have one ounce of truth to them, but the people of Sheridan Falls didn't care to see things sensibly. Some people loved small towns, but Shayla hated them. Hated that, no matter where she went, someone was looking at her. No matter what she said in her own defense, people believed what they wanted to. In coffee shops and on street corners everywhere, she had been the topic of discussion after the murders—with the theories about her taking a worse turn every time the story was retold.

Shayla hadn't even been able to grieve the loss of her friend without the scorn of the people in Sheridan Falls. In a town where often the worst news of the day was who had burned their apple pie, a real-life double murder had consumed the townsfolk and they had come after her like piranhas devouring their prey.

Shayla glanced in the rearview mirror. The black SUV was still behind her. Maybe someone *was* following her?

She indicated and went into the right lane. So did the SUV.

Shayla's breathing began to accelerate. Surely no one from Sheridan Falls would know where she was right now. Unless someone had happened upon her on the highway and seen her Florida plates. Everyone knew she'd moved to Florida. Dazzle Dance Designs, the store she'd set up there to sell dance costumes and accessories, had even been burned to the ground—by someone from her past, she was sure.

Shayla pressed her foot on the gas, accelerating as she neared her exit. The SUV behind her sped up as well.

"I'm in the right lane," she grumbled. "Just pass me already."

Shayla tried to see into the SUV's front window, but it was tinted and she couldn't see who was driving. She looked ahead just as she was coming up to the ramp for her exit, which she took faster than anticipated. She had to clutch the steering wheel and pump the brakes so that she didn't careen into the guardrail.

The SUV stayed on the highway.

Shayla exhaled sharply. What was wrong with her? Why had she let herself get so worked up? It didn't make sense that anyone would be following her. No one knew the time and the date that she was heading back to her hometown.

As she exited the off-ramp and onto Main Street, she looked out at the landscape. It had changed a little bit. On the left side of the road, there was now a strip mall where there'd once been a farmer's field. And beside it, a new restaurant, an all-day breakfast joint. It was a perfect spot to cater to hungry travelers and give them an opportunity to spend some money between the restaurant and the shops. On the right side of the road, there were still fields as far as the eye could see.

Shayla pulled her car into the restaurant's parking lot, which was her destination. Then she called her cousin, Deedee.

"Hey, Shayla," Deedee answered warmly. "Are you here?"

"Just got off the highway. I'm in the parking lot of 24-Hour Breakfast and More."

"Perfect. Oh, I see you. Come on in, cuz!"

A smile touched Shayla's lips as she gathered her purse and exited her vehicle. It had been years since she'd seen her cousin, and she was looking forward to giving her a big hug.

Deedee was waiting just inside the restaurant doors as Shayla entered. She hadn't aged a day in five years, but she'd put on probably ten pounds, giving her a more robust figure, especially for her five-foot-two-inch height. Her black hair was styled in thin braids and pulled into a bun high on her head. Deedee's complexion, a warm chestnut brown, was flawless. A bit of burgundy gloss and mascara was all the makeup she needed.

Her welcoming smile melted away the rest of the unease Shayla had been feeling about returning to Sheridan Falls.

"Shayla!"

Shayla walked into her cousin's open arms, and the two swayed their bodies as they hugged for several seconds.

"Five years," Shayla mused as they pulled apart. "I can't believe it's been that long."

"And you made me go to Miami in order to see you," Deedee chastised playfully.

Shayla glanced downward before meeting her cousin's eyes again. "And I appreciate that. I know you prefer to be a homebody."

Deedee was a nervous flyer, and generally freaked out when stepping out of her comfort zone. At amusement parks, she preferred to watch the shows and skip the rides—except the merry-go-round.

"It was a fun trip," Deedee said, "but, whew, if I never step foot on another plane again, it'll be too soon."

"After everything, you know that it was easier for me to stay away."

"I know," Deedee said softly.

"You could have come back to see me over the years," Shayla said. "Driven down, of course. I think you enjoyed yourself much more than you thought you would when you came to Florida." And, at least in Miami, no one was specifically watching her every move, waiting for a chance to hurt her...

"I did love visiting you in Miami, but there were too many people for me. Too much traffic. I felt claustrophobic."

"You liked the beach though, didn't you?"

Deedee nodded. "Yes, the Atlantic ocean was gorgeous. But the lake here is far more peaceful. Without the threat of sharks."

Shayla threw her head back and laughed. "You never fail to make me laugh."

Deedee had tried to make light of her fear over sharks, but Shayla had known that she wasn't joking. She remembered her cousin dipping her toes into the warm, blue waters of the ocean while eyeing the deeper waters with a hint of fear. "You promise I won't get eaten by a shark?" she'd asked.

While Shayla swam and enjoyed the water, Deedee had been far more cautious, and Shayla knew that she hadn't enjoyed the experience as much as she should. Most of the time, she preferred to stay on the beach, claiming she was happy just taking in some sun. Shayla knew that her cousin had let her fears get the best of her.

"Anyway, come on in." Deedee grabbed a menu. "Have a seat right here." She placed the menu at the first booth. The restaurant was about seventy percent filled. It was definitely in a great spot right off the highway, and no doubt did good business. That's why Deedee had invested in this property, after all.

"Can I grab you a coffee or a tea?"

"I'd love a coffee," Shayla answered. "Cream and sugar."

"I'll be right back."

Shayla glanced around the restaurant as she took a seat in the booth. Most of the faces she didn't recognize. But there were a few familiar ones. Tammy Taylor seated with John Hetrick. They'd been a couple in high school, and the toddler in the high chair beside them had Shayla realizing that Tammy and John must have gotten married.

Deedee returned with the cup of coffee, the sugar and creamers on the side. "Have you had a chance to check out the menu?"

"Gosh, not yet," Shayla said. "But I assume you have some sort of home fries and scrambled eggs?"

"That comes with three pancakes as well."

"Okay by me," Shayla told her. "I'll take the works."

"The works it is. You've gotten way too thin."

Deedee was right. Stress did that to a person.

As her cousin ambled away from the table again, Shayla looked in Tammy's direction. Saw that Tammy was staring at her. Shayla offered a small smile, but Tammy didn't return it.

Shayla looked away, then played with her phone to pass the time. She checked emails and then spent some time browsing social media. She sent a text to her mother to let her know that she'd be at her place very soon.

"Here you go!" Deedee said in a cheerful voice several minutes later.

Shayla looked up to see her cousin placing the plate of scrambled eggs, home fries and a stack of pancakes on the table. She would never be able to eat all of this, but she welcomed it nonetheless. "Thank you, Deedee. This looks and smells amazing."

Deedee slipped into the seat opposite her. "How do you feel being back?"

Shayla swallowed a mouthful of scrambled eggs before speaking. "Well, it feels strange. It's been so long. Like I'm a stranger, yet also at home." She lowered her voice and added, "I saw Tammy Taylor over there. I smiled at her, but she just gave me a stony look."

"I know people here have long memories, but I think everyone will calm down once they hear you're back. Tammy's probably more surprised than anything."

"You're probably right," Shayla agreed. "But you know I told you that I got that email from someone. Basically threatening to harm me if I came back to Sheridan Falls. I assume it's someone who knows my mom is sick and would expect me to be returning."

Deedee's lips twisted with concern. "I'm sure it's just someone trying to be a pain in your butt."

"That's what I want to think but… It does give me pause. As I was heading to the Main Street exit, there was this black SUV that seemed to be following me. If

I switched lanes, it switched lanes too. I literally started to panic. But then I got off at my exit and the black SUV kept going."

"See?" Deedee said, and reached across the table to squeeze her hand reassuringly. "It's just nerves. I understand, it's gotta be difficult being back here after so much time. And after…everything."

"Yeah." Shayla sipped her coffee. "I guess I'm just stressed about being back here, hoping that people still don't hate me as much as they did after Hayley and Jonathan were killed."

Deedee nodded. "You know, it does worry me that you still get threats after all this time. I was thinking about something, so hear me out. I think you should consider hiring a bodyguard."

Shayla chuckled, as if the idea were absurd. "A bodyguard?" She shook her head. "No."

"Like I said, hear me out. Tavis Saunders, you remember him?"

At the mention of his name, Shayla's heart stuttered. How could she forget Tavis? He had been three years her senior, and Shayla had been secretly crazy about him. Tall, beautiful brown complexion, a smile that could tempt any woman. Of course, he never looked at her as anything more than Hayley's friend—he'd been Hayley's older cousin. And after Hayley's death, he had hated her just like everyone else.

"Of course I remember him," Shayla said.

"Well, guess what? He's a bodyguard now. He used to be a cop for a bit, now he's got an agency where he protects people."

"Really?" That surprised Shayla. But she wasn't entirely sure why. He'd loved football. She'd assumed he might end up playing professionally or maybe coaching. But once she had left Sheridan Falls, she hadn't talked to him again or tried to find him online. Nor anyone else for that matter, except her few closest friends and her cousin.

"Yep," Deedee said. "So he's someone you know, he's from this town, so he knows the people, and I think you should hire him just to be on the safe side."

"I thought you just said you didn't think the threats were real."

"I want to believe they're not real. But why take any chances? With someone like Tavis, you can be protected twenty-four-seven."

The very thought made Shayla's pulse race. But with desire or fear? She remembered how she had run into Tavis's arms after the murders, hoping for comfort. And for a few glorious seconds, she had felt safe in his arms. But as he'd pulled apart from her, the look on his face had been unforgettable. Confusion, hurt and anger all mixed together. "People are saying you had something to do with this."

"What?" Shayla had been stunned to hear him say that. "You know that's not true. How could you even say that? Hayley was my best friend."

"Where's Lucas?" he had asked. His expression had been hard. Unwavering.

"If I knew where Lucas was, I would tell you. But I really don't think he had anything to do with this."

"He just disappears after Hayley and Jonathan were at his party? Come on, you're his girlfriend. You have to know where he is. Please, do the right thing and tell me."

But Shayla hadn't, and no matter what she had said, Tavis hadn't believed her. Just like the rest of the townsfolk.

"No," Shayla said. "I'm definitely not hiring a bodyguard. Especially not Tavis."

"I don't think you should dismiss the idea, but obviously it's your choice."

Shayla nodded. Then Deedee rose from the table. "I'll

let you eat your food. I'm going to make the rounds, check on the customers."

"Thanks again."

Deedee smiled at her. "Of course. You're family. I'm always here for you."

Her cousin's words reassured her and helped her feel better about being back in town. Shayla then dug into the meal in earnest, eating most of the scrambled eggs, the home fries and one of the pancakes. When she was finished, she was stuffed.

She was sipping the last of her coffee when she saw Tammy and John heading toward the exit with their son. Tammy definitely made eye contact with her, and once again Shayla offered her a smile.

"Shayla," Tammy said, her tone unreadable. "You're back in town."

"Yeah," Shayla said. "I'm not sure if you heard, but my mother is sick."

"Yeah, I did hear. I'm sorry about that."

Shayla felt the tension in her shoulders relaxing. Tammy was being cordial.

"Of course, the stress you put her through over the years certainly hasn't helped her health."

The words were like a dagger in Shayla's heart. She didn't even know how to respond.

"She's stronger than most women," Tammy went on. "I do hope she pulls through."

"Thank you," Shayla said, her tone clipped.

"I hope you don't plan on going to the vigil this week," Tammy continued. "If you have any respect for the victims' families, you'll stay away."

"Tammy, I'm not here to make anyone feel—"

Shayla's words died in her throat when she saw the swift action of Tammy's hand scooping up the water glass.

And the next thing she knew, cold water was hitting her in the face.

Shayla gasped. She heard others in the restaurant do the same.

"You've hurt enough people in this town," Tammy said. "No one wants you back here."

"That's enough," John said to Tammy. "Let's go."

And then Tammy hustled through the door with John and their son, leaving Shayla sitting at the table, embarrassed and crushed.

Chapter Two

Deedee rushed over to Shayla's booth the moment Tammy and John stepped out of the restaurant. "Oh my goodness! Shayla, are you okay?"

Dabbing at her face with a paper napkin, Shayla looked up at her cousin. "Yeah. I'll live. I guess this is what I should have expected coming back to town. No one is going to be happy to see me."

Deedee passed her more napkins from the adjoining booth, then also began to wipe off the table. "*I'm* happy to see you. Your mother's going to be happy to see you. There are others who will be happy to see you too. Tammy was close with Hayley—she's never gotten over the murder."

"And I am the number one hated person when it comes to that." Sometimes it seemed as though people hated her more than they even did Lucas, the one who had committed the crimes.

Shayla blew out a frazzled breath then fiddled with a strand of her shoulder-length curly hair. It was wet now, and it would frizz, but at least she wasn't heading anywhere after this where she needed to look great. And if she could convince her mother to relocate for treatment, she wouldn't even have to stay in this town for long.

Deedee wiped off the seat on the opposite side of the booth, then slipped onto it. "Look, you might want to rethink hiring Tavis. I mean, I know Tammy didn't physically strike you, but if others are going to get any crazy ideas to come and accost you… I think that having Tavis around will be a good idea."

Shayla nodded, but didn't actually voice an agreement to the suggestion. She didn't need to tell her cousin that she could never hire Tavis. Maybe it was silly, but the crush that she'd had on him had been real, and the disappointment after he had seen her through the same lens as the other people in this town had been too hard to endure. Sure, that was a long time ago, but she didn't feel like spending day and night with a man who couldn't stand her.

And right now, she didn't want to have that discussion with Deedee. She wanted to get out of there and head to her mother's place. That was most important.

But she was curious about one thing. "Tammy mentioned something about a vigil?"

"Yeah, there's a vigil every year. Didn't I tell you that?"

"On the anniversary of the deaths," Shayla said. "Of course. In four days. I didn't realize the vigils were still happening now."

"People say they'll have the vigils every year until the killer is brought to justice."

What had happened to Lucas? Shayla wondered. If she knew where he was, she would serve him up on a silver platter so that everyone in the town could finally get the closure they wanted—herself included.

Four days from now would mark the nine-year anniversary of the murders. The date was forever etched in her mind. Beginning of June, right after the school year had ended. Everyone had been happy to start summer break, their last summer together before they would head off to college or other post-graduate pursuits. It had been a time of hope and promise that had been tragically cut short for all of them.

"People get together at the high school, send up balloons, hold candles. Pray." Deedee paused. "Don't think you have to go just because you're in town."

"Hayley was my best friend."

"But if someone's upset with you... And the first one you went to nine years ago didn't end well."

It hadn't, because Hayley's and Jonathan's families had accosted her for being there. Their words had been ugly, and they had ultimately forced her away.

Now, Shayla steeled her shoulders. So much she had endured. Tammy's unexpected assault had had her feeling sorry for herself for a moment and questioning why she'd come back. But she needed to remember that she had nothing to feel guilty for. She might not like being here, and the people of Sheridan Falls might not want her here, but she needed to hold her head high knowing that she'd had nothing to do with what had happened to Hayley and Jonathan. There was no need for her to slink away and hide.

"I'll see how I feel on the day," Shayla explained. "If I do go, I'll stay at the back of the crowd." She shrugged. "I don't know. What I do know is that I need to get to my mother right now. See how she's doing. It's been way too long."

"Of course," Deedee agreed. "Call me later."

In the car, Shayla had even more resolve to face this town with the guts she hadn't had when she'd run away. Maybe by running she'd given them all more fodder to talk about.

It had been easier to leave because she hadn't been able to grieve the loss of Hayley and Jonathan or even to process all that had happened under the scrutinizing eyes of everyone in Sheridan Falls. The judgment had been too much for her, so she had taken off when she could, built a life for herself somewhere else far away.

But had it been a life? She had thrown herself into work,

had few friends and barely socialized. Except for one six-month relationship with Paul, the firefighter who'd gotten frustrated with her inability to open up, she had only dated a handful of times. She had always been too afraid to let anyone get close to her. And she'd constantly worried that someone would make good on any of the numerous threats on her life. So, for the first several months while she'd lived in Miami, she had looked over her shoulder everywhere she'd gone until she'd started to feel a modicum of peace and safety. The peace had lasted for a while—until the day her store had burned to the ground four years later.

She had adjusted, setting up a digital storefront, where she still moved a lot of product, not just in South Florida but across the country and even internationally. The world of dance was intense, with costumes and accessories in high demand. It was something she knew, so she'd found a way to make a living from it since she'd stopped competing after Hayley's death. She thought one day she could possibly coach, but she'd run even from that idea, preferring to live in her own small corner of the world where she felt she was safe.

As she headed to her mother's place, Shayla realized that the way she'd lived hadn't been much of a life at all.

She put those thoughts behind her as she neared Belmont Street. The street she had grown up on.

She turned right and, within moments, was at number fifteen. Her house. It would always be her house, wouldn't it? The place she grew up never ceased being home.

She exited the car, straightened her shoulders in case any neighbors were watching, and headed up the driveway and then the front steps. Though this was still technically her house, she rang the doorbell. The nurse was expecting her and it seemed better that she announce her presence rather than just use her key to get in.

Less than a minute later, the door opened. The dark-haired woman greeted Shayla with a warm smile, her blue eyes brightening. "You must be Shayla."

"And you must be Jennifer."

"I am," Jennifer said, holding the door open wide. She was wearing royal blue nursing scrubs that complemented her eyes.

Shayla stepped into the house. Her eyes roamed over the place that had been her home for the first eighteen years of her life. Not much had changed. Her mother's sprawling houseplant was still growing along the wall, though its leaves and stems stretched farther now, over the piano. The sofas were the same, with the floral design that was outdated, but her mother had refreshed the ornament on the coffee table. It used to be home to a horse sculpture, but now there was a vase with fresh flowers. She wondered if that was the nurse's touch.

"How's my mother?" Shayla asked, sadness pulling at her heart. She wasn't looking forward to seeing her mother sick.

"She's awake now. This is the perfect time to go and see her."

Shayla nodded. "Thank you." She headed down the hallway, already knowing that her mother had been moved downstairs for her home care.

The main level den, having been converted to a bedroom to house her mother, made it more convenient to get her to the bathroom, and easier for the nursing staff in general.

The room looked completely different. There was a hospital-style bed on the far right, and some shelving set up on the left, where there were medical supplies, from what she could gather. The sofa was gone, but there was an armchair. The other belongings in the room had been put into boxes that were now placed against the back wall.

But Shayla quickly looked past all that and focused on her mother, whose eyes were closed. Had she fallen asleep?

She walked toward the bed quietly. "Mom?" she said softly. "Are you awake?"

Her mother's eyelids flitted open. And then a smile spread on her lips. Shayla's eyes moistened. Her mother had the same warm smile, but her body was much smaller than it used to be. It hurt to see her like this, knowing that cancer was ravaging her body.

Shayla stepped forward and took her mother's hands into hers. "Mom. I'm so sorry I haven't been here for you. Why didn't you tell me you were sick sooner?"

"I didn't want you to worry. I know you have your life in Miami."

"*You* are my life, Mom." Unfortunately, her mother had decided to keep her cancer diagnosis to herself. Maybe she'd been unable to face it, or maybe she'd thought she was protecting Shayla. But Shayla wished she'd learned about the colon cancer before it hit the fourth stage.

And before the cancer had spread to her liver and abdomen.

If only Mom had agreed to move to Miami with her. She knew her mother was stubborn, the type who believed that whatever was going to happen should happen. It didn't help that to some degree she was afraid of doctors. But she'd let her situation become too grave too quickly by ignoring the signs.

"How are you feeling?" Shayla asked her.

"I've been better." She closed her eyes as if in pain and then reopened them. "I'm getting meds for the pain. And you see I have an IV attached here for fluids. The nurse is taking good care of me."

Shayla didn't want to cry in front of her mother, but tears escaped her eyes nonetheless. She brushed them away. "I'm here now. Anything you need, I'm here. You're going to get through this. Okay? *We* are."

Her mother merely squeezed Shayla's hand tighter. Shayla didn't know how her mom felt about fighting. It had to have been devastating to have received a cancer diagnosis. And she'd heard that chemotherapy made you sicker before you got better. Did her mother believe she was going to pull through, or did she think this was the end?

Shayla could not, and would not, accept that this was the end for her mother. As long as she was here, she was going to fight and help Mom fight. Maybe what she needed was her daughter in her life to show her she had more to live for.

"I'm gonna get my stuff from the car, get settled in. But if you need me, let the nurse know. I'll be here for you anytime you want me. Always."

"I know, sweetheart. You go on and get your things and get settled in. We'll catch up a bit later."

As Shayla left the room, the tears hit her full force. Seeing her mother having lost at least twenty pounds was crushing. Her mom had always been strong, independent, and had raised her fearlessly when her father had abandoned them both. Life wasn't fair, that was for sure. But Shayla was going to do whatever it took to help her mother get through this. She refused to believe this was the end.

Jennifer was standing in the hallway, her arms crossed over her chest and a sympathetic expression on her face.

"Thank you so much for being here for my mother," Shayla said. "I really appreciate it."

"No problem," Jennifer told her. "I'm happy to be here, happy to help."

"You must think I'm a bad daughter. I've been away for so long. But I didn't know the extent of what my mother was going through. I guess she wanted to protect me."

"That's exactly what she was doing. And I don't judge you. Your mother speaks so highly of you."

The words filled Shayla with pride. "That's nice to hear."

"Um," Jennifer hedged, "do you mind if I say something?"

"Sure. What's on your mind?"

"I know this might be a touchy subject, but I just wanted to say that from all of my interactions with you on the phone, and talking to your cousin and your mother, I don't believe that you had anything to do with what happened to your friend and her boyfriend nine years ago."

Somehow, Shayla managed to stop herself from reeling backward at the statement. That wasn't what she'd expected. The nurse didn't even know her. Why would she broach this topic?

"I'm sorry if I'm stepping out of line here, but this is a small town and everybody knows what happened. When I first got the job taking care of your mother, a couple of the neighbors talked to me and made me aware of what went on. And… I'm sorry, I've offended you."

"No," Shayla said, though she wasn't being completely honest. "But I am confused."

"I guess I figured I should just put it out there, let you know that I heard some of the rumors, but I don't believe them at all."

"As long as you're here for my mother and doing the best for her, that's what matters."

"Of course," Jennifer agreed. "We don't have to talk about this again."

"I'm going to go to my car, get my stuff," Shayla said, then walked past Jennifer and headed outside.

Why on earth had the nurse brought that up? Though she did understand that this was a small town and people talked, and maybe the nurse felt she was being supportive in some odd sort of way. Instead, her comments were intrusive, but Shayla was going to let it slide. She'd meant what she'd said. As long as the nurse was taking care of her mother, that's what mattered.

Shayla retrieved her suitcase and small travel bag from the car and returned to the house. She headed upstairs to her bedroom, pausing a moment before she opened the door. It had been so long…

She opened the door and peered inside. The room looked exactly as it had the day she'd left. The pink-and-blue comforter on the bed. The giant stuffed bear Lucas had given her propped up against the pillows. The photos on the walls of her in various dance outfits, either in the middle of a dance routine or posing with a trophy. Some photos of her and Hayley laughing and being silly.

It was almost eerie seeing everything as she'd left it. As if time had stood still in this room while the rest of the world had moved on.

Shayla stepped into the room with her belongings and closed the door. Her Sheridan Falls High letter jacket was still hanging on a hook behind the door, just where she'd left it. She had loved that jacket, but after the murders, she hadn't wanted any reminder of her high school days, so she'd left it behind when she'd taken off for Florida.

She stroked the red leather now, remembering all the sports she and Hayley had been involved in during high school. Dance, soccer, track, the swim team. They'd been overachievers when it came to sports, mostly because being involved in different activities kept them in shape for dance, their greatest love.

Shayla brought her bags to the foot of her bed. Again, she looked at the giant stuffed teddy bear. Lucas had given it to her the week before the murders, after they'd been dating for a month. Why she'd kept it, she didn't know.

She'd just left it behind, along with other things she hadn't wanted to pack for her new life.

She went over to the teddy bear now and scooped it up. Then she tossed it into her closet where she wouldn't have to see it again.

Home, she thought as she returned to the bed and bounced on the soft mattress. It had taken nearly nine years, but she was finally home.

"I'M BORED OUT of my mind here, Tavis," Griffin Woodward said. "All this girl wants to do is go from one high-end store to the next, buying makeup and dresses, and God knows what. Days like this, I could just shoot myself."

Tavis chuckled into the phone. "She's paying a pretty penny, remember that."

"I know," Griffin said, "which is why I haven't cocked my gun yet. I don't think there's any real threat to this girl. She probably just wants the prestige of having a bodyguard following her around."

"Which is fine by me," Tavis said. Sure, he enjoyed the adrenaline rush that came from a high-stakes case where there was tangible danger, but he preferred cases where there was no actual threat. Socialites who weren't in any real danger paid the bills just as much as celebrities who worried about stalkers.

Of course, with his line of work—personal security— there was no guarantee that any detail would be without danger. Even the rich, who wanted protection where there was no specific threat, could have angry people who wanted to hurt them. Enemies came in all forms, from jaded business partners to jealous peers, to bitter exes bent on doing harm. Tavis was prepared for all of that, and enjoyed performing the services of being a bodyguard for a myriad of people.

At least as the owner of his own company, he got to

make all the rules. Unlike when he had worked for the Buffalo Police Department.

"Oh, got to go," Griffin said. "She's heading out of the store now."

"Update me if there's anything exciting," Tavis told him, a hint of humor in his voice.

"I doubt that, but yeah, I'll talk to you later."

Tavis was glad to hear that. He wanted an uneventful day.

As the sole proprietor of Forged in Steel Protection Services, he had two guys who worked for him. Griffin Woodward and Lenny Pinter. Lenny was currently out of town, providing protection services to a businessman at a convention. With a new and innovative product the man wanted to launch, he was worried about competitors who might pose a problem for him. But so far, there had been nothing eventful. Uneventful was always preferable.

Tavis's phone rang and he glanced at the screen. It was a number he didn't recognize with a prefix from Sheridan Falls. "Forged in Steel Protection Services."

"Tavis?"

"Yes, this is he."

"Hi, this is Deedee McKenzie. Shayla's cousin."

"Yes, of course. How are you?"

"I'm doing okay," she told him. "But I'm calling about Shayla."

Tavis rubbed the back of his neck. "Is she all right?"

"She just got back to town and I'm a bit worried about her. I've asked her to call you to see if she can secure your services. As you know, many people here don't like her, and I'm worried someone might want to hurt her."

Tavis rose from the chair where he was sitting in his home office. "What's going on?"

"She got a threat not too long ago. Someone who told her that if she returns to Sheridan Falls, she's going to be killed."

Tavis frowned, dragging a hand over his shortly cropped hair. He knew that after the murders years ago, Shayla had gotten several death threats. People in Sheridan Falls had been angry that two young people had been killed—understandably so—and with Lucas Carr on the lam, all of their anger had been directed at Shayla.

"Was it a phone call, email, something on social media?" Tavis asked.

"Email," Deedee answered.

Nine years later, and people were still threatening her. No wonder she'd left Sheridan Falls. Tavis himself felt a modicum of guilt over how he'd treated her in the wake of his cousin Hayley's death. He had firmly believed that Shayla had been hiding information about Lucas, despite her protests. It had just never made sense to him that she hadn't gone to the party that night. While he didn't think she'd asked Lucas to kill Hayley and Jonathan, he had been fairly certain that she'd known more about Lucas's whereabouts than she had admitted.

"You think the threat is credible?" Tavis asked.

"I've been telling her that I don't think the threats are real, but maybe that's just wishful thinking. She stopped by my restaurant for a bite to eat when she got back to town, and Tammy Hetrick was here. She had a few words with her and then threw a glass of water in her face. It hit me then that, despite the time that's passed, there are some people here who are still very, very angry with Shayla."

Tavis remembered that Tammy had been great friends with Hayley, but she'd also been friends with Shayla. Throwing water in her face, while not something that would physically hurt her, was still an attack.

"Have you asked her to call me? I happen to be available right now. I've got time. I can do the job."

"That's the problem," Deedee said. "I suggested that she hire you, but she's completely against the idea. She doesn't think she needs protection. You might remember, Shayla can be very stubborn."

"If she doesn't want to hire me, it's going to be pretty hard to protect her."

"I guess I just wanted to know if you're available, and I'm hoping I can convince her to call you in the next couple of days at least. Or…maybe you can drop by and see her? She's at her mom's place."

Should he drop by and pay her a visit? The idea gave him pause. He remembered the last time he had seen Shayla, and how their interaction had gone. She'd been devastated when he had pleaded with her to tell him where Lucas was. He could still remember the look in her eyes, the disbelief that he would even ask her that. He didn't know if stopping by to see her was a good idea.

"How's her mom doing?"

"Honestly, she's not really doing well. A few weeks ago, she was up and active. Then suddenly she got very weak. The doctors have told her that the chemo isn't working anymore. The cancer is eating her away."

"Man, I'm sorry to hear that."

"Thanks. She has nursing staff with her twenty-four-seven, but now that Shayla's back, she wants to be the one taking care of her mother most of the time. A nurse will still come by during the day, but Shayla intends to spend some quality alone time with her mom."

"That's understandable."

"Anyway," Deedee said, "I wanted to give you a heads-up, let you know what's going on, and hopefully my cousin will reach out to you."

"If she does, I'll be ready."

BY THE NEXT MORNING, Tavis hadn't heard from Shayla. Not that he had expected to, but Deedee's call had stayed with him throughout the night. The anniversary of the murders was coming up in just a couple of days, and because of that, tensions were probably high. The fact that someone was still threatening Shayla so many years later had him concerned. He was inclined to think the threat was real. Or, at least, should be taken seriously.

He decided to head over to her mom's place. He would take Shayla for coffee, and the two could talk. He hoped to penetrate her stubbornness and make her see reason.

Though Tavis had worked for the police department and founded his protection agency in the City of Buffalo, he still lived in Sheridan Falls. It wasn't a far trek to the city. Only thirty minutes outside downtown Buffalo without traffic, Sheridan Falls was a quieter area to live. Besides, Tavis had wanted to keep his roots in Sheridan Falls as he searched for clues to find Lucas.

It didn't take him long to get to Belmont Street. He drove slowly, and as his eyes wandered toward the Phillipses' house, they narrowed. Shayla was standing in the driveway, beside her vehicle. He could see her wide eyes even though he was around sixty feet away.

And then suddenly she turned and sprinted into the house, as if the devil himself were chasing her.

She hadn't seen him, had she? No, her gaze had been fixed on her windshield.

Tavis pulled to the curb and jumped out of his GMC Sierra. He surveyed his surroundings as he started up the driveway, searching for any visible threats. But it didn't take long for him to figure out what had spooked Shayla.

On the windshield of the car with Florida plates, he saw the words painted in white.

YOU WILL DIE.

Chapter Three

Shayla stood in the kitchen with her hands bracing the counter, her head reeling from the words painted on the windshield of her car.

YOU WILL DIE.

Who would have dared to put that there? And when?

The threat she had received just last week seemed far more real now. Not just someone trying to rattle her. Someone knew she was back in town, and they'd come to her mother's place to leave her a warning. This person clearly wasn't joking around.

Where was the nurse? Shayla had only started to head to her car because she'd wanted to pick up some cream, and Jennifer was running late. She hadn't even called to explain where she was. Shayla had sent her a text and gotten no reply.

The doorbell rang. It was probably Jennifer, and Shayla was irritated with her tardiness and lack of communication. She had a key. Why was she ringing the doorbell?

The doorbell rang again followed by a blurted "Shayla!"

That was a man's voice. A familiar voice...

"Shayla, open up. It's Tavis."

Tavis! Shock hit her like a punch to the gut. Why was he here?

But she quickly headed to the door, opened it, and as

she stared into the face of her one-time crush, she felt an odd rush of sensation. Medium brown complexion, closely cropped hair. He looked the same, but different. The young man she'd once known had grown up. Eight and a half years ago, he had been tall and lanky. His once-thin frame had filled out with well-honed muscles. The once-boyish face now had a five-o'clock shadow, making him look a lot more mature. All of his new muscles were set in a six-foot-three-inch frame. The man was gorgeous.

Not that it mattered.

"Tavis," she said, hating how breathless she sounded. "What are you doing here?"

"Are you okay?" he asked. Then he looked over his shoulder at her car. "I saw you run into the house. When did that happen?"

Shayla exhaled sharply. "Come in."

She stepped backward, holding the door open, and Tavis entered the home. She led the way to the living room.

"Did you see anyone?" Tavis asked. "Hear anything?"

"No. I was heading to my car because I needed to run to the store to grab some cream for my coffee. The nurse is supposed to be here, I don't know where she is, so I was just going to run out for a moment while my mother is sleeping. And then I saw that written on my car. At first, I couldn't believe it. I thought my eyes were playing tricks on me. So I went closer... And saw that there really *was* a threat written on my windshield. It spooked me, so I turned around and ran back into the house."

Tavis cursed under his breath. "Deedee called me, told me that she thinks you could use a bodyguard."

"Oh, good grief. I'm sorry about that. I specifically told her that I didn't want a bodyguard."

"Actually, I'm glad she did. She was worried that calling me may be an overreaction on her part, but she figured why not be safe as opposed to sorry. Now you're in town for one day and you have a threat written on your car? Someone came to the house and put that on your car. I think you have to consider that this is a real threat, Shayla."

Shayla was momentarily taken aback by the way her name sounded on Tavis's lips. Maybe she was more rattled than she thought, because she wouldn't mind curling into his arms and having him hold her.

If he were the Tavis she'd known before the murders... But that Tavis had turned into someone else, someone angry and unforgiving where she was concerned.

"I guess it is," Shayla said. "But it's probably just someone else trying to scare me. I saw Tammy Taylor—Tammy Hetrick now—at Deedee's restaurant yesterday. She threw water in my face."

"Yeah," Tavis said. "Deedee told me."

"So I'm sure she got on the phone the moment she got home, or even before, and let everybody know that I was back. People know my mom is sick, and I'm sure they figured I would show up at some point. I just didn't expect that they would still hate me so much."

A moment of silence passed, then Tavis said, "I don't think everyone hates you. Obviously there are some people who have issues and haven't gotten over the murders—but that's because no one was ever brought to justice."

"How could anyone think that I would ever want to hurt Hayley?" she said in frustration, then clamped her lips shut. She didn't want to have this conversation with Tavis. Not now. Not after he had pretty much believed the worst about her as well nine years ago.

"How is your mother?" he asked softly.

"She's...not great," Shayla said, the words heavy in her throat. She didn't want to say what her heart didn't want to accept. "But I'm here now, and I'm going to help her get through this. I know I can."

The sound of the front door opening had both of them

turning in that direction. Jennifer breezed into the house, offering an apology.

"Where were you?" Shayla asked, sounding harsh. But she hadn't expected someone who was being paid to take care of her mother to not even respond to her calls and texts.

"I'm so sorry. My phone died, and I had a flat tire. I'm sorry. It won't happen again."

Shayla's anger softened. "You didn't have a charger in the car for your phone?"

"It broke. And I stupidly forgot to charge my phone last night." Jennifer held up a charger in a package. "I picked this up at the gas station once I got the spare tire put on. But I just raced here instead of calling as I was only a few minutes away."

Shayla wanted to be angry, but she found herself wondering why. Because of Jennifer's mess-up or because of anxiety? Lord knew that with the stress she was under, she wanted to lash out at someone.

"All right," Shayla said. "I'm glad you're here now and that you're safe."

"I'm really, really sorry," Jennifer reiterated. "Has your mother eaten yet?"

"No, she's been sleeping."

"Then I'll get to work on something for her to eat." She scooted past Tavis and Shayla, and went into the kitchen.

"I think you should call the police," Tavis said.

"Huh?" At first Shayla thought he was referring to the nurse, then caught on. "Oh, I don't think so."

"Why not?"

"Because… I don't want to make a bigger deal out of this than it is."

"A threat to your life is a big deal."

"Let me give it a couple of days. See if there's anything else." As Shayla looked at Tavis, she could see the disbelief in his eyes. He didn't understand why she wouldn't call the police. Shayla didn't know if it would make a difference calling the authorities. Would they be able to find out who'd actually done this? The person had probably been smart enough to wear gloves and not leave any prints. Besides, it was just one other thing for her to deal with now, and she had enough on her plate.

"So you haven't had coffee yet, based on the fact that you said you were heading out to get cream," Tavis said.

"No. Maybe that's why I'm extra cranky." She offered him a wry smile.

"Someone left a threat on your car. Of course you have a right to be cranky."

Shayla nodded as she folded her arms over her chest. He was right. But how concerned should she be? Was someone simply being a thorn in her side, trying to make her life miserable? She certainly hoped that was all it was.

"How about we go get a coffee together, talk for a bit? The nurse is here now. Is that okay?"

"I... I guess." Though sitting down and sharing coffee with Tavis wasn't exactly what she wanted to do. He probably felt a bit sorry for her, given what had happened, and she didn't want his pity.

"Honestly, you should be calling the police," he told her. "I know you don't want to, but this should be reported. Think about it. You can call later today, if you change your mind."

"Honestly, Tavis, it was probably just someone being an idiot." She was trying to convince Tavis of that fact as much as herself. "I'm used to this. Have been for nine years."

"You've still been getting threats all this time?" he asked.

"Not every day, but often enough. So, yeah, I'm used

to it. If I called the police every time I got a threat, they'd probably bounce all my calls to voicemail."

"This one was on your car," Tavis said. "It's different than an email threat. But it's your choice. Just think about it."

"One second," Shayla told him. Then she went to the kitchen, where she saw Jennifer peeling potatoes.

"Do you mind if I take off for a little bit? I'm gonna go get a coffee."

"Absolutely, go enjoy yourself. I'm here."

Shayla nodded. "Call me if there is any issue at all."

"I will."

Shayla was about to ask the nurse if she'd seen what had been scrawled on her car, but didn't bother. With Jennifer running late, she'd probably run right into the house and not even noticed.

"I'll see you later, then," Shayla told her. "Remember, call me if you need me."

"Take your time and enjoy your coffee," Jennifer said.

Shayla went back into the living room and smiled at Tavis. "All right. I'm ready to go."

No more than five minutes later, Tavis was pulling his vehicle into a spot in the center of town on Main Street, right in front of Molly's Café. He hopped out of the GMC Sierra, then went around and opened the passenger door for Shayla.

While he wasn't officially protecting her, he surveyed the area nonetheless before offering her a hand and helping her down from the vehicle. He saw Mr. and Mrs. Chen sauntering hand in hand, which they said they'd been doing for the past fifty years since they'd gotten married. A woman on the other side of the street was walking a golden retriever. A couple of teenage girls dressed almost identically strolled by with their fancy frozen-coffee drinks.

No threats that he could see.

"Molly's Café," Shayla said as she stepped onto the sidewalk. "Molly Baxter?"

"The one and only."

"In high school she always said she wanted to open a café," Shayla said. "Good for her."

Tavis opened the door, and the door chimes sang. The coffee shop was fairly full, and again he looked around to make sure that he didn't see any specific sign of a threat.

Not that he knew what he was looking for.

Almost every head turned in their direction. And then mouths opened and eyes widened as people saw who was entering.

Shayla.

Tavis had expected this. Nine years ago, Shayla had been the topic of discussion for several months, even after she'd left town. People were now looking at her as though they were seeing a ghost.

He looked over his shoulder to where she stood rooted in the doorway. "Come on," he said. Moving to stand beside her, he placed a gentle hand on the small of her back. "People will get over this in a moment."

He walked into the café, and Molly, who was behind the counter, looked at him and gave him a smile. Then her eyes wandered to Shayla and her entire face lit up.

"It seems at least one person doesn't hate me," Shayla muttered.

Tavis guided her to the line of customers, where two people were ahead of them: a man in a suit and a young woman scrolling through her social media feed. It took a few minutes to fill their orders before Tavis and Shayla stepped up to the counter.

"Hello, Tavis." Once again, Molly's eyes lit up as they landed on Shayla. "And is that really you, Shayla Phillips?"

"In the flesh," Shayla said, sounding pleasant.

"You've got to give me a hug, girl." Molly gestured for Shayla to lean across the counter. Tavis was shocked when he saw Molly heave her butt onto the polished black marble. But it was the only way to hug Shayla with the counter between them.

"It has been so long!" Molly said as she slid off the counter. "It's really good to see you again."

"It's really good to see you too," Shayla said. "I see you made your dream happen."

"Yep. Molly's Café." She sprayed down the counter and began wiping it. "I figure I drank so much coffee as a teen, I was destined to make a career out of it somehow." She chuckled. "My dad died the year after you left town. I used the money he left me to invest in this place."

"I love it," Shayla said.

"I was so sorry to hear about your mother," Molly said.

"Thank you. She's not doing that great, but I believe in keeping the faith until there's no more faith to be had."

"I agree with you. I'm praying for her. I'm sure all of the town is praying for her."

"Thank you. I do appreciate that."

Molly smiled again, her gaze volleying from Shayla to the lineup gathering behind her. "I'd better get your orders started. Tavis, I know you want a black coffee with two sugars."

"You know it. I keep it simple every day."

"Shayla, what can I get for you, hon?" Molly asked.

"I'd love a cappuccino. Caramel flavored," Shayla added, eyeing the menu on the back wall.

"One caramel cappuccino coming right up. You two go on and take a seat. I'll bring the coffees out to you."

Tavis paid then led Shayla through the coffee shop toward an available table near the back. The two-seater with plush chairs was by a window that faced State Street. He could feel the tenseness radiating from Shayla's body as she walked by each table, her gaze fixed forward despite the heads turning in her direction. And he couldn't blame her. The townsfolk in the coffee shop were blatantly staring as only people in small towns dared to do.

"I hate that everyone's looking at me like I don't belong here," Shayla said as she took a seat at the table.

Tavis took a seat across from her. "Ignore them. Like I said, people will get used to the fact that you're back before long. And life will go back to normal."

"Will it?" Shayla asked, a challenge in her voice. "It's been nine years and they haven't forgotten."

"You know how people are in this town. They will forget, trust me. They'll go back to their normal lives once they find something else worthy of talking about."

Shayla glanced down before meeting his gaze again. "I hope you're right."

"Molly was happy to see you. Not everyone here hates you."

"I guess not everyone." She opened her mouth as if she were about to say something else but then thought better of it.

"I know you're hesitant to hire me, but I want to let you know—"

"Tavis, why would you want to protect me?" Shayla said, interrupting him. "You don't even like me."

Her words hit him hard, at his core. He figured that was what she'd been about to say a moment earlier. It wasn't true, of course. He did like her. In fact, he'd always found her attractive, if a little young for him. Three years his junior had seemed like a world of difference back then. Now, of course, they were both adults…

Tavis quickly put a stop to that train of thinking, wondering why on earth that had even popped into his mind. Shayla was beautiful, with her bright brown eyes and long lashes, her thick head of curls and chocolate-colored skin.

There was an effortless sexiness about her. Even with no makeup and dressed casually, her beauty radiated. Clearly, it had been too long since he'd been with a woman that just being in Shayla's company had the direction of his thoughts heading where he hadn't expected.

"You think I don't like you?" he asked. "That's not true, Shayla. I've always liked you."

Molly arrived then, her smile wide as she placed their orders on the table. "One black coffee with two sugars and one caramel cappuccino."

"Thank you," Shayla and Tavis said in unison.

The moment Molly was out of earshot, Tavis continued. "We haven't been in touch since you left town, but I was always your friend."

"And you were angry with me," Shayla said. "You think I forget our last conversation? You were livid. You believed I was protecting Lucas. That was the moment you stopped liking me, Tavis."

"That's not true." Tavis was silent for a moment. He sipped his coffee. "Hayley had just been killed, and I wasn't sure if you knew more than you were saying. I realize now that I was hard on you. But I was only trying to get answers."

"Everyone else in this town had turned on me and then you did too," Shayla said softly. She fiddled with her coffee cup before bringing it to her lips.

He stayed silent, letting her have a moment to enjoy the coffee. Though, given the faraway look in her eyes, he wasn't sure she was even tasting the beverage.

"I'm sorry that I was hard on you. But trust me, I always liked you. I was grieving my cousin's loss, trying to get answers."

"I was grieving too. I needed..." Her voice trailed off. "It doesn't matter what I needed. It was a long time ago."

"Hey," Tavis said softly. He reached across the table

and put his hand on hers, surprising himself. "You were hurt. It does matter."

"I'm fine," Shayla insisted.

"I'm here for you now," Tavis told her. "And I'm not about to let anyone hurt you. You're an old friend. I'm happy to provide protection services free of charge."

"Oh, absolutely not." Shayla moved her hand away. "I don't want charity."

"It wouldn't be charity. Call it me making up for the past. For me being hard on you when I should have known that you would never protect Lucas."

"Whatever you want to call it, I don't need to be protected. And I wouldn't want you to pass up other work to babysit me."

Tavis sipped more of his coffee, and decided not to push the issue of protection for the time being, but he had something else he wanted to discuss with her. "I know you might not want me to ask you this, considering our last conversation years ago. Especially given what you just said. But did you ever hear from Lucas any time over the past nine years?"

Shayla's eyes widened, registering her disappointment. "I can't believe you would ask me that. You just said that you believed I wouldn't keep Lucas's whereabouts secret—"

"That doesn't mean he didn't call you, or send you a message—even if he never told you where he was. I'm just wondering if you ever heard a word from him in some shape or form."

"I didn't. I've never heard from him. Not once. And I don't know what happened to him after the night of the party. He left town and dropped me, just like he dropped everyone else."

Tavis thought about her words. It was beyond frustrating that Lucas had disappeared without a trace. Tavis had used his resources at the police department to search for him and had never come up with a shred of evidence indicating where he might be. It wasn't impossible that he was living off the grid, or had stolen someone's ID and assumed a new identity. He'd probably hightailed it clear across the country to California, or Washington. Maybe he'd even crossed the border into Canada. All Tavis knew was that he wouldn't rest until he had his cousin's killer apprehended and paying for his crimes.

"Hey," he said softly as Shayla was sipping her coffee and gazing outside. There was tension between them, and he needed to clear things up. "Please know that I never hated you. I was disappointed and upset, and I judged you wrongly."

Shayla said nothing.

"I didn't ask you about Lucas right now because I believed you were keeping anything from me, but we haven't seen each other in almost nine years, and it's possible you could have heard from him during that time. This is the first time we're talking about it. I had to ask."

"And now you know."

Tavis nodded. "Yes, now I know." He paused. "Years ago, I never believed that you would ever *want* to protect Lucas. What I did think was that you were probably scared of him, maybe had even been threatened by him into staying silent. It crossed my mind that if you'd lied originally, you wouldn't ever think you could come clean with the truth, scared that people would be even more angry with you if you admitted that you knew where he'd gone."

When Shayla opened her mouth to protest, Tavis continued. "Hear me out. I said that's what crossed my mind back then. And that's why I pressed you hard for answers. But I can see now—I know now—that you wouldn't lie about that. You loved Hayley like a sister. And you would want her killer brought to justice just as much as I would."

"I did love her like a sister," Shayla said, her voice hitching. Then she straightened her spine. She glanced left for the first time, into the café at large, then gasped softly. "Oh my God, that's Jonathan's grandfather. And the way he's looking at me…"

Tavis quickly looked in that direction. And sure enough, Donny Bozzo was staring at Shayla, his gaze unyielding and serious.

"Ignore him," Tavis said. "That's the best way to handle anyone who gives you a hard time. Do your best to ignore any negativity."

Shayla sipped more of her cappuccino. Her chest rose and fell with a heavy breath. She glanced in Donny's direction once more, this time offering the man a small smile before returning her attention to Tavis.

"You know," she began, "I came back to Sheridan Falls thinking that I needed to hide out and be remorseful and afraid of what people would think. I almost didn't want to say yes to coffee with you because I didn't want to face anyone in the town. But the truth is I have no reason to be guilty about anything. I have no reason to hide my face. I did nothing wrong. And I'm not about to act as though I did."

"Good."

"I just wish it was as easy to not care," she went on. "But I'll get there."

Shayla's eyes wandered toward Jonathan's grandfather again, and Tavis followed her line of sight. The older man was now leaving the coffee shop. Because of her? Well, let him go. At least he hadn't decided to come over to their table and harass Shayla.

"We should probably go now," Shayla said. "I can pop into the variety store next door and get some cream, then we can head back to my house."

Before Tavis had a chance to respond, Shayla shot to

her feet. She reached into her own wallet and put the tip on the table.

Tavis rose to join her. "Thanks for agreeing to have coffee with me. Hopefully it won't be a one-time thing."

Shayla tucked a strand of her curly black hair behind her ear, not meeting his eyes. "Maybe."

Sheesh, why had he even suggested getting together for coffee again? He'd made it sound like an invitation for a date.

"If you want," he said. "You know…to talk."

"Sure," Shayla said softly. "I'll let you know."

Unlike when they'd arrived, she took the lead, heading to the coffee shop's exit, waving at Molly as she passed. Tavis followed her, matching her quick strides.

She opened the door and stepped onto the sidewalk, and then Tavis saw her body seize with fear. A quick glance to the right told him why.

Donny Bozzo stood on the sidewalk with a gun aimed at Shayla.

"Don't you move!" he cried. "Because of you, my grandson is dead. And now you're finally going to pay for your crimes."

Chapter Four

In a flash, Tavis was in front of Shayla, protecting her with his body. "Whoa, Donny. Put the gun down."

"No," Donny said, his resolve steely even though his voice quivered. "It's time she pay for what she did. She had my grandson killed."

"That's not true," Shayla said, but Tavis quickly put up a hand to silence her.

Tavis looked at the old man, assessing the situation. Was he crazy enough to pull the trigger? It wasn't something that Tavis could risk, and he slipped his hand beneath his jacket, placing it on the handle of his gun. As a bodyguard, he had a license to carry. And having been a police officer, he knew very well how to use the SIG Sauer.

But he didn't want to pull his own gun out and make an already-tense situation even worse. However, he wanted to be ready in case Donny decided to do something stupid.

"Donny, lower your gun," Tavis repeated.

"I'm not gonna kill her, which is more than she did for my grandson. But I called the police. They're on their way. They're going to arrest her."

As if on cue, the sirens sounded and seconds later two cop cars whizzed around the corner, coming to a screeching stop in front of the coffee shop. Sheriff Thompson jumped out of the first vehicle, and one of his deputies,

Deputy Campbell, jumped out of the second vehicle, both rushing forward, their hands on their guns.

The sheriff's eyes volleyed between Tavis and Donny. "Whoa, whoa, whoa," he said, sounding surprised. "Donny, what are you doing?"

"There she is," Donny said, pointing the gun in Shayla's direction. "The one who had my grandson killed. Arrest her."

"Donny, lower the gun," Sheriff Thompson said. "We don't want anyone getting hurt today."

"Sheriff, you need to take her in," Donny stressed.

The sheriff approached Donny slowly. "You know I'm gonna do my job. If she is responsible, she will pay. Trust me on that."

"Of course she's responsible!" Donny yelled.

Behind Tavis, Shayla clung to his back. He felt a weird sense of satisfaction that she was trusting him, given the undoubted tension between them. Not that she had much choice, but still it felt good that he was here for her.

So much for idle threats.

The sheriff drew his own weapon, but kept it lowered. "Now, Donny, don't make me tell you again. I don't want to have to arrest you. Leave this matter to the law." He gave him a stern look. "Lower your gun."

"As long as you're going to make sure she doesn't get away with what she did. She's a killer, even if she didn't pull the trigger herself!"

"I will take care of this matter," Sheriff Thompson said.

Finally, Donny lowered his gun, his shoulders slumping, as though all of his energy had oozed out of his body. He began to weep softly.

Tavis knew how intense the grief was. He'd lost his cousin. But this wasn't the way to handle the situation.

Pulling himself together, Donny looked at Tavis with

contempt. "And what are you doing with her anyway? She killed your cousin!"

"As the sheriff said, the law will deal with Shayla as necessary," Tavis said. Behind him, Shayla flinched.

Deputy Campbell moved forward, taking the gun from Donny's hand and then guiding him to his pickup truck. Tavis couldn't help thinking that if this were anyone else, the sheriff and deputy would have taken him down on the ground in a flash. Waving a gun around in the center of town was dangerous. Uncalled for. A clear threat. But they were treating old man Donny with kid gloves.

"You're not going to arrest him?" Shayla asked. "He pulled a gun on me. He could have killed me!"

"Ah, Donny is no harm," the sheriff said, and twirled the edge of his gray, handlebar mustache. "Besides, he's all tore up over his grandson. Can't say I blame him. But Donny…he's all talk, no bite. He called the police, told us that a crime was in progress. That's how he got us here." The sheriff threw a warning glance at Donny over his shoulder. "That wasn't right, Donny. You shouldn't have made a false claim of a crime in progress."

"As far as I'm concerned, a crime is in progress right now. A felon escaping the law as she did nine years ago."

Shayla pressed her face against Tavis's back, and he wasn't sure if she was crying. He turned and gathered her in his arms, and felt her melt against him. He stroked his hand over her hair, not caring that he was maybe getting too close. He just wanted her to feel okay. To feel safe.

"That's enough now," Deputy Campbell said to Donny. "Put the gun back in the glove compartment. That's it." He closed the door once Donny was sitting upright in the driver's seat. "You have a good day now, Donny. Say hello to Emma for me."

"Unbelievable," Shayla muttered. "They just treated him like a two-year-old who dropped an ice-cream cone."

As Donny drove off, the sheriff approached Tavis. "Why am I not surprised to see you mixed up in this?" he asked.

"Mixed up in what?" Tavis asked. "I was here getting coffee with Shayla, we came out and Donny had a gun pulled."

"Always chasing trouble," the sheriff mused. He stepped toward Shayla. "You all right?"

Shayla nodded. "Yes," she said, but her voice was feeble.

"So you're back in town."

"Yes. My mother… She's sick."

"Yeah, I heard. I'm real sorry about that. You convey that to her for me, will you? Let her know that I'm wishing her well."

"Of course," Shayla told him. She paused and said, "So you're not going to arrest Donny? He gets to pull a gun on me without any consequences?"

"Donny took his grandson's death real hard. Now, I know you said you never had anything to do with it, and I believe you. But a lot of people in this town felt you were hiding some vital information. Maybe you were afraid to tell us what you knew?" The sheriff's voice ended on a question.

"No," Shayla said. "I held back nothing."

Sheriff Thompson nodded. "And since you've been gone all these years, have you ever been in touch with Lucas? Do you know where he is now?"

"I have no clue where he is. I never heard from him after the day of the murders. Please," Shayla said, sounding exasperated, "you have to believe me."

The sheriff nodded, seeming to believe her. "All right. But if you hear anything at all, let me know. No one's ever paid for this crime, and it would mean a lot in this town if we could see the killer brought to justice."

"I'm sure it would. I just wish people would stop blaming me," Shayla added with the hint of bitterness.

"Tell him about the threat on your car," Tavis said.

The sheriff's eyes widened. "Threat?"

Shayla hesitated for a moment then spoke. "I don't know if it's really anything. But someone wrote a threat on my car. It read 'you will die.'" Shayla shrugged. "I don't know."

She was downplaying this, but with Donny pulling a gun on her, the threat on her car and even Tammy accosting her in the restaurant, it was clear to Tavis that she still had quite a few enemies in this town. "She's had some email threats as well," Tavis said. "I'm a bit worried that someone might really want to hurt her. So you keep your ear to the ground, sheriff? If you hear anything, make sure you take it seriously."

Sheriff Thompson's lips curled, but there was no cheer behind the smile. "Of course," he said, his tone clipped. "I've been doing this job for a long time, Tavis. I've always got my ear to the ground."

"That's all I ask."

"I hope that means you plan to leave this matter to law enforcement. I can handle the people in this town."

His gaze lingered on Tavis, a silent warning. There was no love lost between the two men. Then he turned and headed back to his cruiser.

SHAYLA SAT CURLED in the passenger seat as Tavis drove her back to her mother's place. The events that had transpired had her shaken. She knew people hated her and didn't want her back in Sheridan Falls. But it was worse than that. Maybe they wouldn't be happy until she was stoned in the town square.

That was likely an exaggeration, but with Donny pulling a gun on her, could she be blamed for her macabre thoughts? The incident had her rethinking her return to her hometown.

She'd had no choice. She had to be here for her mother, no matter the risk.

"Hey," Tavis said softly, interrupting her thoughts. "You okay? Obviously, you can't be fully okay. But how are you doing?"

"I'm wishing I never had to come back to this town," Shayla said honestly. There was nothing here for her, except for her mother. And, of course, her cousin and aunt and uncle, but this was too hard. More than she'd bargained for.

"If it's any consolation, I don't think Donny was going to hurt you. He saw you, was shocked, and obviously overreacted."

"And then got the royal treatment from the sheriff's department." Shayla made a face. "They need to at least take things like this seriously."

"I agree with you. Donny deserved more than a talking-to."

"They barely did even that." Shayla sighed. "What's the point of me calling them about any threat or telling them what happened to my car? I don't think they're going to handle it the way law enforcement should."

"That's where I come in," Tavis said. He glanced at her, and she met his gaze, but she didn't say anything.

"I'm good at what I do," Tavis went on. "For example, I verified the nurse's story with one look at her car."

"What do you mean?"

"She said she'd had a flat tire. When we left for coffee, I saw that, indeed, she did have the donut tire on her car."

Shayla made a face. "Do you suspect her of something?"

"It's my job to check out everything. Everyone."

"But surely the nurse… She was caring for my mother before I even came to town."

"Like I said, it's my job to check out everything and everyone. And at least her story checked out. She's got the donut on her car, so yes, she was late because she had a flat tire. When you don't know where a threat is coming from, you can't dismiss any possible angles."

Shayla supposed he was right. He was the professional, after all.

"I think it's wise to have me watching your back," he continued. "I won't be intrusive. I can shadow you, watch your house, make sure there are no signs of danger. But given the temperature of things around here—and the fact that the anniversary of the deaths is in a couple of days— it's probably best for me to stick around and make sure you're okay until all of this blows over."

Shayla said nothing, because how could she argue his point? Had she been at the coffee shop on her own, what would have happened? Would Donny have gone too far? Would he have been too angry to listen to reason and pulled the trigger?

She shuddered at the idea.

Tavis turned onto Belmont Street and moments later was pulling up in front of her house.

"Thank you," she said, facing him. "For the coffee, for everything."

"You didn't say whether or not you agree to have me provide you protection services."

Shayla offered him a small smile. "Do I have a choice? I don't think you're going to take no for an answer."

"You're right," Tavis said.

Shayla shrugged. She was stuck with Tavis, whether she wanted to be or not. "By the way, it seems like you and the sheriff aren't the best of friends."

"You figured that out?"

"I could feel the tension between the two of you. He was polite as he spoke, but it was clear that he was telling you to back off. And then he made that comment about you always being around when there's trouble."

"Yeah, I'm definitely not one of Thompson's favorite people."

Shayla looked at him, waiting for him to continue. When he didn't, she asked, "Why? What's the story between you two?"

"He and I don't exactly see eye to eye."

Shayla waited. Was that all he was going to give her?

"Remember, I used to be a cop. The whole reason I became a cop was to try to find Lucas and bring him to justice. I didn't apply to the sheriff's department here. I figured I wanted to be in a bigger city where I could ideally have more resources. So I went to Buffalo, applied. Got through there. I also thought maybe Lucas was back in Buffalo, because that's where he'd grown up. I figured it might be easier to find him there, because he clearly wasn't in Sheridan Falls. Anyway, let's just say I did a lot of digging on people in the town and broke a few rules trying to find answers as to what happened to Hayley. Sheriff Thompson always felt I was pushing too far, going around his authority to get answers."

"And were you?"

Tavis shrugged. "I didn't want to leave any stone unturned. The way it seemed to me, Sheriff Thompson had given up. As far as he was concerned, Lucas had taken off and wouldn't be found, so why waste resources searching for him? That wasn't okay with me. And I couldn't understand why it was okay with him."

"So you're a bit of a rebel," Shayla surmised.

"Determined," Tavis countered. "Determined to get justice for Hayley." His gaze wandered off. He was silent for several moments. "But I failed to do that."

As much as Shayla had been the brunt of his wrath and anger years before, she felt for him now. She'd lost her best friend. And because of the way she had been treated, she hadn't fully considered other people's grief. Tavis had lost his cousin. It must have been excruciating for him.

"I'm not sure if I ever said that I'm sorry that you lost Hayley…" Shayla began. "I know, I lost her too. But what I mean is I was so focused on my own grief, my own pain, defending my name, I'm not sure I really considered how hurt you were. As family to her."

"I know you cared. She was your best friend. You loved her same as I did."

"Absolutely," Shayla said. "I still can't believe what happened. All these years later, in some ways it feels like a dream. A nightmare."

"And you have no idea why Lucas would do this?"

Shayla threw her hands up and slapped them down on her thighs. "All I can think is that they were drinking, he was stupid, he had a gun. I don't know… But something went down. Maybe it was a fight with Jonathan, and Hayley was just there. Maybe Hayley took out her anger with me on him. A million things have crossed my mind, but at the end of the day, I don't have any answers because I wasn't there."

"I know."

"Do you? Do you really believe me?"

"I told you earlier, I do believe you."

Shayla's gaze wandered out the window. Then her eyes narrowed. Was she seeing what she thought she was seeing? There was a scratch along the entire right side of her car!

"Oh my God."

"What?" Tavis asked, instantly sitting straight and sounding on edge.

"There's a scratch along the side of my car. Maybe it was there before and I didn't notice. Or did someone else come and do this while we were gone?"

Tavis opened his door, then got out. Shayla did the same, heading straight toward her car. She cursed under her breath when she saw how deep the scratch was.

"I didn't notice that before," Tavis said.

"But did you see all of my car?" she asked.

"I didn't specifically look, no. I was checking out the nurse's vehicle."

Despite the warmth of the day, a chill ran down Shayla's spine. She wrapped her arms around her body. "Did someone come here while we were out? My mother is in the house. She's sick. She doesn't need the stress. And neither do I. I can't handle this…"

Tavis put his hands on her shoulders, and she didn't move away from him. She accepted the comfort he was offering her, trying not to think about how good it felt being so close to him.

"There are a couple of repair shops in town," Tavis began, "you want me to take your car somewhere?"

"No," she said. She didn't want to lean on him for everything. She was independent, and she would deal with this. "I'll take care of it later. Or maybe I should just let it sit. No point fixing it just for someone else to come along and vandalize it again."

"No one is going to be able to vandalize your car while I'm around."

Shayla turned, stepping away from Tavis's touch. Looking up at him, she asked, "Starting now?"

"Actually, if you don't mind, there are a couple things I need to do. Since I wasn't prepared to start this job immediately, I've got to check in with a couple of my guys at the office, catch up on a little bit of paperwork. I'll go home, grab my laptop. Then I can stay in the car and do what I need to do."

"That's perfectly fine," Shayla said. "Especially considering I didn't expect that you would even be doing this job for me. I... I can't pay you—*yet*. With my mother's health care—"

"I already offered to do this pro bono. You're a friend. I'm not going to stand by and let something happen to you. So don't worry about that."

"Okay," Shayla said softly. She knew not to push the issue. But when she could, she would pay him something. "When do you think you'll be back?"

"Give me an hour. Hour and a half tops."

ONCE TAVIS LEFT, Shayla figured she may as well find a local body shop where she could take her car. Though she had contemplated leaving it and letting anyone else in the town have a go at it, she realized she couldn't do that. The idea of looking out every day or even driving the car with that threat on the windshield was something she wouldn't do. So she looked in the phone book and found two body shops. She chose to go to the closest one. Lucky's Auto Shop.

When she arrived and went inside, she saw a familiar face behind the counter. Older, but definitely familiar.

"Chase?" she asked.

"Shayla!" the man boomed. He was her age, twenty-seven, but he looked at least ten years older. He had changed quite significantly since he'd dated Shayla's cousin, Deedee, back in high school. Then, Chase had been a football player, with a full head of thick hair and a muscular body. These days, his once-shaggy blond locks had prematurely thinned on top, he'd put on considerable weight, which hid any muscles, and he had a sizable beer belly.

"I heard you were back in town," he said, sounding pleased.

"Yeah. My mom— You probably heard..."

"I did. Cancer sucks, man."

"That it does."

"What brings you into my shop?"

"This is yours?" Shayla asked.

"Yep. You might remember that I liked to work on cars. They say make your passion your job and it never feels like work, right? So, I decided to open up an auto body shop here in town. We do oil changes, mechanics work and also bodywork. It's been good."

"Then I guess I'm in the right spot. Someone keyed my car. It needs to be repainted."

"Damn," Chase said. "Sorry to hear that."

"And so you're not shocked, something's written on the windshield of my car too. I tried scraping it, but I couldn't get it all off. Someone wrote a threat telling me that I'm going to die." She spoke casually, as if the threat was no big deal. But she couldn't stop wondering if someone truly wanted her dead.

Chase's eyes registered shock. "That happened here?"

"You know people here have long memories. Anyway, can you come out and take a look at it, then give me a quote for how much it will cost and how long it will take?"

"Sure thing."

As Chase headed out from behind the counter and walked ahead of Shayla to the door, she mused at how differently two people could change over the years. While Chase looked visibly older, and more out of shape compared to his fitter younger self, Tavis had grown into an even more attractive and strong man who must have women's heads turning constantly.

But why was she even thinking of Tavis?

Because he was gorgeous and strong and he'd protected her from possibly getting shot. Despite how he'd hurt her, he had been her crush, and seeing a more mature and sexier version of him still stoked a reaction from her.

"I hear you married Lisa Middleton," Shayla said.

"Yep. Eight years now. I guess Deedee told you."

"She did." Along with her commentary about how much she despised Lisa, who had made a play for Chase while Deedee had been dating him.

"Me and Lisa have three little ones now. Two boys and a girl."

"Ah, so sweet," Shayla said. Though years had passed since Deedee and Chase's bitter breakup, they didn't talk. Deedee seemed to have never gotten over the way their relationship had ended. The fact that he was currently married to Lisa was probably the biggest reason why she wouldn't talk to him.

"I think your cousin still hates me," Chase said as he opened the door, smiling wryly. "Which is just as well, I guess. Because Lisa doesn't want me talking to her. I think she still sees Deedee as a rival, even though I married her. And you know what they say, happy wife, happy life."

"Right." Shayla headed to her vehicle, which was parked in the shop's lot. "That's my car." She walked along the right side and pointed to the scratch. "You can see where it was keyed."

Chase bent onto his haunches and smoothed a finger over the scratch. "They keyed you good."

Shayla rounded the front of her vehicle. "And this is the windshield. It's some sort of glossy paint, I think. Hopefully it won't be any trouble for you to get it off."

Chase joined Shayla at the front of her car. "You weren't kidding. That's a definite threat."

"You can clean it up?"

"The windshield's no problem," Chase told her. "But that scratch…it's along the entire length of your car. That means all those panels need to be repainted. If it was just the door, I could do that section alone. But I'll have to match everything, and that means doing almost a full paint job for you."

Shayla winced. Once again, she wondered if she should leave this to be done now, or wait until the townsfolk had fully taken out their wrath on her. What if there was more damage afterward?

But she had already spoken with her insurance company, and she was going to go ahead and do this. She'd filed an official report with the sheriff's department before bringing her car here.

At least with the car in the shop, it wouldn't be in the driveway for a couple of days.

"I can take care of this for you," Chase said. "I'll need two days. Maybe three."

"That's fine with me."

"Let's head back in and I'll get the work order started for you," he said.

The two wandered back into the shop and Chase went behind the counter and got onto the computer. He asked her for further information. She gave it.

"So, you ever hear from Lucas?" Chase asked.

"No, never heard from him. I don't know what happened to him, and I don't know why he did what he did."

Chase harrumphed. "I used to think that Lucas was a nice guy. I mean, he wasn't perfect—just like me and my brother weren't—we did some crazy stuff. But I didn't expect him to murder anybody."

"So maybe three days to fix my car?" Shayla asked. She didn't want to talk about Lucas anymore.

"With the amount of painting on all those panels, yeah, I'd give it three days."

"Okay. I can survive three days." Her mother had a car, if necessary. She could use that. People would probably be less likely to vandalize her mother's car. At least her mother hadn't had to bear the brunt of the wrath for her daughter's perceived sins.

"If you don't mind me saying, I never understood what attracted you to Lucas. You two seemed so different."

"He was new to town, he asked me out," Shayla said by way of explanation.

"Yeah, but he was such a rebel. You didn't care that he sold weed?"

"I really didn't know much of what he was up to."

"Come on," Chase said, then leaned forward and said in a lowered voice, "You had to know some of the stuff he was involved in."

"I heard a lot of rumors after he took off, but before that, I was involved with my dance and sports. And he probably didn't want to tell me about his bad habits. Besides, Lucas and I really weren't together that long. We'd barely been dating when...when..." Her voice trailed off. There was no need to finish her statement.

"Yeah, but you had to have known *some* stuff. Like he probably told you who he sold drugs to, that sort of thing?"

This was the first time anyone had asked her such a question, and Shayla felt as though she were in the twilight zone. "No. I know nothing about any of that. Why are you asking?"

"I just heard some stuff, is all. Wondered if you knew much about it."

"More than the allegation that he sold weed?"

Chase shrugged. "I heard he used to flash a gun around sometimes."

"You and Alex hung out with him a lot. Did you ever see him with a gun?"

Chase's eyes narrowed, as though surprised that she'd turned the line of questioning on him.

"You'd probably know a lot more of what he was up to than I did," Shayla added.

Slowly, Chase shook his head. "My dad's the sheriff,

remember? He wasn't stupid enough to flaunt a gun in our faces."

"I suppose not."

An easygoing smile came on his face. "I guess I've lived in this town too long. We're always nosy. Don't mind our business."

Shayla smiled tightly.

"But I always got the sense that he was connected to something bigger. You know, he'd come from Buffalo, said his parents wanted him to have a change of scenery and get away from his bad friends. I thought he was still connected to the big city. I don't know… I just feel like he was involved in some kind of bigger criminal enterprise. Maybe he was running weapons, that kind of thing."

"Running weapons? That's a bit of a stretch, isn't it?" None of this sounded familiar to Shayla, and the little she knew of Lucas, she didn't believe that he was part of some big criminal enterprise. Leave it to small-town folks to have big imaginations. She knew he had a bad-boy reputation, but she'd always thought he was fronting. Acting tough so no one bothered him. But she hadn't really known him all too well.

"Did you ever talk to your dad?" Shayla asked. "Tell him your theories? Are you thinking he had help killing Hayley and Jonathan?"

"Not sure. Just thinking off the top of my head, I guess. Wondering if you knew anything specific about what he was up to."

"I knew nothing."

Chase went back to typing in whatever information on the computer, then he printed out some paperwork for her to sign. "If you sign here, that authorizes me to do the work. That's the price, but I'll be sending it off to your insurance company. If there are any complications, I can call you and let you know, but I don't expect there to be. This is pretty routine."

"Sounds great." Shayla scrawled her signature on the form. "Thanks so much. I look forward to hearing from you."

"Hey," Chase began, "you need a ride home?"

Shayla hadn't fully thought of that. She considered calling her cousin, or taking a long walk. "Actually, I was going to call my cousin."

"Deedee," Chase said. "How's she doing?"

"She's good. She bought a restaurant. Perhaps you've been there?"

"Haven't been there yet. Lisa has forbid me to ever go there." He chuckled. "Anyway, I don't mind giving you a ride home if you need one. I've got a couple of guys working on cars. They can cover the front for me."

Shayla's cell phone rang. She saw Deedee's face flashing on her screen. "Speak of the devil," she said to Chase. Then she quickly answered the call. "Hey, I was just about to call you."

"Where are you?" Deedee asked, sounding somewhat harried.

"I'm at Lucky's Auto Shop."

"You are?"

"Yeah, I was just gonna call you for a ride home." She glanced toward Chase, gave him a wave and exited the store so she could speak to Deedee outside without worrying that anyone was overhearing the conversation. The warm summer air enveloped her. "Why do you sound so worried? Did you talk to Tavis?"

"Tavis?"

"Deedee, I know you. What's going on?"

"It's your mother."

Shayla's stomach spasmed. "My mother. Is she okay?"

"I'm coming to get you right away."

Chapter Five

Shayla barely breathed as she waited for Deedee to pull up in front of Lucky's. And when she did, she could see the stress on her cousin's face.

"Is she okay?" Shayla asked without preamble as she hopped into the car.

"She started having trouble breathing," Deedee told her. "I was with her at the time and… I'm not gonna lie, it was very frightening."

"Oh God," Shayla whimpered.

"I rushed to get you because I know you would want to be there, but I just spoke to the nurse and she's calmed down now. So don't be too upset. But your mother was asking for you, and she was very irritated."

"Because she thinks this is the end?" Shayla couldn't help asking. Though she wanted to be positive, wanted to believe that her mother was going to pull through, the ugly alternative couldn't escape her mind.

"I'm not sure. All I know is that I was really worried, but thank God the nurse updated me. She said your mother's breathing is regulated."

"Why didn't Jennifer call me?"

"Because I was at the house when it happened, and I told her that I'd track you down."

"And no one called 9-1-1?"

"You know your mother's wishes," Deedee said softly, and she and Shayla exchanged glances.

Yes, Shayla knew that her mother didn't want any life-saving measures. She just didn't agree with the decision.

"What's going on with you?" Deedee asked. "You asked if I'd spoken to Tavis, and you were at Lucky's. Why?"

Shayla quickly filled her in on what had happened with the threat on the car as well as the vandalism. "So I figured I'd bring the car to a body shop, and it turns out that Chase works there."

"He owns the shop," Deedee clarified. "If you'd told me about this ahead of time, I would have told you to go to the other body shop."

There was no love lost between her cousin and Chase, though they'd dated years ago. Shayla remembered Deedee being angry at Chase after the breakup. She'd said he left her for Lisa because Chase was white and Deedee was Black. At least, that was what Deedee believed, though Shayla hadn't been so sure. The one thing that Shayla had liked about this place was that people didn't seem to be hung up on color. Though the town was small, the population was diverse. They looked at each other for who they were, not the color of their skin.

"Something else happened," Shayla said, and exhaled a sigh that signified the magnitude of the situation. "I ran into Jonathan's grandfather. He pulled a gun on me."

"What?" Deedee exclaimed.

"I was with Tavis. He jumped into action to protect me. But I don't think that Donny was going to shoot me. He just wanted to make sure I didn't go anywhere. At least, that's what he said. He'd called the cops to arrest me."

As they neared Belmont Street, Deedee said, "So, have you decided to hire Tavis then? I think it's a good idea. Especially with everything you just told me."

"After what happened with Donny, I don't think if I

told him no, he would listen. So, why not? Better safe than sorry."

"Good. Someone needs to be looking out for you."

Deedee pulled up in front of the house, and Tavis's Sierra was already there. Shayla jumped out and started to rush up the driveway. Tavis exited his pickup and called out to her, but Shayla said, "Deedee will fill you in. My mom needs me."

SEEING HER MOTHER awake and calm had waves of relief washing over Shayla. It had been one thing to hear Deedee say that her mother had recovered from whatever breathing spell had alarmed them all, but another to see her looking okay. Still, Shayla was frazzled nonetheless. She hoped there wasn't another incident like this that had her fearing she might be losing her mother. Thankfully, as her mother's pain had increased and her anxiety grew, the nurse had been there to administer the appropriate medicine to calm her down. Maybe her mother had just needed her to be by her side, because seeing Shayla now seemed to perk her up.

Shayla felt guilty for leaving, but she had needed to take care of her vehicle. And she could never have predicted that at the moment she'd left, her mother would experience a mini crisis. When she'd gone to Lucky's Auto Shop, her mother had been sleeping peacefully.

"I'm sorry I wasn't here for you, Mom," Shayla said softly.

"I'm okay now, baby. For some reason, I woke up and was afraid. I don't fully remember, but I had some sort of bad dream. About you. That you were in danger. And when I woke up and you weren't here… I was so scared."

Shayla hated to hear that she was the cause for her mother's distress. "You don't need to worry about me, Mom."

Her mother chuckled softly, but there was pain behind

the sound. "Oh, you'll understand one day when you have a child. There's no such thing as not worrying about them."

"So I've heard."

"Are you all right?" her mother asked. "I know you never wanted to come back here, and I know people haven't been kind to you. I'm just hoping that when they see you out and about now, they'll be nicer."

Shayla couldn't tell her mother what had happened with Donny, or with Tammy, or even her car. There was no way she would add more stress to what her mother was already experiencing. So she didn't. "I haven't really run into many people, but either people are keeping their opinions to themselves or they've put it behind them," she said. Her mother gave her a doubtful look, but Shayla squeezed her hand. "Please, Mom, I'm fine."

"Okay, darling. But be careful. I don't know why I had that dream, but it left me with a bad feeling. I just want you to be safe."

"What about you, Mom? How has everyone been toward you?" Shayla hoped that they hadn't been horrible to her, that her mother hadn't stayed here despite bad treatment.

"After the initial shock of the murders and people feeling you might've had something to do with it, they really didn't see me as a bad guy. I know they lashed out at you, but there was a bit of sympathy for me after you left town. People feeling bad that you were my only child and now you'd gone, and you were caught up in this mess. Surprisingly, they didn't come after me the way I thought they might."

"I'm glad for that," Shayla said. Her mother had told her as much over the years, yet she wasn't certain she'd told her the truth. But maybe that did explain why her mother hadn't been keen on leaving and heading down to Miami. She'd been more or less treated well in the town, so she hadn't had a reason to escape.

Unlike Shayla.

"Here's one more reason for your mind to be at ease," Shayla began. "You'll be happy to know that I've taken a precaution to make sure that I am definitely safe. You remember Tavis?"

"Oh yes, of course I remember Tavis Saunders. You used to have a crush on him," her mother said, a smile touching her lips.

"That's ancient history. But he has a protection service agency, and Deedee put him in touch with me. He's decided to offer me protection services—out of an abundance of caution—to make sure I'm safe while I'm in town."

"You agreed to that?" her mother asked.

"You know me too well," Shayla said with a soft chuckle. She was glad to see her mother had perked up, that they were having a conversation that was normal. "Deedee felt it was a good idea that I had some sort of protection while I'm here, especially with the anniversary of the deaths coming up so quickly. I know it sounds crazy, but at least if I have someone looking out for me, I can be certain that no one can hurt me."

"It doesn't hurt that he's as good-looking as he is."

"Mom! What's gotten into you?"

"The one thing I would love to see before I leave this world is you with someone who makes you happy. Someone who's going to take care of you. Allow me to dream a little. I know how much you used to like Tavis, and I think he's a good guy."

Shayla wanted to remind her mother how Tavis had made his lack of feelings for her clear after Hayley's death, but she didn't bother. Their conversation was jovial and light. She didn't want to ruin the mood. She stroked her mother's hand then lifted it to her lips and softly kissed it. "One thing at a time," she said with a smile. "The most important thing is for you to know that there's no need to lose any sleep worrying about me. Let's worry about getting you better."

Her mother's eyelids began to flutter. They were getting heavy, and it seemed a struggle for her to keep them open. The nurse had told her that the pain medication caused drowsiness.

Shayla kissed her mother's hand again, saying, "I'll let you get some rest. I love you, Mom."

"I love you too, sweetheart."

Shayla went upstairs to her room, where she closed the door and pressed her back against it. She drew in a deep breath then finally let out the sob she'd been holding in. Seeing her mother like this was the hardest thing in the world. What she'd gone through with the murders and the scorn and the hate paled in comparison to the idea that she might be losing her mom.

"You're not going to lose her," she told herself. "You're going to be strong for her because that's what she needs. You're going to help her get through this."

Shayla glanced at her dresser. And frowned.

Her jewelry box…had it been moved?

Shayla moved forward, eyeing the box. It held only costume jewelry, nothing valuable. But still. She was certain that it had been closer to the corner of the dresser.

Closing her eyes, she shook her head. The stress was getting to her. She was imagining things.

With her eyes still closed, she started thinking about the night her life had changed. She had tried to flee the memories, but here she was, back in her old house and face-to-face with the reality she couldn't escape.

Opening her eyes, she went to the closet and slowly opened the door. She'd thrown the teddy bear in there the other day, but had not bothered to look inside. Because inside, there were many memories she had tried to bury in the deep recesses of her mind. Now, as she turned on the light in the closet, she saw ribbons hanging from nails in the wall, countless trophies. All of her accolades from her world of dance. She and Hayley had been freestyle dancers, and had competed for twelve years. It was something they'd both loved and done well at. They'd competed on teams as well as individually.

And when Hayley had failed to make the cut for the regional competition, everything had gone to hell. Hayley had complained about feeling unwell that day, her stomach bothering her. And she hadn't performed as well as she could have; that had been apparent to Shayla the moment she'd started her routine. But Shayla had been on point, doing her dance exercise to perfection. She'd secured a spot, and Hayley hadn't.

As the days had passed, Hayley's failure had seemed to make her more and more angry with Shayla. Shayla had tried to be patient with her, but Hayley had not been up to seeing any reason.

Then came the night of the party, and though they were talking, it was clear to Shayla that their relationship wasn't the same. She'd tried to make things normal between her and Hayley again, without success. But at least when she'd agreed to go to Lucas's party, she'd thought that things were finally on the mend between them.

Until Hayley had gotten into the car and started to go on and on about the competition again, and how Shayla thought she was so special because she'd made it and Hayley hadn't.

By the time Shayla had driven up to Lucas's place, she'd been in no mood to go to any party. Her best friend was saying things she simply couldn't understand. Had Shayla known that Hayley was going to go off the deep end over all of this, she would have forfeited her spot. It wouldn't have felt good for her to do it, but she would have done it. She wanted Hayley more than she wanted another trophy.

Shayla stifled a sob, hating this trip down memory lane. "Oh, Hayley. Why did you let that competition come between us? Did I do something wrong? Was there something I should have done instead? And now you're gone and we can never repair anything." Her voice ended on a croak.

She let the tears fall. Tears for her friend who had died. Tears for the animosity that had come between them before her death. Tears for her mother. Tears for herself and for what she'd lost.

Then she brushed the tears away and sucked in a deep breath. She couldn't wallow in pain over the past. She needed to move forward. She would never understand what had truly gotten into Hayley, and that wasn't how she wanted to remember her. She wanted to remember the smiling girl with the ridiculous-sounding half snort, half giggle that was totally infectious. She wanted to remember all the happiness she had shared with her best friend.

Chapter Six

Shayla's eyes flew open, instantly greeting the darkness of the room. For a moment, she didn't breathe. She felt disoriented and alarmed. Something had awakened her.

She lay still, concentrating on listening. And there it was again. A sound. Some sort of thump?

Her heart began to race. She was in her mother's room downstairs, her body folded into the armchair. She glanced toward her mother, who was snoring slightly as she slept. The IV beside the bed was dripping slowly, the monitor seemingly undisturbed. So what had awakened her?

Shayla got up, her legs cramping slightly as she stretched her body out from where she'd been curled for so long. Then she exited the den and started down the hallway. When she got to the living room, she saw the curtains by the patio door blowing gently. A draft?

No, she realized, stepping closer. The back door was open!

As fear took hold of her, she quickly whirled around and tried to figure out what she could use as a possible weapon. Someone was in the house…

She rushed to the kitchen, hoping that no one was hiding there. Then she took the biggest knife from the butcher's block. Slowly, acting on instinct, she tiptoed to the back patio door. The curtains billowed with the light breeze.

Shayla drew in even, steady breaths, not wanting to make a sound. She tiptoed toward the patio door. As she got closer, she could hear a voice. A female?

She stepped up to the back door and hit the light switch to illuminate the backyard. And as she peered out, she saw Jennifer sitting at the patio table, her cell phone to her ear. Jennifer quickly threw a glance over her shoulder then lowered her phone.

A relieved sigh rushed out of Shayla's body. It was only the nurse. But why was she there? It was the middle of the night.

"Jennifer?"

The nurse got to her feet. Whomever she'd been talking to, she had quickly ended the call. "Sorry. Did I wake you?"

"Why are you here? Didn't you go home?"

Jennifer gave her an odd look. "Don't you remember I said I would stay later tonight because of how your mother was today? I know it was likely that she was just having a panic attack, but with her breathing difficulties during the day, I told you I'd stay."

Had she? Shayla couldn't remember. But the day had been a blur, with so much transpiring and the fear that her mother had taken a turn for the worse.

"Oh. I don't remember that. But I haven't even seen you throughout the evening."

"I checked in on your mother, and you were sleeping beside her, in the armchair. When I checked your mother's vitals, you didn't even budge. You were out cold."

"Oh. And how are her vitals?"

"They're back to normal. I think her episode today was stress related."

Jennifer's cell phone lit up. It was ringing, but on silent.

"You were talking to someone, weren't you?" Shayla asked. "I interrupted you."

"My boyfriend. You startled me, and I hung up on him."

"Yeah, I know the feeling."

"I'm sorry about that." Jennifer glanced at her phone's screen. "That's him calling back." She swiped to reject the call then typed out a text. When she was finished, Jennifer looked at her with concern. "You look a bit stressed yourself. Can I get you something? Maybe a sleeping pill might help?"

"No. I'm fine." She paused. "Good night."

"Good night. I hope you get some rest."

Shayla wandered through the living room and looked out the front window. Tavis's vehicle was there, as he'd promised he would be.

So he'd meant what he'd said. He would give her round-the-clock protection. Though at some point he needed to sleep.

Should she go out and offer him some food or a drink? Maybe a steaming cup of coffee?

She quickly dismissed the idea. He was an expert at protecting people; he certainly had to be prepared for long nights. Besides, she didn't want to see more of him than was necessary. It had already thrown her for a loop that he was back in her life, and she knew that however nice he was being to her now, he still blamed her to some degree for what had happened to Hayley. He was doing the right thing by her at this point because he was an honorable man, but he probably would be happy to see less of her as well.

With the nurse staying the night and her mother resting, Shayla headed upstairs to her room and crawled into her bed. Hopefully she could sleep the rest of the night without any distractions.

"HEY, TAVIS," Griffin said into the phone. "Something's going on here."

Tavis, who was lying in his bed, quickly threw the covers off. It was four thirteen in the afternoon, but his room showed no sign of daylight due to his blackout curtains. He'd needed rest after being with Shayla for nearly twenty-four hours. And that was why Griffin was there at the house right now.

"What's going on?" Tavis asked, now wide awake.

"Shayla is on the move."

"Where's she going?"

"I just asked her, and she gave me the runaround. She exited the house and headed to her mother's car. That's when I approached her. You want me to give her the phone so you can ask her?"

"Yes. Put her on."

"Hold on."

Tavis heard the sound of shuffling as Griffin exited the vehicle. Then he could hear the faint sounds of Shayla's voice in the background as Griffin talked to her.

"Just going out for a little while."

"But you won't tell me where?"

"That's not necessary. I won't be gone long."

Griffin came back on the line. "She says she's going out and that she won't be long."

"Put her on the phone," Tavis said.

Next came Shayla's voice. "Hello?"

"Shayla, what's going on?"

"Nothing," she said, but her voice sounded a little strained.

"Where are you going?"

"I don't need protection every second of the day. I can go to the store, can't I?"

"Is that where you're going?" Tavis asked her. "To the store?"

She hesitated, and Tavis knew something else was going on. Something she didn't want to tell him.

"Wherever you need to go, I can take you. I'll be there in five minutes."

"Tavis," she protested. "You don't need to."

"Let me speak to Griffin," Tavis said.

Moments later, Griffin came back on the line.

"She's not gonna like this," Tavis said, "but block the driveway. Something's going on with her. I can hear it in her voice."

"I agree. She seems a bit on edge," Griffin said.

"Thanks for calling me. I'll be there soon."

SHAYLA WANTED TO SCREAM. She'd blown it. Blown her chance to escape and make the trip to Buffalo that she needed to make. She could call the sheriff to complain that she was being blocked in her driveway, but she didn't want to take it to that level. She just… She hoped she hadn't ruined the plan.

Tavis pulled up to the curb and exited his vehicle. He went over to Griffin's SUV and spoke for several seconds before the other man drove off. Tavis then turned his attention to where she sat on the front step. He stalked up the driveway, all six-foot-three muscular inches of him, and despite the look of irritation on his face, Shayla found herself reacting to his purely male presence.

"What's going on?" he asked her. "You know the deal is that I provide you round-the-clock protection."

"I just need to go somewhere." She got to her feet. "I can't tell you about it, and I don't need you following me."

Tavis's eyebrows shot up. "You can't tell me about it?"

"Maybe I have a romantic rendezvous lined up," she said, then immediately felt silly. Why on earth had she said *that*?

"You have a date?" Tavis asked doubtfully.

"That's such an impossible concept?" she asked, doubling down on her lie.

"Obviously not," Tavis said. "You're a very beautiful woman. But that's not what's going on here."

Shayla didn't want to think about the fact that he'd just said she was beautiful, or the fact that he knew she was lying.

"Wherever you want to go," Tavis went on, "I can take you there."

"You're going to ruin everything," Shayla mumbled.

Tavis's lips twisted. "Huh?"

Shayla exhaled sharply. How was she going to get out of this? She sucked at lying. And time was ticking. The call had come an hour ago, and she had expected to be in Buffalo by now.

"Tell me what's going on here," Tavis said.

A beat passed. Then two. And then Shayla let it spill. "I got a call. From Lucas."

An expression of stunned disbelief came across Tavis's face and his entire body went rigid. *"Lucas?"*

"I didn't want to tell you because… Because you're going to think that I've lied about everything. But he called me. Out of the blue. And he said that he needs to meet me."

"Lucas Carr?"

It was as much a shock for him as it had been for her. When she'd heard the voice, gravelly and faint, she hadn't been able to place it at first. And when he'd said that it was Lucas and he needed her help, she had been blown away.

"He said he knows I'm back in town, and that what happened on the night of the murders isn't what everyone says. He said he needs my help—help to clear his name." She paused. "I believe him. I always told you I never thought he killed anyone."

"And he wants you to go to Buffalo. To meet him."

"He can't very well show up in Sheridan Falls. He gave me an address. I already looked it up online. It's a house."

"And you were just gonna take off and go there without telling me?"

"He said to come alone. What did you want me to do?"

"I wanted you to tell me because you're sure as hell not going alone. I'll take you there."

"If I show up with anyone, it's going to spook him. He said if anyone else knows I'm meeting him, it could get him arrested."

"So you planned to go there alone." Tavis shook his head, disappointment evident in his eyes. "You thought that was safe?"

Shayla wasn't stupid. She'd considered the danger. But she'd asked him questions about their relationship, the party, and he'd answered them all. "I know there's a risk, but it's a house in the middle of a neighborhood. It's still day. If I can get answers about what happened, isn't that a good thing?"

Tavis gave her a pointed look. Then he said, "We're gonna take my car."

SHAYLA SAT HUGGING the passenger door and staring out the window with a conflicted expression as Tavis drove to the address in downtown Buffalo. He had left her to her thoughts, certain she felt bad about how everything had played out. It was beyond him that she had planned to drive to this address by herself, not fearing at all that she could be heading straight into danger.

Tavis's adrenaline was pumping. All these years he'd been looking for Lucas and, out of the blue, he had re-emerged.

Shayla's cell phone rang. She glanced at the screen then at him. "It's Lucas."

"Answer it," Tavis told her.

"Hello?" Shayla said. "Yes, I'm on the way. I'll be there

in…" She glanced at the GPS. "Seven minutes. Okay, see you soon."

"He's at the house?" Tavis asked once she ended the call.

"Yes."

Minutes later, they were off the highway and heading onto Niagara Street. They passed a fast-food restaurant and a pharmacy, then turned right after passing a grocery store. There were a lot of people milling about on this warm summer evening. This was the inner city, where there was more crime, and Tavis didn't like that Lucas had asked her to come here alone. The man was believed to have killed two people, and now he wanted to see her without anybody there to help her? How had Shayla not considered that Lucas might want to hurt her too? Though her quiet and pensive demeanor told him she was understanding that now.

He didn't want to give her a hard time, but he wanted her to understand that he was offering her protection for a reason. Someone wanted to hurt her; possibly kill her, if the threats were real. Once she'd gotten the request to go to a location in downtown Buffalo, she should have called him immediately.

Slowing, Tavis turned left. On the street corner, a few people were standing with their bicycles.

"It's not a desolate area, as you can see," Shayla suddenly said.

"True," Tavis agreed. But that didn't mean anything. People got hurt in the middle of crowds, in front of witnesses. You didn't always know where a bullet came from.

Tavis pulled up in front of a house. It took him a moment to read the number—thirty-seven—because the metal had faded due to the weather. "This is it."

It was dusk now, the sun dipping farther on the horizon every minute. Shayla reached for the door handle, but

Tavis quickly put a hand on her arm. "Let me go out, have a look around."

"Okay," she said.

Tavis exited his vehicle, glancing all around as he did. Curious neighbors regarded him warily. He offered a small nod in the direction of the couple on the porch two houses over, trying not to look conspicuous. This was the kind of neighborhood where people would be curious as to who was showing up without cause.

He walked up to the front door and knocked. He was greeted by silence. He strained his ear against the door to listen, but heard no sound.

Hearing his pickup door open, he turned to see Shayla exiting the vehicle. "He's waiting for me," she said. "If you call out to him, he's probably going to run. Whatever we do, right now we do it together."

"Fine," Tavis said. "But you stick to my side."

She walked up the steps to meet him. "All I want to ask is that you give Lucas a chance. I know you're going to want to drag him to the authorities, but let's hear what he has to say. If he says he didn't kill Hayley and Jonathan, I believe him. I never believed he would do such a thing."

"I'm shocked that he's still in Buffalo. I thought he would've been far, far away from New York State by now." Some criminals took off to another continent and started a new life to evade the law. Lucas had apparently stuck around.

Shayla knocked on the door. Again, there was silence. She called out. "Lucas? It's me, Shayla."

No one answered.

Tavis tried the door. It opened. As he let it fall open fully, he met Shayla's gaze. She looked up at him and shrugged.

Tavis took the first step into the house. He looked around cautiously, seeing nothing but an empty hallway. On the right was a small, furnished living room. Directly ahead, he could see part of a kitchen. The house was quiet.

Turning around, Tavis nodded toward Shayla, letting her know that it was okay to enter.

Shayla followed him inside. She tiptoed up beside him, and Tavis could feel her energy. She was afraid.

His own heart was pumping, the hairs on the back of his neck standing at attention. Everything in his gut told him that something was off. Why would Lucas have her meet him here? And more importantly, where was he?

"Where is Lucas supposed to be?" Tavis whispered.

"He just said to come to this address. He didn't say anything else."

"Then where is he?" Tavis asked as he stepped farther into the small house. The wood floors creaked beneath their steps.

"Maybe he saw you, or heard you, and took off. I told you that I needed to come alone."

"That wasn't gonna happen."

As they headed toward the kitchen at the back of the house, a door suddenly flung open. A figure appeared, dressed in black. Tavis saw the shape of the gun and in the moments before it fired, had precious milliseconds to throw his body against Shayla's and force her to the floor. A bullet whizzed almost silently over their heads, lodging somewhere in the living room.

Shayla screamed. Tavis quickly shot to his feet, grabbing his gun from the holster beneath his jacket. He gave chase. The shooter, racing for the back door, turned and fired off another shot. It went high, landing in the wall above Tavis's head.

"Tavis!" Shayla screamed.

The shooter flung open the back door and rushed outside, firing another shot over his shoulder as he did.

Tavis had to duck to avoid getting hit.

"Nooo!" Shayla cried.

"Damn it!" Tavis ran to the back door and onto the dilapidated deck, saw the figure in black darting through the alleyway at the side of the house. He wanted to sprint down the alley and catch up with the guy, but he couldn't leave Shayla. He turned and raced back to her. She was wincing, holding her elbow.

"Are you all right?" Tavis asked. He got onto the floor beside her. "Let me see your elbow."

Shayla partially extended her arm, moaning as she did. "It's just hurt. I don't think it's broken."

Tavis took her arm in his hand, gently checking for any damage. "It doesn't feel dislocated. I'm sorry. I had no choice but to knock you to the ground."

"Of course you didn't. He shot at us."

"He got away," Tavis said. "I couldn't go after him, not with you here."

"I think we spooked him."

Tavis looked at Shayla for a moment, dumbfounded. Did she not realize what had just happened? "Shayla, you must realize what happened here. Lucas lured you to this house. Not to give you information, but to get rid of you."

Her eyes bulged and her lips fell open. "No. That's not true. He wouldn't."

"But he did."

"That's because I didn't come alone. He freaked out. Probably thought you were going to take him to jail. He… he shot to scare us, so that he could get away."

Tavis placed both hands on Shayla's shoulders and looked her directly in the eye. "The person who came out of the bathroom was dressed in all black, right down to a ski mask. It wasn't Lucas suddenly scared because you showed up with someone else. That was someone prepared to kill and make a clean getaway."

Shayla's pupils seemed to jump as she registered

his words. She shook her head slowly. "No. It… Lucas wouldn't do that. Why would he do that?"

"He even had a silencer on the gun to minimize the sound. You must understand now that if you had come here on your own, you would've been killed, right?" She didn't speak, as if unable to comprehend his words. "The threat to your life is very real. You have to take it seriously."

"I thought I was going to get answers. I even googled the address to make sure it was a safe location. It's a fairly public place. There are neighbors everywhere…"

"None of that matters when someone wants to kill you," Tavis told her.

She gasped then, finally understanding the gravity of the situation. "But I don't understand why he would want to kill me. After all this time?"

Tavis gathered her in his arms and pulled her to her feet. "I don't know either. But let's get out of here."

As Tavis led Shayla out of the house, he stopped short when he saw two young men standing at the foot of the walkway. Had they heard the shots? Likely not, because the shooter had used a silencer. But there was no guarantee.

"Hey, who are you guys?" one of the men asked, eyeing them suspiciously.

Tavis glanced at Shayla. Then she said, "I was supposed to meet someone here. Maybe you know him?"

"Jenae?" the man supplied.

Though hearing the name hit him like a ton of bricks, Tavis did his best not to react.

"Jenae?" Shayla asked. "You know Jenae?"

"She was living there for a little while, but suddenly she took off."

"When?" Tavis asked.

"Hmm, about a week and a half ago—two," the second guy said around the lollipop in his mouth.

"What about Lucas?" Shayla asked.

"The guy she was living with? Shaker, that's what he went by."

His street name. Tavis asked, "You didn't know his real name?"

Both of the men shook their heads. "Only knew him as Shaker."

Tavis sauntered to the end of the walkway. "If you hear from Jenae or Shaker, tell them to call Tavis. They already have the number."

"Will do," the guy sucking the lollipop said. "Though I'm not sure if we'll ever see them again. She and Shaker took off real quick."

Chapter Seven

All Shayla wanted to do when she got home was go hug her mother and then slip into a warm bubble bath and stay there for a long while. She was relieved that the nurse had agreed to stay again for the night, because Shayla was so shaken by the events that had happened that she was in no proper position to care for her mother. She needed to decompress, take a hot bath and slip under the covers.

If you had come here on your own, you would've been killed...

Tavis's words reverberated in her brain as she sat in the bubble bath, wondering what she'd actually been thinking. Surely, she had to have known that going to see Lucas might be dangerous, but she'd completely pushed any thought of danger from her mind.

It had been hearing Lucas's voice, the way he'd desperately pleaded with her for help, that had her throwing caution to the wind.

I didn't do this. Everyone thinks I did. I can't return to Sheridan Falls without getting arrested. I need you to help me, Shayla. Please. Please help me clear my name. I can't go on like this anymore! You know how many people want me dead?

The plea had been earnest, heartfelt, and how could she have denied him? Especially when he'd gone on to explain that he'd had to live underground, hiding and watching his back—how that wasn't a life at all.

In her own way, she understood.

Had he really said all that just to get her to show up and meet him so he could kill her? Or had he started shooting because Tavis had showed up as well?

Shayla had had another idea; one Tavis hadn't agreed with. But it had occurred to her that maybe Lucas had set up extra security to make sure that she had come alone. Maybe he'd been working with someone else to protect him, and that person was the one who'd been hiding out at the house. Had Shayla gone there alone, the mystery man would have gotten word to Lucas and Lucas would have come to meet her. When she'd showed up with Tavis instead, the guy had panicked and come out shooting.

Tavis hadn't believed that for a second, and now as Shayla rethought the theory, she didn't believe it either.

Shayla eased her body lower into the tub so that her shoulders were covered by the bubbles and hot water. She didn't want to think about any of this anymore. All she knew was that someone had shot at her and Tavis.

At a house where Jenae had once lived.

Despite everything, that had been the biggest shock of the day. The house she'd been sent to had very recently belonged to Jenae Wilkinson.

So what was the connection between her and Lucas?

And did one or both of them want her dead?

HALF AN HOUR after returning to Sheridan Falls, Tavis's blood was still pumping hard through his veins after pretty much coming face-to-face with a killer. Thank God the guy hadn't been a good shot, because he and Shayla could very well be dead right now. And they were no closer to finding Lucas.

"This case just got real," Griffin said. Tavis was sitting

beside him in his Chevy Tahoe. "All these years later, it went from cold to hot."

"That it did, Griffin. That it did."

"You think that was actually Lucas at the house?"

"I'm not sure. I didn't get close enough to him to find out. If it is him, he wants Shayla dead. But why—and why now?"

Griffin lifted his coffee carafe and took a sip. "Are you going to report the shooting to the police?"

Tavis pursed his lips as he met Griffin's gaze. His friend knew him too well. "If I contact any of my former police colleagues about Lucas, they'll probably want to throw *me* behind bars. They don't want to hear anything about it. And you know Sheriff Thompson, he's not going to want to hear that I'm still looking for Lucas. I'll get the police involved when I find some concrete evidence."

Tavis's gaze wandered to Shayla's house. He had told her the same, that she shouldn't breathe a word of what had happened to the sheriff's department. What was the point? They were no closer to finding Lucas, and they couldn't give an accurate description of the shooter.

"Go home, Tavis," Griffin said. "I've got this. You know I'll make sure she's safe."

Tavis looked at his friend. "I know. I just… It's been a long day."

"Which is why you need to get some rest. I'm a phone call away. If anything happens, you know I'll reach out to you immediately."

"Thanks, Griffin." Tavis had some work to do at home anyway. Sleep would have to wait.

He exited Griffin's vehicle and was on his way. What did Jenae Wilkinson have to do with all of this?

Until just last week, Jenae had apparently lived at the address where someone had lured Shayla to kill her. According to Shayla, there was no reason that Jenae would want her dead. She'd been friendly with Jenae years ago, but not friends.

Tavis quickly pulled into his driveway then slammed on the brakes. He needed to dive into his files to see if he could find a connection between Jenae and Lucas. Something he'd overlooked before, or a connection he had failed to make.

"Why can't you just let this go?" Sheriff Thompson had asked him late last year when Tavis had tried to get him to look into a lead about where Lucas could have been. At the time, Tavis had received an anonymous message about Lucas living on the Big Island under an alias. He'd wanted the Sheridan Falls' police resources to track the person down and verify if it was indeed Lucas. But Sheriff Thompson had wanted none of it.

Ultimately, Tavis had gone around Thompson and gotten the information from Deputy Mike Jenkins. It hadn't been Lucas after all.

Apparently he'd been in Buffalo all this time.

Tavis hurried into his modest two-story house. He took the stairs two at a time to the second level, then went into the spare bedroom that he'd turned into his war room. There was no bedroom set in this room, but a desk and table and cabinets with various files. In this room, he had everything to do with the murders.

Tavis stood in front of the wall on which he'd erected a large whiteboard. It had all the visuals corresponding to the case. In the center was a picture of Hayley and one of Jonathan. From there he had lines drawn toward Lucas, and also Shayla, and the other friends who'd been at the party that night. There were family members and more friends from school connected to the pair, with his notes detailing useful points and questions.

He kept his detailed notes in his binder and files, which included the interviews he'd done over the years. But no one had given him anything useful. People offered speculations, theories, and the belief that Lucas was a no-good bad boy who had likely changed his identity and was living undetected somewhere.

Tavis moved to the wall. Jenae Wilkinson had been Alex Thompson's girlfriend, and had left town not long after the murders. She'd headed clear across the country to Oakland, California, for college, and after her degree had returned to Upstate New York. She and Alex had gotten married and had settled in Buffalo, but they'd divorced two years ago.

Something about his conversations with Jenae had always left him unsettled. Her story was both vague and detailed. With what he'd learned today, Tavis wondered if she'd deliberately kept critical information from him.

According to her, she'd been at the party but so high that she hadn't been paying attention to anything. She'd been drinking and smoking pot. Sure, there might've been a few squabbles, but she'd left long before anything serious had happened. She knew nothing.

That had been her initial story. Vague. And then she'd somehow remembered some details with stunning clarity. So much so, that Tavis didn't believe her. His years as a cop had taught him that when suspects were too vague or too detailed, they were most likely lying. And when their stories changed, it was pretty much a guarantee that they weren't telling the truth.

Given her initial lack of recall, when Jenae had suddenly offered Tavis a timeline that was very exact, he'd heard her out but had been wary. According to her, at eight thirty, she'd arrived at the party. By nine o'clock, she'd already had two drinks and had been smoking weed. By nine thirty, she was starting to lose her senses. By ten, she wasn't feeling well and had asked Alex to take her home. At ten fifteen, she'd been crawling into bed. She hadn't been sure if Alex had gone back to the party. Maybe he had? But according to Jenae, Alex had told her that he'd left the party before anything major happened.

For someone so vague on other details, she'd come up with a pretty specific timeline that had Tavis wondering if she'd created that story. But at the end of the day, he hadn't believed that Jenae was involved in the murders.

Now, he wasn't so sure anymore. He wanted to talk to her again. But to do that, he needed to find her.

Tavis picked up his cell phone and called Deputy Mike Jenkins. He answered after the first ring.

"Deputy Jenkins."

"Hey, Mike. It's Tavis."

"Oh, hey, Tavis. How are you?"

"I'm okay. But I have a favor to ask."

"Of course you do. What is it? I can't guarantee I can help."

Tavis knew the routine already. Mike didn't want to cross certain lines. He didn't want to push the rules or break them, but Tavis still reached out to him on many occasions to see if he would do just that.

"Jenae Wilkinson," Tavis said. "I'm trying to find her."

"Didn't you ask me this last year?"

"Well, that was a year ago. I wasn't able to find her then. But I've had this feeling, call it a hunch, and I feel the need to follow up on it."

"You're killing me, man."

"Last year I wanted to talk to her and go through her statement again. I've spent some time reconfirming the statements of most of the people I interviewed. But I've been looking at what she told me. I find it suspect." He didn't want to tell Jenkins about the house in Buffalo… not yet.

"What's talking to Jenae going to do for the case? You

think she killed Hayley and Jonathan and disposed of their bodies?"

"I'm not saying that. But I want to talk to her again. I want to see if she's got more to tell me now than she did before. She could've been afraid the first time. You know how it goes. Witnesses change their stories all the time."

"All right, Tavis," Deputy Jenkins grudgingly agreed. "I'll see what I can do."

Chapter Eight

"Come on, Mom," Shayla said, helping her mother to sit up on the bed. "I know you're weak, but let's get you up. Let's take a short walk to the kitchen."

"Oh, sweetheart. I don't know."

"You need to get a little exercise in. I can't begin to say that I know what you're going through, but I know that you need to move your legs and your arms. I'm with you. I've got you."

Her mother began to shift her legs over the side of the bed, and Shayla helped her. Then she wrapped her arms around her mother's torso and held her, guiding her to the floor.

"Are you okay?" Shayla asked.

Her mother was unsteady on her feet, but after a moment, she said, "Yes. I'm okay."

The pole with the IV was attached to her arm, and Shayla grabbed it so they could walk with it down the hallway. "I am glad that you're here. Maybe you're what I need for this fight."

"I know that I am. There's so much I have yet to do, Mom. And I need you here for all of it."

"I hope that soon you'll find someone nice in your life. Someone to take care of you and give you babies."

Shayla wasn't sure if that was in the cards for her, but

she agreed with her mother to make her feel better. "I'd love nothing more than to give you lots of grandchildren. But you've gotta be here to see them. Deal?"

"Deal." They walked slowly, her mother taking one careful step at a time through the hallway. And then the doorbell rang. They were crossing the threshold into the living room, and Shayla guided her mother to the sofa. "Sit here for a second, Mom. Let me get the door."

Shayla hurried to the front door and opened it. The nurse was out doing some errands, and Shayla didn't expect that it was her. She looked through the peephole, and seeing Sheriff Thompson, she was instantly alarmed. Had he heard about what had happened yesterday? She quickly opened the door.

"Sheriff Thompson," she said, a hint of a question in her voice. "Is everything okay?"

"Hello, Shayla." He tipped his Stetson toward her. "I'm here to make sure you're okay."

Shayla swallowed. "Oh?"

"I hear you took your car in to be cleaned up. My son Chase told me."

"Yes." Shayla smiled softly, relaxing. "I didn't know that that was his shop. He promised he'd fix my car up for me. I should be able to get it maybe by tomorrow."

"He took a picture of the threat written on your windshield and sent it to me. It was pretty ballsy of whoever did it. Just wondering if there's anything else that's happened. Any other thing making you feel unsafe?"

For a moment, Shayla wondered if the sheriff knew about what had happened in Buffalo yesterday. But how could he? Tavis wasn't going to say anything, and she'd agreed to keep silent about it as well. "Only Donny a couple of days ago," she told him. "Since then, things have been okay."

"Is that Sheriff Thompson?" her mother called out.

"Yes, ma'am. Glad to hear your voice."

"Thank you," her mother returned. "I'd come to the door, but I'm not properly dressed."

"That's okay, ma'am," the sheriff said.

Shayla was glad to hear that her mother had summoned the strength to call out to the sheriff, even if she wasn't able to rise to her feet to come to the door. She was in her nightgown, and not dressed for company anyway.

"I was just helping my mother take a little walk around the house. She's still very weak," Shayla told Sheriff Thompson.

"That's okay. I'm not staying. I just wanted to reiterate that if you feel unsafe at all, or if anything happens that's bothersome, please do call me." He withdrew a business card and handed it to her. "You don't need Tavis nor his sidekick, Griffin, tailing you and probably getting you into worse trouble."

"What do you mean 'getting me into worse trouble'?"

"Tavis… I don't know what it is about him, but trouble finds him. He's the type who gets himself mixed up where he shouldn't. Let me just leave it at that. You have a problem with anyone in this town, call me. I'm the sheriff. I'll take care of it."

The sheriff would no doubt see what had happened yesterday as proof of his point about Tavis, though what had happened hadn't been his fault. Shayla tapped the card against her palm. "Okay. Thank you, Sheriff Thompson. But I'm hoping that the incident with Donny was the last of it."

"Me too."

The sheriff turned, about to leave, but quickly pivoted back on his heel. "By the way, I'm not sure if you're aware, but tomorrow there's a vigil for Hayley and Jonathan. It happens every year on the anniversary of their deaths."

"Yes, I heard about it."

"I'm wondering if maybe you shouldn't go, in case you were planning on it. If someone here is angry enough to hurt you, might be best you not give them the opportunity."

"You think I should stay away? If people know I'm here and I don't go, maybe that will give them *more* reason to be upset."

"But you don't want to push your luck, now, do you? I know you didn't have anything to do with killing Hayley and Jonathan. And in their hearts, the people in this town know it too. But that won't stop people from giving you a hard time."

A few harsh words Shayla could handle. Keeping safe from someone who wanted her dead was another matter. Was it Jenae? Or Lucas?

"Don't get me wrong," the sheriff went on. "Many are still angry. They either think that Lucas was defending your honor where Hayley was concerned, or that you know where he went. So, all things considered, there could be some bad blood at the vigil that you might want to avoid."

"I'll take the advice under advisement," Shayla said. "I didn't come back here for the vigil. I came here for my mom."

Sheriff Thompson nodded. "You take care now."

"You too."

AFTER SHAYLA GOT her mother back into bed and once the nurse returned, she went to get her phone. That's when she saw that she had missed a call from Tavis. She called him back and he answered after the first ring.

"Hey, Shayla. Did you get my message?"

"No, I just saw that you called, so I figured I would call you back. I noticed that you're not outside."

"That's why I was calling. To let you know that I'll be on my way soon. I was pretty much up all night going through my files, trying to see if there's something I missed. I still can't find a connection between Jenae and Lucas."

"And I don't know one either. They knew each other, but they weren't friends."

"I assume you called the number Lucas called you from."

"Yes, and it's out of service now."

"Figures," Tavis said, and Shayla could hear the frustration in his voice. "Let's forget about that for now. How are you today?"

"Uh, okay. In some ways, yesterday seems surreal. Like it was a dream."

"And how's your elbow?"

"Much better. I took a long hot bath last night, and a painkiller. I'll live."

"Griffin just texted to tell me that the sheriff was at your house."

"Yeah. Sheriff Thompson came by. He wanted to see how I was doing, and at first I wondered if he knew about yesterday. But he came by to check on me, and let me know that I should be in touch with him if there are any problems or threats. He ended up telling me that I should probably stay away from the vigil tomorrow, considering someone wants to do me harm."

"Really?"

"Yeah. I guess it makes sense. But I doubt Lucas will show up here. Anyone else at the vigil will probably give me dirty looks. Dirty looks, I can deal with."

"I agree, I don't think he'll show up here either." Tavis paused. "I've been searching for Jenae online, but I can't find any information on her. I know she ended up marrying Alex Thompson. I've seen some pictures of the two of them on his social media, as if they're still a happy couple. Have you been in touch with her online?"

"No," Shayla said. "When I left, I basically had to close

all my social media accounts because of the hate. I kept in touch with a few people via phone and texting, but she wasn't one of them."

"I might track down Alex, see what he can tell me. I wonder if she's always had no social media presence, or if this is something new."

"You checked under Thompson, her married name?" Shayla asked.

"Yes, I checked both her maiden name and married name."

"I can ask my cousin if she has a way to reach her. They were both dating the Thompson boys, so maybe they stayed in touch."

"That'd be great," Tavis said. "You can let me know when I see you later."

"Sure thing."

When Shayla ended the call with Tavis, she punched in Deedee's number. "Hey, cuz," Deedee greeted her, a smile in her voice. "What's up?"

"Nothing much. Oh, my mom's doing a bit better. We went for a walk around the house earlier."

"That's great," Deedee said. "Tell her I'll be by to see her again soon. And my parents are coming back from North Carolina later this week, so they'll be visiting her then."

Shayla was looking forward to reuniting with her aunt and uncle, whom she hadn't seen in years. "I was talking to Tavis, and he had a question. He's trying to reach Jenae Wilkinson. I told him maybe you'd know how to get in touch with her?"

"Why does he want to reach her?"

For a moment, Shayla considered telling Deedee what had happened yesterday, but she didn't want to get into that right now. "Sounds like he wants to go over something she told him about the night of the murders. I'm not sure."

"Last I heard, Jenae and Alex broke up and Alex came back to Sheridan Falls. I don't know what happened to Jenae."

"You don't have a number for her? Did you guys ever stay in touch?"

"We stayed in touch for a little while. Here and there, off and on. I'm sure the number I have for her is old, but I can try it."

"Oh, that'd be great. If you reach her, let me know."

"I will. Now, what are you going to do about tomorrow and the vigil?"

Shayla filled her cousin in on the fact that the sheriff had dropped by and ultimately told her he didn't think it would be a good idea for her to attend the vigil.

"I'm inclined to agree with him," Deedee said.

"I don't know if it's because everyone's telling me not to go, or because I feel I should be able to grieve for Hayley since I did nothing wrong. But I think I want to go. What time is it being held?"

"Two o'clock. At the school. It's always at the school because that's where their bodies were found. But, Shayla, I don't think you should go. It's a bad idea."

The more people didn't want her to go, the more she *did* want to go. There was no doubt she had a stubborn streak, and hadn't she let the townsfolk control her enough already?

"I hear you," Shayla said. "I'll make up my mind in the morning."

HOLDING A MUG of coffee, Shayla approached Tavis in his vehicle where he was parked outside of her house. She went over to the driver's side of his GMC Sierra and he lowered the window.

Smiling, she passed him the coffee. "Black with two sugar."

"Thank you. You didn't have to."

"It was no trouble. But… I tried to make a lasagna for you, figuring you were likely hungry, but I ruined it. I was wondering if maybe you feel up to taking a drive to Deedee's restaurant. I can treat you to a meal. And you can talk to Deedee about Jenae."

Tavis perked up. "She knows something?"

"I'm not sure, but I talked to her about Jenae, and she said she has some news. She doesn't want to share the news over the phone or via text. She wants to talk in person."

"Definitely, we can go over there. Now?"

"Just let me grab my purse."

A SHORT WHILE LATER, Tavis and Shayla were entering 24-Hour Breakfast and More. The hostess brought them to an available booth and placed two menus on the table in front of them.

"Your waitress will be with you shortly," the red-haired teenager said.

No sooner than the hostess walked away, a woman with short black hair began to approach their table. But fast on her heels was Deedee. "I've got this table, Amber," Deedee said, flashing the woman a bright smile.

"Oh…okay."

"This is my cousin, Shayla," Deedee explained. "And my friend Tavis."

"Nice to meet you both," Amber said, then sauntered off.

Deedee slid into the booth, beside Shayla. "Hey, Tavis. Good to see you."

"Good to see you too, Deedee."

Deedee glanced around before saying in a lowered voice, "You're trying to reach Jenae?"

"Yes," Tavis told her.

"Why?"

"It's about my cousin's murder. I want to verify a couple of the things she told me."

"After all this time?" Deedee asked. "What could she say now that could possibly help you?"

"Maybe she knows more than she ever told me," Tavis said. "I have my reasons for wanting to speak to her. Do you have a way to reach her?"

Deedee sighed softly. "I wasn't able to contact her directly. The number I had for her is out of service. But I talked to someone who does still talk to her. She conveyed the message that you wanted to reach her, and Jenae said that she has nothing more to tell you and she doesn't want anybody bothering her about the past."

Tavis frowned. "So she won't talk to me?"

"It sounds like she's a bit afraid," Deedee admitted. "Her marriage with Alex ended on bad terms. Like, really bad terms. She doesn't want him getting wind of where she is."

"I would never breach that confidence."

"I'm sure, but I can understand her hesitation. Maybe if you give me the specific questions you want to ask, I can forward them?" Deedee suggested.

Tavis shook his head. "No. That won't work. What I will do is give you my number. Tell her friend to pass along the message that I'd really like to hear from her. If she calls me, then we can talk."

"Okay," Deedee agreed. "Fair enough."

Shayla asked, "Did she ever say anything bad about me, Dee?"

"Not that I'm aware of. Why?"

"Just wondering," Shayla said. "So many people didn't like me. I don't know if Jenae was one of them."

Deedee shrugged. "If she ever said anything, it wasn't to me."

"And what about her and Lucas?" Shayla went on. "I don't remember them being friends, but maybe they were?"

Deedee looked between Shayla and Tavis, her eyes narrowing. "Why, what are you thinking?"

"I've been thinking about everyone who was at the party, and whether or not someone might be inclined to protect Lucas," Tavis answered. "I know you were there, but you left early, right?"

"I did," Deedee said.

"Do you remember what time?" Tavis asked.

Deedee's mouth fell open, but she didn't answer right away. "I don't exactly remember. That was nine years ago."

"But when you left, was Jenae still there?" Tavis pressed.

"I… I honestly don't remember. Maybe she left before me…?" Deedee's voice ended on a question. "I'm not really sure what you're getting at."

"Something happened…" Shayla began. It was time to fill her cousin in. "Yesterday—"

"Someone contacted Shayla," Tavis interjected. "This person suggested that Jenae had possibly helped Lucas nine years ago."

"What?" Deedee couldn't hide her shock. "Who contacted you?"

Shayla looked to Tavis, who clearly didn't want her to tell Deedee about their trip to Buffalo yesterday. When he didn't speak, she did. "Someone called me. Said that Lucas and Jenae were connected…"

"Which is why I'm exploring all angles," Tavis said. "If I can talk to Jenae, she can answer these questions."

Deedee shook her head. "I don't know about that. I think Hayley and Jonathan were the last two people at the party, and that's when something went wrong. Lucas killed them, then freaked out and took off."

"Maybe there's no connection," Tavis admitted, "but I don't want to leave any stone unturned."

"I'm sure Deedee will do what she can to help," Shayla said, offering her cousin a smile. "If she can get a message to Jenae, great." She turned to Tavis. "I promised you a meal." She opened the menu. "Do you know what you want to eat?"

Tavis glanced at the menu. "I'll have a Philly cheesesteak sandwich. To go."

"Sure thing," Deedee said, her tone sounding clipped. She got out of the booth and headed toward the kitchen.

"You upset my cousin," Shayla said.

"I've got to ask questions, Shayla. If I don't ask questions, I won't get answers."

"But you made it sound like you were doubting her." Shayla could see the sheriff's point about Tavis. He was like a dog with a bone, unwilling to give it up. But there was no point upsetting people when you needed their help. "And why didn't you want me to tell her about yesterday?"

"I'd prefer we keep that to ourselves for now. Until we learn more, I don't want word about that getting out."

"She wouldn't tell anyone."

"And she definitely won't if she doesn't know."

Shayla frowned. Tavis was being very hardheaded about this. "You seem upset," she said to him.

"I'm frustrated," he told her. "I know that someone knows something. Someone must. All these years, someone must've heard something."

"I know you want to solve this case. And God knows, I do too. Hayley was your cousin and my best friend. But... what if you can't? What if there are no answers?"

"You still believe that, after yesterday? Lucas contacted you. For the first time in nine years, he's back on the radar."

"But what if he disappears again, this time for good? This case might never be solved."

"I won't accept that. I can't live with that. I am going to solve this case, Shayla. Whether it's now, or five years from now. I'm going to get the answers that my family deserves."

Chapter Nine

I'm really sorry. I don't feel well, but another nurse will be coming in this morning.

Shayla reread the text, stunned. She could accept that the nurse wasn't feeling well. But why wouldn't she have the decency to call?

Shayla pressed the phone icon to dial Jennifer's number.

"Hello?" Jennifer sounded hoarse.

"Sorry to call you," Shayla began, "but I figured it's easier to have a short conversation rather than keep texting back and forth. I'm sorry to hear you're not feeling well. Is this other nurse coming in for eight?"

"Yes. She'll be there in the next half hour. I'll be back tomorrow or maybe the next day. As long as I shake this bug."

"Obviously, take the time you need to get well," Shayla told her, her irritation fading. If Jennifer was sick, that wasn't good for her mother.

"I'm really sorry."

"No need to apologize." At least Jennifer had corresponded with her this time. She'd seemed perfectly fine last night, but sickness could come on instantly. She only hoped that whatever Jennifer had wasn't something that would affect her mother.

"Get well," Shayla told her.

"I will."

THE REPLACEMENT NURSE, Melanie, was an older woman who was efficient and aloof. She set about making oatmeal for her mother's breakfast, and after she'd eaten, Melanie got her up and out of bed. Again, her mother took a walk around the house, and Shayla was glad. Hopefully every day she'd get stronger and stronger.

While Melanie cared for her mother, Shayla spent some time online answering business emails and going through the orders.

A few of the emails she received were complaints. One large order for a dance team had not been delivered on schedule.

Before calling the supplier herself, Shayla called Lyndsay, her assistant manager, to see if the problem had been addressed.

"I'm already on it," Lyndsay told her. "There was a backlog, but the supplier is rushing the order and giving us a discount because of the delay. I'm going to pass the discount on to the customer."

"Good," Shayla said. "Keep me posted."

"I will. Look, don't worry about the store. I'm taking care of everything."

Shayla exhaled softly. "Thank you. I know you're completely capable of handling things while I'm away."

When Shayla had decided to move the business online, Lyndsay would come to her house for the day, where they'd both work together, go through the orders and catalog the inventory delivered to her place. Lyndsay knew every aspect of the business. Dazzle Dance Designs was in good hands.

"Spend time with your mother," Lyndsay said. "How is she, by the way?"

"She seems stronger. She's been up and walking around. With some help, but still."

"I'm praying for her. And for you."

"Thank you."

"And what about you? Are you safe?"

Shayla's eyes ventured to the back of her bedroom door where her purses hung on a hook. She frowned, noticing that an older brown purse was now on the top. She hadn't touched that purse in ages. How was it on top?

"Shayla?" Lyndsay prompted.

"Um, yeah," Shayla said. "I've been safe." Maybe the purse had always been there and she wasn't remembering correctly. That had to be the case.

A beat passed. Then Lyndsay said, "I didn't want to tell you this, but obviously you need to know. An email came in to the store's account. Someone said that if you know what's good for you, you won't go to the vigil."

"When did you get that email?"

"This morning."

Shayla bit down on her bottom lip. "All right, thanks for telling me."

"You know I'm worried about you. Maybe you shouldn't go."

Shayla felt a spurt of anger. How tough this person was, anonymously threatening her. Lucas? That didn't feel right. He had called her and announced himself, so why send anonymous emails? Whoever had a problem with her, they should just make it known. She was tired of dealing with this.

"I have someone who's protecting me," Shayla said.

"What?" Lyndsay sounded shocked. "Like a bodyguard?"

"An old friend. Yes, he offers bodyguard services, and he's watching out for me. So I'm okay. Please don't worry about me."

"Well, I'm glad to hear that, but please stay in touch. Let me know that things are going well."

"I will."

As Shayla ended the call with Lyndsay, she contemplated calling the sheriff to let him know about this latest email threat. But he would just reiterate that she shouldn't go to the vigil.

Instead, Shayla headed outside. Tavis had been there this morning, not having taken a break since last night. He looked at her with concern as she approached the vehicle.

She got into the passenger seat. "I got some news. My assistant in Florida, who runs my e-store with me, told me that an email threat came in again. Someone who doesn't want me to go to the vigil."

"Were you planning to go?" Tavis asked.

Shayla squared her shoulders. "Yes. I am."

"Good. Because I plan to be there as well. That way I can have eyes on you as opposed to having Griffin come to the house to watch you."

Shayla smiled. "Perfect."

Back in the house, she called Deedee. "I hope you have the afternoon off as we discussed yesterday," Shayla said before Deedee could speak.

"You're not going to the vigil, are you?" Deedee asked.

"I am," Shayla said with resolve in her voice. "I'm in town, why shouldn't I?"

"You've already had a threat left on your car and a gun pulled on you. I think the last thing you should do is show your face at the vigil and give someone a chance to hurt you."

If only her cousin knew what had happened in Buffalo. But Shayla was certain that she'd be fine today, with her plan to stay at the back and observe. Besides, there was no way Lucas was going to show his face at the vigil.

"I know," she said. "But if people know I'm in town and

I don't go, they'll have something to say, won't they? So I'm gonna go, stay at the back. Wear a hat. Try to remain unseen. And I would really like it if you'd go with me."

"Considering how stubborn you are, I made arrangements to have my shift at work covered. But I'm not happy about this."

"You'll be happy to know that Tavis will also be at the vigil, so it works out anyway. Otherwise he was going to have to call someone in to replace him to watch me at the house. Now he doesn't have to."

"You have this all worked out," Deedee said somewhat sourly.

"It's eleven thirty now, so that gives you a couple of hours to get here. I think we should leave here at one thirty to get to the school."

"Why do you have to be so stubborn?" Deedee asked her. "I think you're asking for trouble. Stay with your mother and leave the town to do what it always does. You don't need to be there."

Deedee sounded more concerned about the threat than she had before. "You must think someone's really going to hurt me?"

"Why take any chances?"

Had Deedee heard something? In a town like this, Shayla wouldn't be surprised. With her insistence that she not go to the vigil, Shayla wondered if there was something Deedee wasn't telling her. Or was she just being excessively cautious?

Of course, her cousin was the type to be excessively cautious, whether fearing sharks or rollercoasters. Maybe Deedee was simply worrying that the worst would happen.

"I'm gonna go," Shayla said. "If you don't want to pick me up, Tavis can give me a ride there. Just let me know."

"I'll pick you up," Deedee said grudgingly. "And I'll be there early enough so that Tavis can tail us to the vigil.

That's the one thing I'm happy about—that he'll be there. Though, hopefully, he no longer thinks I'm lying about the night of the murders."

"He does tend to push hard," Shayla said. "But he doesn't think you're lying. He's just…determined to get answers."

"He could have fooled me. But I do understand. He lost his cousin."

"See you at one thirty?" Shayla said.

"See you at one thirty."

THE VIGIL WAS to start at two, and at exactly one fifty-five, Deedee pulled her car up in front of the school. The crowd had already gathered on the grass, balloons and candles in hand.

"That's a lot of people," Shayla commented.

"They pretty much shut down the town so everyone who wants to attend can. Two in the afternoon—"

"The exact time that dog walker found their bodies under the tarp at the back of the school by the dumpster," Shayla supplied.

Shayla gazed out at the crowd, nerves tickling her stomach.

"We don't have to do this," Deedee said to her.

"Yes, I do. I'm not here for anyone in this town. I'm here for myself. For Hayley and Jonathan."

Behind them, Tavis pulled his vehicle to a stop. "And my personal bodyguard has arrived." He'd been on a call when Deedee had driven off from her mother's house, so was delayed by a few minutes. "Which was your idea, by the way. So, no need to worry."

Deedee cut her eyes at her. Shayla offered her a tentative smile, then looked in the visor's mirror and adjusted the baseball cap on her head. Satisfied that her identity was adequately obscured, she opened the door. Deedee followed suit.

Together, Shayla and Deedee walked slowly toward the crowd. Shayla didn't want to get too close to the group. She wanted to linger at the back; be part of the throng of people, but safely away from them. With everyone facing the family members who were standing on the school steps at the front, Shayla didn't expect anyone would be spotting her in the crowd.

And it did seem as if much of Sheridan Falls was there. She recognized some of the faces as they turned to look in her direction. Chase was standing with his wife, Lisa, and his brother, Alex. Graham Knight, who'd been one of Jonathan's best friends. Alisha Macklin and Kelly Du-Pont, who'd been on the cheer squad. Almost all of the football team from years before was in attendance, many of them looking visibly older, some not so much. More women who'd been on the cheerleading squad. Other athletes. Molly from the coffee shop.

Shayla stopped walking. She stood behind a taller man she didn't recognize, hoping that she would melt into the crowd. She looped arms with her cousin.

Katie Harrison, who looked almost exactly the same as she had when she'd been a cheerleader, right down to her fiery red hair, was walking toward them with extra balloons. Shayla glanced away, not meeting her gaze.

"Hey, Deedee," Katie said. "Here are some balloons."

Deedee took them, and passed one to Shayla as Katie continued through the crowd.

The sound of someone clearing their throat reverberated through the microphone. Shayla looked to the front.

"Everyone with candles, please light them now," Eric, Jonathan's father, said.

People in the crowd took a moment to light their candles, some sharing the flame with those around them.

"Thank you all for coming today," Eric continued. "Once again, we are marking the grim milestone of Jonathan's and Hayley's passing. Of their *murders*. And, sadly, their killer has not been brought to justice."

Hayley's mother, Victoria, was weeping. Her hair was a thick afro now as opposed to the permed straight style that Shayla remembered. The afro looked good on her.

The tear-filled eyes did not.

She was holding the teddy bear that Shayla remembered all too well. Hayley'd had to sleep with it every night. Even when they went away for dance competitions, she'd brought that bear with her. It was her good luck charm, she'd always said.

Eric hugged his wife, Maria, comforting her as she also openly grieved. "People say time heals all wounds," Eric began, "but I can tell you that's not true. Each year, the pain cuts a little deeper knowing our precious son is still gone. That he's never coming back. Some days it feels like a dream and I think I'm going to wake up and he's going to be in his bed clutching one of those trains he loved so much, but it never happens."

"It's still like it happened yesterday," Maria said, holding her hand against her heart. "I'll never see my son play college football at Kent State as he was going to. I'll never see him married. There have been days I haven't wanted to go on."

Jonathan's younger sister, Emily, hugged her mother. There were more tears. It was hard to watch.

"I want to thank each and every one of you who has been supportive of us over the years," James, Hayley's father, said to the crowd. "My Hayley didn't deserve this, and neither did Jonathan. And while the pain is as deep as it is, I know it would be lessened if the killer could be brought to justice."

He looked through the crowd, seeming to find Shayla

and stare her down. Shayla squirmed on the spot. Had he actually seen her? Or was he just looking in her general direction?

"I know this case can be solved," James went on. "And I know that someone in this town has answers. Think hard, think about what you know, what you remember. And if you've been keeping anything to yourself because of fear, take this time to do the right thing."

He was definitely looking in Shayla's direction. Deedee elbowed her. "You know he's talking to you."

Shayla said nothing. She wiped at the tear that was rolling down her cheek. She wanted to go forward and speak, say something on Hayley's behalf. Yet she knew she couldn't.

But others did. Friends and family went up and spoke about the wonderful people that Hayley and Jonathan had been.

After a good twenty minutes of fond memories and tears, Eric stepped up to the microphone. "The time has come for us to release the balloons. We're going to do that on three, then pause for a minute of silence. One... two...three."

Everyone released their balloons. The pink and blue balloons flew upward, catching on the wind and flying high into the sky. Some people clapped. Others hugged. Others wiped their tears. Then, following the lead of the family members on the steps who lowered their heads and closed their eyes, everyone went silent.

Oh, Hayley, I miss you, Shayla thought. *I hope that you're above, smiling down on us.*

"Thank you," James said after a minute passed. "I pray that by next year this time my daughter's killer has finally been brought to justice. This is too much for her mother and me to bear. Knowing that someone who brutally slayed your child is out there. Out there living his best life while our daughter is six feet under."

"And knowing how scared she must have been," Victoria said. "And I wasn't there to…to protect…her…" Victoria could barely finish the words, and James once again gathered her in his arms.

"Let their memories be a blessing," someone in the crowd said.

And at that moment, everyone blew out their candles. It was done in complete unison, and Shayla realized that that must have been the cue to blow the candles out.

Shayla quickly turned on her heel. She wanted to disappear before the crowd started to disperse. "All right. Let's go."

"Shayla Phillips, as I live and breathe."

At the sound of her name, Shayla stopped dead in her tracks. She glanced to her right, seeing Alex Thompson. Like his brother, he had grown wider around the middle over the years and his hair had thinned. He was a less attractive version of his former self. He smiled at her, as though happy to see her. Though they had never been close years ago.

"Alex," she said, forcing herself to sound pleasant. "It's been a long time."

"It sure has. How you like being back? I know it's not Miami, but Sheridan Falls still has its appeal."

She almost wanted to ask how he knew she lived in Miami, but then, of course everyone knew. People in this town spread any nugget of information instantly. No telephone lines required.

"It's been okay," she told him. "Not much has changed."

"I hear you." Alex chuckled softly. "But we do have a new stoplight near Main Street and the interstate. Right by your restaurant, Deedee."

"How's Jenae?" Shayla asked. "I heard you guys split up. But do you still talk? Where is she these days?"

Alex's grin went flat. "I have no clue where Jenae is. We're not on speaking terms."

"Oh, that's too bad. It's always unfortunate when relationships end and two people who loved each other no longer communicate. I was going to ask if you had a way for me to reach her, I wouldn't mind saying hi."

"Can't help you."

Shayla nodded. She lowered her gaze as people passed, not wanting anyone else to recognize her. "Well, it was nice running into you. But as I'm sure you know, my mom is sick. And I really do need to get back to her."

"Sure thing," Alex said. "See you around then, sometime."

"See you around," she said, then looped arms with Deedee's and hurried with her cousin toward the car.

TAVIS WOULD TYPICALLY be standing at the front of the vigil with his cousin and his aunt and uncle, but instead he sat in his vehicle, eyeing the gathering. He was watching for any threat to Shayla, of course. But he was also taking a look at the crowd from a different vantage point—as an investigator, not a mourner. He had his camera with him, and he was snapping shots of everyone so that he could examine them later.

In past years, he had mentally taken note of all the faces. Pretty much everyone in attendance had been people he'd known from the town. Yet he'd always looked for someone he didn't recognize, or someone who seemed fidgety or somehow out of place. He'd never specifically found anyone who'd been acting suspiciously, and he'd left each vigil with a sense of hopelessness. Because he was waiting for some break, something to happen, that would change the course of his investigation. But each year, he'd gotten nothing.

He slinked down his vehicle as Deputy Mike Jenkins walked from the grass toward the sidewalk. The deputy's cruiser was parked across the street from Tavis's pickup, but the man didn't stop and acknowledge Tavis, which was exactly as he wanted it right now. He wanted to scope out the dispersing crowd.

Sheriff Thompson was on the other side of the school, also watching the crowd. So was another deputy, Deputy Holland. The sheriff's department always came out for every vigil, allegedly doing what Tavis was now—but Tavis wasn't convinced that they were searching the crowd for clues. He figured they were in attendance to show their respect, nothing more. After all, Sheriff Thompson believed that Lucas was gone and never coming back because he would be too stupid to return to the town.

Tavis didn't disagree. Lucas had to know that returning to a small town like Sheridan Falls would be the same as walking into any police station and asking to be arrested.

Again, Tavis marveled at the fact that Lucas was in Buffalo. Had he been there all this time, or had he recently returned there?

Two people who were not at the vigil were Lucas's aunt and uncle, Rosita and Andrew Carr. They'd gone to the first one, and had been chased from the event. Just as Shayla had been. Even now, while they still lived in the town, they pretty much kept to themselves. They'd gotten some death threats in the beginning too, though Tavis had heard that the threats had died down after a few months. Maybe people realized that Rosita and Andrew were no more responsible for Lucas's actions than anyone else in Sheridan Falls. They'd taken in a troubled teen and had never imagined that he would kill two people and shame their names.

Tavis glanced to his left as a black sedan drove by. Speak of the devil, he saw Lucas's aunt in the passenger seat. Rosita and Andrew had come to the vigil after all.

But he didn't think they had exited their car, because he hadn't spotted them in the crowd. Maybe they'd been watching from a distance? Or were they simply driving by the school at this moment?

Looking from the Carr vehicle and back to the crowd, someone caught Tavis's attention. A person in a baseball cap on the far side of the field. Quickly picking up his camera, he zoomed in and took a photo. Who was that? He snapped off a couple of other shots, while the person, alone, walked farther away. Dressed in jeans and a jean jacket, by the shape, he could tell it was a woman.

Jenae?

TAVIS PULLED UP alongside Deedee's vehicle. Deedee wound down the window, and both she and Shayla looked out at him.

"Shayla, are you heading back to your place?" Tavis asked.

"Yeah," Shayla told him.

"I'll be there soon. I have to check something out." His gaze wandered ahead, and Shayla tried to follow his line of sight. The crowd was scattering, and she couldn't see whom he was specifically eyeing.

"No problem," she said. "See you soon."

Tavis drove off, and Deedee started up the car and began to move. She drove carefully, as some people were walking into the street to get to their own vehicles.

"Is that how it always is?" Shayla asked. "The balloons, candles, the speeches."

"Yeah," Deedee said. "It's a time for everyone to reflect and remember, and many people want to speak."

Shayla nodded, once again feeling a wave of emotion at the thought of Hayley being cut down in the prime of her life. She wished that she could have spoken up about her friendship with Hayley and how much she'd loved her, but she couldn't dare. Not when she was public enemy number one.

"At least I don't think anyone really noticed us," Deedee said. "That's what I was worried about, and that people would give you a hard time. Like they did at the first vigil."

"I wasn't going to let anyone force me away this time. I needed to be there. It felt… In a way, it felt like a bit of closure. Not fully, but at least I was able to feel close to Hayley without anyone getting in my way."

"I'm glad you got out of it what you wanted."

Shayla had gotten some of what she'd wanted, but not all. "If you don't mind, I'd like to go to the cemetery."

"Why?" Deedee asked.

"I have something… I want to leave it at the grave. I think it will give me the full closure that I'm looking for."

Deedee's eyes narrowed as she looked at her. "What do you have?"

Shayla wiggled the fingers on her left hand. "The silver band on my pinkie. Hayley gave it to me when we were ten. It's cheap—she won it in a gumball machine. But to me it meant the world, because she said it was proof that we would be BFFs forever. She had one too…" Shayla's voice trailed off. "Anyway, I want to leave it at the grave for her."

Deedee reached for her hand and squeezed. "Oh, hon. I'm so sorry."

"I hope that as she was dying, she knew that I loved her with all my heart. She was the sister I never had."

"I'm sure she did," Deedee said.

"I haven't been able to visit her grave in all these years," Shayla went on. "I feel as though there's unfinished business between us. Words left unsaid. So I want to say them to her. And I hope that wherever she is, she can hear me."

"I totally understand," Deedee said. "Absolutely, I'll take you to the cemetery."

TAVIS SLAMMED A hand against the steering wheel when he realized that he'd lost the mystery woman. With the crowd of people spilling onto the street, he hadn't been able to speed up and follow her. She'd cut sharply around the building, heading toward the back of the school, and he'd pulled up his vehicle several seconds after seeing her head that way, trying to get a better look. His options were either to watch the direction where she was heading and hope that he could drive in that direction and cut her off around the block, or get out of his vehicle and start to follow her.

But the woman, already dodging through the thicket of trees, suddenly started to run.

Tavis pulled the lever to open his door. Then cursed under his breath when he opened it and saw Sheriff Thompson standing there.

"Tavis," he said.

Tavis wanted nothing more than to speed around the block to see if he could catch up with the mystery woman. But Sheriff Thompson was putting a wrench in that plan.

"Sheriff," Tavis said, his voice strained.

"It was a nice vigil today, wasn't it? I didn't see you out there, though."

"I decided to watch from the comfort of my truck."

The sheriff looked beyond him, his gaze landing on the camera with the giant zoom lens. "Doing some sort of surveillance?"

"I always have my gear in my pickup."

"You need all that to provide protection for Shayla Phillips—or is there something else going on?"

"I took pictures of the event. That's not a crime, is it?"

"With that lens? Hmm." The man made it sound like an accusation.

"Yep."

"At least there weren't any problems today. Everything went smoothly."

"Yes, it did." Tavis glanced toward the trees. There was no sign of the woman. "If you—"

"I'm not sure who's been giving her trouble, but I already spoke to Shayla and told her if there are any more threats, she should come to me directly. I'm the one who can help her." He paused. "There haven't been any more threats, have there?"

"Nope," Tavis said, not quite meeting the sheriff's gaze.

"That's good. Then maybe what was written on her car was just someone being a pain in her butt. I doubt anyone's going to do her any harm."

"From your lips to God's ears." Tavis smiled tightly. "But either way, I'm here if there's a real threat or no threat at all."

"I expected you to say that." The sheriff tapped the inside of the Sierra's open window frame. "You have a good day, Tavis."

"You too, sheriff."

DEEDEE WAS DRIVING along Route 1 on the outskirts of town, heading toward the cemetery. She threw a furtive glance into the rearview mirror then said, "Is that guy following me?"

Shayla turned in her seat. There was a large SUV bearing down on them at a rate of speed that was way too fast compared to Deedee's. Route 1 had only one lane in each direction, and when the vehicle on their tail didn't pass them, Deedee sped up.

The SUV accelerated too.

"What's he doing?" Shayla asked, her heart thundering in her chest. Was this just some reckless person on the road? Or someone deliberately following them? She didn't know that anyone had seen them at the vigil, but perhaps someone had. Someone angry enough to—

They both screamed, their bodies jerking forward against their seat belts as the SUV rammed into their car.

"Oh my God!" Deedee exclaimed. She pressed her foot to the gas pedal, speeding up.

"Maybe you should pull over. Let this guy pass you."

"Pull over where? There's no shoulder here. Just gravel, and my car—"

Another jerk, and they screamed again. Clearly, this was no accident. The person behind them *wanted* to do them harm.

Deedee's car fishtailed and she fought to control the steering wheel.

"There," Shayla said, pointing to the county road coming up. "Turn left!"

Deedee hit the gas then slowed a little, anticipating the turn. As she started to turn left, the sound of the SUV's engine revving was all Shayla could register, and her heart caught in her chest.

The SUV slammed into their side. And then the car was spinning wildly. Shayla gripped the armrest on the inside of the door and held on, barely breathing. Gravel exploded in a cloud of smoke as Deedee's car hit the ditch. It spun one final time and then came to a rest on the driver's side. The airbags deployed, hitting Shayla in the face.

For one long moment, there was only silence.

Then Shayla closed her eyes and screamed.

Chapter Ten

Her pulse racing out of control, Shayla couldn't stop screaming. She was dangling in the car, her body leaning left against the seat belt as the Hyundai Sonata was on its side.

Suddenly it hit her. She was the only one screaming. Deedee was silent.

A cold chill sliding down her spine, Shayla was instantly afraid to open her eyes. It seemed like several minutes passed before she dared to do just that, afraid of what she might see.

"Deedee?" she asked, opening her eyes. Her head pounded, making it clear that she hadn't been in some bizarre dream where she'd been stuck on some strange ride at an amusement park, spinning around and around. She was in Deedee's car.

"Deedee…" Shayla's voice croaked as she looked to her left. Deedee sat there motionless, her eyes closed.

Terror seized every part of her body. "Deedee," she repeated, speaking louder this time. "Deedee!"

Deedee said nothing.

The airbag had deployed, and was pressed against Deedee's face. Surely, the airbag had saved her. So why wasn't she moving?

Oh God. No…

Shayla looked to the rearview mirror, remembering the SUV. But it wasn't there. It was just her and Deedee at the corner of this deserted road en route to the cemetery.

Shayla shook Deedee's shoulder. "Deedee, wake up!"

Blood gushed from Deedee's head, and her eyes remained closed.

Shayla had to get out of the car. She needed to get help. She opened the door, which immediately closed as the weight of gravity pulled it down. Shayla then hit the lever to lower the window and, thankfully, it worked. She undid her seat belt, forced herself past the side and front airbags, and squeezed through the window. She crawled onto the side of the car then hopped down.

As her feet hit solid ground and she drew in a deep breath of fresh air, the reality of the situation hit her. Someone had just tried to kill them. Deedee was unresponsive in the car. She needed to get help.

Shayla's cell phone was in her over-the-shoulder bag, and she quickly accessed it. She punched in Tavis's number.

TAVIS LOOKED AT his phone, saw Shayla's number flashing on his screen. He swiped to answer the call. "Hey—" He stopped short when he heard screaming on the other end of the line. "Shayla?"

"I don't know if Deedee's dead!" came her anguished voice.

Terror gripped Tavis's heart. "Where are you? What happened?"

"Someone ran us off the road!"

"Where?" Tavis demanded.

"Um, I don't know. I… I can't think."

"You said you were heading home. Are you at an intersection?"

"We were heading to the cemetery."

"St. Joseph's Cemetery?"

"Yes."

"So you're somewhere along Route 1."

"Yes. Wait, we're at the corner of County Road 5."

"Okay, I know exactly where you are. I'm on my way."

"Deedee's not moving. She's bleeding." Shayla sobbed. "I'm scared."

"I'm heading to you now. Call 9-1-1."

Tavis ended the call. The sound of terror in Shayla's voice had his gut clenching.

He put his pickup into Drive and tore off.

TAVIS SPED ALONG Route 1, not caring that he was going well over the speed limit. He had to get to Shayla and Deedee.

If someone had purposely run them off the road, then Shayla could still be in danger. And Deedee... He didn't want to believe that she was dead.

Behind him, he heard the sounds of the sirens before he saw the flashing lights in his rearview mirror. Tavis slowed for the cruiser, prepared to pull over, but the cruiser sped around him and continued on. The deputy was heading to the accident scene, no doubt.

By the time Tavis got there, the cruiser was parked on the road and he could see Shayla standing in the ditch beside the silver Hyundai. The car's rear was smashed up pretty badly, and it was on its side. The driver's side.

"Damn," Tavis uttered.

As his gaze wandered, his shock intensified. Rosita and Andrew were on the scene. At first, Tavis's brain didn't compute what he was seeing. Lucas's aunt and uncle? What the heck were they doing there?

Tavis pulled his Sierra to a screeching stop several feet from the accident, then jumped out of his vehicle and trotted back toward Shayla. Moments later, the sheriff's car came whizzing onto the scene.

Seeing him, Shayla hurried to him, and he noticed that she was limping. She threw herself into his arms. "Tavis!"

"I've got you," he said. He held her quivering body against his. He glanced at the wrecked vehicle. "Deedee?"

"She's alive," Shayla said. "But I couldn't get her out."

"We should wait for the firefighters to move her in case she has some internal injuries," Tavis said.

More sirens, then a fire truck was arriving, followed by the paramedics. All emergency personnel were responding to this single vehicle crash.

"You said someone ran you off the road?" Tavis asked. "Are you sure?"

"Someone deliberately hit us. Look at the rear. Then he rammed us from the side and we spun out, landing in the ditch."

Tavis released Shayla and went to further inspect the Hyundai's rear bumper. It was dented and scraped from an impact. "Did you get any information?" he asked. "License plate, make and model?"

"It was a dark car. An SUV. Either navy or black. I couldn't see anything else. I couldn't see who was behind the wheel. But they were definitely after us. After *me*..."

Tavis's gaze wandered to Rosita and Andrew as the sheriff and a paramedic made their way toward Shayla. What were those two doing there? Lucas's aunt and uncle conveniently on the scene?

Tavis didn't like coincidences.

He had seen them drive by the vigil, though they hadn't gotten out of their vehicle. Had they been angry? Angry enough to hurt Shayla? Though their vehicle was black, it wasn't an SUV. And more importantly, there was no damage to it. It couldn't have been the vehicle that forced them off the road.

He stepped toward them, wondering how they had come to be here at this moment. Several feet away, he saw Shayla shaking her head and backing away from the paramedic. "My cousin's the one who needs help," she said.

Tavis turned back to the Carrs. "Rosita and Andrew, hello."

"Hello," Andrew said, slipping an arm around his wife's waist. Her distress was palpable on her face.

"How did you end up at the scene?" Tavis asked, getting to the point.

"We were coming from the cemetery," Andrew answered. "Saw the car in the ditch. Heard the screaming. We pulled over."

It was a reasonable enough explanation. But Tavis pressed on. "You're coming from the cemetery?"

"As you know, today was the vigil for Hayley and Jonathan. We never like to go, but we did drive by today. Then we went to the cemetery to pay our respects. No one wants us at the vigil, but we still feel it's important to honor the victims. Not because we think Lucas killed them," Andrew quickly added. "But because that day changed all of our lives. Two children died who didn't deserve to."

The sheriff wandered over to them. "Andrew and Rosita, Shayla tells me you came upon the scene shortly after the accident."

"Yes," Andrew said.

"You know that Andrew is a retired firefighter," Rosita said. "He could never drive by without stopping to help."

"So you didn't witness the accident as it happened?" Sheriff Thompson asked. "You didn't see who ran them off the road?"

Tavis made his way back over to Shayla while the sheriff spoke to the Carrs. She was hugging her torso as she watched the firefighters in the front and back seats, working on freeing Deedee.

"This is my fault," Shayla said softly. "Someone wanted to kill me, and Deedee is the one paying the price. Maybe if I'd told her about what happened in Buffalo, she would have convinced me not to go today. And she wouldn't be…" Her voice ended on a sob.

"We don't know that this is connected to what happened in Buffalo," Tavis said, though he didn't believe his own words. He kept thinking about the woman in the crowd. Jenae?

"Isn't it?" Shayla asked. "First Buffalo, now this, and you think it's coincidence?"

The question was rhetorical, so Tavis didn't answer. But he didn't like coincidence. However, given Shayla's state of distress, he didn't want to tell her that he may have seen Jenae in the crowd.

"I'm the one they're after," Shayla went on. "They must have seen us at the vigil, then followed us."

"You're saying *they*," Tavis said. "Did you get a look at who was in the vehicle? And was it more than one person?"

Shayla's lips parted, but then her eyes narrowed. "I… I don't know. I couldn't see into the vehicle. All I know is that someone in a navy or black SUV ran us off the road."

Tavis would do his best to find everyone in the town who drove a vehicle that matched that description. But there were a number of them in town, including his.

When Deedee's body emerged on a wooden stretcher, Shayla doubled over with relief. "Oh thank God."

The other firefighters surrounding the car hurried to help carry Deedee to safety. At first, Tavis thought she was unconscious, until he heard her moan softly.

"She's going to be okay," Tavis told Shayla, reassured that she was conscious.

Shayla followed the firefighters to the ambulance, while keeping a respectful distance behind them. As two paramedics helped guide Deedee into the back of their vehicle, the paramedic who'd offered Shayla help returned. "We're going to get your cousin to the hospital as soon as possible. Let me check your vitals, check you for injuries."

"I'm fine," Shayla insisted.

"You could have internal injuries. You really need to go to the hospital to be evaluated."

Tavis placed a hand on the small of Shayla's back. "He's right. You should go."

The car made a loud thud sound as it was finally pulled upright. Seeing the mangled driver's-side door made Tavis realize how serious the attack had been. The Hyundai was far more damaged than he'd realized. That meant Deedee and Shayla had been very very lucky.

"I'll take her," Tavis told the paramedic. "I'll follow the ambulance to the hospital."

When Shayla looked up at him, he said, "We're going there for Deedee, anyway. May as well get you looked at. This is nonnegotiable, Shayla. If you have internal injuries that go undiagnosed, I'll never forgive myself."

Her chest rising with a heavy breath, Shayla nodded. "Okay."

She leaned against him, and he wrapped an arm around her. Every time she turned to him for support, he felt an odd stirring in his gut. He wanted to hold her until all the danger had passed.

"I'm worried about my mother," she said softly. "What if I put her in danger too?"

She pressed her face against his chest and, Lord help him, he wanted to stand there with her like that until she was no longer afraid. "I don't think anyone would hurt your mother. But we now know that this threat is not idle. It's very real. I'm going to have twenty-four-hour surveillance at your place at the back and the front. No one is going to get into your house to hurt you or your mother."

"But no one's there now."

"I'll call one of my guys as soon as we get in the vehicle. Your mother is going to be safe, Shayla. And so are you."

Looking up at him, Shayla nodded, and he could see the gratitude in her eyes. "I appreciate this so much. I promise I'll pay you."

"The only payment I want is you staying safe." Then he gathered her in his arms and held her, feeling a sense of satisfaction as her body melted against his.

And maybe something else he didn't want to acknowledge.

AT FIRST, Shayla had been so pumped up on adrenaline that she hadn't felt any pain and didn't think that she needed medical attention. But once they got to the hospital, she felt the pain in her lower back, her ankle and her head.

Thankfully, she had no broken bones, just some muscle aches and bruises. She would be fine—but would her cousin?

Now, as she and Tavis waited for word on her cousin's condition, Shayla had made the call to Aunt Maggie and Uncle Charles in North Carolina. They were making immediate plans to return home.

Dr. Nelson, who'd spoken to both Shayla and Tavis earlier about Deedee's condition, entered the waiting room. Tavis shot to his feet. Shayla sat, afraid of what he might say.

"I know I told you that I was worried about brain swelling and the possible complications of that, but we've run extensive tests on Deedee and, long story short, she's very lucky *and* a fighter. The airbag undoubtedly saved her life and protected her skull. She's got a mild concussion and some contusions, and she may suffer some short-term memory loss, but all indications right now are that she's going to be just fine."

"Oh thank God," Shayla uttered.

"That's the best possible news," Tavis said.

"She'll need to stay here for a couple of days for observation, just to make sure there are no unforeseen complications. And of course, she'll need pain management as well. I suspect that will be her biggest challenge." Dr. Nelson paused. "Someone was looking out for you both today."

"How soon can we see her?" Shayla asked.

"She's sleeping right now, but I would say probably in the next hour or so."

As the doctor walked away, Shayla threw her arms around Tavis. "I'm so relieved."

"I know you are. So am I."

"Since we can't see Deedee yet, I'd like to go home and check on my mom. I didn't expect to be gone this long, and I just want to make sure she's all right."

"Absolutely," Tavis agreed.

THE AFTERNOON HAD been a blur of activity, with Shayla's adrenaline racing at warp speed. But now, as Tavis pulled up in front of her mother's place, Shayla realized that her pulse was returning to a somewhat normal pace.

Being with Tavis had made all the difference. He'd been a calming force amid the chaos.

"Thank you so much for being there today," Shayla said. "I'm not sure I could have gotten through this without you."

"There was nowhere else I wanted to be."

Offering him a small smile, Shayla extended her hand and placed it on his. She held his gaze longer than she'd expected, unsurprised by the flash of heat she felt. Quickly, she glanced away.

How silly was she, once again crushing on Tavis? But every time he'd held her today, Shayla had felt as though there was something more between them. She'd wanted to melt into his strong arms and stay there. For a moment, she'd wondered if he'd felt the same way, but Shayla was fairly certain that the feeling was one-sided.

The one thing she did believe, and it made her very happy, was that Tavis didn't hate her anymore.

"We're going to find out who did this to you and Deedee," Tavis said with steely resolve. "And they're going to pay."

The determination with which he spoke had Shayla believing him. "I know," she said.

"Did you find it odd that Andrew and Rosita were at the accident scene?"

Shayla shook her head. "No, why?"

Tavis's eyebrows rose as he regarded her. "I don't think they're your number one fans."

"True," Shayla said. Rosita and Andrew felt she should have done more to clear Lucas's name. "But they weren't the ones who ran us off the road. You said they told you they were coming from the cemetery. I believe them. I was going to the cemetery for the same reason—to pay my respects away from the prying eyes of the townsfolk."

"I guess I'm grasping at straws here," Tavis said, his lips twisting in a scowl. "It just seems a bit coincidental that they showed up on the scene after the accident—and I don't like coincidences."

"It wasn't them. Nothing about that makes sense."

"There's something else," Tavis said. The silence that followed was heavy. "I didn't want to say this, because I didn't want to upset you. But there was a woman at the vigil today. I didn't get a good look at her, but I was wondering if maybe it was Jenae. If so, that could be the connection here. First, what happened in Buffalo, now this attempt on your life today."

As Shayla digested the words, her lips pulled into a taut line. She couldn't understand this at all. Why would Jenae want to hurt her?

"I can't be certain," Tavis went on. "It's speculation for now. But I couldn't help wondering."

"I saw Alex at the vigil and we spoke for a minute. I asked him if he's in touch with Jenae. His mood changed when I asked about her. He seemed irritated. But he said that they don't talk and he has no idea how to reach her."

"I was going to try to ask him exactly that. You believe him?"

"Oh yeah. Whatever the situation between them, there's no love lost."

Tavis frowned. "Hmm."

"Let's let this go for today. We can rack our brains until they're fried, but hopefully by tomorrow there'll be a clue based on evidence and not speculation. Sheriff Thompson might find the vehicle by then."

"Let's hope," Tavis said, but he didn't sound convinced.

Chapter Eleven

"You gave me quite the scare," Shayla said, unable to contain her smile. She was at Deedee's bedside and holding her hand, her heart brimming with happiness. All things considered, her cousin was okay. A few bruises and bandages weren't reflective of the serious crash she'd been in just the day before.

"You're not getting rid of me that easily," Deedee said.

"I would never want to get rid of you."

With a bit of effort, Deedee smiled. "I know. You talked to my assistant manager?"

"Of course. Don't worry about the restaurant. It's under control."

"And my parents?"

"Will be back soon." They had come to visit bright and early this morning, not stopping at home after arriving from North Carolina. "Your mother said she was going home to make you some—and I quote—'edible food.'"

Deedee chuckled. "Of course. My mother's probably worried that I'll waste away during the time I spend here."

Shayla grinned then swallowed as a spate of sadness hit her. So many years she'd lived away from her mother, and now her mother might not have much time left.

"I'm so sorry," Shayla said, and her happy tone turned

serious. "I never should have insisted that we go to that vigil. If I'd ever known—"

"You wouldn't have gone. I know." Deedee squeezed her hand. "It's not your fault."

"But you didn't want me to go, and I was so determined. Now you're here…"

"Exactly. I'm *here*. A little banged up, but still kicking. And you're still here too."

Shayla nodded. That was the most important thing— that the attempt on their lives had failed.

There was a knock at the door before it opened a smidgen. Deputy Jenkins stuck his head into the room. "Can I come in?"

"Sure," Deedee said.

"I hope you're up to answering some questions this morning. I did get Shayla's statement already, but you might be able to fill in some more blanks."

Deedee began to sit up in the bed, wincing as she did. Shayla slipped her hands beneath Deedee's underarms and helped ease her up.

"I'm ready to tell you what I remember," Deedee said.

Shayla was relieved that the doctor had been wrong. Deedee did seem to have her short-term memory, so that was good. She hadn't suffered any memory loss whatsoever. All things considered, this was a miracle.

Even Shayla's aches and pains and twisted ankle would heal. She only hoped that the person who had done this to them was caught quickly.

The deputy came to stand beside the bed and then dug his notepad out of his jacket. "Tell me what you remember."

"I was driving toward St. Joseph's Cemetery. Then, out of the blue, there was a van behind us." Deedee winced. "A van or an SUV."

"You think it was a van?" Shayla asked.

"Maybe. I mean, I think it was an SUV, but it could've

been a van, maybe. Or one of those pickup trucks on steroids. You know, those big, shiny ones."

"I suppose it could have been a Ford F-150 or one of those monster pickups," Shayla agreed. "Or an SUV. But I don't think it was a van."

"So a pickup truck or an SUV or maybe a van." Deputy Jenkins scrawled some notes.

"And it was black," Deedee added. "I'm pretty sure of that."

"Did you recognize it at all?" the deputy asked. "Have you seen anyone in town with such a vehicle?"

"I'm not sure what vehicle it was, so no, I didn't recognize it per se. But there are a lot of people in town with vehicles that look like that. Chase, for one. He has one of those big pickups, and it's black. But he's not the only one. There are a number of them."

"Chase was at the vigil," Deputy Jenkins said. "I saw him there. And, given the timing when you left, I don't think he could have been the one to run you off the road. He was talking to his father for quite some time after everyone dispersed."

"I didn't say it was him," Deedee pointed out. "You asked if I know anyone with such a vehicle. He's someone I know with a black pickup or an SUV. His brother too. Tavis. Probably thirty per cent of the men in this town."

The deputy scrawled more notes. "And you feel that you were deliberately targeted? This wasn't simply an accident? Maybe kids being stupid?"

"I remember the vehicle speeding up behind me. I started to drive faster, thinking that would appease the driver. But whoever was behind the wheel started to drive even faster. I wanted to pull over onto the gravel to let them pass me, but it was a two-lane road and nothing else was coming in the opposite direction, so I thought the driver would just overtake me. Then the next thing I know, he's hitting my bumper. I thought maybe it was a mistake. Until he hit me again. And then I quickly went to turn, because there was a side road coming up. I started to turn, and that's the last thing I remember…"

Shayla looked at the deputy. "This was deliberate. And I know I was the target. I've already spoken to Sheriff Thompson about some of the threats I've received, and I know this was directed at me. I was really shaken up and distraught yesterday, but today I'm angry. I could've been killed, and my cousin could've been killed. Why? Because people in this town won't let something go that I had nothing to do with. So today, I'm livid. I want this person caught. I want him caught now."

"I understand your frustration," the deputy said. "That's why we have to ask these questions. The more we know, the faster we can bring the culprit to justice."

"This is a small enough town," Shayla went on. "How hard can it be to search a database and find everyone who has a similar vehicle? Then find the person who has either just repainted the vehicle or has it in the shop somewhere."

The deputy gave her a wry smile. "I see you like to watch a lot of crime shows."

Was that meant as an insult? "Some things are common sense," Shayla said. "I'm just hoping that you're on top of this, because what happened yesterday was very serious and could have been deadly. It's a miracle that neither of us was killed."

"I agree." The deputy looked at Deedee again. "Do you have anything else to add? Anything that you think may be important?"

She shook her head. "No. I don't even remember the impact. Maybe that's a good thing. All I remember is at one point waking up and feeling somewhat disoriented and not knowing what was going on. The next thing I knew, I was in this hospital room."

Shayla stroked her cousin's forehead. Once again, she thought of how she could have lost her, and a wave of emotion gripped her heart.

"Please, deputy," Shayla said. "Find whoever did this. And find him quickly."

TAVIS STOOD OUTSIDE the hospital room with Deedee's parents. They had gone home a couple of hours ago and now had returned, Deedee's mother holding a tote bag from which emanated some seriously delicious smells. He had stopped Deedee's parents before they could enter her room, letting them know that the deputy was in with them.

"I hope he won't take too long. I want to make sure my daughter has some good food to eat. Hospital food." She made a face. "It's barely sufficient."

"It didn't take you too long to whip up something that smells amazing," Tavis said.

"Sweet and sour chicken with sticky rice," Maggie said. "I can prepare you a plate if you like. There's enough for two."

A smile tugged at Tavis's lips. He would love nothing more than to indulge in a meal, but he declined. "Deedee's going to need all the food she can get. I know that what they serve at hospitals is paltry and unappetizing. She's lucky she has you."

The door opened and the deputy exited. Maggie and Charles whizzed into the room.

Deputy Jenkins had his cell phone to his ear, and walked a good distance away as he chatted. Tavis couldn't hear what he was saying, but he watched him intently.

Several minutes later, Deputy Jenkins ended the call. Then he headed toward Tavis. "You wanted a word with me?"

"Yes," Tavis said. "Have you been checking local body shops to see if anyone brought in a vehicle for repair?"

"You sound like Shayla."

Tavis didn't ask him to elaborate. "Obviously the vehicle that ran them off the road is going to have some damage. It's going to pop up somewhere."

"I just got some news on that front," the deputy said, indicating the phone in his hand. "Both good and bad."

"Oh?" Tavis's eyebrows shot up.

"The vehicle that ran them off the road has been located."

"Why didn't you say so?" Tavis asked. Finally, there was a break.

"Well, that's where the bad news comes in. The good news is we found the vehicle, but the bad news is, the person it belongs to most certainly isn't the one who ran them off the road."

Tavis's gut began to sink. "You sure about that? You can't rule anyone out."

"The vehicle belongs to Aaron Burke," the deputy said, and let his words sink in. "I'm sure you can agree that Aaron Burke would not be the person behind the wheel of that SUV when Deedee and Shayla were run off the road."

Aaron Burke was one of the town's most high-profile residents. A famous soccer star, Tavis couldn't see it either. He had no connection to the case, though he did know the kids from school.

"Mr. Burke reported his vehicle stolen last night. It was found ditched the next county over."

"Darn it," Tavis uttered. "Hopefully the perp didn't wipe it down."

"He did one better. He torched it."

"Son of a—" Tavis clenched his teeth. Someone was really making sure to conceal their tracks. "Then there were two of them. If the SUV was ditched the next county over, whoever drove it there would need a ride back."

"He could have used a ride-sharing service—which

we're checking," Deputy Jenkins added before Tavis could ask the question.

"Hopefully he—or they—made a mistake."

"At first I thought it might've been a couple kids who were stupid, possibly drinking. But the fact that the SUV was torched tells me this was something different."

"It sure as hell was. And it's a miracle that there were no fatalities because of this." Tavis blew out a frustrated breath. "Man, I was hoping we'd catch a break with the SUV. Instead we're back at square one."

"*I'm* back at square one," the deputy clarified. "The sheriff's department is back at square one. You're not."

Tavis said nothing. He had some leeway where Deputy Jenkins was concerned, and he didn't want to push it. No, he wasn't officially investigating this case, but he'd be damned if he wasn't going to do what he could to find out who was behind the attack. Someone had nearly killed Shayla and her cousin—on his watch. He wouldn't soon forgive himself for that. The only way to atone for it was to find out who'd done it.

"Oh," the deputy said. "I almost forgot. You asked me for a favor."

Tavis stood straight, perking up. "Yes. You have an answer?"

The deputy took a couple of steps, moving farther away from the waiting room area and out of earshot. "I found out that Jenae changed her name," the deputy said in a low voice. "Looks like she wanted to escape Alex."

"That's a pretty serious reaction. Was he abusive?"

"There were rumors that he had a bad temper, but I never heard that he hit her. But maybe once they split, she was afraid of him? Now, I'm not saying he would've hurt her, but she must've believed that to change her name. Or maybe she simply wanted a complete break from him. I heard they had a really ugly divorce."

"Yeah, someone mentioned that. About the divorce." Tavis hesitated for a beat then asked, "What's her new name?"

"I don't know. I spoke with her parents, and all they'd tell me was that she'd changed her name."

"You have a way for me to reach her?" Tavis asked.

"Unfortunately, I don't. Because here's the thing. Her parents said they haven't heard from her in over a week. They're worried. They put in a missing persons report in Erie, where she was living and last seen."

"Erie? I heard that she lived in Buffalo."

"At one time I think she did, but her parents said she very recently moved to Erie."

This didn't make sense. At all. "The parents filed a missing persons report? So you're telling me that Jenae Wilkinson is missing?"

"That's what her parents said."

"For more than a week?"

"Apparently."

If Jenae was living in Erie, then what was the connection to the house in Buffalo? And Lucas?

"Thanks," Tavis said. But he was more confused than ever and no closer to any answers.

ALL NIGHT, Tavis tried to put the pieces of the puzzle together, but couldn't. Was Jenae actually missing? Surely her parents wouldn't have filed a missing persons report if she wasn't. That had Tavis wondering about what Deedee had said.

Deedee had told him that she'd contacted someone who'd contacted Jenae only a couple of days ago. But if that were true, then Jenae *wasn't* missing. Or had Deedee been lying?

But why would Deedee lie? Surely she wouldn't do anything to put her cousin, or herself, in jeopardy. And yet, he had gotten the feeling that she hadn't been completely forthright with him.

Tavis dragged a hand over his face. Maybe he was losing his mind, suspecting everyone and everything. It had been a lot of years of searching for Lucas, investigating every angle he could, and hoping for a break. Maybe it was all getting to him.

Regardless, he needed to talk to Deedee again. But with her still in the hospital, he didn't want to push her while she was recovering. He needed more answers, and maybe the best way to get them was to go directly to Jenae's parents.

"Hey, Griffin," he said into the phone. "You okay to stay at Shayla's house for about thirty, forty, minutes?"

"Sure thing."

"There's something I need to do, then I'll head right there to relieve you."

"No problem. I'm good."

"Thanks, Griffin."

Tavis downed a cup of coffee then headed out to the Wilkinson place. He pulled into the driveway of the old Victorian house, noting that there was no car in the driveway. But the vehicles could be parked in the detached garage.

Tavis exited his GMC Sierra, then walked up the steps to the wraparound porch and the front door. It was a beautiful house, painted a bright yellow. A porch swing moved gently with the breeze, and wind chimes sang.

Tavis rang the doorbell. Waited.

Nothing. He rang the bell again, straining to make sure that he could hear it. It was working. But when again there was no response, he knocked. A full minute later, no one had come to the door.

Tavis stepped to the right and peered through the window, hoping that any neighbors seeing him would not think he was up to no good. He could see the outline of a living room and the kitchen at the back through the sheer curtains, but he saw no signs of life.

He turned on his heel and headed down the steps.

"They're not there," came a voice.

He whirled around, seeing an older woman standing on the porch of the neighboring house.

"Oh?" he asked.

"They haven't been there since yesterday, before the vigil. They took off in a real hurry."

"Took off, hmm?"

"I think they're worried about their daughter. They didn't say much. They just packed up their car and left."

"And they were heading to find Jenae? That's what they told you?"

"They didn't really say. I saw them briefly and asked where they were going, and Laura said that they needed to get to Jenae."

"She in some kind of trouble?" Tavis asked, ambling over to the other house.

"I'm not sure. Such a sweet girl. Shame she has to be worried about that fool she married."

"Alex," Tavis supplied.

"I never thought he was any good. He's made her life hell, he has."

"I heard things ended badly."

The woman harrumphed. "He didn't want to let her go. Though only God knows why. It wasn't like he treated her well."

Tavis pulled his phone from his jeans' pocket. "You have a way for me to reach the Wilkinsons?"

The woman suddenly seemed to think better of her rambling mouth, and now eyed Tavis with suspicion. "What's your business with them?"

"I've been trying to find Jenae. I'm…in the personal protection business. I can help."

"Why don't you give me your number and I can pass it on to them. I'm not sure I can reach them, because I've called a couple of times and haven't heard anything. But I'll leave them a message all the same."

Tavis reached into his back pocket for a business card. "That'd be great."

Chapter Twelve

The next morning, Shayla's cell phone rang. Seeing the Sheridan Falls prefix, she answered. "Hello?"

"Shayla, it's Chase from Lucky's Auto."

"Oh yes. Hello."

"Your car's done. Would you like me to come pick you up?"

"No, that's not necessary. I can get a ride there. I can come anytime?"

"I'm here all day," he said, then chuckled.

"Excellent. I'll see you soon."

Shayla let the nurse know that she would be heading out for a short bit. Aunt Maggie was visiting her mother, so thankfully her mom wasn't alone. Aunt Maggie would head to the hospital in the afternoon to pick up Deedee, who was expected to be discharged after some final tests. Shayla would be home well before then.

Shayla went out to Tavis's Sierra. Seeing her coming, he wound down his window.

"Hey," Shayla said. "I got a call that my car is ready. Do you mind driving me to Lucky's Auto Shop?"

"Right now?"

"Yep. My aunt is with my mom, and the nurse is there. I think we're fine to leave for a little while."

Tavis glanced around then started his ignition. "I agree. Hop in."

Within minutes, they were at Lucky's Auto Shop. Chase smiled when she entered, the smile wavering slightly when he saw Tavis enter the shop behind her.

"Shayla, hello. Tavis."

"Hello, Chase."

"Your car is as good as new."

"Where is it?"

"In the back bay. Follow me."

Shayla did just that, and Tavis fell into step beside her. Together, they went into the bay area of the shop where there was one car hoisted up, another with its hood raised, and then her car, looking shiny and new.

"As I explained," Chase began, "I had to repaint the entire right side in order to match the paint and make it look good. I detailed the whole car to make it look brand-new."

Shayla examined the right side of the car, then the rest of the vehicle. The royal blue looked perfect.

"Thanks so much," she said, now inspecting the windshield. There was no indication that it had ever been vandalized. It glistened.

"You were at the vigil a couple of days ago," Tavis said.

Chase wiped his palms against his navy mechanic's jumpsuit. "Yeah, yeah I was."

"I suppose you heard what happened—someone running Shayla and her cousin off the road?"

"Yeah, I heard." He made a sound of derision as he shook his head. "I couldn't believe it. Who would want to hurt them? You might not know, but Deedee and I used to date. Back in high school."

"Yeah, I remember." Tavis looked around at the other cars, and then outside at the cars lined up waiting for work. "You hear anything? Any word about who might have run Shayla and Deedee off the road?"

"No." Chase shook his head. "But no one would tell me that."

"But this is a small town. You must have people coming in and out of here all day. Word gets out."

"I did hear that the vehicle was found, burned. People like that don't tend to brag about what they've done."

Tavis nodded, acknowledging that fact. "Do me a favor, will you? You hear anything, will you let me know?"

Chase looked at him for a long moment. "I'll let my dad know. He's the one investigating this. The sheriff's department."

Shayla watched as the two men stared each other down. There was animosity between them. Or was she imagining it?

"Thank you," she said to Chase in an effort to put an end to the unspoken tension. "I guess I just need to sign the paperwork and collect the keys, then I can leave."

Chase turned his attention to her, offering a big smile. "That's right. We can go back inside, take care of everything."

Chase led the way, and Shayla followed. Tavis lingered for a moment, and when Shayla looked over her shoulder at him, she saw him glancing around the shop.

Was he looking for something? And if so, what?

"WHAT WAS THAT ABOUT?" Shayla asked when she and Tavis were finished and outside.

Tavis shrugged. How could he tell her that all of the Thompson men rubbed him the wrong way? The sheriff was a thorn in his side, and his sons had always been spoiled and entitled.

"A bit of bad blood," Tavis admitted.

"Because of what?"

Tavis's cell phone trilled. He quickly accessed his phone, happy for an excuse to avoid answering Shayla.

The problems between him and the Thompsons weren't worth getting into.

When he read the text, his stomach dropped.

"What is it?" Shayla asked, and he could hear the alarm in her voice.

"I just got a text," he explained. "It says, 'Stop looking for me, you're going to get me killed.'"

Shayla's eyes bulged. "What?"

He angled the phone so she could see it for herself.

"Who?" Shayla asked. "Jenae?"

"Maybe," Tavis said. "It's a Buffalo number, and she was living there." He pressed the number on the screen, and it began to dial. He brought the phone to his ear.

"The number you are calling cannot be reached. Please check the number and try again."

Shayla stared at him expectantly.

"The number can't be reached." He frowned. "Probably one of those apps. You can text but you can't call someone back."

"But why would Jenae send you such a message?" Shayla frowned.

"I went to her parents' place. I was hoping to find them and see if I could locate her." At least he knew now that she'd gotten the message. He explained the interaction he'd had with the neighbor and that he'd left her a number to pass along to Jenae's parents so they could reach him.

Tavis sent a reply text, hoping it would go through to the sender.

Who is this? If you need help, I can help you.

"I sent the person a text," he said. "I hope it goes through to whoever it is and they'll respond." Staring at his phone, he made a face. According to Deputy Jenkins, Jenae had been missing for over a week. Her parents were clearly worried, which had him wondering if she'd met with foul play.

Suddenly, it didn't make sense that she was the one who'd sent the text.

"Listen," Tavis began, "I need to talk to your cousin about something. But I won't do it yet. I know she's recovering, and I don't want to upset her. But I got news from Deputy Jenkins. According to him, Jenae's been missing for over a week. That's why her parents left, apparently to try and find her. But Deedee said she spoke to someone who relayed my message to Jenae only a couple of days ago. If her own parents can't reach her, how could a friend?"

"Deedee wouldn't lie. If she said she got word from Jenae, then she did."

"Shayla, I'm told her parents filed a missing persons report."

"You don't think Jenae sent that text?"

"Maybe it was Lucas?" Tavis suggested. "Unless Jenae isn't missing, but she's gone underground. I'm going to do a records search on that house in Buffalo, see who owns it."

"I feel like we're fighting a ghost," Shayla said.

"I wonder if it's possible that Jenae was in the crowd at the vigil."

"You just said she's missing."

"Yeah, but there was a woman at the vigil. I didn't get a good look at her. I took pictures, but with what happened to you and Deedee, I haven't gone through them all yet. Maybe you can come to my place and go through the pictures with me. See if you recognize anyone that I may not. We might even get an idea of who might have followed you and run you off the road."

"Now?" Shayla asked.

"Now's as good a time as any," Tavis said. "We don't

have to take too long. Maybe thirty minutes to go through the photos?"

"I guess my mother should be fine in the meantime. The real threat is to me—and if anyone has been watching, then they'll know that I'm with you. Besides, it's the middle of the day. I doubt there'll be any problems right now. I'll just text the nurse to tell her that I'll be back later than I expected."

"Great," Tavis said. "Follow me to my place."

SHAYLA FOLLOWED TAVIS through the main streets of Sheridan Falls until he turned onto a tree-lined street with modern houses, built probably within the last ten to fifteen years. Halfway down the street, he turned right into a double-car driveway and she did the same. As she turned off her car, she looked out at the two-story, redbrick home. It had a moderate-sized lawn that was somewhat parched, but the shrubs surrounding the front porch were a vibrant green.

Shayla exited the vehicle and followed Tavis up the steps to his front door. Her gaze wandered from his home to him, taking in the sight of him from behind, from head to toe. His wide shoulders and muscular back, and those very strong biceps. As far as bodyguards went, she couldn't do better. Tavis made her feel protected and safe.

And he also made her feel something else. Looking at him now, she was suddenly very aware of him as a man. He was strong, sexy and undeniably hot. But she hadn't spoken to him in nearly nine years, and there'd been animosity when they had. So how was it that she still felt any level of attraction for him now?

She turned and gazed out at the quiet street. Two young children were playing on a lawn three houses over, squealing with delight as they jumped through a sprinkler. It made her think for a moment of the life she hadn't considered. A life with a husband and kids, and being normal. Not a life where she felt shame and fear because of the tragic incident that happened in her life years ago.

"You coming?" Tavis asked.

She spun around at the sound of his voice. "Yes. Of course."

She followed him into the house, and instantly took note of the cream-colored walls, which were mostly bare except for a couple of black-and-white photos of city skylines. To the right was the living room, with a large black leather sectional and a giant flat-screen television. The pictures in the living room were of abstract art. There was nothing in particular that made this place his. No pictures of him or his family.

It was the quintessential bachelor pad.

"I have everything upstairs," he told her.

Shayla followed him to the second level. She blew out a haggard breath. The idea of going upstairs with him had her thinking of something else entirely—which made no sense. It wasn't as if Tavis had invited her here for a romantic date.

When he opened the door to a bedroom, all misplaced thoughts of attraction fled her mind. She immediately saw the wall with pictures of Hayley and Jonathan and her and Deedee and Alex and…pretty much everyone they'd gone to school with. Everyone who'd been at the party anyway. He had an entire wall with tons of pictures and notes and arrows pointing between people.

She stepped into the room. "What is this?"

"Everything I've come up with regarding the murders. Everyone who was at the party, everyone who had a story to tell me about what they believed happened."

She looked up at him. "I wasn't at the party."

"No, but you were connected to Lucas." He pointed, showing her how the line from Lucas led to her and the words written there. *Does she know where Lucas is? Did he tell her what he was going to do?*

"You know now that I don't know where he is. You know that he never told me what he was up to."

He used his fingers to wipe away what he'd written between the line connecting her and Lucas. "I haven't updated it."

Shayla looked at the board, folding her arms over her chest as she inspected all the work he had done. "Wow. This is everyone."

She frowned when she realized he had written something else, which must have been recent.

Rosita and Andrew? At the scene coincidentally?

She whipped around to face him. "Didn't you tell me that you don't think they had anything to do with the accident?"

"I don't believe that they do, no. But… I like to put everything down just to be sure. Sometimes it sparks another question, and I can go back to something and see things differently."

"You put a lot of work into this."

"And that's not all." He walked toward one of his filing cabinets, opened it and withdrew a binder. "In here, I have interviews with everyone. I transcribed them all."

She wandered over to him, saw the amount of pages and gasped softly. "Tavis…"

And it struck her then just how determined he was. But his cousin had been killed. Of course he was determined.

She looked at him. "I didn't even imagine how much this has been eating at you. I…"

She reached for his arm, gently laid her hand on it. He looked at her, holding her gaze for a long beat. Shayla had the overwhelming urge to put her arms around him and offer him the kind of comfort he had offered her yesterday.

Before she could, he stepped away. He moved to the

desk where his laptop was and opened it. "I uploaded all of the photos from the memory card. You want to go through them now?"

Shayla went to stand beside him. Her heart was beating faster than normal. "Sure."

The first picture was of the crowd at large, with the grieving families up front on the school steps. Tavis rose and grabbed another chair so she could sit. When she did, he continued clicking through the photos.

Chase and his wife. Alex. Her and Deedee. Many of the people she'd seen in the crowd. Most of them familiar faces. No one in town she specifically knew would want to hurt her, except Jonathan's grandfather, who'd pulled a gun on her, and maybe Tammy, who'd thrown water in her face.

"These are all the townsfolk," she said. "Everybody I know."

Tavis continued going through the photos. "What about her?"

Shayla squinted to see, but the photo had been taken from a far distance. "It's a bit fuzzy. I can't fully see her."

He zoomed it in. "Today, I was wondering if that might be Jenae with an altered appearance, though I don't know. She looks different. But something about her got my attention." He went to the next picture, a closer version of the woman.

And Shayla's mouth fell open as she realized who the woman in the baseball hat was.

"Oh my God."

"You know her."

"That's my mother's nurse." She looked at Tavis, who met her with a questioning gaze. "The day of the vigil, she called in sick. She told me she had the flu and she couldn't make it in to take care of my mother."

"You're sure?" Tavis asked.

"Yes! That's her!" She pointed at the screen, stopping

short of jabbing it. "But she wasn't sick, obviously. Which means she lied to me."

"I thought she had dark hair."

"She's definitely not blond, so that must be a wig," Shayla said. "Unless she dyed her hair."

"I've never seen her in this town before. Have you?"

"No. Never. I only met her when I came back here. So if she's not even from Sheridan Falls, what the heck was she doing at the vigil?"

Chapter Thirteen

Shayla raced back to her house. Suddenly, she was terrified for the safety of her mother. Even though she had left her there with her aunt and the replacement nurse, knowing that Jennifer had been at the vigil and had lied had her feeling a sense of betrayal she couldn't quite explain. Was the home care nurse's whole appearance in Sheridan Falls based on false pretenses? Had she taken the job in an effort to get close to her?

Shayla rushed into the house, immediately greeting Melanie, the replacement nurse. The woman looked at her with concern. "Is everything okay?" she asked.

"Jennifer. The other nurse who has been here. Do you know her?"

"No. The agency called me to replace her. Why?"

"Have you ever met her?"

The door opened and Tavis entered. The nurse looked between Shayla and Tavis, a sense of growing unease obvious on her face. "What's this about?"

"I have reason to believe that she is not who she said she is. And she's been in this house with my mother."

"I… I don't know what to tell you."

"How did you hire her?" Tavis asked Shayla. "Through an agency?"

"Yes. An agency out of Buffalo. I had no reason to be concerned." She looked to Melanie again. "My aunt left?"

"About twenty minutes ago. She said she needed to get to the hospital."

Shayla rushed down the hallway to the den. Seeing her mother sleeping, a relieved breath eased out of her. She didn't know what was going on, but she didn't like it.

"If the other nurse has done something, I suggest you call the agency to report her. Or I can, if you'd like."

"No," Shayla said forcefully. "Do not call the agency." She took a deep breath. She didn't want this woman to be alarmed enough to call the agency, because maybe Jennifer would never show her face again. And she needed Jennifer to show her face again to get answers.

"There's no need," Shayla went on. "I… I just need to clarify something. Maybe I've misconstrued the situation. Understandably, I'm very protective of my mother."

"Of course," Melanie said. "I can tell you that your mother has been taken care of very well. From the notes I've seen, nothing is out of order. But you can ask Jennifer tomorrow. I've already gotten word from the agency that she'll be back."

Shayla threw a glance over her shoulder at Tavis.

"Tomorrow." She smiled. "Perfect. I'll talk to her then."

Tomorrow couldn't come fast enough as far as Shayla was concerned. Thankfully, the evening provided distractions from her obsessing over the situation with Jennifer. Deedee had been released from the hospital and Shayla, along with her aunt and uncle, had helped get her settled at home. Afterward, she went back home to her mother, tipped Melanie generously for agreeing to stay a couple more hours, then when Melanie was gone, curled up beside her mother and played a movie for them to watch.

Tavis hadn't wanted to leave, not with the word about

Jennifer. So he hadn't had Griffin relieve him. Instead, Tavis was planning to stay outside Shayla's place the entire night.

He was going above and beyond, and she definitely appreciated him for that.

At about one in the morning, Shayla couldn't sleep. Tavis was out in his vehicle, keeping watch over her house, and that didn't sit right with Shayla. The least she could do was offer him a comfortable sofa.

Shayla slipped into a robe then went outside. Crickets chirped, the only sound at this hour. She made her way to Tavis's pickup. She heard the locks click open before she could knock on the passenger's-side window.

Shayla opened the door. "Why don't you come inside? I hate the idea of you being stuck in your truck all night."

"I'm fine here."

Shayla glanced around. The street was quiet, and seemed safe. "I'd prefer you come inside. I... I'll feel better. Safer."

"Are you sure?"

"Let me get you something to eat, something to drink. You can still do your job, but from inside my house. Arguably, it could be better for you to be inside. What if someone tries to access the house from the back? I know you're the only one here tonight."

"All right," Tavis agreed.

Shayla walked back into the house, leaving him to gather his belongings. She stepped into the kitchen and started the kettle.

When she heard Tavis enter, she went to the foyer to meet him. In a quiet voice, she said, "I started the kettle. Would you like some tea? Or if you like coffee, I can make that."

"I'm fine with tea. Two sugars."

"Now what about something to eat? There's some fried chicken in the fridge as well. Can I get you a plate?"

Tavis hesitated then nodded. "I'd love a plate."

Shayla felt good as she set about preparing some food for him. He was giving her so much, she wanted to do something nice for him.

She set the plate and the tea on the kitchen table for him.

"This smells amazing, thank you," he said.

"Feel free to set your laptop up here," Shayla said.

Tavis dug in, moaning happily as he ate a piece of the chicken. "This is delicious."

"I'm glad you like it. The least I can do is give you a decent meal."

Tavis sipped some tea. "I think it's a good idea if I set up a couple of cameras in the backyard—until the person who wants to hurt you is caught. I'll always be out front, or one of my guys, but setting up a camera or two at the front is probably a smart idea too."

"Tell me what I need to get. I'll go buy it."

He nodded, unable to speak as he ate some of the mac and cheese.

"You know," she went on, "I was thinking about something. You asked me if I knew what Lucas was up to—and I didn't, of course. People seem to keep asking me about him and if I'd known about his criminal enterprise—which I didn't. But when I think back to that day, he had seemed a bit anxious. I'm not sure why. But he'd even asked me the day before if I would consider leaving town with him."

Tavis lowered the piece of chicken he'd been about to bite. "He asked you to leave town? You knew he was planning to leave?"

"I didn't know that he was going to leave for sure, just that he asked if I would go with him. I told him that I couldn't do that. For one, we'd only been dating for like a month or so. I found the request bizarre. But the big thing

I'm remembering now is that he seemed on edge, uneasy about something. I don't know why I didn't consider that before. I don't know if it has anything to do with why he left, or why he did what he did. And he didn't tell me what was bothering him. Maybe nothing was, and I'm reading too much into the memory. Or maybe he knew he was planning to leave and he didn't want our relationship to end?"

Tavis pursed his lips. "I don't know what to make of that."

"Neither do I. But I thought I'd tell you. I don't know... Maybe it's nothing."

Shayla left Tavis to eat and returned to the counter, where she decided to use the time to unload the dishwasher. Once it was cleared, she put the few dishes from the sink into the dishwasher.

"Where's your green bin?"

Shayla whipped around, throwing a hand over her heart. Somehow, Tavis had appeared right beside her and she hadn't even heard him.

"Under the sink," she told him. "Right here."

She opened the cupboard, took the plate from him and scraped the bones into the green bin. Then she put the plate and utensils into the dishwasher.

"Where's your bathroom?"

"Down the hall, first door on the left."

Tavis disappeared, and Shayla made sure that everything was put away in the kitchen. Then she wandered down the hallway and checked in on her mother. She was sleeping. When she turned around, she met Tavis as he was walking away from the bathroom.

"Do you want a pillow, a blanket? I can get that for you if you think you might want to take a little nap on the sofa. You've been here all day."

"I don't want to sleep on the job," he told her.

"Let me get you a pillow and a blanket anyway. I feel... I feel safe with you here regardless."

She quickly went upstairs to the linen closet and got a comforter and a pillow. She returned downstairs with the items, placing them on the sofa. "And if there's anything else you need, just let me know."

The lamps were off in the living room, but the light from the kitchen provided soft illumination. Shayla looked up at Tavis, and he looked down at her. "I really do appreciate you being here for me," she said, her voice soft. "For everything you've done."

And then she was stepping toward him and placing a hand on his chest. She held his gaze, wondering what had come over her. They'd been through so much over the last few days, and Shayla felt a growing connection to him. The idea of heading back to Miami and not seeing him again was a thought she'd already had, and she didn't like it. It was silly, she knew, but there was something about him that excited her. Years ago, and now.

Her chest rose and fell with an anxious breath as she waited for him to reject her, to put a stop to her crazy fantasy. Instead, he slowly ran his fingers up her arm and then across her shoulder blade.

His touch set her skin on fire. And the look in his eyes told her that her attraction wasn't one-sided. Slowly, he leaned toward her. Shayla tipped up on her toes. Their lips met tentatively, and then he slipped both arms around her, held her close and deepened the kiss.

Everything inside Shayla's body came alive as his hands roamed her back and his tongue swept over hers. She looped her arms around his neck and held on.

"Maybe we shouldn't," he said on a raspy breath.

"Why not?" she asked. "I'm a big girl. I want this."

And she did. She wanted one night with her old crush.

One night where she got to fully feel what it was like to have a man like him love her.

She took him by the hand and led him upstairs. She giggled slightly, imagining having done this as a teen— sneaking a boy up to her room. She hadn't done it as a teenager, but now was doing it as a twenty-seven-year-old.

She led him into her bedroom, closed the door and then took her robe off. Tavis slipped his hands beneath her nightshirt, and when his fingers moved over her breasts, she moaned. His touch felt like heaven.

She pulled her nightshirt off and tossed it aside, while Tavis removed his gun and holster and then his shirt. Moonlight and streetlight filtered through the blinds, and Shayla took a moment to admire his muscular chest. What a specimen of a man!

He moved toward her and kissed her cheek softly. Then the other cheek. And then he began to softly kiss her lips. She melted against him, surrendering to this man who had always excited her.

"I probably shouldn't be doing this," he said. "But I don't want to stop."

"I don't want to stop, either." One night with her crush…

Tavis led her to the bed, where they kissed and worked at getting out of the remainder of their clothes. Then Tavis pulled her into his arms, and Shayla gave herself up completely to the sweet heat consuming them.

MAKING LOVE WITH Tavis had been incredible, and provided Shayla some time where she wasn't obsessing over Jennifer. He lay with her in bed for half an hour afterward, making Shayla feel as though the sex hadn't simply been sex. Though he had only just returned downstairs to resume his protection duties, she missed him.

Not that they were about to sail off into the sunset. The

sex had been something they'd both wanted, and perhaps needed, given all the stress of the recent days.

And the morning was going to bring more stress once she confronted Jennifer.

When Shayla got up bright and early and went downstairs, Tavis wasn't in the house. He'd packed up his laptop too. Shayla looked out the front window. His vehicle was there.

He'd returned to his Sierra.

Maybe he hadn't wanted to be inside the house when the nurse came? Or maybe he'd considered that he might startle her mother if she got up in the night?

Shayla checked on her mother, found her sleeping. Thankfully. Hopefully, she continued to sleep when Jennifer arrived so she wouldn't overhear any of the conversation. To be on the safe side, Shayla closed the door to the den.

Ten minutes later, as Shayla was drinking a cup of coffee at the kitchen table, she heard the nurse enter the house. Nerves fluttering in her stomach, she got up and headed to the foyer.

Seeing her, Jennifer greeted her with a bright smile. Gone was the blond hair, meaning she'd been wearing a wig at the vigil. "Good morning, Shayla. How are you today?"

"I'm great," Shayla said. "You're feeling better?"

"Yeah, nothing that a couple of days of rest couldn't cure."

"You look good. The rest agreed with you."

There was a knock at the door. It had to be Tavis.

"Let me go check on your mother," Jennifer said.

"Definitely. I'll get the door."

Jennifer ambled off down the hallway, and Shayla headed to the front door. As she opened it, she realized that her heart was beating fast. Tavis looked down at her, and she nodded. "Let's do this."

Tavis entered the home, and she guided him into the living room. She didn't want to confront the nurse while she was with her mother. A few minutes later, Jennifer was walking into the living room, her eyes widening when she saw Tavis.

"You remember Tavis," Shayla said.

"Yes." Jennifer smiled. "Good to see you again."

Shayla was ready for the charade to be over. "What were you doing at the vigil, Jennifer?"

Her eyes grew wide. "Wh-what?"

"The vigil," Tavis supplied. "Two days ago. I saw you there."

"You're mistaken. I wasn't at the vigil. Why would I be at the vigil?"

Tavis took his phone from his pocket and, seconds later, zoomed in on the photo of Jennifer wearing a baseball cap. "That's you in a blond wig. You can't deny it."

"So what were you doing there?" Shayla demanded. "First of all, you lied to me about being sick. Then you're at a vigil for people you don't know?"

"And Shayla and her cousin were run off the road and nearly killed shortly after that vigil." Tavis gave her a stern look. "You'd better start talking."

Jennifer's eyes flitted between them and the front door. She was clearly contemplating a way to escape. She made a little cry.

"You're not going to get far," Tavis told her, "so I suggest you start talking."

"And I'm happy to call the sheriff if you don't want to talk to us," Shayla added. She held up her own phone, making it clear she was ready to punch in the number in a second.

"I'm sorry," Jennifer said.

"Why were you there?" Shayla pressed.

Jennifer looked pained and shifted her weight from one foot to the other. "She's going to kill me."

"Who's going to kill you?"

"I… I just went to…see who was in the crowd."

"I need you to start telling me exactly what you're getting at," Tavis said. "Who's going to kill you?"

"Jenae."

At the mention of her name, both Tavis and Shayla shared a look.

"Jenae?" Shayla asked.

"Yes. Jenae."

Shayla looked toward the back door. She didn't want her mother hearing any of this in case she woke up. "Can we speak outside? I don't want to wake my mother or worry her with anything we're talking about."

Jennifer crossed her arms over her chest and nodded tightly. "Yes."

She sounded pained, terrified. But all three of them went to the back deck. They stood, neither of them taking a seat.

"You're working for Jenae?" Tavis surmised.

"Kind of."

"Where is she?" he asked. "I need to speak with her."

"That's the thing. I haven't heard from her in over a week."

"You just said that you went to the vigil because of her."

"Yes. Because I hadn't heard from her. Because I'm worried about her. When she wouldn't get back to me, I wondered if maybe she would show up at the vigil. I didn't know. So I went, hoping to find her. I've been out of my mind with worry."

Shayla held up a hand. "Whoa, wait a second. You're saying you haven't heard from Jenae?"

"No. Not since last week."

"I'm gonna need you to back up and tell me this story from the beginning," Tavis said. "How did you end up working for Shayla's mother?"

Her shoulders drooped. "I'm a real nurse, if that's what you're wondering. It just so happens that I'm friends with Jenae. In Buffalo. She knew your mother was sick, she'd heard about her cancer. And then when the call came to this agency for a nurse, I pulled a few strings and got this job."

"Why?" Shayla asked. She felt betrayed.

"I want you to know I've been doing nothing but giving your mother the proper care she needs."

"But why did you want to be here? What was so important about working for my mother?"

Jennifer whimpered softly. "Because Jenae said you probably have something here in the house. Something that can help her."

"Me?" Stunned, Shayla stared at Jennifer for a long moment. "Jenae and I weren't even close. How could I have anything that could help her? And help her *what*?"

"It has to do with the murders," Jennifer said. "Obviously," she added when she saw the looks on Shayla's and Tavis's faces. "She was concerned about Lucas."

"Has she heard from Lucas?" Tavis asked.

"She just said that there's some proof somewhere, proof of what Lucas did. And if I could find it, it could help her. So I… I came here. Because she thinks… She feels certain that Lucas gave it to you."

Shayla shook her head. "Lucas gave me nothing," she said. "I don't know why everyone thinks that I was so important to him that he would share any of his criminal plan with me. Why would he?"

"Jenae wasn't certain exactly what I should be looking for. She just said I would know it when I found it."

The nurse's words hit Shayla like a ton of bricks. And

she suddenly realized why she'd thought she'd seen things in her room out of place. At first she'd thought she had been imagining things, but now it made sense.

"You were in my room? Going through my things?"

Jennifer started to cry softly. "I was trying to help Jenae. You would do the same to help a friend."

"That's where you're wrong," Shayla said. "I would never lie and sneak around and access someone's private property to help someone else. You could have just come to me and been honest. Instead, you got to my mother as a way to get to me."

"I never hurt your mother. I've given her nothing but amazing care."

"What is it Jenae is looking for?" Tavis asked. "If she asked you to find evidence, you must know."

"She didn't say exactly. Just that I would know it when I saw it. A letter, a gun… I don't know."

"A gun?" Shayla gasped. "You think Lucas gave me a gun?"

"I know it sounds like I'm lying, but I'm not. I think Jenae wasn't sure, just grasping at straws."

"You don't sound like you know much for someone with an agenda who's gained access to private property and private citizens." Tavis's look was unwavering. "You realize we can call the sheriff right now, have you arrested."

"I didn't hurt anybody. I was only trying to help."

"Where were you after the vigil?" Tavis asked. "Because I saw you take off behind the school, as though you didn't want to be seen by anyone. Did you go to a waiting vehicle, one that was stolen? Did you follow Shayla and Deedee and force them off the road? Are you the one who nearly killed them both?"

"No!"

"Then why were you there, and why this whole subterfuge?" Tavis asked. "Because I don't believe that you were at the vigil looking for Jenae. That doesn't make sense."

"I'm not lying."

"But you did lie to me," Shayla said. "You accessed my house, you went through my things, and did you find anything?"

"No. I didn't find anything useful."

"Does Jenae want Shayla dead?" Tavis asked.

Jennifer's eyes widened. "No. Of course not."

"What do you know about the attack on Shayla in Buffalo?" Tavis pressed on. "Is Jenae working with Lucas?"

"What attack on Shayla?"

Tavis filled her in. "One of the neighbors asked us if we were looking for Jenae. Shayla was lured there, someone tried to kill her—*us*—in a house where Jenae lived. Now we find out you're here working on Jenae's behalf. So tell me, why does Jenae want Shayla dead?"

"She doesn't! She's never said such a thing. She's only said that Shayla probably has some information that can help her."

"Are you denying that Jenae lived at that house in Buffalo?" Tavis asked.

"No," Jennifer said. "But… Maybe her ex found her and that's why she took off. Jenae's relationship with Alex was volatile. She didn't want him knowing where she was. Or…or someone might be setting her up. I'd ask her, but I can't find her."

"That's all you know?" Shayla asked. "Or that's all you're going to tell us?"

"I've told you the truth about everything," Jennifer said. "I swear."

"Good," Shayla said. "Now leave. And never come back."

"Wait," Tavis said. "You mentioned Jenae's ex. I heard

that Jenae changed her name so he couldn't find her. What's her new name?"

"She only changed her surname. But I don't think—"

"What is it?" Tavis asked.

"Taylor," Jennifer admitted, her voice barely audible.

"Jenae Taylor," Tavis said. "I'm gonna need her number."

The nurse whimpered. "She won't want me to give you her number."

"Do you want me to call the sheriff?" Tavis countered.

Jennifer angrily brushed a tear away. "Fine. I'll give you her number."

She opened up her phone, found the number and rattled it off.

"Now, what's her connection to Erie, Pennsylvania?" Tavis asked.

"Erie... I think she mentioned having a friend there."

"She never mentioned that she was going there?"

Jennifer shook her head. "No. I don't know anything else." Then she looked at Shayla. "I'm sorry about all of this. I don't expect you to let me stay on."

"How very astute of you," Shayla said.

"I'm sorry," Jennifer repeated. "I really am."

"I'm going to have to call the agency," Shayla said. "You've breached my confidence, and my mother will need another nurse."

Jennifer started for the back door. "Fine. Do what you have to do."

Then she whizzed into the house, grabbed her belongings and was out the front door in a flash. Shayla wanted to follow her, but what would that get her?

Tavis placed a hand on her arm. Shayla looked up at him. "You said you and Jenae were never close. But do you think she hated you because of what happened to Hayley and Jonathan? This nurse was in your house because of her. And she doesn't have answers that make sense to me. And now Jenae is missing. Maybe she went off the deep end, wanted you out of the way for some reason. Maybe she blames you for what happened to Hayley—it could be as simple as that. Or Jonathan. Maybe she's been holding a grudge all this time, saw an opportunity and took it."

Shayla shuddered. "We have to find her. And we have to find her fast."

Chapter Fourteen

Tavis wasn't sure if he should have let the nurse go, but he'd gotten the make and model of her car, plus the license number. He'd have a way to track her down if need be in the future.

He didn't know exactly what was going on here, but something suddenly occurred to him.

"Shayla," he said softly. She was sitting on her sofa, a faraway expression on her face. "Hey, this isn't your fault."

"Isn't it?" Shayla asked, meeting his eyes. "I brought her into my house. I allowed her to be close to my mother."

"But you couldn't have known. How could you have? Their plan was genius. How could you or anyone ever suspect them? Yes, Jennifer got close to your mother, but you can't blame yourself for something that you couldn't have even anticipated."

"But maybe I should have anticipated that coming back here was going to put my mother at risk. My cousin at risk."

Tavis got up from the armchair and joined her on the sofa. He slipped an arm around her shoulders. "Don't do this."

He stroked her hair softly, and she folded her soft, feminine body against his. And, God help him, he wanted to stay here with her like this, simply holding her and making her feel safe. What had gotten into him?

He cleared his throat, trying to force himself to stop thinking of her as a beautiful and desirable woman. "You said that Lucas asked you about leaving town with him."

"Yes." Shayla angled her face to look up at him. "And Jennifer's comments made me think of something else. I'm pretty sure he mentioned something about having a stash of cash and an insurance policy…? I didn't know what he meant at the time, except that he had money and that we could live off of that when we left. But now I'm wondering if he meant something else."

"There's got to be *something* to be found somewhere. I don't know what it is, but you had more than one person ask you about it, and now Jenae is trying to find something that you allegedly could have? Lucas must have left something somewhere. I don't know what, and I wish I could talk to Jenae to get an answer. But something is somewhere."

"But where?" Shayla asked. "It's not here. Jennifer said she went through my stuff—" She shuddered again, and Tavis knew that she was thinking about the nurse violating her privacy. "So, where?"

"Where he was living. With his aunt and uncle."

"You think so?"

"It's worth a shot, isn't it? All I know is that when Lucas disappeared, his aunt and uncle experienced wrath from the town. I don't know that the sheriff's department interviewed them with any compassion, and the way they've kept to themselves since, I'm thinking not. Maybe it's time I pay them a visit and ask them these very questions. Maybe…" Tavis's voice trailed off. Then his eyes lit up. "Maybe Lucas was afraid of something. You said he seemed on edge. Maybe there's something he knew, something he was worried about…"

"What are you thinking?"

"I don't know," Tavis said, making a face. "All this time we've believed Lucas is the killer. But what if he's a witness?"

TAVIS WAS DETERMINED to get to the bottom of this. If there was any such evidence of an insurance policy anywhere, the best place for it to be would be his aunt and uncle's home. Unless it was stashed somewhere else. But if Shayla didn't have it, he needed to get to Rosita and Andrew's and have a look around.

Was it possible that Lucas had been a witness? He wasn't sure. He wasn't even sure what he was trying to find.

He drove to the Carrs' place, a modest older house in the middle of town, and went to the door. When he knocked, Andrew opened within seconds, as if he'd seen him approaching. The man looked at him with suspicion.

"Hello, again," Tavis said. "I'm wondering if you would mind if I ask you some questions about Lucas?"

Rosita appeared then, standing beside her husband. "We have nothing else to say about Lucas," she said, her tone defensive. "Everyone crucified him in this town years ago. Aren't you done yet?"

"That's the thing," Tavis said. "I'm wondering… Maybe Lucas wasn't the killer. Maybe he was a witness?"

"What's brought about this change in thinking?" Andrew asked. The edge to his voice said he didn't trust Tavis.

"A few things have happened, and it has me questioning the big picture. Some things just don't make sense."

"Lucas killing anyone doesn't make sense," Andrew said. "We tried to say that in the beginning. That we knew Lucas would never hurt anybody. No one believed us."

"May I come in?" Tavis asked. "I promise I want to

hear everything you have to say. If no one ever listened to you before, I'm sorry for that. But I'm prepared to listen to you now."

SHAYLA HAD WANTED to go with Tavis to the Carrs' place, but she'd had to stay behind to wait for the replacement nurse. And it was probably a good thing that she hadn't accompanied him. She was starting to get too used to him being around. Every time she was upset, he was there to turn to. He was like an anchor in a raging sea.

It was clear that she wasn't going to be able to get through this crisis without him. And what about afterward? That was what she was beginning to fear. How would she go back to her old life now that she'd shared a special moment with him? It may not have meant anything to him, but it meant a lot to her.

The arrival of the new nurse, Kathy, had her putting thoughts of Tavis on the back burner. Kathy was a heavy-set woman in her fifties, and she seemed both pleasant and no-nonsense.

Shayla gave her the general rundown of her mother's situation. "Though, of course, you must have all of this information in her file," Shayla added after she'd spoken.

"I'll give your mother the best possible care," Kathy told her. "I'll make sure to get her up and moving. Help her through this."

"Thanks so much."

As Shayla let the new nurse get acquainted with her mother, she called her cousin. "Deedee, how are you?"

"I am doing very well for someone who shouldn't be alive," Deedee said.

"Don't joke about that."

"I'm feeling great. I mean, I've got some pain, but nothing serious, all things considered. And of course my mother is doting on me. I probably gained another five pounds in the past couple of days."

"Good. I'm glad to hear that." She filled her cousin in on what had happened with the nurse, and the fact that Jenae had actually been behind it. "She thinks that Lucas left something for me, some kind of proof. But proof of what, I don't know."

"That's what she said?"

"Yeah. She said that it would be something that could help Jenae. I have no clue what she could be talking about, and there was nothing in my house."

"That is totally creepy."

"Tell me about it. But you know, it got me thinking. Lucas seemed a little bit skittish before the murders. Like he was afraid of something. He didn't tell me what, but he did ask me if I would leave town with him, and he talked about having money and an insurance policy... I didn't know what he'd meant, but Tavis is wondering if it means he *did* leave something here. He's wondering if maybe Lucas wasn't a killer, but may be a witness."

"How does that make sense?" Deedee asked.

"I don't know. We're grasping at straws."

"This whole thing is giving me a headache," Deedee said. "You don't think Lucas is back in town...that he's the one who ran us off the road?"

"If he got away with murder and has been able to avoid the law all these years, why would he risk coming back to town now? Tavis is wondering if maybe Jenae is behind the car accident. Honestly, I don't know. But the crazy thing is, Jennifer said she hasn't heard from Jenae in over a week. Tavis said he got word that she's missing. But you spoke to someone who spoke to her... Right?"

"Yeah," Deedee said. "I relayed the message to you just as it was told to me."

How was it that Deedee had been able to get a message

to Jenae when even her parents couldn't reach her? "Who did you contact?" Shayla asked.

"What?"

"You said you got a message to Jenae through a mutual friend. Who is that friend?"

The sound of Deedee's indignant chuckle filled the phone line. "What is this, Shayla?"

"A simple question."

"It sounds to me like you don't trust me."

"There's something else that happened," Shayla said. "I didn't tell you before because Tavis wanted to keep it quiet. But Lucas called me—or someone pretending to be Lucas—and asked me to meet him at a house in Buffalo. I went there thinking I was going to get answers. Instead, Tavis and I were shot at. In a house where Jenae once lived. So if you have a way to reach her via a mutual friend, you can see why I'd like to know."

"Shayla, I'm so sorry. Oh my God. I… Okay, I'm going to tell you this and please don't be mad. I didn't really talk to anyone who talked to Jenae. I… I just wanted you to drop all of this, because I was worried about you."

"So you *lied*?"

"To protect you. Yes."

So Tavis had been right all along. Deedee hadn't been truthful. "Protect me from what?"

"You just told me you were shot at. Maybe if you let all of this go, forget the past, whoever wants to hurt you will move on."

"If only there were a guarantee of that. Anyway, Tavis is at the Carrs' place right now. He's thinking that if there was something that Lucas left behind, it might be there."

"After all these years?" Deedee sounded doubtful.

"It's worth a shot. This whole thing is one giant mystery and, until we solve it, I'm not going to know who's after me. And we need to find that out, because the last thing I want is for you, my mother or anyone else I love to get hurt. And of course I don't want to get hurt either."

"Keep me posted," Deedee said.

"Of course."

"Lucas came to live with us because he'd been getting into some trouble in Buffalo," Rosita said. "My sister-in-law was at her wit's end and knew that he needed a change."

"So we agreed to let him come live here," Andrew said.

"Lucas might have always found trouble," Rosita began, "but he was always a follower. You know, the type of kid who wanted to look tough. He followed the crowd, did what they were doing, but he was never the instigator. The idea that he would shoot anybody, and especially over some dance competition squabble, was completely ridiculous. I knew it wasn't true."

"He was selling drugs, right?" Tavis asked.

"If he was, it was a small amount," Rosita said. "He wasn't a big-time drug dealer."

Tavis wondered how much Rosita would know. Kids weren't honest about things when they were involved in illegal activities.

"Was he ever in any other trouble?" Tavis asked. "Did he hang out with other kids who were in trouble, or have meetings with people you didn't recognize?"

"Only those guys from school. I never liked them. Especially the Thompson boys. Chase and Alex. He was always with them, out late, drinking. Smoking pot. I always thought they were trouble. Spoiled. Always pulling some kind of prank, from what I heard from Lucas. I told him to limit his time with them, but he was always attracted to the bad ones. And Jonathan too. They always hung out together."

Tavis thought about that for a moment. Did Chase and Alex know more than they had let on? They'd been at the party that night. But based on their accounts, they'd left before any conflict had happened. They'd left, and Hayley and Jonathan had stayed behind, and the next thing they knew Hayley and Jonathan were dead.

At least, that's the story they'd told.

"Did you notice anything different about Lucas in the days before the murder?"

"No," Andrew said. He looked at his wife. "My wife and I had left town. We'd gone on a cruise." He hung his head low for a moment. "Do I ever regret that now. Had we been here, Lucas never could have had that party here. And whatever happened could never have gone down."

Tavis thought about something that he'd discovered when he was working as a cop. "The forensics team was never able to find evidence of the murders in the house, right? No blood, no bullet casings, nothing?"

"No," Andrew said. "Their theory was that Lucas gave Hayley and Jonathan a ride home. Remember, Shayla had dropped them off and then left. So Lucas was the one to drive them home, but something happened and instead he drove them to the school and shot them. That's what the police believe. And that he took off after that… Disappeared. There was never a car to test for any evidence."

"All we know is that Lucas was gone," Rosita said, "and they pinned the murders on him. But the more I think about it, maybe he could have left because he was afraid."

"Why do you say that?" Tavis asked.

"I don't know. It was just a feeling I had. When we left for the cruise, he was extra loving. He hadn't been quite so loving when he first got here. He didn't like our tough rules. But before we left, he told us how much he appreciated us, hugged us, really just loved on us. I kind of felt… And Andrew thinks the same now… I kinda think that he was saying goodbye."

"Goodbye." Tavis's eyebrows shot up. "Really? So that

could mean he was planning to leave?" That aligned with what Shayla had said about him asking her to leave town with him.

"I don't know," Rosita said. "I wish I knew. All I know is that, in my heart, I don't believe he did what they said he did. But did he witness the murders and leave because he was afraid? That, I can believe."

Family members never believed the worst. They could see their loved one pull a gun on someone and they would still find an excuse to justify what happened. You always had to take a loved one's perspective with a grain of salt.

But Tavis was intrigued by the fact that Rosita had the same general sense that Shayla did. That perhaps Lucas was uneasy before the murders and may have been planning to leave town.

"I'm sure the police looked through your place years ago," Tavis began cautiously, "but I'm wondering if there might be something here that can help Lucas. Maybe some sort of evidence? Something he left behind?"

"We searched the room from top to bottom," Andrew said. "We found nothing. And the police didn't find anything either."

"All the same, would you mind if I had a look around?" Tavis asked.

Rosita and Andrew eyed each other. Perhaps because this was the first time anyone had addressed them with any concern for Lucas, their demeanors had changed considerably from when they'd first answered the door. Gone were the tense shoulders and angry expressions, replaced with a more relaxed posture and genuine curiosity.

"That's fine with us," Andrew said.

He led him upstairs to the room that had been Lucas's. It had a bed with a plain white spread on it, and not much else. There was a chest of drawers and a closet. Posters of Kanye West, Jay-Z and Eminem filled the walls.

"We left his stuff as it was in the drawers and the closet, on the off chance he ever came back. But he never did."

Tavis started to look through the drawers. Socks. Briefs. T-shirts. There were some school notebooks, and he flipped through those but didn't see anything of particular interest. He searched every drawer, looking through all that was there to see if there was anything that might be some kind of proof.

But proof of what? He went to the closet and spent time going through folded jeans, checking pockets, hanging clothes, and when he saw the duffel bag on the floor, he thought he'd hit pay dirt. But the bag contained gym clothes, a binder and a few science fiction books. School stuff. Nothing that led Tavis to believe that there was any sort of proof of anything. And certainly not any insurance policy. This was a typical teen's room.

Tavis stood, his gaze downward as he tried to think of something he might be missing. And that's when he saw it. The piece of wood flooring that seemed to be a smidgen higher than the planks around it. It was hardly noticeable. But maybe it was something?

Secret compartment?

He might well be grasping at straws, but he quickly dropped onto his haunches nonetheless. He tried to pull at the edge. It didn't move. He took out his keys and continued fiddling with the plank. And, lo and behold, after several seconds, the wood panel popped up.

"My goodness," Rosita said. "That's a secret hole in the floor?"

Tavis quickly took a picture before he dug farther into the hole. He soon realized that three pieces of the wood paneling came up. Inside the floor was a cardboard shoebox. He pulled it out and opened it. His eyes widened when he saw the gun and a wad of cash.

"That's a gun!" Rosita exclaimed. "That's been here all this time?"

"You've never seen this before?" Tavis asked.

Rosita shook her head. "No. Of course not."

"We never knew that he had a gun," Andrew said.

Rosita curled into her husband's side, placing a hand over her mouth to hide her horror.

Tavis took more pictures. Then he used a T-shirt from the duffel bag to lift the gun. It was a revolver.

"He couldn't have killed those kids," Rosita said, sounding distressed. "He just couldn't have."

"If he did, this wasn't the weapon," Tavis said.

Rosita's eyes grew wide as she looked at him. "How do you know?"

"Because this is a revolver. The gun that killed Hayley and Jonathan was a pistol." He lifted the wad of cash, which was secured with an elastic band. Hundred-dollar bills. "And I'd say this is about five grand."

"You can't tell the sheriff about this," Andrew said. "No matter what you say about the type of weapon, they'll find a way to tie it to the murders."

"That's not how it works," Tavis said. "They have evidence from the shootings. If this gun doesn't match—"

"You think we trust the police?" Rosita asked. "If they know that a gun and thousands of dollars are here, they'll believe everything they assumed about Lucas is true."

"This could clear him of the murders," Tavis said.

"But implicate him of what else?" Andrew countered. "We let you look around to help Lucas, not to hurt him."

Tavis got to his feet. He knew that he should call this in. Was the gun connected to another crime? But the bigger question was why Lucas would leave town without a gun and without all this cash.

"I think you should let the sheriff know about this," Tavis said. "But I'll let you sleep on it and decide later."

Was the cash the insurance policy that Lucas had alluded to? "Can I call you tomorrow?"

"You can call us tomorrow," Andrew said, "but I'm pretty sure we won't change our minds. The people in this town have already vilified Lucas. We don't need to give them any more ammunition."

SHAYLA COULDN'T BELIEVE it when Tavis filled her in. "A gun and a wad of cash?"

"Yes. I know I should call the sheriff, but the Carrs don't want me to. They don't want Lucas's name further dragged through the mud. If I were still a cop, I'd have no choice but to report this. But they let me go through Lucas's room as a favor—hoping I'd find something to exonerate him, not implicate him. I know they've gone through a lot because of the murder case, but I told them they needed to reconsider. What if the gun was used in another crime?"

"There's not a lot of crime in this town," Shayla said.

"Maybe not here, but in Buffalo. Although…" Tavis's voice trailed off.

"What are you thinking?"

"Remember the summer before the murders? There was an old guy who'd been shot downtown. The Elm Street murder."

"That's right," Shayla said. "That case was never solved?"

"No, never. The old guy, Norman Harris, had no known enemies, and certainly no reason to be gunned down. He was in his late seventies, a widower. Took a walk downtown every morning to stay in shape."

"I remember," Shayla said. "His twin granddaughters were high school freshmen."

"All leads went nowhere. In the past, I wondered if possibly the two separate murders could be connected. But Harris's killing seemed entirely random, senseless.

Hayley and Jonathan were teenagers who were allegedly killed after an unknown argument—people believed it was about the dance competition, or perhaps something else that went wrong at the party."

"Two entirely different killings," Shayla said.

"I'm going to do some digging, see if I can find out the weapon used to kill Harris. I expect Sheriff Thompson to throw up roadblocks. He wants simple answers to the problems in this town, and if something can't be solved, he's happy to let it go. I'll have to go around him, but if it turns out that Harris was killed with a revolver, maybe Lucas's gun can be checked against that... I'm thinking out loud now, but this is starting to feel right."

"Surely, Sheriff Thompson would want to solve this case," Shayla said.

"You don't know him like I do. And if I'm the one who brings this to him, he most certainly will ignore the issue at hand."

"Why?" Shayla asked.

"This is going to sound crazy, and petty, but it's the truth. It has to do with the sheriff's wife. Ex-wife."

"His wife?"

"She was a 9-1-1 dispatcher, so I knew her. We talked. Were friendly. There was a time that she and the sheriff were having problems. I didn't know that, and she was suddenly hitting on me. She even hired me for protection, allegedly from him, although she didn't specify that at the time. She was quite a bit older than me, but that didn't stop her interest. When I understood what was going on, I let her know that I didn't reciprocate her feelings. But the sheriff saw me as making a play for his wife. Nothing I said to him got through to him. And that's why he hates me. He sees me as being the cause of the end of his marriage."

"That is crazy," Shayla said. "What ended up happening?"

"I passed her off to someone else in my agency, and she

wasn't happy. Eventually she canceled the protection contract. She left the sheriff and ultimately remarried. She's still in town. I see her from time to time, and she pretends I don't exist. That's fine by me."

"It seems a bit immature for the sheriff to ignore anything you have to tell him about a case just because of that."

"It is immature. But if I say black, the sheriff says white. Whatever I tell him, I think he deliberately ignores. So I'm going to investigate what I can about the Elm Street murder, see what I can find. Then I'm going to talk to the Carrs and see if I can get them to turn over the evidence. That's the best I can do."

Chapter Fifteen

Shayla called Deedee and filled her in. "I can't believe it, but Tavis found a gun at Rosita and Andrew's place. And get this… It's not the gun that killed Hayley and Jonathan."

"How could he know that?"

"Because it's a revolver. Hayley and Jonathan were shot with a pistol. And get this… He's wondering if maybe this gun was used in another crime. Remember, there was an old guy who was killed the summer before Hayley and Jonathan and no one ever found out who did it? The Elm Street murder."

"Yeah, Mr. Harris. I remember. You think Lucas was the one behind that?"

"I… I would hate to think so. It would mean I knew him even less than I thought I did. It's all premature—maybe the gun isn't related at all. But maybe we're getting closer to figuring this out."

"So what about an insurance policy?" Deedee asked. "Did Tavis find anything like that there?"

"The cash, he's thinking. But Tavis makes a great point. If Lucas left town, why would he leave five grand worth of cash there? And the gun? Nothing about that makes any sense."

"I don't know. But maybe you should just stop all of this. I don't know where this is leading. Lucas left. He never came back, obviously. He's the one who killed Hayley and Jonathan. The fact that there was a gun at his place shows that he was a bigger criminal than we ever thought. Don't you think? Maybe when he killed Hayley and Jonathan he had to take off quickly. That's why he had to leave the money."

That was likely, Shayla couldn't deny it. But still. She didn't know what to make of it all, but the idea that Jenae had been looking for some sort of proof had her feeling like Tavis had just unearthed something important.

"Shayla, I think you need to stop looking into this stuff. Immediately. Someone wants to hurt you. If it's connected to the Elm Street murder, do you really want to be digging into something that could get you killed?"

Shayla made a face. "You say that as if you think that's the scenario. But how could you know that?"

Deedee hesitated a moment. "I'm not saying that I do know that. I'm just… This is a lot. Tavis keeps digging, you keep asking questions and you're going to make someone angry. It's common sense."

"I made someone angry before I even got back here. Someone wanted to hurt me before I started asking any questions."

"Shayla, I love you. But your stubborn streak is too much. You need to stop. Stop asking questions and putting yourself in harm's way."

As Shayla ended the call with her cousin, she couldn't help wondering why Deedee's suggestion seemed more like a warning as opposed to a general concern.

Did her cousin know something that she wasn't telling her?

THE NEXT MORNING, with Griffin outside the house and the nurse tending to her mother, Shayla decided that she should go see Rosita and Andrew. She could share what she had known about Lucas, and get their perspective. She kept coming back to the idea that Jenae was looking for some sort of proof, some sort of insurance policy. Maybe it was somewhere else in the Carrs' house?

But when Shayla drove onto their street, she saw the fire trucks and smoldering smoke in the distance.

Was it…? Her heart leaped to her throat.

And as she got closer, she saw the devastating truth.

The house that had been Rosita and Andrew's no longer existed. It had burned to the ground.

WHEN TAVIS SAW Shayla's name flashing on his phone's screen, he quickly answered the call.

"Tavis!" she cried before he could speak. "They burned down the Carrs' place. They burned it down!"

Tavis shot up in his bed. "The house is burned down?" he asked for clarification, his groggy brain coming to life.

"I just drove by there. I wanted to go see them. There are fire trucks everywhere. The house is completely gutted. I don't even know if they're okay!"

"Where are you now?" Tavis asked.

"I'm outside the Carrs'."

"Where's Griffin?" Tavis asked.

"He's behind me. He followed me here."

"Go home." He reached for the T-shirt on the chair beside his bed. "Go home and I'll meet you there."

THIS WASN'T A COINCIDENCE. Just yesterday, Tavis had found the secret compartment at the Carrs' place. Now, before he'd even been able to alert the police or turn over the evidence, the house had burned down.

That meant somebody knew something. But who? Shayla was the only one who Tavis had spoken to about what he'd found.

As he drove up to her place, she came out to meet him.

He unlocked his vehicle and she hopped into the passenger seat. She looked shaken.

"How did this happen?" she asked. "And why now?"

"That's exactly what I want to know," Tavis said. "This isn't a coincidence." Other things that happened had been possibly coincidental, but this was deliberate. "Who would know that I went to the house?"

Shayla hesitated. Then she said, "I only spoke to Deedee. But Deedee knows the situation."

"Deedee." Tavis said her name through clenched teeth. "You told Deedee?"

"Yes."

"You told her what I found?"

"Yes. But Deedee is my cousin… She was nearly killed in that accident. Why wouldn't I tell her?"

The vein in Tavis's temple began to pound. First, there was the alleged message from Jenae that Deedee had received at a time when no one else had heard from her. Now, Deedee was the only other person who knew what Tavis had found at the Carrs' place—and it had burned to the ground.

"Something's not right here. And unless you went and told somebody else, we have to consider that Deedee was the one who talked to someone."

"No! She wouldn't."

"How do you explain this fire?" Tavis asked. "Just a coincidence the day after I find evidence there? Evidence that I don't even get to turn over to the police? Any connection between that gun and the Elm Street murder or any other unsolved case is now gone."

"Deedee knows what's at stake. Are you trying to tell me you think Deedee's involved in this?"

"Call her. Ask her if she told anyone else."

Shayla looked at Tavis and gasped. "You want me to call my cousin and essentially accuse her of sabotaging this case? You think she also wants to see me hurt, or worse? It doesn't make any sense."

"Call her."

Shayla dialed her cousin. She put the phone on speaker.

"Hey," Deedee said.

"Deedee, I'm here with Tavis. The Carr place burned to the ground last night. You're the only one that I talked to about what was found there. And he's wondering…" Shayla's voice trailed off. She made a face before continuing. "You told me yesterday that I should drop this. Stop looking into this. What did you mean?"

Tavis's eyebrows shot up. So, Deedee *did* know something.

"What are you asking me?" Deedee asked.

"Deedee," Tavis said, "if you know something, this isn't the time to stay quiet. You need to tell me."

"What can I possibly know?" Deedee asked. But there was a higher pitch to her voice, and Tavis didn't believe her.

"Why did you tell me to stop looking into this?" Shayla asked. "If you know something, please tell me."

"It's…common sense," Deedee finally said. "I was nearly killed, remember? The more you ruffle feathers, the more someone's going to be upset. I just… I don't want anything to happen to you."

"Did you talk to anyone about this?" Tavis asked, direct.

Deedee hesitated a beat. "No. Of course not."

She was lying. He couldn't prove it, but he knew it in his gut.

Shayla ended the call and turned to Tavis. "See? My cousin wouldn't do this. She was nearly killed, remember? Now you're acting as though she possibly could be helping whoever wants to hurt me."

"I'm trying to figure this out. Deedee's the one you spoke to about this—unless there's someone else and you're not saying."

A flash of hurt streaked through Shayla's beautiful brown eyes. "Do you really believe that? After all that I've been through, you think I wouldn't tell you the truth now?"

"I have to ask."

She placed her hand on the door handle and pulled. "Of course you do. Because no matter what we've been through, you don't trust me. You never did."

She hopped out of the vehicle and took off toward the house.

No sooner was Shayla in the house, her phone whistled, indicating she'd received a text. It was from Deedee.

Stop looking into this. I can't tell you how I know, but they're angry. You won't be safe if you keep looking.

Shock hit Shayla like a tidal wave. Deedee knew something!

She quickly called her cousin. "Deedee, what are you saying?"

"I don't want to talk about it on the phone. But just know… You're not safe. You gotta let this go. In fact… I think I might go away for a couple of days."

"Deedee, tell me more. You have to."

"If you know what's good for you, you'll stop asking questions. If you stop asking questions, I think they'll let it go. But if you don't…"

"Deedee, I'm your cousin. You can't… You can't leave me hanging like this." Tavis was right. Deedee had been hiding something.

"Okay, I'll tell you this. Lucas… Lucas is dead. He wasn't the one that called you to the house in Buffalo. He's been dead since the night of the murders. There weren't two casualties that night. There were three. Hayley, Jonathan *and* Lucas."

Shayla was stunned. All these years later and now her cousin was telling her this? How could she ever have kept it from her?

"How come they never found his body?" Shayla asked.

"Because he needed to be the one who took the fall for killing Hayley and Jonathan. You just have to listen to me. I don't want to say any more over the phone."

"Where's his body?" Shayla asked.

Deedee didn't answer right away. "Somewhere it'll be impossible to find."

"Impossible?"

"Not unless someone knows where to look. Probably a hundred kids have been there since and wouldn't know."

"Wait, what are you saying?" Shayla asked.

"I've said enough. Too much. Please, stop this. Stop looking. Let it go."

The line went dead, and Shayla slumped onto the sofa, unable to believe what she'd just heard.

Lucas was dead. He had been since the night of the murders.

He himself had been a victim.

She had to tell Tavis. So she went back out to his truck. When he saw the look on her face, his own face morphed with concern.

She climbed into the vehicle. "What is it?" he asked.

"I think you're right. About Deedee. She…she…" Shayla could barely get the words out, her chest was suddenly feeling tight. It was hard to draw in breath.

"Calm down," he told her. "Breathe in slowly."

She did as he said, calming herself.

"Deedee said… Lucas is dead. He has been since the night of the murders. She said that he was a victim. Just like Hayley and Jonathan."

"Get her on the phone."

Shayla called her cousin. But Deedee didn't answer.

"Of course." Tavis cursed. "This makes total sense. No wonder I couldn't find Lucas anywhere. Not a shred of evidence about the man over the last nine years. Because he wasn't alive."

"I can't believe it," Shayla said.

"If Deedee told you that, she knows who did the killings. Do you think… You think she was involved?"

"Absolutely not. My cousin… She wouldn't…" But what did Shayla truly know? No. She knew her cousin wouldn't be involved in the killing of anyone. Somehow she must have solved the crime on her own, and now was afraid for her life.

Shayla called Deedee again. Again, the phone went to voicemail.

"Now she's ignoring you," Tavis said.

"She begged me to stop looking into this because she said *they* are getting angry. She said if I keep looking into it, my life will truly be in danger."

"Your life is already in danger."

"She's afraid, Tavis. So afraid that she's going to take off for a few days."

Tavis looked at her, and she could see the doubt in his eyes. "I know you can find out where your cousin is. And when you do, you need to tell me."

"That's all she said. I'll try to keep reaching her, but I can't make any promises."

Several hours later, when Shayla still couldn't reach Deedee, she called Tavis and told him exactly that. And she realized then the big mistake she'd made by turning to him for comfort.

"I think you're protecting your cousin," he told her. "She's been lying to me from the beginning. She doesn't want me to know where she is, and you're protecting her."

"After all of this, after everything I've told you, you think I would protect Deedee."

"She's involved in this, Shayla. You know she is. But she's your cousin. Families go to incredible lengths to protect family members even when they're guilty of the most heinous of crimes."

"So you think Deedee is responsible for the murders and that I'm protecting her. That I know where she is and I'm not telling you. You think someone ran me and Deedee off the road and, despite Deedee nearly dying, that was all…what? A well-orchestrated plan?"

"Maybe it was. Maybe it went wrong and Deedee got hurt."

Shayla's mouth fell open. "I can't believe you would say that to me. Deedee wouldn't risk getting herself killed. And she definitely wouldn't try to get me killed."

Ending the call with Tavis, Shayla felt crushed. She thought that she had garnered some trust with Tavis since returning to town. Foolishly, she'd slept with him, thinking that they had reached a new level of understanding.

But the only thing that mattered to him was solving Hayley's murder. She was just a tool to do so.

Shayla needed to finally take matters into her own hands. She'd been trusting Tavis to get to the bottom of this. But her cousin's life was at stake, as was hers. It was time she turned to proper law enforcement.

So the next morning she dug out the card the sheriff had given her. She called him.

"Sheriff Thompson? I have some news for you."

Chapter Sixteen

The next morning, Tavis went to Shayla's door briefly before leaving. He asked her if she'd heard from Deedee, and she told him no. But her voice had been devoid of emotion and her answer so instant that he wasn't sure he believed her.

She was protecting her cousin. She had to be.

Deedee knew more than she was saying, obviously. But she loved Shayla, so why give her half answers? Wouldn't she tell her more details so Shayla could be prepared for whatever danger she was referring to? Why be vague?

Unless Deedee was protecting herself.

And Shayla must have realized that, which is why she wasn't forthcoming about her cousin's whereabouts.

Tavis left Griffin at the house, as he needed to follow up on this lead. He found out that Rosita and Andrew were staying at a hotel, and he went to pay them a visit.

Though he'd already gotten word of the initial finding of arson at the scene, the Carrs shared the details of their harrowing experience. They'd been asleep when they'd heard the fire crackling, and had barely made it out of the house without being overcome by smoke. Someone had doused the entire outside of the house with gasoline, and also had broken some windows and thrown gasoline inside to ensure the fire quickly engulfed the house. The fact that they'd made it out with their lives and no injuries had been a miracle. Andrew's quick thinking to wear their winter coats had saved them from being burned.

"And the evidence?" Tavis asked. "Was it still in Lucas's room?"

"We left it where we found it. Everything's gone."

Tavis left the Carrs and called Deputy Jenkins. "Where are you?" he asked the man without preamble.

"At Molly's Café, getting a muffin and a coffee. Why?"

"Can I see you? This is urgent."

"I'll wait here. How long will you be?"

"Give me five minutes."

When Tavis arrived at Molly's, he saw Deputy Jenkins standing outside his vehicle. He was speaking with a middle-aged couple, and Tavis approached slowly. Jenkins saw him, nodded, and then Tavis joined the man at his cruiser as the couple walked away.

"Maybe we should sit inside your car for this," Tavis told the deputy.

Moments later, they were both seated in the deputy's vehicle. "Obviously, you heard about the fire at the Carr place," Tavis said.

"Yes. Such a shame. It was arson."

"It wasn't a coincidence," Tavis said. "This has to do with Lucas and the murders nine years ago."

"Come on, Tavis. How could it?"

"Because I went to see them the day before yesterday. And I found something in Lucas's room. I found a box with a gun and a wad of cash. There was a secret compartment in the closet floor. Nobody knew about it. Obviously, it was missed by investigators in the past. Someone must've gotten word as to what I'd found. And they torched the place."

The deputy looked doubtful.

"Come on, you're a cop. You know there's no such thing as coincidence."

The deputy sighed. "Tavis, why is it anything you get yourself involved in ends up getting worse?"

"Spare me Sheriff Thompson's analysis. This situation is getting out of hand because somebody knows I'm getting close." He paused, glancing out at the street as a mother with two young children walked by. Sheridan Falls was an idyllic little town. But there was a dark secret here, one that was finally coming to light.

He turned back to the deputy. "All I have are pictures of the revolver and the cash that I found in the secret compartment. But I was thinking about the Elm Street murder, how that was never solved. I'm wondering what type of gun was used to kill Norman Harris. Because if it was a revolver…"

"If it was a revolver, we'll never know if it was the one at the Carrs' residence."

"Listen to me. There are three murders in this town that need to be solved, and I know you're not like the sheriff. I always thought it was probably some kids who'd killed the old guy, some dumb drunken activity. Or maybe an initiation. Rosita and Andrew said that Lucas hung out with Alex and Chase and Jonathan. They said they always thought Alex and Chase were no-good influences on their nephew. I'm thinking now that maybe Alex and Chase know more than they ever told me."

Deputy Jenkins glanced around, as though making sure no one was within earshot even though they were behind the closed doors of his cruiser. "You didn't hear this from me. But years ago, there was some speculation that Alex and Chase were involved in that shooting. The Elm Street murder."

"You're kidding."

"But the idea was quickly dismissed. They're the sheriff's boys. They wouldn't do anything so heinous. Anyway, it was just a rumor, and the sheriff figured people were just being bad-minded, going after his kids. The whole concept was quickly squashed."

Tavis's gut began to tighten. The gun and the cash at the Carrs' place—the insurance policy? It made sense. "So this isn't the first time that someone considered this?"

The deputy shook his head. "No. But just because the idea was thrown out there doesn't mean that they did it. And by your own admission, you found a revolver in Lucas's closet. When he came to this town, he was always known for being a troubled teen. So maybe he killed Hayley and Jonathan and he also killed Mr. Harris."

"There's something else," Tavis said. "And for now, I'd like to keep this between us. But I got word from someone that Lucas is dead. That he was killed the night that Jonathan and Hayley were killed. And if that's true, then he didn't kill them. Someone else did."

Alex and Chase? Tavis wondered.

Deputy Jenkins looked at him with a disbelieving expression. "Who told you that?"

"I can't say right now. But if you can find out and let me know the weapon that was used to kill Mr. Harris, maybe I can finally start putting these pieces together in a real way."

"I don't need to look into the file because I worked the case. The weapon that killed Norman Harris was a revolver."

"Thanks," Tavis said. "I know I'm close, and I'm going to solve this case."

SHAYLA KNEW THAT leaving the house with Griffin watching was going to pose a bit of a problem. So before she got into her car to leave the driveway, she approached his vehicle.

"Hey," she said, forcing a smile onto her face. "I'm just running to the store for a few minutes. Maybe ten, fifteen. I'd really appreciate it if you'd stay here and guard the house, because I'm worried about my mother. Tavis might have told you that we had an issue with the previous nurse and, while I trust this one, I just prefer that someone be here to watch over her. In fact, I'd prefer that you stay in the house."

When Griffin looked slightly concerned at her request, Shayla summoned a tear and forced emotion into her voice. "I'd never forgive myself if anything happened to my mother because of me. Please, stay in the house until I get back. Make sure my mother's safe. I won't be more than ten, fifteen minutes."

"All right," Griffin agreed. "As long as you agree to call me if you need me."

"Yes. I'll absolutely call you if I need you." She dabbed at her eyes and flashed him a soft smile. "Thank you."

She led Griffin into her house, introduced him to the nurse, then got into her car and headed for town.

SHERIFF THOMPSON WAS waiting outside the building when Shayla pulled into the department parking lot. He waved a hand and smiled as she got out of her vehicle.

"Hello, Sheriff Thompson," she said. "I'm glad you could meet with me."

"No problem," he told her. "It sounds like you have something serious to discuss with me."

"I do." She blew out a frazzled breath. "I got word from someone, and I think this makes sense. Lucas Carr is allegedly dead."

The sheriff's eyes grew as wide as saucers. "Dead?"

Shayla nodded. "Apparently murdered. The same night as Hayley and Jonathan. And if that's the case, then that means he didn't kill them. Someone else killed all three of them."

"My God," the sheriff said. "Do you know where the body is?"

"Um, not really." Shayla hesitated. "But, I was thinking

about that all night. There's this barn on the outskirts of town. We used to hang out there. Kids would drink, or smoke pot, party. It was a great location because the property was abandoned. If anyone wanted to get rid of a body so that it wouldn't be found, my guess is they'd bury it there."

"Can you show me?" Sheriff Thompson asked.

"I… I guess. Though I'm not sure if his body is there."

"But let's go check it out," the sheriff said. "You could be on to something."

Shayla's phone began to ring. She saw Tavis's name and number flashing on her screen. She rejected the call.

"Ready to go?" Sheriff Thompson asked. "I'll drive, and you can lead me to this barn."

Shayla nodded. She wanted answers as much as the sheriff. "Sure."

TAVIS FROWNED WHEN his call to Shayla bounced to her voicemail almost instantly. He called again, and again the same thing happened.

Was she rejecting his calls?

He understood that she was upset with him, but he needed to talk to her.

Everything made sense now. Alex and Chase were the ones behind the killings of Hayley and Jonathan. Of the guys who used to hang out and cause trouble, only Alex and Chase were still alive. They'd killed Old Man Harris on Elm Street. Maybe Lucas had been involved. Jonathan too. Though they'd all been close, something had happened and they'd ended up killing Jonathan and Lucas. Maybe to silence them as witnesses?

He tried calling Shayla again, and when again the call went to voicemail after the second ring, he sent her a text instead.

Call me. It's important.

SHAYLA SWIPED TO reject Tavis's call.

"That's Tavis?" the sheriff asked, glancing at her.

"Yes."

"That man acts like he has a thorn in his backside. Always on edge, never letting a situation go."

"Tell me about it," Shayla said softly.

"You did the right thing by coming to me. I'm the sheriff in this town. If what you say about Lucas is true, we'll find his body, and I promise you I will investigate this to the fullest extent and find out what happened to him."

"Thank you. If we can find out who's trying to hurt me, I can finally be free of this."

She scrawled out a text to Tavis.

I'm with Sheriff Thompson. We're going to look for Lucas's body. I'll be in touch later.

Then she turned off her phone.

WHEN SHAYLA'S TEXT came in, Tavis's heart sank. He quickly called, but the phone didn't ring at all. Just went to voicemail. He tried to text her, tell her to not go with the sheriff anywhere, but she didn't respond. He called again, then again. Each time, he was told to leave a message.

He needed to find Shayla. If she was with the sheriff, she was in danger. Because for Alex and Chase to have gotten away with murder all those years ago, they'd had to have help. And who better to help them than the town's top law man, their own father?

Tavis had seen it a million times. Family members going to all sorts of lengths to protect their loved ones from facing justice. Even if that person wore a badge.

How far would the sheriff go to make sure his boys avoided the law?

Tavis didn't want to find out.

He called Deedee's number, and it rang and rang. At least her phone was on. He drove to her house, found her parents there. They confirmed what Shayla had already told him. That Deedee was gone. Said she'd needed to get away for a couple of days; her parents didn't know why.

"If you know where she is, I need you to tell me."

Deedee's parents looked at each other with concern. "What's this about?"

"This is a matter of life and death. I'm worried about Shayla, and I think Deedee's the only one who can help me."

"She told us not to tell anyone where she went."

"Then do me a favor. If you have a way to reach her, call her. Tell her to call me immediately. Let her know that I think that Shayla is right now in mortal danger, and I need her help."

IT DIDN'T TAKE more than ten minutes for Tavis's phone to ring. He answered right away. "Tavis Saunders."

"It's Deedee."

"Thank God. Deedee, I don't care what you knew and when, but I care about finding Shayla. I think she's in danger. She's with the sheriff right now."

Deedee gasped, confirming his suspicion. "So, I'm right. She's not safe with the sheriff."

"Where are they?"

"Shayla said something about going to see if she could find Lucas's body." Tavis paused for a beat. "Tell me everything. Because I know that you know. And you're the only chance I have of finding Shayla."

"If she's with the sheriff, she's in danger. They've been warning me since she got back. Afraid that she was going to get close to the truth."

"Alex and Chase?" Tavis asserted.

"Yes. They killed Jonathan and Lucas because they were in the car when Alex and Chase killed that man on Elm Street. They were getting paranoid, thought that one of them was going to talk. Hayley just happened to be there that night, and they couldn't let her live."

"Where would the sheriff be taking her?"

"All I can think is that Shayla figured out possibly where the body could be buried. I kind of hinted at it, but I wasn't specific. We used to hang out there. You remember the old abandoned barn on the edge of town? Kids would hang out there, party, drink."

"Yes."

"Either she guessed that's where I was talking about when I said Lucas was buried where he'd never be found, or the sheriff suggested taking her there."

"Thank you, Deedee," Tavis said.

"Find her," Deedee said. "Find her before it's too late."

TAVIS QUICKLY CALLED Deputy Jenkins. "Jenkins," he hurriedly said when the man answered the phone. "Shayla's with the sheriff. And I think she's in danger."

"Tavis, come on."

"Hear me out," Tavis said. And then he filled him in. "This is a credible witness, someone I know personally. What she says makes sense. Think about it. You said yourself that Alex and Chase were suspected in the Elm Street murder. But nothing ever came of that. Don't you think it makes sense that Sheriff Thompson covered up their crime? These are his boys. He wasn't going to let them go down for murder."

"I hope you're wrong," Jenkins said.

"Listen, I'm calling you because I need to find Shayla. She and the sheriff are apparently going to the old abandoned barn at the edge of town. I'm heading there now. And I need to know that you have my back. I think he's going to hurt her."

"Damn, this is a mess," Jenkins said.

"Yeah, it is. Can I count on you?"

The deputy exhaled sharply then said, "You can count on me."

THE SHERIFF PULLED his car into the long driveway that led to the abandoned barn. When he stopped and cut the engine, he and Shayla exited the vehicle.

"Show me exactly where you guys used to hang out," he said.

Shayla looked around. This place was still exactly as she remembered it. The peeling red paint. The broken windows, the missing wood panels.

"We used to hang out either in the barn, or sometimes outside of it. It's crazy when I think about it. The stairs leading to the second level in the barn were so unstable, but that didn't stop us from climbing them anyway. Some teens would seek privacy in the old horse stalls and make out." Shayla looked around. "But Lucas wouldn't be in the barn. There's a firepit at the back." Shayla led the way there. "Right there," she said, pointing. "We liked to hang out there too, sometimes roasting marshmallows and making s'mores. This was the perfect place to hang when we were in school. Somewhere we knew we wouldn't get caught."

"And where's Lucas's body?"

Shayla whirled around to look at the sheriff. "I don't know. I just assume it's probably out here somewhere." She looked toward the field behind the barn. The area was vast. "I couldn't begin to tell you. But maybe if you guys get cadaver dogs—" Her voice stopped abruptly when she turned again to look at the sheriff. For a moment, she couldn't register what she was seeing.

And then she did. He had a gun. And he was pointing it at her.

"What are you doing?"

Gone was the smile on his face, replaced with a dark, evil look. "You should've let this go," he said.

Shayla's mouth fell open, her brain scrambling to make sense of the situation. How was this possible? The sheriff wanted to kill her?

"You...you want to kill me?"

"It's not that I want to. But I have to. You were getting too close. Asking too many questions. Putting it all together. Eventually this was going to be a problem."

"I... I don't know what's going on here."

"Oh, I think you do."

Keeping his gun trained on her, the sheriff went to the back of his cruiser, popped it open and removed a shovel. Walking back to Shayla, he tossed it at her. It landed on the ground in front of her feet.

"Pick it up!" he bellowed.

Shayla quickly lowered herself and picked up the shovel.

"Very good," he told her. "Now walk."

When she didn't immediately move, he shoved the gun in her back, and she started to walk. "Where?"

"Toward the well."

Shayla moved one foot in front of the other, heading toward the well that was on the property. Once they had passed the well by about twenty feet, the sheriff said, "That's enough. Stop right there."

She stopped, and looked over her shoulder at him. Her chest was rising and falling with rapid breaths.

"Start digging."

"Is this where Lucas is?" Her voice was a croak.

The sheriff chuckled, a hollow, evil sound. "Oh, you're cute. But since you seem to be continuing to play the innocent act, let me be clear. You're digging a grave. *Your* grave."

Chapter Seventeen

Tavis raced toward the edge of town, his heart in his throat every step of the way. This was his fault. He'd come down hard on Shayla once again, and she had done the one thing that made sense. She'd turned to the sheriff for help. Instead of him.

Because she couldn't trust him.

Couldn't trust him to have faith in her. Couldn't trust him to be there for her.

He mentally chastised himself and promised that if he ever got the chance, he would never fail her again. Deedee had kept her in the dark as well. He would find out later the extent of what had gone on that horrible night nine years ago, but he had painted Shayla with a tarnished brush. The same brush he'd painted her with all those years ago when he'd suspected that she hadn't been honest about Lucas.

He hadn't meant to offend her. He'd just been so desperate to get to the truth.

Too desperate. Desperate to solve the murder of someone who was already dead and gone, as opposed to cherishing a person who was alive and well.

Alive and needed protecting.

And if she died at the hands of the sheriff, this would be on his watch. His responsibility.

Griffin couldn't stop apologizing, but Tavis didn't

blame him. This was his fault. He'd sent her running to the sheriff because she couldn't trust him to be there for her.

There was nothing Tavis could have done to protect Hayley, but he could have protected Shayla.

And he'd failed.

"Hold on, Shayla. I'm coming."

He hit the accelerator.

SHAYLA'S BROW DRIPPED with sweat from digging. She didn't understand why the sheriff was doing this. And if she was going to die here, she deserved to know why.

"Why are you doing this?"

"You were going to find out sooner or later, because that cousin of yours couldn't keep her mouth shut. But I couldn't let my boys go to prison. Do you understand? No one meant to kill Hayley. She was just in the way. But Lucas and Jonathan? They were gonna try to take my boys down."

"For what?" Shayla asked.

"You know I'm talking about the Elm Street killing. Now, I never condoned them killing Old Man Harris, but his life had already been lived. My boys were young. Made a stupid mistake. They didn't deserve to lose their lives over something like that."

Alex and Chase... They were behind the Elm Street murder!

How did Jenae fit into this? Had she known? She must have, just like Deedee. Is that why she'd taken off? Was Jenae even alive?

And then it hit her. Jenae and Deedee had been dating Chase and Alex at the time of the murders.

"Did you kill Jenae too?" Shayla asked.

"If she knows what's good for her, she will never come back to this town. And she'll keep her mouth shut. You are going to be the example to anyone else who thinks that opening their mouth will get them anywhere. It won't. I'm the law in this town. I run things here."

"You don't have to do this," Shayla said. "I won't say anything, I promise."

"You won't, because you'll be dead."

"So if Lucas is dead, who tried to kill me in Buffalo?"

Sheriff Thompson snorted. "Alex messed that up. It would have been the perfect setup. Jenae tried to hide, but he found out where she was living. You were supposed to die there, then everyone would think she'd killed you. With her own murder charge, she wasn't going to be a problem anymore— Who told you to stop? Keep digging!"

Shayla pushed the shovel into the dirt, her chest heaving. What if she swung the shovel backward and whacked the sheriff in the head? Could she hurt him enough to disarm him? Or would he just get angry and then shoot her?

"I can see what you're thinking. But don't. Because if you make me kill you, I won't make your death quick. I'll make you suffer. But if you dig your grave, I'll give you one bullet that will take you out and you won't feel a thing."

"And my mother? You would take me away from her when she needs me?"

The sheriff hesitated, as though for a moment considering his conscience. "This isn't what I wanted. But this is your fault, Shayla. At least now Lucas's insurance policy has been destroyed in the fire and there's nothing tying my boys to the Elm Street murder."

"I promise you, I'll say nothing."

Gone was the sheriff's momentary glimpse of conscience. His expression darkened. "Dig, or I'll make you suffer."

Shayla whimpered and continued to dig.

TAVIS SLOWED DOWN on the road in front of the barn. The last thing he needed was to approach the property with tires squealing and alert the sheriff that he was there. The property was large, but he was hoping that he would be able to find the sheriff and Shayla fairly quickly. He would need stealth and quiet as he advanced.

He parked his Sierra on the road. The sheriff's cruiser was down the length of the driveway. At least the barn was close enough to the road. The field behind it was vast. From memory, he knew there was at least another building back there as well, but they could be anywhere.

He exited his vehicle, got his gun, and cut across the gravel and weeds that led toward the barn. As he made his way around the side of the building, he strained to listen for sound. He heard nothing.

As he got to the back of the barn, he peered out carefully. And in the distance, he saw them. Shayla with a shovel. She was digging. And the sheriff had a gun trained on her.

His back was to Tavis, and so was Shayla's. But damn it, they were a distance off.

There was a thicket of trees to the right. He could go that way and try to get closer.

He took out his phone and opened the camera app. These new phones had amazing capabilities, and his was no exception. He was able to zoom in close enough to capture the sheriff with his gun on Shayla. He took the picture and texted Deputy Jenkins.

I'm at the property right now. The sheriff looks like he's ready to kill Shayla! Here's the proof.

Then he sent the picture.

Now, Tavis needed to get close. At least close enough to take a shot if need be. He went around the other side of the barn toward the thicket of trees at the side. And then, hoping the trees would cover him, he began to advance.

"Can you hurry it up?" the sheriff said. "I ain't got all day."

Shayla really wished she could take the shovel and pummel this man. How dare he expect her to dig her own grave so that he could kill her, and do it without any complaint? But what could she do? Maybe the best thing to do was to make her move, and then try to run for it. It was her only way...

She felt so stupid now, not trusting Tavis. He had been the one person in this town determined to make sure she was okay. Even her cousin had betrayed her. Whatever Deedee had known, she should have told her a long time ago. It could have spared her this right now.

She couldn't even turn her phone on at the moment without attracting the sheriff's attention. She had stupidly turned it off. There was no way for anyone to find her.

"You don't have to do this. Whatever you think I'm going to say, I won't. Hayley's death was a long time ago. All of this is ancient history. No one needs to worry about it anymore."

"Yeah, but there's something to be said about loose ends. Loose ends and loose lips. I know that your friend Tavis is never gonna let this go. I'm sorry, I genuinely like you. But there's no other way."

"Sheriff Thompson!"

A sense of shock hit Shayla like a sledgehammer to the chest. When she realized the voice wasn't a figment of her imagination, euphoria quickly took hold. She threw her gaze to the right, toward the trees. And then she saw him. Tavis. His gun drawn.

"Tavis Saunders." The sheriff laughed without mirth. "I should've known you'd end up here. But you know what? This is good. Even better than I'd imagined."

Shayla wanted to throw the shovel and run to Tavis, but the sheriff would shoot her dead in a second.

"Put the gun down," Tavis demanded.

"Really?" Thompson asked. "You're going to tell the sheriff to put the gun down? Not gonna happen. But it's a good thing you came here in time to join your girlfriend. Because now, when she dies, I'll have been here to save the day. You blamed her for Hayley's death, and that's why you killed her. Unfortunately, I'll have no choice but to shoot you dead."

"This is over, sheriff." Tavis spoke firmly.

Shayla didn't know what to do. She only knew that, finally, she felt a sense of hope.

"Drop the gun, Tavis. Kick it over here. Or I'll make your girlfriend suffer."

Tavis held up his phone and, for a moment, Shayla was confused. And then he explained.

"I've already taken a picture of you with your gun trained on Shayla. I sent it to Deputy Jenkins. By the end of this day, everyone in town will know that you're a fraud. We know what happened. We know you covered for Alex and Chase. We know you covered for them killing Lucas. I don't have all the other details, but that's enough. You gotta love technology," Tavis added, chuckling. "There's nothing you can do now to escape this. Everybody in this town is going to know you're a corrupt sheriff who let murders go unsolved and even committed murder to save your boys."

The sheriff's face fell. Shayla gazed at him, wondering if he was going to shoot her. His gun was still on her, but he quickly threw it in Tavis's direction. "You sent a picture?" he asked through clenched teeth.

"The killing stops," Tavis said. "You're not going to kill another person to save your two spoiled sons who you couldn't control."

In the distance, sirens sounded. Shayla's knees buckled and she almost dropped to the ground. These few seconds would be precarious, but she felt a surge of hope. Tavis had come to save the day.

Sheriff Thompson's eyes widened at the sound of the sirens. And as Shayla watched, he did something she didn't expect. He turned the gun from Tavis and put the muzzle in his mouth. Then he fired.

SHAYLA SCREAMED. Tavis ran toward her and scooped her in his arms. She cried, clinging to him, and he clung to her. She was alive. He'd gotten to her in time. Waves of relief washed over him.

"Oh my God, Tavis!"

"Sweetheart," he said, breathing into her hair, inhaling the scent of her just to make sure this moment was real.

"He was going to kill me. I thought I was going to die."

"I told you I would take care of you. I failed for a moment, and I'm sorry for that. But I'm here now."

As he pulled back and looked at her, and brushed away her tears, he brought his mouth down on hers and kissed her fiercely. He wasn't thinking, but feeling. Feeling this incredible sense of relief and something else. Shayla was safe in his arms. And he didn't ever want to let her go.

TWO DAYS LATER, after the dust had settled and the town learned the truth of the horrifying acts that had happened nine years ago and what had almost happened to her, Shayla was finally getting to breathe.

Hayley, completely in the wrong place. Lucas and Jonathan, caught up with the wrong crowd. Alex and Chase—monsters.

At least they'd been arrested, and with their father dead and gone, they were certain to pay for their crimes this time.

Deedee couldn't stop apologizing. She'd come to see Shayla and explain everything. "I was afraid. What more can I say? I thought that being silent was going to protect you, protect me. But they were scared. Totally scared of you being back and finding the proof that Lucas left."

"Why didn't you just tell me? You didn't trust me to keep a secret?"

"They told me that if I ever told anyone, they would kill me and kill my parents. I saw what they'd already done. How could I doubt them?"

"But I never would have betrayed your confidence. You know that."

"But what if just knowing the truth caused you to react somehow differently? Like when you brought your car to Chase? If you'd known he was responsible for Lucas's murder, you might have looked at him differently. Instead, at least when you went to his shop, you were pleasant with him, and he was none the wiser."

"And yet, they still tried to kill me."

"I know. I thought I was doing the right thing."

"You got into the jail to talk to Chase?" Shayla asked. Her cousin had promised she would before she came to see her. To get answers about the recent attacks on her life.

"Alex was the one who stole the SUV and ran us off the road. He was at the vigil and left right when it was over so that he could follow us. Heading to the cemetery gave him the perfect opportunity to try and kill us. I guess he figured if he killed me too, it would make their lives easier. I certainly couldn't tell you anything if I were dead."

"I can't believe them. All these years, they got away with what they did and hung around this town and acted as though I was the evil one."

"But they're going to pay for their crimes now. That's what matters. And you're safe."

Shayla looked at her cousin. So much had happened, so much that was hard to believe.

"I'm sorry," Deedee said, and her voice broke.

Shayla put her arms around her cousin and hugged her. "I know you are. Deedee, I love you. I don't blame you."

Deedee wept, and Shayla held her, the two of them finally able to feel the relief that came from knowing there was no longer a threat to their lives.

TWO DAYS LATER, Tavis approached Shayla's house. He hadn't heard from her, and it was gnawing at him. He knew that a lot had happened and she was dealing with so much. Her cousin, the aftermath of this absolutely crazy ordeal, the emotional distress of everything. Not to mention her mother's illness. But still, he wanted to see her.

She answered the door and looked up at him with those bright brown eyes, her mouth forming an O. How lovely she was.

"Hey, Shayla."

"Hi."

"I know I haven't heard from you, and I understand you might be upset with me. I just wanted you to know that I'm sorry."

"It's okay."

Was it? "I judged you harshly and I shouldn't have."

"But you do that, don't you?" she asked, a tinge of sadness in her voice. "With Hayley, you judged me. And with Deedee, you judged me."

"I was wrong, and I'm sorry. But...what about us?"

"I'll always be grateful that you saved me, but I know that everything that happened between us... We were caught up in the moment. I understand, and I'm at peace with everything."

"What if I don't agree that we were simply caught up in the moment?"

There was sadness in her eyes. "I don't know what I'm going to be doing," she went on. "Probably heading back to Florida. And you'll be staying here. We don't have to have an awkward conversation about what happened. It is what it is, and I'm okay with that. I'm just glad this whole thing has been solved and we can both move forward."

Her words were like a punch to the gut. Had their one night meant nothing to her? Heck, he didn't know fully what it meant to him. He only knew that he didn't want their relationship to be over.

"I'd like for us to have a conversation at some point," Tavis said. "When things have calmed down."

"Is there any point in prolonging the inevitable?" she asked.

When he said nothing, she continued. "I'm going to see my mother now. Unfortunately…" Her eyes began to well with tears. "Unfortunately, she's taken a turn for the worse."

"Shayla, I'm so sorry."

"Thank you."

She closed the door, and as Tavis walked away from the house, he felt a very odd and distressing sensation deep in his heart.

Odd and Super

Epilogue

Two weeks later, the sun was shining bright in the sky and a flock of geese flew overhead just as the crowd finished singing the last verse of "Amazing Grace." Shayla looked at the coffin that had just been lowered into the ground, and dropped her yellow rose onto it. Her mother's favorite.

"Goodbye, Mom."

Deedee hugged her, and Shayla turned into her cousin's arms, holding back her tears. Her mother wouldn't want her to cry anymore. There'd been enough tears already.

This wasn't what she'd wanted for her mother, but the truth was, her mother had been gravely ill, something Shayla hadn't been able to accept until the final days of her life. Shayla would have to cherish the memories and the time she'd shared with her mother these last weeks. She could never regain the time they'd lost, but she knew that her mother was at peace now, in a better place. And she would always be with her.

Her aunt and uncle hugged her, as did others in the crowd. Many of the townsfolk had come out to see Michelle Phillips laid to rest. It was a wonderful send-off.

As Shayla looked up at the cloudless sky, she felt a sense of renewed hope. The mystery was solved. Her name was cleared. Her mother was at rest. And the future ahead of her would no longer be tainted with fear.

With Deedee's arm around her waist, Shayla began to walk away from the grave. She saw someone in the distance in a skirt and sandals walking toward her. A familiar face. Jenae!

Shayla stopped walking, and Jenae came right to her.

"Hello, Deedee, Shayla."

Shayla swallowed. She didn't know if she was happy to see Jenae or not. The fear had been that she'd been killed. "Jenae."

"I'm sorry for your loss," she said, and her face filled with sorrow.

"Thank you," Shayla said.

"I just want you to know, I'm sorry about how everything played out. But I was afraid. You know the story now, I'm sure," she said, throwing a glance at Deedee. "I was married to Alex and I knew exactly how dangerous he was. When I got away from him, I changed my name so that I could be safe. But this murder that happened years ago always hung over my head. I was always afraid that he would kill me because I knew the truth.

"The night of the murders, Lucas mentioned something about an insurance policy. Before they killed him, he said they'd never get away with it because of this insurance policy. We searched high and low, but couldn't find anything, and I finally started to think he may have left it with you. That's why I sent the nurse to your house. What I wanted was proof that I could take Alex down with, so that I could be safe. I never wanted to hurt you."

"I understand now," Shayla said.

"I thought changing my last name would keep me safe from Alex, but he still found me. That's when I went into hiding. I got involved with another guy and he promised he'd protect me, but you can never be sure. I was convinced Alex was going to kill me."

"Shaker?" Shayla asked, remembering the name the guy on the street in Buffalo had mentioned.

"Yes, his real name is Henry. He prefers his street name, though."

"Thank God you got away from Alex," Shayla said. Jenae's story tied up the last loose end. "I can't believe his father…" Shayla's voice trailed off.

"Sheriff Thompson didn't get to hurt you," Jenae said. "That's what matters."

"I know."

Jenae opened her arms, and Shayla accepted the hug she offered. "I can now get back to my life," Jenae said. "And I hope you can too."

Shayla nodded. "That's the plan."

Jenae turned and walked away, and Shayla hugged her cousin a little tighter.

"Have you heard from Tavis?" Deedee asked.

"No," Shayla said. "Look, I know he was being nice to me because he felt a sense of obligation. And he didn't want anything to happen to me, and I'm glad he was there to save my life. But that's all there is to it."

"Are you sure about that?" Deedee asked.

"Of course I am. He never liked me. We just had…a moment."

Deedee's eyes wandered off, and Shayla followed her line of sight. She sucked in a breath when she saw Tavis standing near a tree, dressed in a suit and sunglasses. Looking every bit as incredible as he ever had.

"I think you might be wrong," Deedee said, a smile on her face. And in her voice. Then she stepped away.

Shayla's heart was beating fast as Tavis approached.

As he neared her, his lips pulled into a grin. "It's good to see you, Shayla."

"Likewise," she told him. Why did she feel so flushed suddenly?

His face grew serious. "I was sorry to hear about your mother."

"Thank you."

"I stayed away, because I know you were going through a tough time. And because you were mad at me."

"Tavis, none of that matters now."

"It does matter. Because… I don't know what your plans are, but there's no threat to you here in Sheridan Falls anymore. And this was always your home. You mentioned you have an e-store, so your business is operated online. I'm hoping… Maybe you'll consider staying here?"

"The thought has crossed my mind," she said honestly. With her business online, Lyndsay could still work for her. There were logistics she would need to work out, but it was doable. She'd spent so much time running, and Florida was nice, but it had never felt like home. Here, she could be in the place where she had loved growing up and had spent so many wonderful years with her mother.

"Or maybe you would consider coaching young dancers here. You mentioned once that you'd wanted to coach."

"You seem to have it all figured out," Shayla said.

"I want you here," Tavis said bluntly.

Her breath caught in her throat. He was holding nothing back.

"Shayla, what happened between us wasn't just some isolated moment. There's something special between us, don't you feel it?"

"Yes," she admitted breathlessly. But she'd spent the last couple of weeks telling herself that this couldn't be possible. That Tavis didn't feel anything for her. It was easier than getting her hopes up.

He slipped an arm around her waist and pulled her close. "Stay in Sheridan Falls. Stay with me."

The deep timbre of his voice rumbled through her body, followed by a wave of happiness. She'd always had a crush on him. And now the crush had blossomed into something more...

"Do you really mean it?" she asked.

"Absolutely. I want you here. I want you in my life."

And to prove the point, he lowered his head and kissed her. Softly. Sweetly. A kiss that proved without doubt that there was something special between them.

Something worth staying here and fighting for.

* * * * *

CONARD COUNTY
PROTECTOR

RACHEL LEE

Prologue

"Guilty."

In a hearing room, the General Court Martial has concluded. The judge announces the verdict of the five jurors, a unanimous decision of *Guilty*.

It is the only word the defendant hears. It rolls through him like deafening thunder. He knows what it means: he has been convicted of war crimes, to be stripped of his rank, his time in grade, any future retirement. He will go to prison.

He stands at attention, outwardly accepting the judgment. As he is taken away, he looks at his sister, standing straight in her Marine uniform. He sees his own fury reflected in her eyes.

The defendant believes he has done nothing wrong. It was war, after all. He was just doing his job.

An unjust verdict.

It should have been *Not Guilty*.

Chapter One

Jasmine and Adam Ryder's wedding reception in the Conard City Park had become quite an affair. White fairy lights had been strung among the autumn trees, placed by neighbors and friends far beyond the number of strands originally planned by the bridal pair. They cast a glow that illuminated an open grassy space and many of the wooded paths through the park. The trees had begun to don their autumn cloaks and the fairy lights brightened them from beneath as the evening took over from daylight.

Long folding tables groaned beneath food as potluck dishes were added to the original offerings of sandwiches, sliced cheeses and crackers. Plastic flutes glimmered golden with champagne, poured from magnums, and bottles of beer poked out from ice chests. Stacks of paper plates had been replaced by blue plastic with matching utensils.

Voices filled with laughter and happiness nearly drowned the brass quartet from the community college.

The bride, dressed in a white wool dress, had shed her short veil and donned a thick white wool shawl, her black hair and blue eyes gleaming. She gazed around at the magical setting and murmured, "Wow." Then Jazz Ryder looked at her new husband, Adam.

"Wow," he agreed, taking it all in.

His best man, Master Gunnery Sergeant Jackson Stone, stood beside him. Dressed in his Marine Corps blues, Jackson, or Jax as he was familiarly known, had been glad to fly across the continent for this wedding. Adam had been his only real friend here since early childhood.

"I guess," said Jax, "that I won't have to make one of those ridiculous speeches."

Jazz laughed. "At least you don't have to recall any of Adam's funny moments from years ago."

The three of them, along with the bride's identical twin sister, Lily, had already made a joke about the similarity of their nicknames: Jazz and Jax.

The ad hoc gathering had mostly ignored any idea of formal clothing, except for a few in their Sunday best. The rest unapologetically wore jeans and boots.

As the evening chill descended, no one seemed to care. What had started as a small reception had turned into a huge party, the kind of event Conard City enjoyed.

Jax watched the bride and bridegroom begin to move among the crowd, greeting everyone they could, thanking them for this outpouring. Then he eased to a quiet area, aware that his uniform stood out, and he didn't want to draw attention away from the couple. This was *their* night.

He didn't stand alone for long. "Hello, Jackson."

He turned his head, looking down at a small elderly woman who held the leash of a harlequin Great Dane that seemed almost as large as she was. An odd pairing.

."I don't suppose you remember me," she said. "I'm Edith Jasper."

His memory of her surfaced. "Miss Jasper! You taught senior English."

The woman's smile broadened. "I think you're old enough to call me Edith now. You were so quiet. I always wished you'd speak up because you were one of my best students."

Jax didn't know how to answer, especially because he'd had no idea.

Edith patted his arm. "You've come a long way. Now meet my dog Bailey."

Jax held out his hand, palm up. Bailey sniffed, then seemed to grin. "Big, isn't he?" He hardly had to bend to stroke the huge dog's head.

"People keep expecting him to knock me over or drag me, but he's a good boy. He's always known my limits. Anyway, it's nice to see you again. Now get out there and meet more people who remember you."

He doubted many of them remembered him at all. He scanned the crowd casually, wondering how Adam was taking all of this. Adam had confided that after three tours in Afghanistan he'd come home with some PTSD and couldn't stand to be in crowded places for long. Cities could be torture for him, although this one boasted a population of only around five thousand. Small in some places, but large enough in Wyoming, where the biggest city had a little over sixty thousand residents.

Jax wasn't aware of any PTSD on his part, but that might not mean anything. Experience in the Corps had taught him how to master his mind so, while the threat might be lurking somewhere inside him, he didn't know it. But then he hadn't been wounded like Adam.

"Hello, Jackson," said a redheaded woman as she approached. She wore a silky green dress that slithered over her ample curves.

She clearly remembered him, but he couldn't place her. She appeared to be about his age.

"We nearly dated in high school."

Dated? Astonishment filled him. He'd never come close to dating in high school but instead had avoided it. Not that anyone had expressed interest back then. "Nearly?" he repeated.

She pursed her brightly lipsticked mouth. "Well, you used to smile at me across the classroom. You liked me then. I'm Madge Kearny, remember?"

Jax racked his brains. "It's been a long time…"

She laughed flirtatiously. "Too long. You went and joined the Marines before anything could happen between us. You…"

She was interrupted by another woman, one with thick, long auburn hair and bright green eyes, dressed in a gray slacks suit. She was smiling and said, "Now, Madge, let Jackson get his feet under him." She turned to Jax. "I hear you're staying for a little while."

"Thinking about it." Carefully neutral. Women were drawn to this uniform like flies to honey. He didn't credit himself with any of their attraction.

"You see, Madge?" the woman said. "You'll have plenty of time to get reacquainted. Isn't that Joe over there looking for you?"

Madge scowled at her and flounced away.

The woman laughed quietly. "Always on the hunt, that one. Hi, I'm Lynn Macy. You won't remember me, but I was three years behind you in school. You and Adam were close, as I recall."

"Yes."

"I'm sure he's very glad you were able to come." Her smile grew gentle. "Trust your own memory. I bet a lot of people would like to claim you as a buddy now."

Then she moved off into the crowd, leaving him feeling uncomfortable in a whole different way from Madge. He kind of liked it.

LYNN GLANCED OVER at Jackson Stone while she fell into conversation with Judge Wyatt Carter and his father, Earl. The two of them had played a big part in helping her keep the house her late husband, Matt, had willed to her.

My, Jackson had changed, she thought. From diffident, introverted string bean to a well-filled-out man who stood confidently. The years away had served him well in that regard. And although she hadn't known him directly, being three years younger, everyone knew *of* everyone.

A group of men over by some trees began to sing a bawdy song. *Drunk*, Lynn thought. Then she heard a gravelly voice behind her.

"I hope I don't have to get official tonight."

Lynn recognized the voice immediately. Sheriff Gage Dalton. She turned, smiling, and saw that his redheaded wife, Emma, had her arm through his.

Emma shook her head. "This guy never gets a night off. Come on, Gage. There are enough deputies around here tonight to handle drunkenness."

It was true, Lynn thought. Quite a few of them, in street clothes, were enjoying the party, and it wasn't as if Gage would have to stand in himself. "I'm voting with Emma," she said.

"Me, too," both Carters said in unison.

Gage shook his head, the burn scar on his cheek making his smile a bit lopsided. "I'm being ganged up on."

"Your wife would like you to take a night off," Emma said on a laugh. "Come on, Gage. The judge has ruled."

That caused Wyatt Carter to grin. "Yeah," he said. "Ruling from the bench."

As the Daltons walked away, Earl Carter, a plump lawyer, leaned toward her. "Is Luke leaving you alone?"

Luke was her late husband's brother-in-law. "He stops by once in a while. I know he's unhappy with the legal decision."

"Damn," said Earl. "It's not your fault Luke and Matt's father left the house to Matt. As I recall, Jed Macy had his own good reasons for that will. Loose cannon, that boy Luke."

"Dad," Judge Carter said. "This is supposed to be a happy night. Don't go reminding Lynn of bad things."

Lynn spoke again. "It's okay, Wyatt. You two helped a lot. I can deal with Luke's resentment."

And she could, even if she suspected Luke would like her to fall off her roof while she was repairing shingles.

Well, he'd never hurt her. Too much of a coward.

She moved along, speaking to friends and acquaintances she'd known during her entire life in Conard County. It was a great gathering.

WHEN LYNN ARRIVED back at her house, she noticed the lights showing from the second floor of her house. Her college roomers seemed to be burning the midnight oil. Probably upcoming exams.

She stepped through her front door, hearing dueling music from above. Apparently, they'd taken advantage of her absence to turn up the volume. Amused, she moved

to the dining room to look once again at the list of remodeling items she planned to buy soon.

This project was more than Matt's legacy. Remodeling and repairing this house had become her most en-
joyable activity. Matt's father had let it run down, and
when he died, Matt had been in the Army, unable to do
much about it.

Lynn had tinkered with things while Matt was away
but hadn't wanted to make major changes until he ap-
proved. Now it was her project alone and she felt as if she
were spreading her wings, finding new interests and new
things she loved to do. Even a few years ago she couldn't
have imagined herself taping and mudding drywall, re-
vising the house's layout and handling a circular saw with
the ease of familiarity. Or painting a three-story house,
her biggest project to date.

Now the four upstairs bedrooms took roomers com-
fortably and her own apartment was complete. Her next
project would be dealing with the water damage in the
living room, a bad surprise when she'd ditched all the
ancient furniture.

Pleased with her steady progress, she climbed the two
flights of stairs to her own apartment in the attic. She'd
turned the overhead trapdoor into a stairway, one she'd
built herself specifically for this purpose with a door at
the bottom.

As she flipped on the lights, she looked around, loving the warmth she'd created in the large attic. What a
discovery it had been when she'd finally explored what
she had thought of as storage space.

All the walls and high-peaked ceiling were covered
with gleaming wood that she'd stained and polished; the
floors were built of wider wooden planking to match.

Two full-size windows graced the ends of the attic, allowing plenty of light to enter.

She'd turned it into her own studio apartment with a bath in one corner, a small kitchenette under the back window and her bed in a corner. She'd discovered comfy chairs and ottomans discarded up here, but bright yellow upholstery and some new springs had fixed them up as good as new. Colorful rag rugs dotted the floor.

She wouldn't have changed anything about it now even if she'd initially been uneasy about her decisions. Matt would have loved it, too, she was certain.

Its only problem was that it could get chilly in the winter, and she'd dealt with that by installing an electric fireplace that added to the coziness on cold nights.

She showered quickly—at least the three boys below had left her enough hot water—donned her flannel pajamas and crawled into bed with a good book on her tablet.

She felt sorry for Jackson Stone, though. He'd been a standout at the reception and she wondered how many people would now claim to be his long-lost friends.

Of which he'd had none back when he'd lived here. Despite how confident he appeared now, perhaps his personality hadn't changed that much, considering how he'd stood aside at the reception.

But dang, he was sure an attractive man.

Chapter Two

The fire at the La-Z-Rest Motel started around 2:00 a.m. A smoke detector squealed a shrill, nearly deafening, alarm.

With flames licking two walls of his room, Jax managed to pull on his camos, grab his laptop and his Marine blues, which hung in a garment bag. With them and his desert boots in hand, he raced out into the chilly night to join the other guests who gathered across the highway to watch the burgeoning conflagration. A crowd grew as truckers left their rigs to gawk, too.

He laid down his laptop and suit bag so he could jam his feet into his boots and tie them. Then he stood and watched for a few minutes with the others as fire trucks arrived and tried to put out the blaze. The old motel appeared to have been built from wood that had grown tinder-dry over the years, and the fire had taken over the whole building.

Someone was watching everything they'd worked for going up in flames. He had no desire to rubberneck a tragedy.

While the firefighters began to work, he turned and headed into the truck stop diner. Engines growled all around him as he opened the door and stepped in to be greeted by delicious aromas.

"You okay?" asked the grillman, a lean, tall man of middle years. Over his white T-shirt and jeans he wore a denim apron, and on his head a white baseball cap. "That fire…"

"I'm all right. I hope everyone else is."

"Yeah, it's bad. Well, there's just me here tonight, and I suppose a lot of hungry people are going to show up shortly, so before I get rushed, what'll it be? Coffee's fresh, menu's limited at this hour."

"Hamburger? Fries?"

The man grinned. "You're in my ballpark. Want any pastry, let me know." He snorted. "At least I don't have to cook *that*. I'm Hasty, by the way. You grab a seat. I'll be right with you."

Jax did so, laying his suit bag over one brown vinyl-covered bench and putting his laptop beside him on the other.

By the time Hasty brought Jax his meal and a mug of coffee, others had started to trail in.

Hasty spoke, jabbing a finger at the parking lot full of trucks. "We're not usually too busy at this time of night, so I let my whole staff take off for the wedding. That's why I'm the only one here, and from the looks of it, I'm in for it. Bad snowstorm in the mountains out west. Too many switchbacks coming down the other side, so they're all waiting."

Jax nodded.

"You that Stone guy everybody's talking about?"

Jax felt momentarily taken aback. He glanced toward the growling trucks, wondering how the drivers could have heard.

Hasty chuckled. "Might surprise you, but some of my customers are locals. They like my food. Anyway, a few came in for a midnight breakfast and mentioned you. If it *is* you."

"It is." Jax held out his hand. "Jackson Stone."

Hasty shook his hand with a firm grip. "Pleased to meet you. But a sad way to do it." Then he walked away to deal with the steadily growing crowd at the counter, the fire on everyone's tongue. Because Hasty was alone, the truckers carried their own meals to tables.

Jackson figured he was going to spend the night here before deciding what to do in the morning. A diner wasn't the best place to sleep, but as he recalled, the La-Z-Rest was the only motel for many miles. Right then he didn't know if his rental car had survived. He doubted it. Sure as hell, most of his clothes hadn't.

Then he laughed at himself. He'd survived worse conditions, conditions that came without a hot meal or a roof.

He got a second meal at the counter, and Hasty heaped on a larger order of fries.

Back at his table, he ruminated over the day. It had been good to see Adam so happy. The last time they'd met it hadn't been pretty. A bunch of insurgents had been firing from a clifftop at an allied convoy, and Jax's unit had taken them out. Once they'd secured the area, he and his squad had slip-slided their way down to the convoy, where bodies lay about, some of them badly burned in the raging fire that had taken a troop transport and a Humvee. They offered as much aid as they could while waiting for choppers.

Then he'd turned one man over and recognized the face of Adam Ryder, his lifelong friend. Badly shot up, close to death. For the first time on the battlefield, Jax had felt tears wet his cheeks. *My God, Adam.*

Jax dragged his thoughts away from a memory best forgotten, instead rambling over the wedding, a pleasant affair. More than pleasant, actually. When he'd learned that neighbors and friends had gone over-the-top with food and decorations, he'd been surprised and then realized he shouldn't be. Even in his shy youth, he'd known that people here took care of one another. Besides, a big party was probably the best entertainment around.

And those two women. That Madge had been pushy, really pushy, and he was quite sure he'd never given her any cause to think they were an item. He hadn't been an item with anyone back then, hadn't wanted to be. All he had wanted was to be *out* of this place.

But Lynn Macy had been very different, jumping in to silence Madge before he was forced to say something rude. And then walking away casually, pressing him not at all. Just friendly. And quite beautiful. His gaze had wandered over her, taking in a compact figure that a gray slack suit couldn't fully conceal. Much more attractive to him than Madge.

Through the window beside him, he could see only the truck parking lot. He wondered if the fire was out, then wondered why it should matter to him. He'd lost only some clothes. Others had lost a whole lot more and he couldn't help.

Full of good food and strong, hot coffee, he finally turned his head to look around the diner. The truckers were happy enough to wait at the counter and carry their own food to their tables, but not as quick to clean up. Even paper napkins had been left crumpled on tables and plates, although there were plenty of trash cans around.

Too many new arrivals were simply shoving dirty dishes to one side to make a space for themselves.

No way was Hasty going to be able to deal with this while grilling nonstop, and his staff shouldn't have to face this mess when they came in the morning. Nor should *he* be sitting on his duff.

Annoyed by the mess, he rolled up his sleeves and got to work clearing tables. With a bus bin full, he went to the counter.

"Hasty, what can I do with these?"

Hasty looked over from the grill where he had six burgers frying along with potatoes and onions. He raised his brow. Then he grinned. "I thought you guys never volunteered."

"Sometimes I buck the rule. So where?"

Hasty pointed with a jerk of his head. "Dishwasher's in back. Just shove the pan on the counter beside the dishwasher. I'll get to it all later."

Jax didn't leave it at that. He knew how to use the commercial dishwasher, even though it appeared to be as old as Hasty. He sprayed away remaining food, then put cups and plates on the rack. As each rack rolled through the hot wash and rinse, he went to clear a few more tables.

Lead by example. That had long been drilled into him, and it seemed to work here as drivers began to clear their own tables and stack dishes at one end of the counter. Jax was amused. He hadn't intended this, but it was good to see nonetheless.

At last, just around dawn, the traffic tapered off. Hasty even had time to take a smoke break outside the door. Jax stepped out with him, needing some fresh air.

"Thanks for all that help. Want another meal?" Hasty

asked him. "This time on the house. I'd give you a steak if I had one."

Jax smiled. "Just plenty of coffee, if you don't mind."

Hasty flashed a grin. "Now, why would I mind? You saved me in there. And my staff, come to that. They'd have wanted to put my head on a pike if they came to work and saw that mess."

"Could you blame them?"

"Hah! Couldn't say I would." Hasty ground the cigarette butt beneath his heel. "Gotta get back to the grill, and you start thinking what you want to eat besides coffee. Not like you have any place to go right now."

It was true. Jax stood staring up at the sky, breathing the refreshing night air that was tinged with the smell of wet ash, wondering why in the hell he'd wanted to come back to this one-horse town. It wasn't as if it held many good memories.

Across the highway, impossible to ignore, rose the blackened skeleton of the motel. One fire truck was still there, dousing the remains to make sure embers wouldn't start another fire.

He saw the sheriff, Gage Dalton, approaching him just as dawn began to redden the eastern sky. Aside from meeting him briefly at the reception, Jax remembered him from his childhood before Gage took over from the old sheriff, Nate Tate. Back then he'd been called *hell's own archangel* by locals because of his fire-burned face and his darkly determined isolation.

Dalton shook his hand. "Gotta ask you some questions about last night."

No surprise, given that he was newly arrived. "Fire away."

"At my place, if you don't mind."

His place. The Sheriff's Office. Momentary uneasiness niggled Jax. "Let me get my gear."

IT WAS STILL EARLY, but a few people were about, eyeing Jax curiously as he rode in the front passenger seat of the official SUV. He wondered how that would hit the grapevine, which was as effective in this town as any in the military.

Inside, walking through a squad room in serious need of upgrades with only the computers looking like recent models, he followed Gage down a back hallway to his office. The desk had a computer on one side and a stack of papers on the other.

"Have a seat," Gage said, waving him to a seat facing the desk. Gage walked around it, wincing as he settled into a chair that creaked its age.

Gage smiled, that lopsided smile that looked as if the scar tissue on the side of his face wouldn't allow him more. "So you're a master gunnery sergeant now. Do I call you Master Guns?"

Jax shook his head. "How about just Jax?"

Gage's smile widened just a shade. "Then call me Gage. No formalities here." He leaned forward, wincing slightly again as he rested his forearms on the desk. "I remember you just before you left. You were so thin you looked like you'd blow away in a strong breeze."

"Never happened."

Gage laughed. "I'm looking at you, aren't I? Listen, I didn't want to talk to you because I suspect you of anything. I'm just collecting any information I can get about the fire. In case it was arson."

Jax nodded without surprise, having considered the

possibility because Gage wanted to talk to him. The idea disturbed him. "Was it?"

"Don't know yet. I'm moving ahead before any memories fade or change. You know how malleable memories arc?"

"I do." He'd had more than a little experience of that, watching how Marines' minds could grow and change a story in the telling and retelling and then totally believe it.

"Some welcome home," Gage remarked. "Anyway, what do you recall?"

"The back wall and side wall of my room flaming. Fire was creeping toward the door. Well, creeping isn't exactly right. It was moving fast."

"That place was tinder, all right. And then?"

"I jumped into my camo, grabbed my laptop, suit bag and boots. Out of there faster than a bat out of hell."

"I hear you didn't hang around to gawk."

Jax shrugged. "Why would I? I've seen plenty of fires and all I could think was it was sad for the owners. Everyone got out, I hope?"

"The guy next door to you didn't."

Jazz stiffened. "Damn, if I'd known…"

"If you'd known, we'd have more than one crispy critter."

Jax wasn't offended by the black humor. A familiar survival mechanism. Dealing with ugliness had to be handled somehow for sanity's sake.

Gage continued. "You ought to understand as well as anyone that courage is sometimes useless."

It was true, but for the first time Jax let feeling emerge from his lockbox. He knew all about what fire could do to a person. Too much. It sickened him. "I still feel bad about it."

"Of course." Gage nodded and leaned back. "So you didn't hear anything, see anything?"

"Not that I'm aware of. I'll rack my memory, but frankly I was dead asleep."

Gage nodded. After a moment, he asked, "What are your plans?"

Jax heard the subtle implication in the words. He was an unknown factor in this town and therefore suspicious. Naturally. "None yet. I suppose my car is a total loss."

"Between the fire and the water hoses, not to mention axes, there might not be enough left for a scrapyard."

"The rental company is going to be thrilled."

Gage shrugged. "I'll give you a police report for them. So, *are* you staying in town?"

The implication was not as subtle this time. Jax spread his hands. "Has a new motel sprouted anywhere?"

"Hardly. Listen, I know a lady who runs a rooming house. As I recall, she has a spare room or two."

Great, Jax thought. He was going to be stuck in this town for a while. Any plan he'd had of going to Denver to look for quarters for himself had gone up in smoke with the fire.

Without asking, Gage riffled through an old-fashioned circular card file. "Old sheriff used this," he remarked. "Too much trouble to move it to the computer, especially since I've been adding to it because I can't mess up cards."

Soon Gage was speaking into the phone. "Hey, Lynn, you got a room for a guy who got burned out of the motel last night?"

Jax could hear a woman's voice faintly, first sounding appalled, then quieter.

"Thanks, I'll bring him over. Jackson Stone. Yeah, ten minutes, if that's okay?"

Gage hung up. "You got yourself a room. Ready?"

JACKSON STONE? FOR some reason, Lynn was surprised. At some level she must have known he was staying at the motel but had been shocked nonetheless when Gage told her. She'd only just heard the news about the fire from one of her roomers, a college student named Will. Will sported a bright orange thatch of red hair, a ton of freckles and an infectious grin. He hadn't been grinning earlier when he delivered the news.

Dang, Lynn thought. That motel was a local landmark, having stood since the 1950s, back when long road trips had become popular. These days it survived on truckers who occasionally didn't want to sleep in their cabs.

She had two rooms of her own left, both reasonably ready, but unlike her students, who were given a list of items to bring for themselves, mostly bedding, Jax would have none of that. Diving into an upstairs closet, she checked to make sure she had enough spare sheets and pillows.

Since she had two empty rooms, she decided to give him his choice.

When the front doorbell rang, she didn't bother to tuck her work shirt into her jeans. She had a lot to do today. Instead she got an unexpected and unwelcome surprise.

"Mom!"

Nancy West stood there, smiling. Behind her, her rental car blocked the end of Lynn's driveway. "Hello, sweetie. It's been too long."

The same thing her mother always said, even though

it hadn't been *that* long, and Lynn offered her usual response. "Why didn't you call and let me know?"

"This trip was a whim."

They always were, Lynn thought as she stepped back to allow her mother inside. The woman wore a beige business suit and low heels. Her short salt-and-pepper hair was perfectly coiffed. Nancy always presented a flawless appearance.

She walked in, scanning her daughter with faint disapproval, then looked around the entryway. "I can see you've been busy. Do you still have those college kids staying with you?"

"Three," answered Lynn, wishing she could make this situation vanish. Her mother had objected to her taking roomers since the start. She loved her mother, but the frequent criticisms, implied or overt, were enough to make her gnash her teeth.

"Well, I hope you have room for me! I'm your mother, after all."

Lynn contained a sigh. "The room you usually take. At the back of the ground floor. Make yourself at home." As Nancy always did.

Nancy West beamed. "My bags are in the trunk." She handed Lynn the keys then said suddenly, "Oh, who's that?"

Lynn turned to see the sheriff's car pull up. "A new roomer," she answered.

"In a sheriff's car? I hope he's not a criminal…"

Nancy's voice trailed off as she saw the tall, broad-shouldered man in belted camouflage climb out carrying a suit bag and a laptop case.

"Ooh," murmured Nancy. "A soldier."

"A Marine," Lynn corrected her. Already she was starting to feel a little annoyed. *Ooh?*

"They're all the same." Nancy laughed lightly.

"I wouldn't tell a Marine that."

Nancy eyed her. "Do you already know him?"

"Jackson Stone. I grew up with him. Now, let it go, Mom."

"Funny," Nancy mused as Jax approached. "I don't remember him."

Few people honestly remembered him, Lynn thought. As he reached the foot of the porch steps, Lynn called out, "Hi, Jax. Work your way around my mother and come in."

He smiled. "I appreciate this, Lynn."

"My pleasure. Just drop your stuff in the living room. We'll have some coffee before I show you to your room."

"Coffee sounds great. I'm addicted."

"Tea for me," Nancy said brightly.

"Of course." Knowing her mother, Lynn figured Nancy didn't want to miss one bit of this interesting development, especially since it involved a handsome man in uniform. She offered Jax another smile. "I just need to get Mom's bags from her car first."

"I'll help," Jax said promptly. He took his laptop and suit bag quickly into the empty living room and returned. "Ready."

Lynn walked with Jax to her mother's car and unlocked the trunk. Before she could move, Jax hefted both large suitcases, then carried them into the house behind her.

"Where do you want them?" he asked.

She pointed. "The bedroom in the back, please."

It was all Lynn could do not to frown. She'd planned

to give that room to Jax, the only room with a private bath. Trying to keep her face smooth, she walked into the kitchen.

Nancy followed, her heels tapping. "How nice to have a man around," she said.

"It's temporary and I'm in no hurry to have a man around. What kind of tea do you want?"

"Earl Grey, please."

Lynn started the electric kettle, salvaged the teapot from an upper shelf, then turned to begin making coffee.

Jax returned to the kitchen. "I wasn't sure if I should put the suitcases on the bed, so they're standing beside it."

"Thank you so much!" Nancy beamed. "That's fine."

Nothing like a man to perk her mother up, Lynn thought. Instead of being annoyed, she suddenly felt amused. This might be fun to watch.

The Earl Grey was perfectly steeped just past three minutes, the way her mother preferred it. No milk, no sugar. The coffee wasn't far behind.

They sat at the long wooden refectory table that filled the middle of the kitchen like an outsize island and provided extra counter space. The only seating it offered was benches. Lynn planned to use it in the dining room when she was finished with the repairs and painting. The table was a fine piece and just needed some love to remove all the cut and burn marks. Or maybe she'd leave it looking distressed. There was plenty of time to think about it.

Nancy looked around. "You really need to do something about this kitchen, Lynn."

"With my roomers using it all the time, I'm not terribly concerned about it. They seem happy. At some point I'll get to it."

She looked around anyway. The room hadn't been remodeled at all since Matt's mother had done it at least three decades ago and she hadn't changed out the appliances. Those definitely needed replacing, especially the fridge, which *had* to be ready to die at any moment. As it was, she had to clean it out often. Her boys, as she thought of them, were pretty good at cleaning up after themselves, but the fridge? Some of the things they left forgotten were gross enough. A dead refrigerator would only make it worse.

There were plenty of knife cuts on the green laminate countertops despite a ready stack of cutting boards. She'd have to get something more impervious to carelessness. And she was honestly tired of the green everywhere.

"Maybe my next project," she told her mother. "I'll see."

Jax spoke. "Are you remodeling?"

Nancy answered before Lynn could. "Constantly. I think she keeps busy to suppress her grief over Matt."

Lynn clamped her teeth together to avoid snapping. "I enjoy it" was all she said. She thought she caught a glimmer of sympathy in Jax's dark eyes. For what? Matt's loss or her mother's bald assessment?

"How long are you staying for, Mom?"

"A few weeks."

An unsatisfyingly vague answer.

Nancy spoke again. "What do you do in the Army, Jax?"

Lynn cringed. *Here she goes again.*

"Marine Corps," Jax corrected her with a half smile. "I give a lot of orders, shoot a lot of guns and take my Marines to hell. And you, Mrs. West?"

The kitchen was suddenly as silent as a grave.

LATER LYNN TOOK Jax upstairs and pulled clean sheets and pillows out of the linen closet for him. Towels, too.

Jax thanked her again for the room and told her to just drop the linen on the bed. "I know how to make it up."

"Bathroom is down the hall—you can't miss it. Sorry you'll have to share."

"Like I never have before?"

"I bet you have. Anyway, I give my students strict rules about keeping it clean. I hope they haven't let me down. Every couple of weeks I check it out, mop the floor, maybe scrub the tub if they haven't in a while. No guarantees about what you'll find right now. Certainly no spit and polish."

"Wasn't expecting it. Now how much rent do I owe you, Lynn? Seriously."

She flushed. "Nothing. I wouldn't charge anyone who'd been burned out of their only bed."

He shook his head. "How much? Please."

She looked straight into his rugged face and dark eyes and sensed the pride in the man. No handout would be acceptable. She told him what she charged each of the boys. "But that's monthly. If you don't want to stay that long…"

He shook his head. "I'll get it to you later today," he promised. "I don't think I melted my ATM card or it would be fused to my butt."

She laughed, truly amused. Then she left him and headed back downstairs to try to keep an eye on Nancy. When her students came home later, they were apt to get the third degree.

A pleasurable little shiver ran through her, though, as she descended. Jax was certainly an attractive man.

And she wished even more that her mother hadn't chosen this time to visit.

JAX EASILY REMEMBERED the way to Freitag's Mercantile on Main Street. A few people on the street studied him curiously, but left him alone. That was fine. All he'd ever wanted when he'd lived here was to be left alone. Except by Adam.

Their friendship had begun early when their mothers, both ranch wives, had gotten together on occasional Saturday afternoons for a coffee klatch. He and Adam had no other friends out there in the wide-open spaces and had cemented their relationship, even though Adam was a couple of years older. At first, Adam had acted as an unofficial babysitter, but when Jax grew old enough to have a strong interest in playing with miniature cars and making roads in the dirt, they'd become fast friends. Jax grew up a little faster in those early years by keeping up with Adam, and nothing had ever disturbed the bond between them.

So what was he doing here, now that Adam had gone off on his honeymoon? Damned if he knew, except that the sheriff didn't want him to leave. He should have been on his way to Denver this afternoon or tomorrow.

He just hoped Adam enjoyed himself. He'd confided to Jax that cities, large towns, large crowds, always made him jangle, made him hyperalert. He was going to dive into all of that for Jazz, to make her happy.

Well, Adam must have taken part in the planning. Maybe he was ready to step out and see what happened.

In Freitag's he found everything he needed to get him through a week or so. Jeans, of course, some sweatshirts and hoodies for the growing autumn chill, and underwear, a long-sleeved shirt. At the last minute he added a medium-weight navy blue jacket and leather gloves.

With his purchases packed into a new black duffel bag,

he crossed the street to the bank to get the rent money
for Lynn as he'd promised, then headed back to Lynn's
house. He was glad that his wallet and cell phone had
been in his camo pocket when he'd dashed out of the
burning motel. The cell phone had become an essen-
tial item for military personnel who might need to be
reached at any time.

Well, he was stuck here for a while, even though his
plans had been vague at the best. Gage Dalton had made
that clear, however obliquely.

Well, why not? He'd been a loner as a kid and had
suddenly showed up in town for the first time in fifteen
years. Then the place where he was staying burned to
the ground.

If Jax were the sheriff, he might want to keep an eye
on himself, too.

The thought almost made him smile.

Chapter Three

By midafternoon, Lynn could have cheerfully packed her mother back into her car and sent her home. Even the process of making dinner had become a headache.

"Why don't you have anything decent in the refrigerator?" Nancy demanded, peering inside. "Soda. Leftover pizza. Milk."

"The boys…"

"You live here, too," Nancy said as she opened the freezer. "Toaster pastries? Frozen waffles? Frozen dinners? Lynn!"

"Mom, the boys…"

Again Nancy interrupted as she began to look through the cupboards. "Look at all these sweet cereals. You need something with bran in it. Don't you ever cook?"

Lynn rubbed her temple with her hand, feeling the approach of a headache. "I live upstairs, not down here."

"No, you live in your *attic*. What is wrong with you?"

This was a full-bore attack. Her mother rarely criticized so harshly, preferring sly innuendos or brief, tart remarks, but the woman was on a tear.

"I *like* my attic," Lynn said firmly. "If you'd come up and take a look, you'd see how nice it is." Not that she really wanted her mother to go there and start criticizing her private space.

"I'm not climbing two flights of stairs. You know my arthritis…"

"I'm sorry. How could I forget?"

"Because you hardly keep in touch!"

Lynn nearly gaped. With Nancy dropping in for irregular stays multiple times each year, there hardly seemed to be any point in Lynn traveling to visit her.

Nancy put her hands on her hips. "You've become as bohemian as those boys you rent to. I suppose you'll expect me to eat at that diner again."

"That diner has some great food," Lynn said, wishing she'd just learn to shut her own mouth and let Nancy run out of steam. "Anyway, since you're here, I'd planned to go to the market and get things you'll like for your meals. Are you still off eggs?"

Nancy waved her hand. "Turns out they're good for you in moderation. I'll come with you to the market."

Feeling almost desperate, Lynn shook her head. "You need to unpack. I *am* capable of grocery shopping." *And I need a break.*

Nancy merely shook her head and started the kettle boiling. That was another thing that annoyed Lynn. Her mother insisted on a whole pot of tea, then would drink one single cup because it only tasted good when it was freshly made.

Lynn escaped. Hopping in her car gave her a temporary sense of freedom and she was grateful for it. Lord, had her mother been that bad the whole time she was growing up?

It was possible she hadn't noticed it as much when

she'd been wrapped up in school, in her shop classes and her friends. Now she was getting distilled Nancy.

And Nancy would make it difficult to get on with her remodeling project. Always.

No wonder her dad had bugged out when Lynn was fourteen. Her mother was a born micromanager.

Then she felt ashamed. She shouldn't allow her frustration to make her unkind. Still, she often thought marrying Matt had been her wisest decision ever. Not only had she loved him deeply, but she'd gone away with him whenever she could follow him to his current station. A stronger, more independent Lynn had emerged.

Thinking of Matt saddened her deeply. The grief came more rarely now, but sometimes when it struck her, it speared her as badly as it had during the first weeks and months.

Sighing, she climbed out of her car at the grocery store, retrieved her reusable bags from the trunk, and went inside to deal with the prospect of cooking for her mother. Maybe she'd invite Jax, too. His first night, and everything.

Plus, he might be a good buffer.

She nearly giggled out loud. Was that fair to him? No. Would a good home-cooked meal make up for it? Maybe.

NANCY HAD CHANGED into more casual clothes, a pair of knit blue slacks, a long-sleeved turtleneck pullover in a lighter blue and black ballet slippers.

"If you're going to remodel anything," she said as Lynn brought in the grocery bags, "it should be that bathroom."

"All in good time, Mom." She placed the bags on the trestle table.

"I don't understand why you keep putting me in there."

Lynn faced her. "It has the only private bath on the first two stories right now. *And* there's your arthritis."

For once, Nancy held her tongue.

JAX HAD DECIDED to jog around town after dropping off his duffel, taking in the sights, trying to see how much he remembered after all this time. He hadn't exactly been familiar with these streets during his youth, having spent most of his time on the ranch and coming in only for school and occasional weekend shopping trips under his father's watchful eye, nor did any of it elicit good memories. It was all simply neutral, even Good Shepherd Church. His parents hadn't been churchgoers, which had been fine by him. He was sure he wouldn't have wanted to be there. Not back then.

He recognized most of the downtown, however, and saw only a few changes. The bakery for one. Then a door with an inscrutable sign that he didn't remember. The corner hardware store remained, probably serving people who needed last-minute items for some project. The lumberyard handled most larger purchases.

Maude's diner still bore the fading name City Café, although even in his childhood everyone had referred to it as Maude's. He was pleased to see it. He imagined that café was such a pillar in this community that the whole town would collapse without it.

There was a small new market for organic food. He wondered how they were hanging on. Something must have changed around here.

Then he saw a boarded-up storefront bearing a sign, Tex-Mex Restaurant, Coming Eventually.

A snort of laughter escaped him. He wondered what

kind of problems the owners were dealing with but handling with a sense of humor.

By the time he arrived back at the boardinghouse, he'd learned that nothing held any attachment for him. Not even a hint of nostalgia.

God, what a dork he'd been back then.

Since he was stuck here until the sheriff concluded he wasn't an arsonist, he decided to make the best of it. Otherwise he'd have left tomorrow at the latest, having satisfied his curiosity, having shown any interested parties that he wasn't that dork anymore. The desire wasn't an angry one. Just answering an old need to be *somebody*, even in this backwater.

But tomorrow he could pick up a knapsack, a few supplies, and head toward the mountains to hike. It had always been one of his favorite things when he could escape, hiking in those mountains.

When he arrived back at the house, the first person he saw was Nancy West, stepping out of the kitchen. The delicious aroma of roasting chicken reached him.

"Join us for dinner, Jackson," she said with a broad smile. "We'll have plenty."

How could he politely refuse? "Thanks. I need to shower first."

So that was the way the wind was blowing, he thought with a tremor of amusement. Nancy West wanted to play matchmaker. He suspected her machinations would mortify Lynn.

This could get interesting.

MADGE KEARNEY HAD her own ideas of *interesting*. They all involved Jackson Stone. She'd tried to get his attention in high school, mostly because she'd wanted to be the first and only girl who could. It wasn't even that she really wanted *him*, but that wasn't the point. Then one day he'd smiled at her and she'd believed she'd crossed the first hurdle. Before anything else happened, he'd left for the Marines.

She was ready to try again, but then that officious Lynn Macy had intervened. And now it wasn't simply a matter of counting coup. He had turned into one hell of a gorgeous man, and that uniform!

Unfortunately, she'd already heard he was rooming with Lynn because the motel had burned down. She'd have to find a way past that before Lynn snared him.

The contest was on.

MUCH TO LYNN'S RELIEF, her mother decided to join some friends for cards that evening after dinner. Nancy might have moved away years ago, but she kept some ties with old girlfriends.

Nancy walked out, free as a bird, leaving the dinner cleanup to Lynn. Lynn didn't mind. A brief release from her mother's needling was welcome. And Nancy still hadn't mentioned how long she intended to stay.

She heard a footstep behind her and looked up as she cleared the table.

"Let me take over," Jax said, smiling. "If I could clear up Hasty's diner last night, I can sure do the dishes for a lady who cooked dinner."

"I can do it," Lynn said automatically. *I can do it* had been a refrain of her entire life with Nancy, and it always burst to the forefront when her mother was around. *Look, Mom, I can do it by myself.*

Inwardly, she shook her head. What was it about parents that brought out the child in everyone?

"I'm sure you can," Jax answered. "Hell, near as I can tell you're rebuilding this entire house. I saw the stack of drywall and ceramic tile on one side of the…dining room, I guess it is?"

Lynn laughed. "Eventually. For now, it's storage."

"So let me help with this. My mother raised me to believe the cook shouldn't have to clean up. Just grab a seat and supervise the putting away."

She sat, still smiling. "If you're up to tolerating my boys."

"Your boys?" He began filling the sink with soapy water.

"My roomers. I suppose that's what I should call them. That or my students. It's what I usually do, but somehow *my boys* fits these three better. Especially Will. You'll see when you meet him. They should be trailing in soon, bringing doggie bags or cold pizza or whatever they think will stoke their fires for a night of studying. So they'll move in on the fridge."

"No problem. If necessary, I'll step out of the way. So how did you get into taking roomers?"

She put her chin in her hand, frankly enjoying the sight of his broad back and narrow hips as he washed. "It helps with my overhead. I'm plowing a lot of Matt's insurance money into fixing this place up. It was his family home and it had started to go to ruin after Matt's dad died and while Matt was away so much. My own little project."

"It hardly looks little. I'm sorry about Matt. As I recall, he was one of the good guys."

"He was." That tide of grief began to well in her, and she tried to push it away. It'd be there later. It always was.

"So what has been the hardest part of this project so far?" Jax asked.

"Gingerbread," she answered emphatically.

He turned from the sink just enough to look at her. "Gingerbread?"

"You see all that fancy trim on the outside of the house, running along all the eaves and the front of the porch? Even the porch railings?"

"Yeah. It's charming."

"Now it is. When I took over, it was a total mess. Try scraping off all that flaking paint and then repainting it. If this place weren't on the historical registry, I'd have pulled it all off."

"How'd it get on the registry?"

"Must have been Matt's father. I don't know. What I *do* know is that I have to keep the outside exactly the same. So the gingerbread remains."

He was making fast work of the dishes. "Pain in the neck, keeping it the same?"

"Only that gingerbread, and I couldn't afford to hire anyone to do it. Painting the whole house except for the gingerbread would have been cheap by comparison. But it looks good now and should stay that way for at least another five years. Which, if I jump on it right away, means I won't have to do the scraping."

He rinsed the last of the silverware. "Towel?"

"In the drawer on the left of the sink."

"Tell me where to put everything."

"Silverware drawer to the right. Just open the cabinets and you'll see where everything else goes."

He nodded and set to work. "What changes are you making? Or are you making any?"

"Well, I finished off my attic apartment, got rid of a lot of ugly furniture and replaced flooring. And I put new drywall in the rooms I rent."

"Why new drywall?"

"Because the walls needed a heck of a lot of spackling, and a ton of old wallpaper needed to be steamed off. Drywall turned out to be easier and less expensive, believe it or not. I was even able to save the wainscoting. Next, I need to get onto the living room. Water damage from before I replaced the roof."

He finished drying the washed dishes and reached for the roasting pan.

Then the boys arrived together. As predicted, all of them carried bags or pizza boxes. Ready to burn the midnight oil.

As a group they came to the kitchen with their loads of treasure and paused.

Lynn made the introductions as Jax was drying the roasting pan. "Will, Barry and Tom," she said, pointing each one out. "Jax Stone. My new roomer for a little while."

Jax stepped to one side after saying hello, roasting pan in his hands. "Help yourselves to the fridge. I can stay out of the way."

But she could see the three lads were a little intimidated. Not only was Jax obviously a mature man, but muscles showed through his sweatshirt and jeans. He was, she thought wryly, clearly not a college student like them.

"Why only a little while?" asked Will of the bright orange hair and freckles. The other two leaned toward the nondescript.

"I got burned out of the motel," Jax answered. "Lynn was kind enough to offer me a room. We sorta grew up together."

Attended the same schools more like, Lynn thought

wryly. Several years apart. "And, guys, my mom's visiting. She's in the downstairs bedroom."

The three of them looked a little overwhelmed. They were used to pretty much having the house to themselves, except for Lynn.

"Great," said Tom cheerfully. "Lynn won't be so alone."

They stuffed some of their goodies into the fridge and carried the rest upstairs with the excuse of exams.

"Ouch," said Lynn as she listened to them thunder up the stairs. "I won't be so much alone."

"Well, you won't be," Jax answered. "Like it or not. Where does this go?"

"I keep all the pans in the oven."

And now came the difficult part, Lynn thought. At this time of evening she usually sought out the peace and privacy of her attic apartment, but she couldn't send Jax to his room. It seemed rude to just leave him on his own down here. Why? He was simply another roomer.

Then he spoke. "I think the sheriff suspects me of arson."

Shock stilled her for several seconds. Then, "Come up to my aerie," she said impulsively. "It's more private."

She could see he was startled, but then she had startled herself.

She led him through the door that closed off her private stairway at the bottom, feeling a bit strange to invite him up here. The only people she'd invited before had been some of her girlfriends.

After she reached the top, she flipped on the lights and turned around to watch him mount the last few steps.

He paused, taking in the entire studio apartment. "I really like this. I never thought an attic could look like this."

"I'm fond of it. I used to think it was just storage space, but then I saw all this fine wood. All it needed was some TLC. Grab a seat. Want a beer?"

"Love one."

He settled into one of the padded armchairs in front of her electric fireplace. As she passed it to give him a beer, she flipped the logs on, producing heat and a warm glow.

"One heads-up," she told him. "No alcoholic beverages in the downstairs fridge. My boys aren't of legal age yet and there's no point in tempting them."

"Not a problem."

She took the other chair, ignoring the recliner to one side. "What's this about being suspected of arson?"

He took a pull on his longneck. "It's subtle. I was gently brought in for questioning, asked about my plans, and then Gage called you immediately to see if you'd rent me a room. That quick offer of a room made it clear."

"Wow," she breathed, astonished. "But was it arson?"

He shook his head. "No one knows yet, according to Gage. He said he's getting ahead of the game before memories change. And I *am* the new guy in town."

"Well, except for the itinerant truckers." She bit her lower lip. "That must have been scary, waking up in a burning room."

"I didn't have a chance to be scared. Besides, I'm no longer as easily scared as I might once have been."

Sipping his beer, he looked around again. "Lynn, you've done a fantastic job with this. I'm surprised you ever leave."

"Work must be done. And despite what my mother said, I'm enjoying it. There's something deeply satisfying about working with your hands and seeing the results. I've also learned a lot."

JAX LOOKED AROUND once more, then turned toward her. "If I'm overstaying, just let me know. This apartment feels private." Like a personal retreat. He'd been surprised when she asked him up here, and he'd seen her own startlement in the way her head jerked, a very small movement. That invitation had slipped out. He'd felt awkward about accepting it, but knew he'd be rude if he didn't. Now he felt uncomfortable staying up here.

She surprised him with a gentle smile. "If you don't feel right about being here, you know where the stairs are. They're hard to miss. In some ways you haven't changed, Master Gunnery Sergeant."

He stiffened a bit. "Meaning?"

"I remember the old days. Somewhat. I *do* remember that you must have felt like a fish out of water. I guess this place is making you feel that way again, because you sure can't feel that way on the job."

He shook his head, feeling almost dissected. "Of course not."

She leaned forward, placing her beer bottle on a small table that stood between the chairs. "I used to be terribly shy," she confided. "I finally found a way around it."

"What's that?"

"To have a role to play. A place where I know exactly what I'm doing and what to say."

He gripped the beer bottle tightly, his gaze straying away to land on a framed wedding portrait of her and Matt that was sitting on top of a bookcase. She must still hurt.

He rose abruptly, looking for a place to put his empty bottle. "I need to go."

"Leave the bottle on the table. Sorry I was so forward."

"No, you weren't. It's okay."

He waved her to remain seated while he strode to the stairs. He hadn't realized anyone could strip him so bare in such a short time.

She'd hit the nail on the head, though. Right on the head. Master Gunnery Sergeant Jackson Stone had a clearly defined role.

Jax Stone, back in his hometown, didn't really.

Chapter Four

Mom!

The word in her head slammed Lynn from sleeping to waking in an instant. The woman would be downstairs, brewing her inevitable tea, and trying to interrogate whatever unfortunate soul passed by the kitchen. Her boys didn't deserve to be made uncomfortable that way.

Sheesh!

She hurried through her washing up, then, wrapped in her green velour robe with fuzzy slippers on her feet, she hurried downstairs to provide protection for her boys.

As she feared, Nancy was in the kitchen holding Will captive by courtesy, the youngster not knowing how to escape politely.

"Will?" Lynn said briskly. "You're going to be late for class."

Will looked so relieved it was almost funny. "Yeah. Thanks for reminding me, Lynn." He dashed away.

"Such a nice boy," Nancy said, sipping her tea.

"Then why were you giving him the third degree?"

"I was doing no such thing!"

"I know you, Mom. Leave my boys alone."

A frosty silence descended, which was fine by Lynn.

God, she needed some coffee before facing more of this. She crossed the icy space to start brewing a pot.

"You know," Nancy said finally, "you can't get to know people without talking to them."

"Questioning descends to a whole other level." Lynn turned, leaning back against the counter while the coffeepot gurgled and steamed behind her.

"Why do you think I was questioning him?"

Lynn swallowed a sigh. She spoke quietly. "Because I know you. You really don't need to discover everyone in Will's family tree, or why he decided to go to the college here, whether he has a girlfriend and what his future plans are."

"It's just ordinary interest. Besides, you've invited three strangers into your home—I'll leave Jackson out of this for the moment—"

"Thank God," Lynn muttered.

"Anyway, I'm a concerned mother. How did you choose these boys?"

"The college chose them. They send me students they believe won't cause me any trouble."

"*Believe?* You don't check into them yourself?"

Lynn turned to pour herself a cup of coffee. This morning she indulged herself in some cream. "Believing the college has served me well over the last two years."

At last, she sat facing Nancy across the trestle table. Her mother was, as always, dressed in high-quality clothes, the businesslike image she'd cultivated since Lynn's dad had walked out. Today her color of choice was a creamy rose with a white scarf loosely wrapped around her neck.

Lynn herself hadn't worn much but work clothes since Matt's death. She liked it that way. Right now, however, given the chill of the night that still clung, she was grateful for her comfortable robe.

Surprising her, Nancy poured a second cup of tea from the same pot.

Lynn sipped her coffee, then put her chin in her hand. More was to come, so she tried a stalling tactic. "How's life in Cheyenne?"

Nancy brightened. "So much better than it was here. There's plenty to do, and I really like working part-time as a paralegal. Which reminds me..."

Of course, Lynn thought. Turnaround. Fast enough to cause whiplash.

"Why must you take roomers?"

"It only makes sense. This is a big house. The rent helps. And honestly, I like the feeling that the house isn't empty."

"You must be burning up Matt's life insurance with all the remodeling you're doing."

Lynn felt her face freeze. Financials were off-limits. "Far from it," she said flatly, trying to close the subject.

"Well, I guess all this work is making the property worth more."

In fact, this house was something of a white elephant in a town that always seemed to be verging on going bust. But she didn't care. It was Matt's legacy, his father's legacy.

"Mom, I like my mornings quiet. Time to wake up."

Nancy smiled. "You always were a sleepyhead."

But at least her mother fell silent, finishing her cup of tea and going to make fresh.

Lynn enjoyed her first and second coffees in magnificent silence, but as her brain slipped into waking mode, she had a question. "Do you have plans while you're here?"

"Just to catch up with my daughter." Nancy smiled.

"I'm going to be working."

"That's all right. I'll watch."

Lynn could have groaned. She loved her mother, she really, truly did, but Nancy was easier to take from a distance.

"What's your current job?" Nancy asked brightly.

"The living room. There's water damage to the walls from before I reroofed the house." Right now she was hoping that when she pulled out the old walls she didn't find rotted wood.

Nancy frowned. "You shouldn't have done that roof by yourself."

"I didn't. I just helped." As if she could have brought in pallets of shingles and raised them by herself. Not to mention replacing all the rotting plywood up there. A patch job she could do alone, but an entire roof? She knew her limits.

"I hope you brighten up that room. It's so dark right now."

Fashions left over from the old days. The long-ago old days. Wallpaper that had never been bright to begin with and that had darkened with age. Even the bay window didn't provide enough light to make a difference.

Matt's father had shown little inclination to change anything. So had Matt's mother, come to that. When they'd both died, his father to a stroke, his mother to cancer, Matt had inherited this house that hadn't been updated in over fifty years, maybe more.

Old items, she'd been discovering, could be endlessly

repaired if she wanted to keep them. Newer stuff not so much.

"I do hate this green in here," Nancy remarked.

"Me, too." For once they agreed.

Nancy settled in with her fresh pot of tea. "Are you seeing anyone?"

Lynn just looked at her mother. "Do I feel you stepping on my toes?"

Finally, Nancy laughed. "You're right. None of my business. Well, if you don't mind, I'll go to the grocery and get something to cook for dinner. Maybe we should invite that nice soldier."

"Marine, Mom."

"Well, I just don't see the difference. Anyway, I'm off!"

Invite that nice soldier. Let the matchmaking begin.

Alone in the kitchen at last, Lynn giggled. Her mom was such a trip. One that had to be kept under light control, but still a trip.

She wondered if she should warn Jax, then decided he would figure it out himself. It might even be fun to watch.

IN THE AFTERNOON, while Nancy buzzed around the kitchen wearing an old apron she'd discovered near the back of the pantry, Lynn studied the living room walls, trying to decide where to begin. Obviously all the floor and window molding needed to be removed before anything else, but the ceiling molding should stay if she could save it. Or was she going over-the-top with that? Remembering how miserable it had been to paint all that gingerbread, she wondered how much time she wanted to spend on those ornate moldings that had, unfortunately, been painted. Stripping and refinishing them might take longer than the rest of the room altogether.

Still, she had to find out at least some of the damage behind the plaster walls before she made any other plans. It killed her to have to remove the plaster, knowing she couldn't replace it, but there was no choice. Water stains marked the wallpaper, especially the outside wall.

Regretting it, she picked up a large hammer and smashed the wall near the biggest stain. Lath greeted her, although she should have expected it under plaster. Oh, man, that stuff was irreplaceable, too. Too bad, she decided. She *had* to know how much damage the leaking porch roof had done. Plaster tumbled around her feet and made a small dust cloud.

"You ought to be wearing a dust mask."

Lynn turned and saw Jax standing in the doorway. "I know," she admitted. "I'm just taking a peek. Trying to determine the extent of the damage. I'm hoping none of the wood frame has rotted."

She noted his dark blue jogging suit. "Been out for a run?"

"Yup. I kinda feel like a prisoner even if I'm not. Strange. Anyway, I'm not used to just hanging around. If you want any help with the demolition, let me know." He grinned. "I'm good at smashing things."

"Too bad you weren't here when I moved the furniture out. That stuff was *heavy.*"

He laughed, increasing the level of attraction she felt toward him. Making her heart flutter.

Oh, God, she didn't need this. She wasn't *ready* for this. A man in uniform. A uniform had gotten Matt killed. Guilt plagued her, too, a sense that her reactions

to Jax were like cheating on Matt. She told herself the
guilt was ridiculous, but it clung anyway.

JAX JOINED THEM for dinner that night. Instead of letting
Nancy steer the conversation, he turned to Lynn. "How's
it going?"

"Well, I made a few more holes, then spritzed some
water to bring down the dust level," she answered. "Next
I'm going to have to rip out some of the lath. Then I get
my snake inspection camera and look inside the wall.
My primary concern is that the wood frame might have
rotted. Or worse, grown black mold."

He nodded, slicing a piece off his pan-fried chicken
breast. "That would be a huge problem. Any idea how
the wall got wet?"

"Maintenance wasn't the best before I took over," she
answered, helping herself to more asparagus. "Since there
was no damage to the wall upstairs, I'm thinking the
water came from the porch roof. The flashing was loose."

"That'd do it," he agreed.

Nancy laughed. "I know nothing about flashing."

Lynn answered. "It's the metal that joins the roof to
the house and prevents water from getting in."

Nancy nodded understanding. "A bad problem."

"Worsened by the fact that most people don't discover
it until they have some interior damage. Or until they replace the roof. The roofer I hired reckoned the roof was
well over thirty years old. I'm lucky the damage wasn't
worse."

Nancy spoke again. "I still think this house is a white
elephant and you should dump it as quickly as you can."

Lynn couldn't answer. Her throat tightened and it became difficult to breathe. Her mother just couldn't seem

to understand her emotional connection to this house through Matt. Or how much she still missed Matt.

Jax surprised her. "I don't think it's a white elephant. It's a great house and Lynn is making it beautiful."

She shot him a look of gratitude, suspecting he understood more than her mother did.

While they were clearing the table, Lynn heard a knock at the front door. "I'll get it," she said, wondering who it might be. She wasn't expecting any deliveries, and with autumn nights setting in earlier, casual drop-ins during the evening were rarer.

She opened the door with a pleasant smile formed on her face, then felt it freeze as she saw her brother-in-law, Luke.

"Hi, Luke."

EVEN IN THE KITCHEN, with the clatter of dishes and running water, Jax heard Lynn's tone change.

"Aren't you going to invite me in?" a man's voice said.

"We're just finishing the dinner cleanup, Luke. This isn't the best time."

"Hey, I'm family."

"That's a matter of opinion."

The man's voice spoke again, wheedling. "Look, you won the lawsuit. At least be nice."

That did it. Jax wiped his hands on a kitchen towel and stepped into the small foyer. A man of average height with shaggy blond hair brushed his way past Lynn, forcing her to close the door behind him or let the cold night in.

"It's settled, Luke," she said tautly. "There's no more to say."

Luke looked past her. "What's this? A bodyguard?"

"Is there a problem, Lynn?" Jax asked. He stood with arms akimbo and sternness filling his face, the way he looked at troublesome men under his command.

"It's just Matt's brother," she said over her shoulder. "No threat but a major nuisance."

"Is that any way to talk about me?" Luke asked. "The issue is settled, now it's time to make up."

Lynn threw up a hand impatiently. "I don't feel like making up, Luke. You put me through legal hell for two years while I was still grieving. All because you thought you should have part of an inheritance your father and my husband didn't want to give you."

Luke frowned. "That wasn't fair, either."

"Maybe not. But it wasn't my decision and I'm sticking by Matt's. So what do you want?"

Luke spread his hands. "Like I said, we're family. Time to make amends."

"Not yet and not now," Lynn replied firmly. She reached to open the door. "Next time call first."

Anger reddened Luke's face, but he followed her implied order, stepping out into the darkness. Lynn slammed the door behind him.

Jax watched her turn, then look uncomfortable. "Sorry about that."

"What was going on?"

"Oh, I can tell you," Nancy said from the kitchen doorway. "Dishes are done and I'm making fresh coffee for the two of you. And how about some key lime pie? It's just about defrosted enough for serving."

Jax didn't want to turn down the invitation. Nancy amused him. "Sounds good to me. Lynn?"

Her cheeks had pinkened. "I behaved rudely."

Nancy shook her head. "You weren't rude. That slithering snake doesn't deserve the time of day."

Jax raised his brows and wondered if Nancy would share the story behind this. *Slithering snake?* The phrase made him want to laugh, but now he honestly wanted to know what was going on.

One thing he'd discovered in a rush: he didn't like to see Lynn upset like that. Nor did he like to hear her apologize for a situation she hadn't created.

With the three of them seated at the trestle table, Jax noted that the passage of Lynn's anger and embarrassment had left her looking incredibly tired.

Maybe it wasn't his place, but he asked anyway. "Who was that guy?"

Lynn didn't answer but Nancy did. "Her brother-in-law. *Ex* brother-in-law.

"Ex?"

"Matt's brother."

Lynn spoke wearily. "Mom, don't."

"Why not? Everyone in this town knows the whole ugly story. Just sit there and eat your pie. Jax has a right to some answers because I think he was prepared to defend the battlements." She eyed Jax favorably.

"It's a hideous story," Lynn said quietly. "Let's not."

"Let's do," Nancy said firmly.

Part of Jax wanted to shut Nancy down when Lynn clearly didn't want to discuss this. Another part wanted to know what was going on, why Luke had tried to barge in that way. And since he was going to be around indefinitely it seemed, he wanted to know what Lynn was up against in case he could help. But he'd also noticed there was no good way to stop Nancy when she had her mind made up. The two women were alike more than they probably knew. Stubborn.

Nancy served him another slice of pie. He hadn't realized he'd wolfed down the first. Stuffing his mouth to keep quiet, he supposed.

"At its root," Nancy said, "it's all very simple. When Matt's father died, he left the house to Matt. Not a single thing to Luke."

"Why not?" Jax couldn't resist asking.

"Luke is a ne'er do well, a ladies' man, a wastrel. Burned through every dime he ever got, apparently lives off whatever woman he happens to be with at the time. Then there was a short prison sentence for drug possession. I think those boys' father had had enough. So he left it all to Matt. Probably hoping that Luke wouldn't get Matt into his financial mess because he owned half the house."

Jax could understand that, but he could also understand how that must have made Luke feel. There couldn't be anything quite like the sting of being cut out of your own father's will.

"Anyway," Nancy continued, rising to refresh coffee cups and her own tea, "Matt apparently didn't feel much different about Luke. Their dad's will didn't change a damn thing. Luke was still running around, mooching off women and friends and living the high life on other people's dimes."

Jax looked at Lynn and saw her nod sadly.

She spoke. "He was so messed up, Jax."

"Still is, from what I hear," Nancy said. "Anyway, if Matt had wanted to, he could have given Luke half stake in this house. Evidently he didn't, because he left everything to Lynn."

Jax nodded understanding, but he was beginning to see how this story was playing out. Terrible for Lynn.

"The long and the short of it," Nancy said, "is that Matt was hardly cold in the ground before Luke filed a lawsuit to gain half ownership in this house. He lost his appeal just three months ago."

Lynn sighed.

"And now," Jax remarked, "he wants to be friends."

"Exactly!" Nancy's answer was emphatic. "Not likely, not after dragging my daughter through a legal mess when she should have been grieving."

"I *did* grieve," Lynn said flatly. "He couldn't prevent that. But more than once I just wanted to throw in the towel and let him have it. But Matt's wishes…" She trailed off.

Jax now saw Lynn in a different light. She wasn't just a vivacious widow with a project. She was a strong woman with a mission. Remarkable.

He repeated a phrase he'd heard more than once. "Nobody ever grows younger from a lawsuit."

He saw a faint smile crack Lynn's weary face.

"This Luke sounds vengeful," he added.

Lynn shook her head. "All hat and no cattle. Apparently he's past being nasty to me."

"I wouldn't count on it," Nancy said. "For heaven's sake, Lynn, he's been taking women for a ride since he was eighteen. Hardly does a lick of work from what I've heard. Mark my words, now he'll be all sweet, trying to get something from you."

"Well, he won't," Lynn answered firmly. "I'd have been a softer touch before the lawsuit, before he grew nasty with me. That ship has sailed."

Later, upstairs in his room, listening to the sounds of

music and voices from the students' rooms, Jax turned the story around in his head.

Bad enough to lose your husband without his closest relative dragging you into court. He was glad Nancy had ignored her daughter and explained the situation.

But he felt awful for Lynn. In a town this small, Luke would be hard to escape. And the streak of vengeance he'd already displayed boded ill.

Damn!

Chapter Five

In the morning, Jax received an unexpected phone call
while he was out taking a walk near the junior college.
He was officially on leave, all his friends knew it, and
phoning for casual chats wasn't customary. It had to be
official, he thought grimly as he tugged his phone out of
the breast pocket of his camo.

The call came from Lieutenant Hugh Briggs, a prosecutor with the Naval Judge Advocate's office. The two
had become acquainted after the war crimes trial of Theodore Albright a year or so ago.

"Master Gunnery Sergeant Stone," Hugh said. "Briggs
here."

The use of his military rank rather than his first name
put Jax on immediate alert. He responded formally.
"Something wrong, Lieutenant?"

"Well, that depends on how you look at it. This isn't
an official call, by the way, so let's skip the ranks. I used
yours just to, ah, get your complete attention. Because
while this isn't official, neither is it a joke. Put your ears
on, Jax."

"Copy."

"You alone?"

"Right now. I'm walking through cattle country. Any

mooing you hear isn't me." His tension wasn't easing any despite his joking. Briggs needed to get to the point.

Hugh laughed. "Got it. Wide-open spaces populated by prime rib and T-bone, huh?"

"The cattle might have a different idea."

"Might could be," Hugh answered.

Silence crackled a bit with static while Jax stood still, waiting.

"Okay," Hugh said. His voice had tensed. "There's something I want you to be aware of. Again, it's not official. No determination has been made."

"Understood."

"You remember the court martial? When you were a juror?"

"Yeah. The only one I've served on, not something I'll ever forget." The photos alone had twisted his gut, and he'd seen plenty in battle. The testimony from Albright's fellow soldiers had made them even worse.

"Well, here's the thing. Again, no one's certain, but the first steps are being taken in an investigation. An investigation that might take months or years, so a heads-up is the least you deserve."

Jax's insides tightened, a tingling crept along his spine. Not fear, he knew fear intimately. Preparedness. "Shoot."

"Two of your fellow jurors are dead. The first was put down to suicide but the second one… Let's just say questions arose. Two jurors within such a short time frame struck a few people as suspicious. Maybe not, maybe a coincidence."

"How likely would this be, Hugh? One in a million?"

"Marines are mostly young and healthy as you know, and while military suicides are sadly common, the second death wasn't easily explained away. So just listen.

Like I said, an investigation will take next to forever. There wcre people in Albright's own squad who denied he'd done anything wrong despite the testimony from others. People who consider him a brother. You know the dynamics."

Indeed Jax did. Brotherhood was forged on a battlefield. He'd thought it stunning that any of the squad had stepped forward with their stories of atrocity. But they had, which made the acts even more sickening. When your brothers-in-arms condemned you, it was bad. Worse than bad. Maybe evil.

"I'm in the back of beyond, not in Denver yet, Hugh, if this is a warning."

"Consider it one. Like I said, no proof, but dangerous to ignore. And when has being in the back of beyond ever protected anyone from a determined Marine? Remember that."

"I guess I should thank you, Hugh."

"As long as you don't shoot the messenger. Just keep high alert. Don't let your guard drop. These two guys were near a military base. You're hanging out there somewhere like a staked-out goat."

After the call disconnected, Jax stuffed his phone back into his pocket and resumed walking, but his head was turning over what Hugh had just told him.

He was quite sure Hugh should have kept his mouth shut, but had decided to buck the rules to call him. Which in itself meant plenty.

Someone was killing jurors from the trial? It was mind-boggling.

And entirely possible.

The idea so offended him that his stomach turned hollow. Then rage crept in. Everything in the code should

prevent this. But apparently someone had gone well past
the code onto a plane of his own.

Above the law.

WHEN HE RETURNED to Lynn's house, he heard some hammering from the living room and poked his head in to
see what she was up to. She was knocking out more plaster, but wearing a mask this time. She had also pried out
some narrow strips of wood.

"How's it going?" he asked casually.

"Well enough. I'm kicking up too much dust. I need
to cover that door with plastic, but I didn't get out my
ladder." She shrugged and gave a small laugh. "I don't
know why, but I'm tripping over myself today, doing
things out of order."

"Got that plastic anywhere?"

"In the next room." She brushed her hands together
and stood looking at the mess. A Shop-Vac stood nearby,
but she didn't reach for it.

"You find anything wrong?"

"I need to check a few places after I pry out some
more of the lath. When the dust settles, I'll bring my laptop and camera in here and start looking around. Cross
your fingers for me, Jax. I don't want to have to replace
the framing."

"Fingers crossed," he assured her. "I'd like to help if
you'll let me." As if he'd be around long enough to do
anything majorly useful.

"Bored?"

He could almost see her smile behind her dust mask.
"I like to keep busy." Certainly true.

"Help is always welcome."

He glanced around. "Where's Nancy?"

"You mean because she didn't leap out at you?" Lynn asked drily. "She headed out with some girlfriends. Tea at the bakery or something. Anyway, I need to clean up."

He stepped back from the doorway. "Let me get that plastic up for you." He scanned the wide door frame. "Looks like I won't need a ladder."

"Quit bragging about your height."

He flashed a smile. "Accident of nature."

Twenty minutes later he had the heavy plastic stapled up across the top, locking in all the dust.

"Thanks, Jax. I really appreciate it."

"Always glad to be of service." He paused, wondering what he was thinking and why he was going to ask. "Like to join me for lunch at Maude's?"

She tilted her head to one side. "Yeah. I would. Sounds good. Let me get rid of this dust and we can go. I'll only be a minute."

JAX CERTAINLY WASN'T the introverted high school student any longer, but he was still reserved. Very reserved. His face revealed little, if anything, and sometimes she wondered if his feelings were as well contained as everything else.

Probably.

She didn't waste a lot of time up in her apartment, just washed her face and hands, brushed plaster dust out of her hair and put on fresh jeans and a bright blue flannel shirt. After a quick look in the mirror, she grabbed a blue bandanna to tie back her auburn hair.

That would do for Maude's. Pulling her jacket from a hook by the attic door, she met Jax in the vestibule. Still wearing his camos and desert boots, with an olive web belt around his waist, he held one of those billed hats with an eight-point crown. Matt had told her about them. *Utility cover.* Different from the other services.

"Sorry to keep you waiting," she said.

He shook his head. "You didn't. I expected you to take longer."

She flashed a grin at him. "Thought I was going to do all that girlie makeup stuff?"

That drew a smile from him. "You don't need it and I'm glad you didn't."

Nice compliment, she thought as they stepped outside. He put on his cover while she pulled on her jacket. The breeze had stiffened and grown chillier.

"I guess Jazz and Adam had their wedding just in time," she remarked, zipping up. "Winter's breath is blowing. Do you want me to drive us? Are you cold?"

Jax shook his head. "I'm fine with walking if you are."

They strode along the sidewalk at a fairly brisk pace that felt good to Lynn. She worked hard physically, but nothing like the stretching her muscles enjoyed from walking.

The sun peeked from behind a cloud and cast buttery light everywhere.

"I've sometimes thought," Lynn remarked, "that I can tell the season by the color of the light. Silly, I guess, when the sun is at the same elevation in both spring and fall. But something about autumn sunlight seems more golden."

"That's an interesting thought. I never really noticed."

She shrugged. "I'm weird."

"I wouldn't say so."

They turned a corner, getting close to the diner. "Heard anything about the cause of that fire yet?" she asked.

"No," Jax answered. "But it probably takes time to make a determination."

So calm, she thought. Stable, without any apparent emotional ups and downs. He didn't even seem in a rush to learn about the fire that might have killed him. Inevitably she wondered if this was training or if this was the real man. But how could she ask? None of her business.

But that didn't keep the question from escaping anyway. "Does anything excite you?"

He stopped walking and he transfixed her with a pair of very dark eyes. "When it matters, a helluva lot."

"So the fire doesn't matter to you?"

"What matters is that someone lost their livelihood and one poor bastard lost his life. As for why, that's not for me to discover. I'm used to awaiting the outcome of investigations."

Lynn shrugged inwardly as they approached the diner. He was right, of course. But among friends she was used to hearing speculations of all kinds, and sometimes talking things to death.

Jax evidently wasn't like that. Which meant that even casual conversation might be difficult with him.

They stepped inside Maude's and conversation came to a sudden halt as everyone at the tables turned to look at Jax. *The grapevine must be afire*, Lynn thought with amusement. The prodigal returns? Or just, *Hey, have you seen what that strange kid has become?*

Lynn had to stifle a giggle. Maybe when she caught up with one of her friends she could find out.

Conversation, along with the clatter of crockery and flatware, resumed as fast as it had halted.

Lynn pointed out a table near the back and headed that way, unzipping her jacket as she went. Jax had already removed his hat, and when they sat, he placed it on the far end of the table.

Maude's daughter, Mavis, a stocky woman, arrived promptly with coffee mugs and the plastic menus.

"Thanks, Mavis," Lynn said.

"Might be a few minutes," Mavis grumped. "We got busy."

"That's good, right?"

"Depends on who's making us busy."

As she stomped away, Lynn looked at Jax to see the corners of his eyes crinkled with amusement.

"I know," she said. "I wonder what's been going on here."

"Your guess is probably better than mine."

Maude and her daughter were the county's most famous grumps, but Lynn had never heard them complain about their clientele. She looked around the room, wondering what subsurface currents she couldn't detect.

Jax spoke, interrupting her thoughts. "I wonder if Maude has half a rhino on the menu."

She grinned. "That hungry?"

"For some reason, yeah. I promise not to embarrass you, though."

"As long as you don't eat that rhino raw, I won't be."

He laughed quietly.

Wow, another laugh, Lynn thought as her heart did that fluttery thing again. Maybe he wasn't as staid and sober as he usually seemed.

Mavis returned carrying a brushed aluminum carafe. She slammed it on the table in front of them. "It's hot and fresh."

Lynn looked at the carafe in amazement. "When did you get these?"

"Last week. Ain't nobody got time to be running around filling coffee cups all the time. I figure that'll take care of you, but if you need more, I'm not invisible."

A laugh escaped Lynn, and Mavis completely astonished her by winking. "Bringing up Ma," she said quietly, then stomped away with their orders.

"I guess I missed something," Jax remarked.

"Only that Mavis is bent on changing her mother's ways, I gathered. The carafes must be the start."

He nodded, smiling faintly. "A good one. I never came here much when I was a kid. I don't exactly remember the way things were."

"They certainly didn't include insulated carafes. Mostly slamming coffee cups. And now you can get a latte, too, if you want."

He nodded. Well, Lynn thought, there didn't seem to be much to say about it. Conversational dead end.

Their burgers arrived, thick and juicy. Jax had ordered two of them, along with a side of broccoli. Lynn had chosen the side salad. In between them stood a heap of hot fries. She could have laughed at the way Mavis had decided they were going to share them.

They'd hardly started eating when a familiar voice said, "I hope you don't mind me joining you," Madge Kearney said sweetly. "The place is too crowded for me to find my own table."

"Help yourself," Lynn answered with a smile, indicating the chair beside her. But instead Madge took the seat beside Jax. Lynn stifled an urge to laugh.

Madge wore a red dress with a low neck, allowing her ample cleavage to show. A bit too much for the weather and this diner. Over the back of the chair she'd hung a red jacket.

"Oh," said Madge, "those burgers look heavenly. Mind?" She helped herself to a fry.

Lynn looked at Jax and thought she saw a smile in his eyes. Did that mean he wasn't fooled or that he was enjoying the unexpected attention? She'd have to wait it out and see.

For all Madge claimed the burgers looked good, and freely helped herself to another fry, she ordered the chef salad.

"Have to watch my figure," she said on a girlish laugh.

Jax glanced her way. "Physical work tends to do that, too."

For an instant Madge looked miffed, but then her face smoothed. "I bet you do a lot of that," she said to Jax.

"You might say so. Lynn does a lot, too."

Madge's gaze drifted toward Lynn. *My*, thought Lynn, *she's angry with me.* Not that it mattered.

The salad arrived quickly, along with an icy diet cola. Madge returned her attention to Jax after she speared a small piece of lettuce. "You were burned out of the motel?" she asked.

"Yes," Jax answered when he'd swallowed and could speak politely.

Lynn bit into her juicy burger and dabbed her chin unapologetically. Good stuff. And with her mouth full, she had an excuse not to speak or let her tongue run away with her.

"How ever did you find Lynn's place?" Madge asked after another nibble.

"The sheriff arranged it." Jax wiped his own mouth with a napkin and looked at Madge. "I'm under suspicion, you know."

Madge's eyes widened.

Lynn wondered why he'd chosen to say that.

Madge cleared her throat. "But you wouldn't have…"

"I might have," Jax answered flatly, then took a big bite of his burger.

"No one could think that!" Madge protested. "You only just got back here and you were always so—" She broke off without finishing, as if trying to find a nice way to say something.

Jax turned his head to look at her. "I've been away a long time, Madge. It *is* Madge, right?"

The woman nodded.

"Funny, I don't remember you. Are you sure you remember me? Or just the reclusive guy who never talked and came home wearing Marine blues?"

Now Lynn could really have laughed. Jax was handling Madge very well. Madge fell silent and returned to pecking at her salad. She probably wanted a stiff drink about now. Whatever her hopes with Jax, they'd just moved further away.

Jax finished his burger and broccoli and devoted himself to eating some fries. "I think a piece of pie will be in order."

"Not for me," Lynn answered. "This burger is huge. You were the one who wanted half a rhino."

He flashed her a grin, then returned his attention to Madge. "So what do you do, Madge?" he asked.

Madge, who had been moving steadily from feeling abashed to feeling angry to judge by her face, turned toward him with an artificial smile. "I work at the dentist's office."

Jax nodded. "Hygienist?"

Madge sighed, her voice somewhat muffled. "Receptionist."

"I bet you brighten up the front office."

Madge just shook her head, threw a few bills on the table and rose. "See you around, Jax," she said, nearly purring as if to make up for her earlier silence and missteps.

"Sure," he answered indifferently.

As Lynn and Jax walked back to her house, Lynn said, "You handled Madge well."

"Did I? I just wanted to be polite without stirring up anything. You said she was always on the hunt."

"She is and has three divorces to show for it."

"*Three?* In so few years?"

"Busy little bee."

"I guess so." He shook his head.

"Anyway," Lynn continued, "you're welcome to borrow my car if you want. Now that you're here, you must want to do something besides hang around my place. Take a look at the old ranch or something."

"I'm not sure about visiting the old place. And I'm only in town because of Adam. Why is your mother living in Cheyenne?"

Lynn shrugged. "My dad took off when I was fourteen. Mom had always felt constricted here. She wanted some bright lights, I gather. Anyway, as soon as I met Matt, she moved away. She seems happy in her new life."

"But not so much she isn't bugging you."

Lynn laughed. "I guess not."

Later in the day, while Lynn was busy drawing up a remodeling list, Jax had time to do some serious thinking about the call from Briggs that morning.

A suicide and a disturbing death, both of jurors in the Albright trial. As Hugh Briggs had said, the suicide, unfortunately, wasn't terribly unusual. War left deep scars that some simply couldn't endure.

But a second death? Hugh was right about Marines being young and healthy. An OD on drugs wouldn't have started an investigation. Something else had happened. Something serious enough that it couldn't be passed over, nor the link to the trial overlooked.

He would have liked to know what had caused this consternation, but if someone was out to kill jurors, he'd been sloppy with that one. He also knew that no one, but no one, not even Hugh, would share any of the details of the investigation.

Hugh had already crossed a line by warning him. He was also correct that Jax's whereabouts could be discovered. He'd been required to provide a general outline of his plans, although his listed time here was two days for a wedding, then on to Denver.

The information was supposed to be confidential, but that protection wasn't impossible to get around. Nor, in the ordinary way, would it matter.

But this time it might.

Inevitably, his thoughts turned to the hotel fire. No, he told himself after a moment. It was only his second night in Conard City. Very unlikely anyone could have found him that fast.

But Hugh's words rolled around in his mind. Don't discount a determined Marine.

Maybe he should find somewhere else to stay until the sheriff made it clear that he could move on. He sure as hell didn't want to draw Lynn into any kind of mess.

Certainly not a deadly one.

Chapter Six

Luke didn't give up easily, as Lynn saw yet again when two days later he arrived at her door. Wrapped in a drab jacket, his too-long blond hair ruffled by the frigid breeze, he looked chipper despite the cold-reddened tip of his nose.

"Just a cup of coffee, Lynn," he said with a smile. "I promise."

She wanted to close the door in his face. This guy had more annoying persistence than a fly, but Nancy's voice emerged from the kitchen.

"Let the boy in, dear. Might be time to find out what he wants now."

Lynn had to swallow a laugh. Count on Nancy.

"I don't want anything at all," Luke protested as he stepped inside. "Just to talk."

Right, Lynn thought. Her mother was correct. Maybe they could suss out Luke's motives.

"Are you a coffee or a tea man?" Nancy asked Luke as he and Lynn entered the kitchen. "Lynn has this place so torn up I can't invite you into a living room."

"Coffee is fine and so is the kitchen," Luke answered. He settled at the trestle table, and much as Lynn didn't want to sit, she took a seat, too.

Luke looked at Lynn, his gray eyes clear and innocent. Lynn wondered how many women he'd practiced that look on.

"You're doing quite some remodeling," he said.

"She certainly is," Nancy answered, filling two mugs and setting them down. "And this place needed it. It had gone to rack and ruin."

Not quite, Lynn thought, but she saw no reason to dispute her mother's judgment. None of Luke's business.

"You're really lucky," Nancy continued, "that you didn't inherit half this mess."

"Am I?" Luke's smile remained, but his eyes hardened a bit.

"Of course you are! Your father didn't maintain anything at all. But why would he after your mother died?"

Lynn didn't like the direction of this conversation and diverted it. "Mom, Luke was hurt. I can understand that. Let it go, please."

Nancy sniffed, but remained quiet.

Lynn returned her attention to Luke. "I haven't heard. What are you up to these days?"

"Oh, I've got a job out at one of the ranches. Keeps me busy."

Lynn doubted the job was full-time or that it involved any physical labor. That wasn't Luke's style. "What about a special someone?"

Luke's smile broadened. "She's a teacher. Jillie Banton. Know her?"

"Vaguely, I think. Cute." And maybe not so bright. Lynn wondered why so many women were attracted to men like Luke. Too many seemed not to mind supporting a layabout. A far cry from hardworking. A far cry from a househusband. Hah! She could just imagine Luke chasing kids, cooking, cleaning, doing laundry. Oh, yeah.

"I'm glad you have someone," she said lamely.

"She puts a smile on my face." Luke sipped coffee. "So, Lynn, are you restoring the entire house?"

"Most of it needs some restoring. Some serious water damage on the living room wall, too. I need to get in there and find out how extensive the damage is."

Luke shook his head. "That could be a pain."

"She needs to get around to remodeling this kitchen," Nancy said tartly. "It's impossible to keep counters truly clean when they're full of knife cuts. And don't forget the burn marks."

"I haven't forgotten, Mom. One thing at a time."

Luke nodded sagely. "An awful lot for one woman to take on."

One *woman*? Luke had no idea how close he came to having his head torn off.

"That big guy," Luke continued. "He's that Marine, right? How long is he staying?"

Lynn shrugged. "I'm not sure. He came for Adam Ryder's wedding. And he used to live around here."

Just then, the front door opened and her three roomers entered the house with laughter, carrying their laptop cases along with bags that emitted delicious aromas.

"Hi, Lynn," they called out, then stepped into the kitchen.

"Room in the fridge?" Barry asked, holding up a bag.

"You know there always is."

Nancy looked as if she weren't so sure of that. Lynn wondered if she'd gone out to plunder the grocery.

All three of them politely greeted Luke, then after the

mysterious bag disappeared into the fridge, they stampeded up the stairs, laughing once again.

"High-spirited," Luke remarked.

"Noisy," Nancy added.

Lynn spoke. "They lighten the atmosphere in this place. I enjoy them."

LUKE HUNG AROUND awhile longer, possibly hoping to cadge a dinner invitation, one that Lynn would never offer him. She'd seen his ugly side during the lawsuit and wasn't going to risk facing that part of him again. Gone were the days when she'd tried to make him into family because of Matt. He'd pretty much shredded that goodwill.

She felt a twinge of conscience as she closed the door behind him, wondering if she was being too unkind, then decided not.

Luke had been pleasant enough during her marriage to Matt, not that he'd ever visited that often. But pleasant. Until a few days after Matt's funeral when he'd dropped the pretense.

Lynn wasn't terribly suspicious by nature, but during the legal battle she had concluded that all that niceness had been meant to get a share of Matt's estate if anything happened.

It had happened, the very worst, and Luke had taken off the gloves. Even though the law had sided with her, Lynn still felt emotionally bruised. While she stood amidst the wreckage of her life, Luke had come after her with both barrels blazing.

Now he wanted to make up? Too late. Far too late.

Sighing, she decided to help her mother make dinner. She wasn't ready to face the mess she might find behind that living room wall. Since it wasn't collapsing, she could wait another day.

"Where's Jax?" Nancy asked as Lynn peeled carrots and potatoes.

"What? Is he your type?"

Nancy laughed but added, "I thought he might be yours."

"Hardly. Uniforms are a put-off for me now."

"I guess I can understand that. I just wanted to invite him to join us for dinner. Seems the courteous thing to do."

He was also just a roomer like the others, Lynn thought, but didn't say so.

Because he didn't exactly feel like a roomer.

"So where is he?" Nancy asked again.

"I have no idea. He has the right to come and go as he pleases."

That ended the subject. Thank God.

SEVERAL BLOCKS AWAY, in the house she owned thanks to the settlement in her first divorce, Madge was still smarting from the way Jax had treated her at lunch.

As if she were a stranger. She wasn't! She'd seen that look he'd given her toward the end of their senior year. And they'd been together in school all those years.

It had to do with that damn Lynn Macy, she decided. If Lynn hadn't been there, the entire conversation would have gone differently. She was *sure* it would have.

She had to find some way to take Lynn out of the picture. Some way that would make her utterly unappealing to Jackson Stone.

While Madge's mental wheels spun, she made herself

another daiquiri, her preferred poison. More elegant than beer or a shot of whiskey, she believed.

Yup. There had to be a way to remove Lynn from the competition. She just needed to figure it out.

Sitting back in the comfy wing chair she'd inherited from her second husband, she sipped her drink and inhaled the lime aroma, imagining herself in an elegant bar.

Madge pretended a lot. She just didn't realize it all the time.

JAX HAD CHANGED into workout clothes and gone for a long run. He had the worst feeling that everything hung in a state of stasis, that more was going to happen, but he had no idea what or when.

Or maybe that was leftover mission-think. He couldn't imagine a more generally peaceful locale than this county. Sure, bad things happened, but most people still left their doors unlocked.

It wasn't as if nothing had changed since his departure fifteen years ago. It had almost surprised him to get broadband Wi-Fi at Lynn's house. The internet might have been around for a long time, but when he'd lived here, most people had to go to the library to use it.

The town, however, looked a little more ragged. The years hadn't been kind. He took in the paint that had faded on some houses, in places peeling away, and all he could do was admire Lynn's determination and her faith that her work would be rewarded.

Or maybe the work itself was reward enough. He wondered if he should ask.

But there was a strong part of him that still hung back from asking questions he had no right to ask, from putting himself forward.

In the Corps he was fine. No problems, set rules, set limits. He knew who he was. Out here in the hinterlands he felt a touch of that young boy returning.

Enough of that, though. That wasn't him any longer.

He thought about going by the ranch house where he and Adam had cemented their relationship over all those years. When they had been the only friends out there in the wide-open spaces.

But no, there were bad memories there, too, like his father's brutality. Only later did he realize the man had no right to whip him like that. Only when he was eight and happened to be home had he learned how violently his father had treated his mother.

He'd heard her crying one night, "Samuel, no! Please…"

He'd crept from his room and peered from the top of the banister to see what was happening. He'd seen too much, his father pummeling his mother even after she fell to the floor.

At the time he'd had no comparison. He thought that was the way things should be, especially when he heard it happen repeatedly. But he hated it. He also never spoke of it, not even to Adam, for fear of getting his mother into more trouble.

Maybe that had birthed part of his reticence, his introversion. Did it matter now?

All he knew was that when he was sixteen, his father had sent his mother to the hospital with a broken jaw.

And that was when Jax, string bean that he was, had learned to stand up to that ugly, abusive man. Never again.

His mother had left shortly after she got out of the hospital. His dad had started drinking himself into a stupor all the time. When Jax left for the military, everything was lost. The ranch foreclosed, his father settling the last of it by eating his shotgun.

And not one sliver of sorrow had troubled Jax.

He'd kept in touch with his mother for a few years until cancer took her. That *did* sadden him, but he figured she was better off.

No, he didn't want to go back to that place. It was seeded with some great memories, but also with many more memories he didn't want to flood him.

Off-limits.

Instead, it was easier to think about a Marine stalking him. Far easier. *That* was the kind of threat he could handle.

LYNN'S ROOMERS WENT out again for dinner and dates, she gathered. She was happy, however, when she heard Jax return. It was not at all like the comings and goings of her boys.

The pork tenderloin was almost done, roasting with potatoes and carrots. The aroma made her mouth water.

Nancy beat her to the kitchen door. "Dinner, Jax? There's plenty."

Lynn hid a smile. She'd never doubted that Jax was also on her mother's menu. She did, however, notice that he hesitated before answering.

"Don't put him on the spot, Mom."

"I'm sure the man knows how to decline, Lynn."

Jax must have heard her warning to her mother, Lynn suddenly realized with a sinking feeling. Oh, hell. She didn't want him to think she was reluctant to have his company, but she also couldn't dash out there and press him further about eating with them.

She needed to learn to keep her mouth shut. And ignore the niggle of hope that he would accept the invitation. She enjoyed his company, reserved as it was, more than she should.

"I'd like that very much, Nancy," Jax answered. "I need to change and wash up first."

"There's time," Nancy answered brightly.

When his boot steps disappeared upstairs, Lynn looked at her mother. "You *do* have a thing for him."

"I do not. He's way too young for me."

"No December-May relationship then?"

Nancy snorted. "I don't need a trophy husband. I'm enjoying my freedom way too much."

Lynn hoped it was true that Nancy was enjoying her freedom. She certainly seemed like it. But *trophy husband*? She nearly laughed out loud.

She turned from the sink, where she was washing a few prep dishes, and was annoyed to see her mother placing a couple of candles on the table. Candles and holders that Lynn had put away a long time ago.

"Too much, Mom."

Nancy stood back, surveying the table that at present held only dark green place mats. "Do you think so?"

"I know so."

"But it's so boring."

"Fine, but it's better than a romantic candlelit dinner. Cut it out."

Nancy sighed, but for once didn't argue. The candles and holders disappeared back to their place in a corner of the pantry. "We need a tablecloth."

"Sure, and who's going to wash and iron it?"

"They make those that don't wrinkle."

"I don't need a tablecloth. I usually eat in my apartment upstairs. By myself."

"But you never know..."

This time Lynn didn't bother to answer.

Nancy was good at laying out food, however. By the time Jax joined them, the sliced tenderloin sat on a platter surrounded by browned potatoes and carrots.

Lynn set the places with the best unchipped dishes she could find and flatware that was scratched with age. No point even thinking about it. It was all she had.

"Dinner smells great," Jax said appreciatively as he took his place at the table.

"Something to drink?" Lynn asked.

"Just water, please. No ice."

After Jax had tasted everything, he remarked, "I don't think I've ever had pork this tender."

"Lynn cooked it," Nancy said. "I just helped."

Lynn resisted rolling her eyes, hearing the subtext *Lynn not only remodels but she can do the feminine thing, too. She can cook.* What was up next? Her mother extolling her virtues as a laundress?

She glanced at Jax and caught the twinkle in his eyes. He must have heard the subtext, too.

"It's really good, Lynn," he said promptly, obviously taking the hint.

Lynn hurried to change the subject. "Did you have a good day, Jax?"

"Fair to middling," he answered. "I wandered a bit, thought a bit about the past." And about the present threat, but he wasn't going to mention that. No way.

"Did you visit the old homestead?" Nancy asked.

"No."

The word was flat and forbidding. Lynn looked at

him, and other than a slight tightening around his eyes, she saw total impassivity. He'd locked something away deep inside him.

"I'm sure you can borrow my car if you want to get out there," Nancy offered.

Lynn wanted to tap her mother's leg under the table. She wasn't getting it. Jax's single word had said enough.

"Very kind of you," Jax said after a moment. "But I think not." He resumed eating. A minute or so later, he asked, "How was your day, Lynn?"

"Wasted mostly," she admitted. "I couldn't face looking into that wall yet, so I puttered around taking some measurements for new kitchen cabinets and counters. And no, Mom, I'm nowhere near ready to do that. Just thinking about it."

"Sounds productive to me," Jax replied.

"You should consult me about the counters," Nancy said. "I've had experience with all the different types and, believe me, some are vastly overrated. Fashionable, but hard to take care of."

"I'd like to hear about that sometime," Lynn said, heading off potential hostilities. Not that a discussion with her mother would ever become hostile, but it could sure turn difficult.

"Have you heard anything from Adam and Jazz?" she asked Jax.

He smiled. "On their honeymoon?"

Nancy spoke. "I think it's so odd that Jasmine is called Jazz and Jackson is called Jax."

"We joked about it at the wedding," Jax answered. "Pure coincidence."

While the food was wonderful, Lynn wished this dinner would be over. Tension crept across the table as

Nancy prattled on about things best left alone, everything from Jax's family to his reasons for not wanting to visit his old home.

As the dinner progressed, Jax grew more monosyllabic, offering no explanations. And why should he? It was no one's business but his own.

Lynn smothered a sigh and was glad when she could at last stand up and start clearing the table. Jax immediately rose to help.

"Mom, why don't you go find something on TV? Or a good book. You worked so hard on this dinner."

Nancy smiled, looking from Lynn to Jax as if this were just what she'd hoped for. "A great idea, Lynn. I'll see you in the morning."

"Not if Jax can escape first," she said under her breath when Nancy disappeared.

To her astonishment, Jax laughed. "Too bad she's out of luck."

Lynn's heart stumbled. "Oh?" she asked, wondering why she should even care.

"I doubt either of us can be maneuvered as easily as she seems to think."

He had a point. Relaxing again, Lynn stacked scraped plates beside the sink. "It doesn't bother you?"

He shook his head and began washing dishes. "It amuses me. Don't let it bother *you*. But I wonder if she has any idea how transparent she is?"

That drew a laugh from Lynn. "I'm not sure."

"It doesn't matter. Just relax. I've handled far worse."

Like Madge, Lynn thought. But Jax was subtle. She wondered if Madge understood that she'd been given a major brush-off.

The woman's nerve astonished her, though. She knew

Madge was a flirt, always looking for another man, as if she had no other way of measuring her own self-worth. But claiming an old friendship when there had been none? That seemed more problematic than her usual flirtations.

Shaking her head, Lynn started drying dishes.

LATER, UPSTAIRS IN her private aerie, music from her boys' rooms rising quietly through the floor, Lynn sat with her tablet on her lap, her eyes focused elsewhere even when the screen darkened to save the battery power.

A small fire burned in her electric fireplace. Warm lamplight filled the room, but she wasn't seeing any of it.

Jax had been tense. Not overly so, but she felt the difference from when he first arrived. It couldn't be Madge; she wasn't important enough to disturb him.

Remembering how abruptly he had responded to her mother about visiting his old home, she felt the tension that lay there. At least inside him.

Given how silent and distant he had remained the whole time he'd lived here, at least according to those who had known him better than she had, maybe something other than his nature had driven him to keep his distance.

Rumors flew around this town endlessly, but she'd heard none about Jax or his family. Not a single whisper, which would lead her to believe they'd been boringly ordinary.

Then there was Adam, his friend since before he'd started school, from what she *had* heard. Wouldn't that be a good memory? Something he could recall out at the old ranch?

Why wouldn't he want to follow those pathways in his past?

As she sat there, she grew increasingly convinced that something truly bad had happened to Jax. Something he had locked inside his silence and introversion.

She stared into space for a while, then sighed. He'd never tell her, and she was probably all wet anyway. Speculating about his past wasn't going to do a damn bit of good.

Instead, she forced her thoughts to the kitchen she'd begun measuring today. No small project, especially since she wanted to do more than replace countertops and appliances. She envisioned gutting the entire room, rearranging everything, adding more cabinets and counter space. The electrical work was going to be expensive, never mind the rest of it.

But if she was going to do it, she was going to do it right. Make it a workable space, rather than a cobbled-together room from an earlier time when the minimum was enough, when a table had to substitute for counters.

Definitely more cabinets because those along the one wall beside the sink simply weren't enough. A built-in dishwasher rather than water-wasteful handwashing.

The measurements she'd taken today hadn't been of what was already there. They had been measurements of the space and the beginnings of rough sketches of how she could change the room without sacrificing too much of the area.

A nice diversion, especially since she had other tasks that were far more pressing like that damn living room wall.

She looked down at the tablet on her lap but didn't turn it on again. Instead she leaned her head back and thought about Matt.

Matt, that wonderful guy who'd swept her off her feet.

His smile, the sound of his laughter, his warm hands caressing her. Her other half.

She'd gotten to the point where she could think about all the good things and mostly ignore the horror at the end. The blessing of time.

But as she dozed off, Matt's face became mixed with Jax's. The two came together seamlessly as if part of her whole. And in dreams, there was no reason to feel guilty.

ONE FLOOR DOWN in his own bedroom, Jax stretched out on the bed with his hands behind his head. He pictured Lynn upstairs in her attic and felt his body stir.

With each passing hour, his attraction to her grew. He didn't seem to be able to prevent it, but he sure as hell could ignore it. He had to. He was convinced that, after Matt, Lynn wouldn't want to get involved with another military man. And he had no intention of leaving the Corps early unless a severe enough wound or injury made him unfit for duty. In five years he'd be able to retire if he chose, but he often thought about extending past that.

He'd be only thirty-eight, and that seemed too young to hang up his uniform.

Nor did he believe he'd be any more acceptable to Lynn because he'd just been given command of recruiting centers in Denver. The position was an honor and physically safe, but it could end at any moment if he was needed in the field. Nope, not secure enough to offer a woman widowed by war.

He shook his head at the unwanted direction of his thoughts. Why was he thinking about her in the long term anyway? They hardly knew each other and he sure as hell wasn't going to have a fling with her. Leave it alone. It could never be. Don't allow these feelings to strengthen.

He thought about Madge for a few minutes, a safer place for his mind to wander. He was still astonished by her insistence they'd had something going in high school. She seemed to be stalking him, judging by the way she'd joined his table at Maude's. It wouldn't be the first time that had happened since he'd put on the uniform.

But that was a minor matter. The problem would end when he left.

Which turned him in a different direction. He was pretty much stuck here until the arson investigation was completed, which meant he was going to have to deal with Madge and the amusing Nancy for longer. He kind of liked Nancy West and her determination to push Lynn to her way of thinking, especially since Lynn clearly wasn't going to allow herself to be pushed.

He wondered, though, how much Nancy sometimes embarrassed Lynn. The question brought a faint smile to his face. Two strong-willed women. They must clash quite often.

The amount of work Lynn had put into this place impressed him. She must be at it nearly all the time. He envisioned her on ladders, scraping and painting all that gingerbread, and there was a lot of it.

He bet that standing in the front yard, he'd have gotten a very nice view of her butt.

Ah, hell. He rolled over, trying to squash the images.

Better to focus on the call from Briggs. Could he be right that someone was out to kill the jurors in the Albright trial? Maybe so, since an investigation had begun.

With his eyes closed, it was too easy to remember that trial. Too easy to see the photographs, too easy to hear the testimony from men who had served with Albright. Those who accused Albright were clearly unhappy about doing so, but equally angry that he had ordered them to kill unarmed civilians. Those who had steadfastly stood up for him had insisted that he had done nothing wrong. It was war, after all.

Those who had accused him had probably killed their own careers and knew it. After that, no one would want to serve with them again because they had violated the code of brotherhood, no matter how justifiably.

Good men had risked everything to stand up for the right. Raising their voices to say that morality had its place even in the midst of war.

Yeah, war was an atrocity-making situation. Atrocities happened because they couldn't be avoided. But to *intentionally* commit them?

No.

The jury's deliberations had taken some time. None of them wanted to convict a fellow Marine of war crimes. The whole idea of convicting one of their own had run counter to their grain. They'd spent a lot of time looking for exculpatory evidence, as if there was any.

They'd spent almost none considering whether Theodore Albright had committed the acts for which he was standing trial. The evidence and testimony were too undeniable.

The inescapable verdict had been rendered with heavy hearts. No sense of satisfaction at all. No sense of self-righteousness. As disgusted as Jax was that Albright was a Marine, he had taken no pleasure in convicting him.

If someone really was killing jurors, he doubted Albright was directly behind it. He was in too much trouble already and still had the hope of an appeal.

Ah, hell. This train of thought wasn't helping, either. Sleep was determined to elude him.

Then he remembered Luke Macy. He didn't like the guy at all and didn't trust him. Nancy had it right when she'd called him a slithering snake.

Imagine him wanting to be friends now with Lynn after a lawsuit. The man had made her life hell, and Luke, after losing the case, should have gone away with his tail tucked. The man clearly knew no shame.

What could Luke hope to gain now? Money? He doubted Lynn had much to spare with the cost of re-modeling this house. But Luke might suspect otherwise, given that she was spending so much.

God, he was surrounded by messes. With his face in the pillow he nearly laughed. And he'd thought he'd be bored hanging around here?

It was a damn TV drama.

Chapter Seven

In the morning, over toast and eggs, Lynn announced, "It's time to get started on that living room wall whether I want to or not."

Jax, who'd made breakfast for the three of them, lifted his head. Nancy was busy shaking hers.

"What can I do to help?" he asked.

"Catch me when I collapse," Lynn answered wryly. "God, I'm dreading this."

"You should call a contractor," Nancy said.

Lynn sighed. "Like it or not, I can do this myself. And it may not be as bad as I fear."

"I hope not," Nancy replied. "But since you're going to be banging around and stirring up dust, I think I'll go out."

Lynn nodded. "Might be for the best. Meeting friends?"

"I'm going to call them, maybe arrange for lunch or an afternoon tea." Nancy favored her with a smile. "Have you looked outside yet? Cold and gray. A good time to stay indoors and visit. Before lunch, though, I may go shopping at the Mercantile."

"I doubt they'll have anything to suit your style," Lynn couldn't resist saying.

Nancy waved a hand. "You never know. Sometimes the larger world actually reaches this far."

"Just don't buy anything for me."

Nancy laughed. "Banish the thought."

Lynn looked at Jax. "She keeps wanting to dress me up." It had been an ongoing argument since Lynn's childhood, and Lynn still wasn't sure she'd won it.

"Hopeless cause," Nancy replied tartly. "Anyway, I'll stop at the grocery on my way home. Maybe I'll find something tempting."

"I could thaw the chicken that's in the freezer."

"No," Nancy said. "I most definitely do not want chicken again."

Dishes done, Nancy sailed out the front door dressed in emerald green wool.

"That's how she wants you to look?" Jax asked after the door closed behind Nancy.

Lynn smiled at him and shrugged. "She used to want me to wear frilly things. Maybe she still does. I'm just practical, and that suit she was wearing is *not* practical."

"Not for what you're doing."

She gathered up her inspection camera from the toolbox she kept in the dining room and grabbed her laptop as well.

"Everything the camera sees will show up on my computer screen," she said, then looked at Jax. "I'm sorry. You probably know that."

"As a matter of fact, I do. One of the lessons of my job."

God, he looked good this morning, Lynn thought. Yummy. Scrumptious. She was glad he was wearing jeans and a sweatshirt, not either of his uniforms, so she wouldn't swoon.

Hah! *Swoon.* Where had that word come from? Besides, she was still struggling with a feeling of guilt. Anyway, Jax was leaving soon and she didn't want a fling. That went against her nature.

Together, they traipsed into her living room, letting the plastic over the door fall behind them.

"Have you made enough holes?" Jax asked, pointing to the gaping spaces in the wall. He grinned.

Lynn laughed. "Enough that this wall could never be patched now. But I knew that when I started." She'd also pulled pieces of lath out of all those walls, enough to peek inside. They were dark holes right now.

Little light fell into the room through the window. Nancy had been right about the day's grayness. Looking outside, Lynn saw the wind blowing autumn leaves from the trees.

Oh, well, winter always came as sure as the sun rising in the east.

She turned on two of the work lights that stood on tripods, then knelt, opening her computer and starting the correct program.

Jax squatted beside her. "Want me to feed the camera in while you watch the screen?"

Lynn nodded. "That would definitely save me some time."

"I doubt it, but it'll make me feel like less of a fifth wheel."

She plugged the camera into the port on the side of her computer and saw the curtains show up on her screen. "It's working. Okay, let's go."

"Just tell me which way you want me to turn the camera when it's inside."

"Dang," she said, feeling butterflies in her stomach.

"I don't think I was this worried when I first discovered the water damage on the wall."

He had dropped to his knees, holding the camera, and agreed. "I imagine dealing with the roof was easier than having to reframe this wall would be."

"By far. I really don't like unpleasant surprises, like seeing the water stains when I evicted the old furniture. New walls, and the flooring is warped as well. I need some good news in here."

"We can hope." He turned to the wall. "Ready?"

Not really, but she'd put this off long enough. "Go ahead."

Grimly, she returned her attention to the screen. Fiber optics ran through the cable, not only returning the image but delivering light at the camera end. She was now looking at studs.

"No insulation in here?" he asked.

"None. These old houses rarely had any, unless they used newspaper. No thanks."

"Tinder," he agreed.

At her direction, he ran the camera through the entire bay, up the studs as far as the camera would reach, then back down again and across the bottom plate.

So far so good. She blew a sigh of relief. There was a little blackening of the wood at the bottom, but nothing major. Maybe it was good there'd been no insulation.

Five more holes and she was satisfied. "No new frame required."

She switched off her computer and sat back on her bottom, braced by her arms. "What a relief! Now I can just go ahead with the drywalling."

"And insulation? Will you add any?"

"Blown in, like I did upstairs. Easy-peasy."

He laughed as he coiled the camera wire. Sitting cross-legged, he faced her. "You have an interesting idea of easy."

Lynn shrugged. "Why? Because I'm a woman?"

"No, absolutely not. Just because most *people* wouldn't undertake this task."

She liked the way he was smiling at her, liked the tingle inside that ran all the way to her toes. Once again she felt sideswiped by the attraction she felt. Wow!

All that because of a smile. She averted her gaze and tried to reach equilibrium. God knew how she'd react if he ever touched her. She closed her eyes, envisioning herself turning into a puddle. A hot puddle.

It had been a very long time since she'd felt like that.

She jumped up suddenly, shaking herself. "I need to get the mail."

It was a good excuse to run, except he followed her. Before she reached the curb, however, he'd taken over an Adirondack chair and leaned back, crossing his legs, one foot on the other knee.

It *was* chilly out here, she thought. She wondered if Jax was thinking about sitting out on the porch long enough to turn blue.

She pulled the door of the box open, started to reach in, then squealed and jumped back.

Jax leaped instantly to his feet and charged down the short sidewalk. "Lynn, what's wrong?"

She pointed, her hand shaking. "Snake. There's a snake…"

JAX PEERED INTO the box and saw a small snake coiled inside atop some mail. Maybe two feet long, max? How the hell did it get in there? And why? He could certainly understand Lynn's shock.

He started to reach in, but Lynn cried, "Stop! God, it's a rattlesnake!"

He glanced over his shoulder. "It might look like one, but it's a milk snake."

"How can you be sure? It has a diamond pattern!" Her eyes were huge.

Her fear was natural, especially in someone who probably didn't see many snakes. "I recognize this type of snake, even used to play with them sometimes when I was a kid. Not that the snake appreciated it. Anyway, at most I'll get a little bite."

Moving slowly, he was able to get his fingers around the snake just behind its head. "It's logy because it's so cold. It's okay, Lynn."

Jax pulled the snake from the mailbox, holding its head, and watched it coil slowly around his hand and forearm. "See? It's trying to get warm by wrapping around me."

"Ugh." But she leaned closer to look. At last she said, "It's kinda pretty. But I don't like snakes."

"A lot of people don't."

"Aren't you going to kill it?" she asked when he took two steps down the street.

He paused to look back at her. "I don't know how it got in your mailbox, but it doesn't deserve to die for it. I'm going to find a safe place to let it go."

He felt her eyes on him as he walked down the street, thinking this snake needed a decent space with some tall grass to hide in. He'd seen one by the college, he thought.

But he couldn't imagine how it had gotten into her mailbox. Someone must have put it there.

"A PRANK," LYNN said decisively when he at last got back to the house. "It had to be a prank."

She'd changed into a green sweater, but still had her arms wrapped around her. Jax wondered if she was cold or still shaken.

"Your roomers pranking you, maybe? Or some neighborhood kid?"

To some people the snake might be funny, especially kids in their teens. He hadn't gotten the impression from her roomers that they'd do something like this to her, but it was possible.

She spoke again. "Well, it's obvious that creature couldn't have crawled in there on its own. But I don't think my boys would prank me that way."

He shook his head. "Can I make some coffee? And I know from experience that young men can get up to the craziest things."

As indeed he did, having commanded many of them during his term of service as he rose in rank.

"Why? Did you do crazy things?"

He put a filter into the basket while he chuckled. "I didn't, but I'm in the military, remember. Plenty of young people. I've been working with them all along, had to discipline some of them for acts of utter stupidity."

He turned to reach for the canister of coffee as she turned toward him at the same instant and brushed his arm against the peak of Lynn's breast. He froze, then snatched his hand back. *Hell!*

He looked at her, getting ready to apologize, but the

expression on her face silenced him. Somehow her green eyes had turned almost smoky, and her lips had parted.

Stillness filled him in the instant before his blood surged.

Seeing his yearning reflected in her gaze almost tipped him over the edge, into drawing her close, into stroking her, learning her curves...

Then she saved him from himself by turning quickly away. He stared at her back, hoping that accidental touch hadn't offended her.

When she spoke, her voice sounded a bit husky. "I'll ask my boys about it. I doubt they did it, but they could have some idea of who might have."

He cleared his throat. "Good idea." But all he could feel was the precipice he hovered on, and the desire to carry her over it with him. With difficulty, he banked his internal fire.

This woman deserved better than a short-term tumble in the hay. She was a long-term type of woman.

No way could he be that for her, especially when his own ideas of marriage were so polluted by his past. He couldn't trust himself.

LYNN, WRAPPED IN a hot haze, knew she had to escape before she did something she'd regret. Like throwing herself into Jax's arms. Was that desire she'd seen in his eyes? Electric tingles were coursing through her own body, but she doubted what she'd glimpsed in him. No man since Matt had looked at her like that. Which was how she wanted it. Right?

"I'm going upstairs for a little while," she said, trying to regain command of her voice.

Then she hurried away. Hurried to solitude. Hurried

toward a chance to get a grip on herself. Fled from needs she wasn't ready to handle.

By the time she reached the sanctuary of her attic, she began to feel ashamed of herself. She'd never been one to run from anything, but she was running from perfectly normal feelings. Feelings that didn't have to come to fruition.

And she felt some guilt. Guilt because of Matt. Guilt because she had the niggling sense that she was cheating on Matt as if he were still alive.

God, she was a hot mess.

To an extent, her mother was right, damn her. She *had* been burying her grief in all the remodeling. But she loved the work, and while it kept her preoccupied, there were the long nights when it did not. Not at all.

She flopped on one of the comfortable chairs she had reupholstered but ignored the matching hassock. She was too agitated to fully relax.

Matt's photo, in dress uniform, stood beside her bed on one side. Their wedding photo occupied the bookshelf. On the other end of the bookshelf she had built along one side of the room, there was another enlarged photo of Matt smiling at her. There were also five photo albums filled with prints of pictures she'd taken of him and he of her, plus all the cell phone photos she'd had turned into prints. They included his childhood photos, such as they were, as well as hers. Even a few other relatives, long since buried.

A family history of sorts, and she still looked through them. Especially the photos of Matt and the two of them together.

Each time she did, she felt a mix of happy memories and heartache.

So much of her life had gone with him. Too much.

These days the happy memories came more often. A good thing, because for a while, Matt's death had banished them all. She could still remember that period when the world had turned gray and life had felt too difficult to live. The light had gradually returned, and along with it a desire to live.

But the words *you need to move on* still irritated the hell out of her. She was moving on at her own pace, and nobody telling her to, however kindly meant, had helped at all. In fact, they'd implied something was wrong with her because she hadn't moved on the way others believed she should.

She had a tight-knit group of friends who'd remained blissfully silent except to listen to her and sympathize. Never suggesting how she should handle her sorrow. But there were plenty of others, causing her to narrow her world to a small group of people.

That was probably bad for her, but here she was, buried in work she loved with little spare time on her hands. Although when her mother was here, she had almost no choice about making the time.

She sighed, looking again at her favorite photos of Matt and smiling. He'd been wonderful. Oh, he had his faults like everyone, but she'd had hers, too. In her mind, however, he was as close to perfect as anyone could be.

She remembered the day she'd met him. Oh, she'd seen him around school, knew who he was. Conard City was small enough that no one could escape notice.

But that day, as she'd crossed the college campus in Laramie, he'd walked toward her in his ROTC uniform. A handsome figure, drawing her gaze. But then he'd stopped in front of her.

"Excuse me," he'd said politely. "You're Lynn West, aren't you? I'm Matt Macy."

She'd smiled. "I recognized you."

"Well," he said, taking a deep breath, "every time I see you, I want to date you. How about some coffee?"

Three months later they were engaged, and six months after that meeting on campus, they'd married.

Almost a fairy tale.

She cherished that memory, hugged it close to her heart. *Fated*, she often thought. For a while.

She didn't think she'd ever have that feeling again and wasn't at all sure she wanted to. Not all fairy tales had happy endings.

She turned her thoughts to Jax. A mystery, really. She knew almost nothing about his past except that he'd been reclusive. In fact, unlike a great many people she knew around here, she didn't know Jax at all.

Best to keep away, she told herself sternly. Wearing a uniform by itself didn't make him trustworthy. Neither did feeling a strong attraction to him.

She glanced at the clock on one of those bookshelves she'd been staring at and realized the afternoon was waning. Her mother had gone out with the express determination not to eat roast chicken tonight. Lordy, what might she have brought home?

Time to get down there again, face her demons and help deal with dinner. And maybe save Jax from the third degree.

NANCY HAD GONE all out. She smiled as Lynn entered the kitchen and said, "Wait until you see!"

Lynn braced herself. "Just tell me it's not raw oysters."

Nancy wrinkled her nose. "I know you hate them."

"Slimy and salty," Lynn agreed. "I'll leave them to those who like them."

"I'm sure they'll be grateful. No, I found some decent shrimp and I thawed them for shrimp cocktail. I *know* you like that."

"One of my favorites." Her mouth watered at the mere thought.

"Then, being in a mood, I got some frozen lobster tails and some fillets. Surf and turf tonight, my dear."

Lynn plopped down in a chair, astonished. "Wow," was all she could say. "Just wow. Can you afford it?"

"I have a healthy bank account these days. Lawyers are generous to paralegals. Which they should be, considering how many things we deal with for them. Halfway to lawyers ourselves. Anyway, I hope Jax doesn't have a seafood allergy." Now Nancy looked a trifle worried.

"Mom, he's a roomer, not a guest. He doesn't have to eat with us. Where is he?"

"Said he was going out to run, get rid of some excess energy. He must have a lot of it."

"Probably isn't used to being cooped up," Lynn remarked.

"Maybe not. Anyway, my dear daughter, tonight I cook and you relax."

Lynn grinned. "Sounds good to me."

MADGE WAS STILL angry about the brush-off she'd received from Jackson Stone. He'd been rude, overtly or not.

Worse, the sheriff had evidently thrown him into Lynn Macy's arms by putting him in Lynn's rooming house.

It was all too disgusting. Smarting, she planted herself in Mahoney's bar and drank perhaps too many daiquiris. She'd always loved frozen daiquiris. They went down so easily and smoothly, and Mahoney always made them the way she liked, with extra lime to give them a bite.

Well, there had to be a way to undermine Lynn before she and Jax really got together. It wasn't as if Lynn wasn't pretty enough, even though she didn't have Madge's endowments.

At some point, maybe during her fourth daiquiri, a man sat down beside her. She turned her head and saw Luke Macy.

"Guess you've been burned, too," Luke said.

"Whadya mean?"

"Lynn. Stone. But mostly Lynn."

"Yeah, she's too much. And *so* not feminine. I don't know what your brother ever saw in her."

Luke smiled charmingly. "Me neither. Cute, I guess, but that's it. Can you believe her depriving me of my inheritance?"

"Yeah. I can't believe that. What's wrong with a little sharing?"

"That was my thought. Not too much to ask. It was the Macy family home, after all."

"You got that right." Madge finished her daiquiri and tapped on the bar for another. Mahoney paused, then nodded. But first he drew some drafts for the other people.

"Let me get that for you," Luke said when Mahoney brought the drink, then looked at Mahoney. "Put Madge's drinks on my tab, and any more she has."

Mahoney rolled his eyes, as if that tab was getting too big, but said nothing.

"*Lynn* should be buying us drinks," Luke said as he took a pull on his own bottle of some fancy brand of beer.

"She ought to be doing more than that."

Luke raised a brow. "What did she do to make you so mad?"

"Jackson Stone," Madge answered. "He was mine and now he's at *her* house."

"I didn't know that," Luke remarked thoughtfully. After Madge had finished half her daiquiri, he spoke again.

"You know," he said slowly, "maybe if we pool our resources we can take care of both our problems."

Madge looked interested. "I'm listening."

NANCY'S INVITATION TO dinner was framed in a way that, short of an allergy, Jax couldn't refuse.

"I made something special for dinner tonight, Jax. And I bought enough for three. Surf and turf. I'd hate to waste any unless you're allergic to shellfish."

Lynn's cheeks heated. Her mother certainly had a talent for getting her way.

"I like shellfish," Jax answered, smiling faintly as he looked at Lynn and probably saw her heightened color.

Damn, she'd thought she'd gotten past the blushing stage years ago. Well, Nancy. 'Nuff said.

"How do you like your steak?" Nancy asked.

"Medium rare. I just need to wash up. Be right back."

Lynn wished her mother would let her help, even though surf and turf was an easy meal to put together. Her mom had already found her cast-iron grill, which would sear the meat perfectly.

But sitting there on her hands like a queen didn't suit her, and less so when she was irritated. Not because Jax would be joining them, but because her machinations must be apparent to Jax as well. A few more days of Nancy and he'd probably head for the hills.

If the sheriff let him anyway.

Before long, Nancy served the three of them a beautiful dinner. Drawn butter, too, although Lynn seldom bothered to clarify the butter on the rare occasion she treated herself to a lobster tail.

"This always used to be a favorite of Lynn's," Nancy said as she joined them at the table. Behind her, the counters and the stove looked as if a whirlwind had hit. Lynn wondered if her mother made such messes at home. And if she cleaned them up.

Nah, she probably ate a lot of her meals at restaurants.

So what had brought this on? The candles weren't on the table, so dinner couldn't have been intended to be romantic. Not that it could have been with her mother there.

Lynn gave up her irritating reflections and settled in to enjoy her meal. Her mom had been right—it was always one of her favorites and enjoyed so rarely. Maybe she was being unfair to Nancy, acting out of a reflex from over the years rather than this moment.

"It's perfect, Mom."

Jazz seconded her and Nancy beamed. "I'm not the best in the kitchen, but I do some things well."

Then she turned to Jax, diving in yet again to a clearly sensitive area. "I don't remember hearing much about your family while I lived here."

Jax's face stiffened. "Nothing worth telling. Ranch life is hard."

Nancy nodded as if she knew, when she'd never ranched a day in her life. "Hard on a boy, I imagine."

Jax didn't respond.

Lynn decided it was time to change the subject. "Still haven't heard anything from Adam or Jazz?"

He shook his head. "I guess they're having a great time."

Lynn smiled. "I certainly hope so."

Nancy spoke. "I don't think I ever met Jazz on one of my visits."

Lynn turned to her. "You met Lily, though."

"Oh, yes. And her darling daughter, Iris. And Jazz?"

"Lily's identical twin. Jazz came for a few weeks while Lily was working in Europe to keep an eye on Iris. That's when she and Adam met."

"Ooh, a fairy tale. I love those."

Jax took the wind out of Nancy's sails. "Very little is a fairy tale, Nancy. Those happen in books. And have you noticed how many of the old tales have unhappy endings? They were meant as lessons."

Nancy was taken aback. "I wasn't thinking of those, certainly."

"Of course not." Jax resumed eating while Lynn grinned inwardly. The man knew how to drag her mother back to reality.

Lynn spoke to prevent the silence from growing awkward. "I don't think some of those fairy tales should be read to children. I don't understand why people think fairy tales of that kind are meant for kids. They're folk tales intended for adults."

Jax nodded agreement.

Nancy delicately sliced a small piece from her steak. "A lot of them have been turned into children's books." She sounded defensive, a rarity.

"You're right, of course," Jax answered. "And probably softened by the storyteller and artist."

That certainly softened Nancy. She began smiling again.

The rest of the meal passed without any more uncomfortable moments. When they all professed themselves satisfied, there wasn't a morsel left.

"Compliments to the chef," Jax said with a smile.

"It was wonderful, Mom," Lynn agreed. "Now let me take care of the cleanup since you wouldn't let me help with the cooking."

That pleased Nancy. "Oh, good. My favorite TV show comes on in a half hour."

Nancy vanished into her own room and Lynn looked around the kitchen, her lips quirking. "I think she never heard of the chef's motto *clean as you go.*"

Jax laughed. "Likely not. Well, you're not alone with this."

They cleared together—then they followed their new routine of Lynn scraping, Jax washing and Lynn drying. Then he scrubbed all the pans, halting only when he came to the cast-iron grill. "Any special directions for this?"

"Scour only with water, heat dry on the stove, then lightly oil the surface."

Then it was all done, dishes dried and put away, the grill sitting on the stove top.

"Someday I'm going to have a built-in dishwasher," Lynn remarked.

"You'll have to tear this kitchen apart."

She laughed. "Exactly what I intend to do. Thanks for all your help."

"No thanks needed."

Then that moment happened again. That moment of hot connection as their eyes met. An instant when Lynn felt as if she were turning into syrup. His dark eyes seemed to blaze with a banked fire.

Oh, God, no. No.

He dragged his gaze away as if she had spoken aloud. "I wonder if the sheriff will let me go soon."

A warning? she wondered. To her horror, her heart sank. "You have to get back so soon?"

He nodded his head. "I'm taking over a new posting in Denver. I was planning to hunt for a place to live before I go on duty."

"Well, this must be bollixing things for you."

He shrugged a shoulder. "There *is* the internet. I need to go look online. Good night, Lynn."

Right after he headed upstairs, her boys came in, laughing and talking among themselves. She was grateful to hear them because there'd been an instant where this house had felt so empty.

"Hey, guys," she called and went out into the entry. "You know anything about a snake in my mailbox?"

Their eyes widened and they all shook their heads.

"What happened?" asked Barry. He was a handsome twenty-year-old with light brown hair and blue eyes.

"I went out to get the mail and was shocked to find a milk snake inside the box. Probably a prank, but I wondered…"

"Wondered if we'd prank you," said Tom. He was mostly identifiable by a large nose. "Nope. I don't think any of us would pull something like that. But we can ask around."

Lynn just shook her head. "There are plenty of younger people around here who *might* think it very funny. I didn't really believe it was any of you, but I thought I should ask."

They all nodded, then headed upstairs.

In spite of herself, Lynn felt a niggle of suspicion.

They had more cause to want to prank her than any other youngster around here.

But it seemed so unlike them.

As the night deepened and the streets emptied, Terri Albright walked around the town. This wasn't a place where she could blend in as a tourist, so she kept to the darkness, dressed in dark clothes but being careful not to look suspicious.

She was angry. Angry beyond words. She was going to kill Jackson Stone for what he had done to her brother. She could hardly wait for the moment and hoped she could do it at close range so she could see the light go out of his eyes.

But even as she relished the idea, she knew she had to be cautious. After Stone there were two more jurors, and she didn't want to make Stone's death so obvious that the entire Naval Criminal Investigative Service crashed down on the problem. Bad enough that her friends had mentioned there was already a quiet investigation.

She'd tutted along with all of them. How awful that anyone would want to kill men who'd only been doing their duty. Unbeknownst to her friends, she didn't think it awful at all.

What was worse was that she couldn't get to those nine men who'd testified against her brother. Too many. Eyes were apt to focus on her, but if she left those men alone she could still look innocent, for surely she would have gone for them. Right?

Instead, she'd have to be satisfied with watching their careers crash and burn. Rats, all of them. Violating the unwritten code on which so many lives depended.

But the jurors could have turned the outcome, and

for that she would never forgive them. They should have seen her brother for the honorable man he was, a man acting under the pressures of war. Doing things many others had done.

Anyway, she hated this damn town. It was too small to make her comfortable, too small to carry off the murder of Jackson Stone except in the most indirect way possible.

She'd hoped by setting that motel fire, she'd drive him on his way to his new posting in Denver. A larger city would make her mission easier. Safer.

Instead, he had planted here and was now living in a rooming house filled with other people. Harder to reach than at the motel.

Maybe if she'd set a bigger fire he'd be dead already, a clearly accidental death.

But she'd been focused on pushing him to Denver. She blamed herself for that slip. Poor planning, inexcusable in a Marine.

Okay, then. She'd messed up. She wasn't going to mess up again, however. Unless she saw an opportunity in this ink spot of a town, she'd have to wait for Denver.

A wait wouldn't be easy, though. She'd waited long enough already.

Chapter Eight

Three days later the cause of the motel fire still hadn't been discovered. Gage Dalton said the inspector was leaning toward arson but hadn't yet discovered the means.

Jax was stuck a little while longer. He chafed under the restriction, then wondered at himself. He was a Marine for Pete's sake, used to following orders, even ones to stay in place.

But this was different. When those orders came, he'd either been in a combat situation or otherwise occupied.

Point was, he'd been busy. Busy enough to make the hours pass. Here there was little of interest to preoccupy him. Moreover, since Hugh Briggs's call, he'd been forced to follow procedures for a threat he didn't honestly believe would reach for him here.

That chafed, too.

He needed to be working out, at least. He was avoiding open spaces that might make him an easier target, so that meant running up and down the streets of this small town.

A quiet town, except for a few brawls at Mahoney's. Folks here were pretty well rooted in their familiar lives. Good for them, not good for him. It made him wonder if recruiting would be a good fit for him. But at least then he'd be able to work out decently and frequently. At least he'd have a command to watch over again.

Right now he was rootless with nothing to do.

Well, except for Lynn and her mother. That Nancy West was something else. Her supposedly covert attempts to get him and Lynn together were fun to watch. He doubted she had any idea just how transparent she was. No, not likely or she wouldn't be doing it. And the way Lynn's eyes sparked or her jaw tightened... Well, Jax felt a lot of sympathy for her.

Lynn, though, was becoming a problem for him. The more he saw of her, the more he wanted her. Now, when he went to bed, he was acutely aware that she was one flight of steps away. Sleep eluded him because he couldn't help fantasizing.

God, he needed to break the back of this before he became addicted. She was a military widow, unlikely to want to become involved with a Marine. She was planted here in Matt's family home, on a mission of her own, a mission that demonstrated how deep her ties to her late husband remained.

Then there was himself. After the way he'd grown up, he couldn't trust himself. What if he carried the seeds of his father? What if somewhere deep inside him all that violence wanted to emerge?

He should stay away from the house more. Stay away from Lynn more. Except there was nothing in Conard City to keep him busy.

Well, she'd begun to tear down a whole lot of plaster and was about to begin pulling out the lath. Surely she'd want help with that, and it would give him a good chance to use muscles that ached for something, anything, heavy-duty to wear them out.

He'd probably sleep better at night, too.

Sighing, he shoved his thumbs into his jeans pockets and turned toward the rooming house. The autumn was steadily sliding into winter, more rapidly now, and the light jacket he wore over his sweatshirt wasn't quite warm enough.

Too bad. He'd experienced far worse cold in Afghanistan.

Since Jazz and Adam's wedding such a short time ago, leaves had been pulled by the wind from the trees, scattering them everywhere. A brightly colored path. Overhead, the remaining leaves still wore their autumn cloaks, but a lot of bare branches showed through now.

Before long the world would shift into browns and grays. Right now, the sky had the rest of the world beat with its gray layer of clouds.

Suited his mood anyway.

As he walked, he kept scanning rooftops and the taller green pines. Threat could come from anywhere, although the Marine in him suggested that it wouldn't be a gunshot. Not here, not in such a quiet place.

But he didn't know the mind of his enemy. Knew nothing at all about the person behind these murders, the person who even now might be coming for him.

If they were inexperienced in tactics, they might just try it, planning to escape fast. If they'd started that fire, they'd certainly not thought it through. As fast as that motel had gone up, they could have done a much more successful job of arson.

Not that he wouldn't have escaped anyway, unless smoke had overcome him in his sleep. Possible anyway.

He had serious doubts that the fire had been intended for him. On the other hand, who would have wanted to burn down that local landmark? Someone who thought they'd been overbilled?

He snorted. Nope, the other possibility was a firebug, but where were the other fires?

When he got back to the house, he heard pounding and crashing from the living room. Yup, Lynn was hard at it. He poked his head in past the plastic and saw her surrounded by pieces of plaster and a ton of plaster dust. She held a sledgehammer and took another swing. More plaster pieces, more dust. At least she was wearing a dust mask.

"Want any help?" he asked.

A lock of auburn hair had escaped her blue bandanna and, as she turned toward him, she brushed it back, smearing the side of her forehead with white dust.

"Anything you want to help with," she said from behind her mask. "There are extra masks in that box beside the door."

"Be right back." Then he paused. "You need a drink or some coffee? You can come out here and we can deal with that first."

"Right now I'd like a double shot of bourbon, neat." Then she laughed. "Sure. I'll wash up a bit at the sink."

He caught sight of her brushing as much dust as she could from her jeans and green plaid shirt.

Hopeless task, he thought with a smile as he headed to the kitchen. Nancy wasn't there. Well, she probably had more ways to occupy herself around here.

She had friends to visit. He didn't. The only statement he'd wanted to make had been at the wedding. Done. And despite Lynn's comment that a lot of people would want to claim friendship with him now, not a one had tried. He was still a stranger to them, drifting through.

Not that it much mattered to him one way or the other.

The coffee finished brewing just as Lynn entered the kitchen.

He eyed her. "You clean up well for a snowman."

She laughed. "I slapped myself with a few rags." She went to the sink and began washing her hands and forearms. "Man, this stuff gets yucky when it's wet."

"Got an alternative?"

She shook her head. "These clothes are going in the trash when I'm done, though. I don't want to clog up anything."

He poured two cups of coffee and placed them on the table. "Time for a break. Then I'll swing the hammer if you want. Or I'll start cleaning up."

"The cleanup's going to be a pain. I still can't believe there's no mold inside that wall. Talk about luck."

"I agree."

"But sadly that lath has to come out, too. I'm not even going to try to replaster the wall." She dried her hands and arms on paper towels and came to join him at the table.

"Where's your mom?" Jax asked.

"She said something about shopping." Lynn smiled. "I hope she goes to the grocery because I haven't spared a single thought about dinner."

"I can go to Maude's and pick up something," he volunteered.

"It may come to that." She shook her head. "I often don't think about these things when I'm in a mood to work."

"I can take care of myself, Lynn."

She eyed him with a faint smile. "I'm sure you can. But there's my mother."

"That woman is a trip. I'm enjoying her, though."

"Ahh," she said after taking a sip of coffee. "Ambrosia. Thanks for making it."

"Well, I wanted some, too," he answered, drawing a laugh from her. "It's grown a lot chillier out there."

"My cell phone was pleased to tell me we might see some flurries later. Jazz and Adam tied the knot just in time apparently."

"Well, they could have stood out there in a gentle snowfall, looking like something out of one of those globes."

She grinned. "It wouldn't have been as beautiful with everyone bundled up in coats."

"Currier and Ives?" he suggested.

"Hah! Listen, how about a sandwich? I just realized I haven't eaten since breakfast."

He rose at once. "I'll make them. Just point me and tell me what you like."

"I was thinking peanut butter."

"Can do. One or two for you?"

"One please. Bread in the breadbox over there."

LYNN WATCHED JAX as he made the sandwiches, thinking his every move suggested he was a man in excellent control of his body. Smooth and easy. Not the slightest misstep. No wasted motion. Impressive.

Well, everything about him was impressive. Matt had been impressive, too, but in a different way. It wasn't just the military bearing, or the comfort within his body, which both men shared. It had also been Matt's sense of humor, ever at the forefront and ready to burst out. He'd been the master of the non sequitur, among other things. And his puns!

Jax had a more somber mood. As if he had delved into some very dark places. But no, that couldn't be quite right, because Matt had delved into those same places when he'd been deployed.

She sighed and decided she'd better drop the comparison game. Different men, differently attractive. Different natures, different personalities.

But she'd loved Matt.

After they ate, she went to the sink to clean up and was suddenly speared by sorrow. *Matt.* For all she'd begun to collect the good memories of him and the grief struck less often, it still surged at times. At night she still sometimes cried herself to sleep. She still wished she could share this remodeling with him. Wished they could be building their dreams together.

Seldom, however, did grief pierce her like this, freezing her in place, filling her eyes with stinging tears, demanding its due. She gripped the edge of the sink, wishing she could shake free of her sorrow, at least briefly. She wasn't alone. Not a good time to break down. That was for her private moments.

But her chest tightened until she could barely breathe. Her throat hurt as if a wire wrapped tightly around it. The tears didn't spill but hung from her eyelashes until all she could see was a blur.

A gentle arm wrapped around her shoulders. Another slipped around her waist and turned her until Jax surrounded her in a warm embrace.

"It's okay," he murmured. "Just let it happen."

And it did. Wrenching sobs escaped her, the tears spilled in hot streams down her face and onto his shirt. His steely strength supported her, but softened enough to welcome her. Her fingers gripped his shirt, hanging on for dear life.

It seemed impossible that she would ever escape this wrenching, clawing feeling. That her insides would unknot and her chest loosen enough to breathe again. That life would ever feel normal again.

But as always, with the passing minutes, grief slowly released its hold. Setting her free. But for what?

Oh, God, she couldn't afford to think that way.

Sniffling away the last of her tears, she tried to step back, but Jax wouldn't let her go.

"Take it easy," he said quietly. "Just give yourself a few more minutes."

She lifted her face, tilting it back so she could dash the remaining tears from her eyes. "I've made you wet."

"I've been wetter."

"I don't usually cry all over people."

"Of course not. You're one hell of a brave, strong woman."

"Not at this minute," she said, her voice cracking from sobbing.

"This is a kind of strength, too. Being able to let it out."

"I've been getting better."

"I've noticed."

He felt so good against her, that hardened body, those strong arms. Suddenly, a spike of fear hit her. What the heck was she doing?

This time when she stepped back, he let her go, his arms dropping to his sides. His expression was grave, however.

"I need to get back to pulling that wall out," she said steadily, grabbing a paper towel and wiping her face. "God, I must look a fright."

"Not possible," he answered. "Let me take care of the lunch dishes and I'll join you in a few minutes."

Letting her flee toward some privacy.

Damn, how did a man like that grow so sensitive?

His childhood, she thought. Something in it had turned him into a total introvert, yet the man he'd become gave the lie to that being his nature.

Now the familiar questions whirled again in her mind as she picked up the sledgehammer and went back to work. What had created the kid he used to be and the man he was now? At the root of that change, there had to be something, a bridge between his past and his present.

She doubted she'd ever know.

On Saturday morning, Lynn's students, Barry, Tom and Will, went to the city basketball courts to play a little pickup. They couldn't do "shirts and skins" in this weather, so they dragged out some athletic wrap and wore neutral wrapped around their upper arms.

It was all going well until some of the gals, watching from the sidelines, said something that Barry didn't miss.

"That Lynn Macy. Who'd have thought?"

Curious, Barry wandered over, wiping sweat from his face with the arm of his blue fleece shirt that was blazoned with the college's white logo. "Hey," he said, sitting nearby and reaching for a bottle of the water the guys always brought with them.

He raised the bottle toward them as if in toast. "At least the water's not warming up in this weather. Next month it'll probably freeze."

The girls all smiled, and one said, "Well, there are indoor courts at the college."

"True, but they smell sweaty."

That sent the ladies off into peals of laughter.

Then one asked, "You live with Lynn Macy, don't you?"

Barry chose apparent disinterest as a better way to find out what was going on. "I *room* there, not live." He didn't question them about why they asked.

"Well, now she's got that guy living there. The Marine."

"He's a roomer, too." And where was this leading? Barry liked Lynn a whole lot, and the way these gals were giggling, he suspected he was going to get angry if he found out what was behind their amusement.

He took a long swig of water, needing the hydration, but wishing it were hot chocolate. Then he looked at the women. "You got a thing for that Marine?"

"Who wouldn't?" one of them sighed.

Their hair almost looked like a rainbow, one blonde, one ginger, one dark. The one with the dark hair sported blue streaks. He kinda liked the ginger hair, though, and she was the one doing almost all the talking. He offered her his best smile. "If you're looking for an introduction," he said, "I'm not sure I can make one. I barely know the guy. Keeps pretty much to himself."

"Except with Lynn Macy," Ginger said, clearly enjoying herself.

Barry wondered how to wade into the matter without making them clam up. He had the strongest feeling he needed to know what they were talking about. And he doubted he was going to like it.

Barry managed to shrug. "He's only been in town a week, planning to leave any day from what I hear."

Blue-streaks just looked amused. Blondie giggled. Ginger sniffed. "Doesn't matter," she said. "That Lynn is a fast one."

Barry's insides coiled tight, but he achieved a friendly but slightly bored tone. "How do you mean?"

"You mean you haven't heard?" Ginger looked amazed.

"Hey, I'm a guy, what can I say?"

That brought knowing grins to three faces. Ginger turned to the two others, then said, "He's living with her. He deserves to know."

Barry looked from one face to another. Question time, he decided. They all now looked as if they could barely contain themselves. "What should I know?"

Ginger couldn't contain the news any longer. "That nearly every time Lynn Macy left town to go visit her *husband* she was actually meeting someone else. Maybe that Marine."

"Huh?" Barry was stunned to his very core. "How do you know that?"

Ginger waved a hand. "Everyone knows. Except you, I guess. Anyway, kinda interesting that guy moved in with her so fast."

Barry couldn't stop himself. "The motel burned down."

"And there are apartments near the college and a couple of other rooming houses. No reason he had to stay with *her*. Or for this long. He could have left right after the wedding."

Oh, my God, Barry thought. Innocent things all tangled up into a story that sounded plausible.

Except he knew Lynn. And he was getting to know that straight-arrow military guy just a bit. What's more, for the love of Pete, Lynn's *mother* was staying there. Talk about a chaperone!

"Well, that's interesting," was all he said. He drained the plastic water bottle and crushed it in his hand before dunking it straight in the recycling bin nearby. He rose, grabbing his sports bag, seeming to forget the girls.

"Guys?" he called to the other players. "I'm headed back. Calc test Monday morning."

They waved to him and he turned, marching straight back to the rooming house. He was sure he couldn't tell Lynn about this. It would only upset her, and that lady had been upset enough since her husband died, as well he should know since this was his second year rooming with her. Anyway, there wasn't a thing she could do about it.

For once in his life, Shakespeare suddenly struck Barry as a smart guy. *Methinks the lady doth protest too much.* Nope, nobody would care what Lynn said about this and might think she was telling an even bigger lie.

Barry clenched his jaw. He needed to find a way to spike this rumor. Fast. But he had no idea in hell how.

Chapter Nine

Saturday afternoon, the rental car company pulled up with a new vehicle for Jax. It had taken a while, but the delivery driver apologized, saying something about needing the police report and whatever.

Yeah, they'd held off until they were sure that Jax hadn't started the fire that had totaled their car. Evidently the sheriff had made the decision about Jax. Which meant Jax was free, although he'd have felt better if Dalton had said so himself.

He also wanted to know what they'd learned about the arson. It had struck close enough to home that he felt he deserved something of an after-action report.

Then Brigg's warning flashed through his mind again. Jax shook his head. He hoped any Marine would do a better job than that fire of taking out a target.

Standing on the sidewalk, keys in hand, he looked at that Jeep and realized he could now just drive out of town. Get on with his plan to find a place of his own in Denver before he returned to duty.

But matters had changed. Suddenly, he wasn't in a hurry to begin this new phase of his life. Instead, he wanted to stay right here.

Lynn. She was the reason, of course. Nothing else on

his plate seemed quite as important. That was so ridiculous he wanted to shake the feeling out of himself.

What the hell was happening to him? How had he invested so much in such a short time? There wasn't anything to invest in anyway. She was a grieving widow. He was moving on, always moving on, and she was planted here in the garden of her friends and everything familiar.

Besides, he kept a better guard on his heart than this. From his very early years he'd learned not to care too much too easily. His heart wore armor for good reason, and it took one hell of a lot to penetrate that armor.

The closer you let people get, the more likely you were to get hurt. Jax was very careful about who he let close, who he trusted. Only a very few had jumped those hurdles quickly. Lynn seemed to be one of them.

So it was time to pack his duffel and take this car on the road to Denver. Before he could hurt her.

But deep in his soul that fear had taken root. He could hurt Lynn, maybe without even meaning to, but he might. That woman had had enough sorrow in her life and she didn't deserve any more. Or to feel used. Or soiled.

That word brought up a sudden unwelcome memory of his father waving a Bible at him and his mother on Sunday morning. Ranting and yelling and reading verses that petrified a young boy. The Stone family might not be churchgoers, but they had their own private congregation headed by Pastor Samuel Stone, a man who shouted fire and brimstone threats of hell.

To Jax all these years later, it seemed his father had used the Bible to justify himself and his actions. It certainly hadn't been intended to improve his wife and son, both of whom had an intimate acquaintance with the "wages of sin," thanks to Samuel Stone. No, it was the way Samuel had justified himself as moral judge, jury and executioner.

Even though Jax had eventually learned that his father's Bible readings had been selective to the extreme, the knowledge hadn't erased all of the effects.

What had he hoped to find in this town anyway? Absolution for the sins he'd apparently committed as a child? Well, if his father had condemned him to hell—and he had when Jackson finally stood up to him—then Jax had gone to hell all right: to war.

Jax returned to the present, a chill like wet leaves on his shoulders. The past? The present? If Briggs were to be believed, he might be stalked. Maybe he should spend more time thinking about that. Apply a little strategic thinking to the possible tactics of the person who wanted him dead.

If that person did. It *could* all be coincidence.

But some battle-hardened sense deep within wouldn't let him accept that. He scanned the rooftops once again, made sure the Jeep was locked, then returned to the house. If Lynn was still banging and prying, she could use help.

At least that was something he could do that would matter.

BUT LYNN HAD showered while he was taking care of paperwork on the new car, and now sat in the kitchen, wrapped in a green robe, wearing fuzzy slippers, with a towel wrapped around her head. She had her hands wrapped around a mug and the room was redolent with coffee.

"Fresh," she said, pointing at the pot.

"Thanks." Jax helped himself, wishing that chill on

his shoulders would vanish. Every time he'd felt it before, it had boded no good. "Finished working for the day?"

"There are times," she said wryly, "when the body says *that's enough*, and I've learned to listen."

"Always a good decision." He sat across from her, studying her lovely face. A beautiful woman in a gentle way. "As you know I now have wheels. I wonder if Gage Dalton isn't as interested in me hanging around town. He hasn't said."

He thought he saw her start, then still, but it was so brief he couldn't be sure. After a moment, she lifted her mug to her lips.

"Good news for you."

"Possibly."

Her green gaze trailed to him. "Why wouldn't it be good? Nobody likes to feel they've lost their freedom for any reason."

"Well, that part's okay." Except he'd begun to like the excuse that kept him in this house. He'd stopped chafing within two days. "Where's Nancy?"

"My mom's always been something of a gadabout. I wonder she can sit still long enough to hold a job, even a part-time one."

Jax laughed. "You seemed to have inherited the gene. She's out all the time entertaining herself, and you spend all your time in here pursuing your remodeling."

That drew a smile from Lynn. "You're probably right. Anyway, she called about an hour ago, said she was going to the market. I wonder what meal she's planning."

"I guess we'll find out. I gather she doesn't approve of what your boys are eating."

Lynn wrinkled her nose. "I'm surprised she hasn't hog-tied them and forced broccoli down their throats."

"There are other veggies."

"Sure, if they top a pizza."

Jax grinned. "Do I hear the Freshman Twenty coming?" He referred to the weight gain many students made in college.

Lynn shook her head. "They play too much basketball. Pickup games. This is Barry's second year with me, and occasionally they forget I'm old and talk to me. Really. We've even played Spades a few times, old-fashioned as it is."

He pretended amazement. "You actually have a deck of *real* cards?"

"Several. Sometimes my friends and I get together for a cutthroat game of Hold 'Em."

"Now that I'd like to see. I'm a Seven Card Stud guy."

"Let's give it a try sometime." Then her face shadowed and she looked away.

Jax figured she had just realized there was no point in long-term planning. She understood that clearly enough, which made him feel…what? Disappointment? Relief? Damned if he knew.

Nancy took that opportune moment to open the front door. "Lynn? Jax? Help with the groceries?"

Lynn rolled her eyes as she started to rise. "I wonder if she bought out half the store."

"I'll help her," Jax said. "You just rest. You've earned it."

There *were* a lot of bags, Jax realized as he reached the trunk of Nancy's car. "You planning to feed an army?"

She shook her head. "Lynn is too low on staples. I'll bet when I'm not here she resorts to frozen meals." She raised an eyebrow at him. "I'd almost bet all those toaster waffles don't belong to her roomers."

"I'll get these," Jax said. "You just go inside and get warm."

Nancy beamed at him. "You're such a nice young man."

Nancy sailed away, her faux fur coat flapping a bit to reveal that today her color of choice was that dark pink, whatever it was called.

Fascinating woman, he thought as he bent to grab bags. Although not as fascinating as her daughter. However dressed up, Nancy couldn't hold a candle to her daughter in jeans and work shirts.

MADGE WAS WELL pleased when the rumor returned to her. In the way of rumors, it made the circuit more than once. Nobody remembered where it had begun, but it got embellished along the way. Her simple supposition, phrased as a question and dropped in a couple of ears, had grown into a full-blown tale with convincing details.

Better than she had imagined. Much better. Just let Lynn try to quash this one. It would be like trying to shake horse manure from her shoes.

Quite happy with herself, she arranged to meet Luke at a roadhouse twenty-five miles deep into ranch country, a place favored by hired hands and ranchers who didn't have time to drive to town for a few too many beers or hard liquor.

Wearing a tight hot pink dress, with just enough cleavage on display for when she took off her jacket, she set out.

Country music played from a jukebox. The barroom was a mix of scarred old tables, creaky chairs and a floor covered with peanut shells. Easier to clean up the spills that way. The bar itself was at least a hundred years old, boasting a real brass footrail that occasionally got polished. Food was limited to things that came out of bags and boxes, all of it salty to encourage drinking.

Not a family in sight. Hardly a woman either, which made Madge the cynosure of all eyes. Fine by her. She enjoyed being admired.

She sat at the bar, her purse and jacket on a stool beside her, and waited for Luke, ordering a beer of her own. It wouldn't be long before somebody sashayed over to offer to buy her a drink, so she hoped Luke wasn't too late. In the ordinary way, she'd have gladly taken the offer of that drink, but not tonight. She didn't want anything to interfere with her talking to Luke.

He showed up maybe ten minutes later, just about the time one of those rangy cowboys, one who hadn't been able to take his eyes off her, appeared to be about to get up. Luke slid onto the stool beside her and smiled.

Man, Madge thought, he had that boyish appeal all sewed up. And she'd trust him about as far as a coiled rattler.

She waited until his beer arrived, then gave him her biggest, most flirtatious smile. Not that she wanted to flirt with him, but she could match his con man smile. "So you heard the rumor I started? It was brilliant, especially the way it took off."

"Genius." He nodded. "Pure genius."

Madge preened. "I'm good."

His blue eyes drifted to her cleavage, then rose again to her face. "Lynn will never shake that."

"And when Jackson Stone hears that she cheated on her husband, he's not going to want to touch her. Maybe he'll even get upset."

"And you'll be a friendly shoulder for him to cry on."

"That's the plan."

Luke shook his head a little. "Come on, Madge, we've known Jackson since he was a kid. He's not one to cry on a shoulder. Maybe less now than ever."

She bristled. "How would you know? He's not the same guy."

"No, now he's hard."

She frowned, tapping her fingernails on the bar, annoyed, but afraid Luke might be right.

Luke soothed her. "Whether he wants a shoulder or not, he won't want Lynn after this rumor gets to him. And you just be there, all pretty and nice like you are."

Well, looks and pretended sweetness had caught her a few husbands, but those marriages hadn't lasted any longer than it took for her patience to wear off. God, guys could be such saps. If they wanted a cook and a maid, they needed to look at someone else.

Luke spoke again. "Now we need to get that rumor into Stone's ear. The problem is I don't think people around here know him well enough to share the grapevine with him."

"It'll get to him because someone will feel they need to warn him that Lynn's a cheater."

Luke turned his frosty beer bottle around a couple of times before lifting it and drinking half of it. "You might be right."

"Of course I'm right," she retorted waspishly. "I told you I could get this whole thing going and you didn't believe me."

"I underestimated you."

That smoothed her ruffled feathers. She raised a finger for another beer, wishing this roadhouse could make something as simple as a daiquiri. Oh, well, she could make one for herself when she got home.

"Now," she said, turning to Luke. "What are *you* going to do?"

"Why, my dear, I'm going to get Stone into some trouble."

"How in the hell are you going to do that?"

"You heard why he's been hanging around, haven't you?"

She shook her head as her curiosity spiked.

"The motel was arson."

"I know that," Madge said impatiently. "So?"

"The sheriff asked him to stay in town. Like he was under suspicion."

Madge shook her head violently. "That's gonna help how?"

"Well," he said quietly, "he was staying at the motel when the fire broke out."

Her eyes widened and she drew a sharp breath. "You're not gonna burn down that house!"

"No, but a little fire will do. Just a little one. Like he's a firebug. How do you think that'll make Lynn feel about him?"

Madge took a long time to think about it, maybe because the daiquiris she'd had at home plus the beer was starting to slow her head down.

Then a grin spread across her face. "I'm not the only genius, Luke."

"Reckon not," he replied, raising his bottle to her and winking. "Reckon not."

TERRI ALBRIGHT'S FRUSTRATION was growing rapidly. Several times a day she had to remind herself that she was on a mission, and missions often required patience.

But this was outside of enough. Hands tied because

this town was too small, and that damn Stone seemed disinclined to head for the wide-open spaces. Must be that woman he was staying with. He must be preoccupied with her.

Great. Just great.

Whatever she did, it was going to have to be fast and permanent. Something that would give her just enough time to get the hell out.

The problem was that she hadn't yet seen an opportunity. Shooting was out of the question while he was in town. That would draw immediate attention, and as tight as this little burg was, someone would be able to point out where the shot had come from. Could she get out of town fast enough after that?

She had good reason to doubt it. And she'd stand out as the stranger. Might as well wear a neon sign. Two bottles of spray purple dye sat on the ground beside her. She was thinking they'd make her look more like a young girl, but she hadn't decided to use them unless she needed to be seen.

She had a seven-inch KA-BAR sheathed on her belt and figured that would have to be her tool if Stone didn't leave soon for Denver. She'd find him soon enough in a big city like that, even if she had to wait until he returned to duty. Because once he showed up there, his privacy would be shot.

But what was killing her now was that she couldn't do a damn thing. Stuck in the mud. Hoping she could take care of Stone because her leave was ticking away. She'd have to return to duty, Stone would be headed for Denver and once she was back on duty, she wouldn't be able to reach him until her next opportunity to take leave.

Rolling over in her sleeping bag, staring up at a sky

that looked as if handfuls of diamonds had been strewn across it, she ignored the cold. She had to find a way. Even here.

Problem was, her role in uniform had never included making plans. She just followed orders. Others made the plans. Her brother Ted would have been better at figuring this out. More experience.

That chafed her sometimes. She was always the little sister, and then the junior rank. Regardless, those petty resentments weren't going to stop her from avenging him.

In the distance, she heard a wolf's mournful howl, soon joined by the harmonizing voices of the pack.

Terri wished she could howl along with them.

Lʏɴɴ's ᴘᴀɴᴛʀʏ ᴡᴀs full now with "staples." Canned goods, jarred goods, dry goods, even stuff in a set of canisters Nancy had bought.

"Mom," Lynn said, "I'm never going to use all that."

"If you *ever* decide to cook for yourself, you don't want to be out of some little thing that you absolutely must have."

Lynn eyed her with amusement. "Seriously."

"I know what I'm talking about."

Lynn wasn't going to argue a truth that her mother believed.

Dinner was late as a result. Night had settled over the world as she served up a beef roast along with mashed potatoes, gravy and asparagus. Lynn loved asparagus.

Jax had agreed to join them, but Lynn was beginning to feel as if he were family and ought to come without an invitation.

Still, Nancy insisted on inviting him, this time by assuring him that she and Lynn couldn't eat all that food and she didn't want to start filling the refrigerator with leftovers. "If we keep that up, the boys won't have any room."

Hah, thought Lynn. They didn't use a whole lot of that space. In fact, they lately hadn't even been making their toaster pastries in the morning. Maybe because Nancy occupied the kitchen like a broody hen?

She also had no idea how long Nancy intended to visit. Her mother hadn't mentioned and it would be rude to ask, a rudeness that Nancy wouldn't overlook.

Still, the boys had kitchen privileges in this house and Nancy had thoughtlessly taken over. But it wasn't as if there was a living room to sit in.

Dang it all, Lynn thought.

Over dinner, Lynn decided to take one bull by the horns. "Mom?"

"Yes?"

Jax continued eating, clearly removing himself from this conversation.

"In the mornings, why don't you take your tea into your room and watch those morning shows you always loved."

"Why would I want to do that? I don't watch them anymore anyway. The news is just too awful. Did you know my therapist told me to stop watching it because there was nothing I could do about most of it? He said it only depressed me and made me feel helpless."

"Your *therapist*?" That floored Lynn.

"Didn't I tell you? The nicest woman. I've been feeling a tad depressed. Not seriously, mind you, but I have. She's a wonderful help. Anyway, no news."

"There must be something…"

"The weather?" Nancy asked drily. "Lynn, what's going on?"

Lynn put her fork down, sighing. She felt that Jax was paying attention, though he revealed it in no way. He simply scooped up another mouthful of mashed potatoes.

"It's my boys," Lynn said after a moment. "They haven't said a word, but I've noticed they don't pop into the kitchen anymore for their breakfasts."

"Because of me?" Nancy sounded incensed.

"Probably," Lynn said frankly. "Not because of anything you're doing, but likely because you're an older woman. You know how kids are. Uncomfortable with older adults."

"Well, really!"

"They have kitchen privileges, Mom. Can you take your tea and a book or whatever, and give them time to pop in and eat?"

"I could cook for them," Nancy suggested.

"I'm sure that would make them even more uncomfortable, Mom."

"So those boys come before me. I'll try not to get in their way. And I'll consider myself confined to my room." Nancy rose and threw her napkin on the table, then walked out.

"That went well," Lynn muttered to no one in particular. Although "no one" was sitting at the table.

"It appears that fences will need mending," Jax remarked quietly.

"Obviously," Lynn answered. "Obviously. But those boys don't deserve to feel unwelcome down here. I don't want that."

"I don't think she's exactly making them unwelcome."

"No, but she's always in here except when she's out to see friends. They must feel like they're trespassing now."

"Why don't you talk to them?" Jax suggested as he finished his potatoes. "Tell them they're welcome whether Nancy's in here or not. Just like before."

Lynn put her chin in her hand and nodded. "I should. Thanks. I just didn't want to put them on the spot." She sighed again. "So I put my mother on the spot. Great job, Lynn."

She ruminated for a minute, wondering how she could have handled this better. It was even more difficult because she didn't know how long Nancy was staying. She couldn't go to her boys and tell them it would only be another week.

If only she had another habitable room down here besides the kitchen. But she didn't, and now her mom was feeling confined to quarters. Sadness filled her. She hated the idea that she'd hurt Nancy. Much as they could ruffle each other's feathers, she loved her mom.

Finally, she spoke. "I wish I had more room down here."

"But you're in the middle of renovations."

"True." Lynn felt her mouth quirk. "I suppose I should be glad I didn't get started on *her* room. I don't know what I'd have done. Especially since she can't climb stairs."

But now she had a mess of a different kind to clean up. Oh, boy.

UPSTAIRS, AS THE evening deepened, Barry, Will and Tom gathered in Barry's room at his invitation.

On Barry's desk—an old table, really—sat two extra large monitors, a high-powered computer and all a guy could need for online role-playing games, one of their passions. It was hard sometimes to keep his mind on schoolwork, but he was determined.

Several opened bags of chips sat on a smaller table along with soft drinks in their cans. Tom and Will busily munched while Barry related what he'd heard that morning.

The munching slowed, then stopped.

Will was the first to react. "You gotta be kidding me! *Lynn?*"

"That's what they're saying."

"Sheesh," said Tom, who was going prematurely bald. He'd started shaving his head just a month ago. The girls seemed to like it.

"I have a stronger word," Will offered.

Barry snickered. "Have at it. We've all used it."

But none of them did.

For a while, they were silent, but slowly Tom started chomping chips again, almost violently. "Damn," he said forcefully, a few crumbs dribbling onto his sweatshirt. "That's…that's…"

Barry filled it in. "Awful. Terrible. I can't think of enough words."

"Well, hell," Will muttered. "Can you believe people?"

"Oh, they've really woven this one into a good story."

Tom shook his head. "I can't believe it. How could anyone?"

"Juices up their lives, I guess," Barry said. "Little enough happens around here. Why not have a good scandal?"

"There's nothing good about this one," Tom growled. "How could anyone believe she had a thing going with Jax before, when her husband was still alive? Is that why he took over two years to get here? And why did he book into that motel anyway, if that's true."

"And just look at the two of them," Barry agreed. "They're a bit skittish around each other. Careful. I've seen how they gaze at each other a couple of times, but you can tell it hasn't gone beyond looks. They don't have that kind of...whatever. There's nothing there. Yet."

"What would be wrong with it if there was?" Will demanded. "Doesn't she deserve some happiness?"

"I've heard her crying up there sometimes at night," Barry offered. "It's quiet, but I hear it. She's not over her husband. She cries less than last year, but it's still happened a couple of times."

Silence fell again, except that it was punctuated by guzzling soda and the occasional rustle of chip bags. Will reached over and pulled another can from the cooler bag they used up here. Lynn was nice about letting them stash cold packs in her fridge.

"I don't like going in the kitchen with her mom there," Tom remarked. "She always wants to talk. I bet she thinks she's being nice, but she always gets around to stupid questions like what am I majoring in and what do I want to do and am I going to a four-year school from here. It's like I'm a little kid again."

"Yeah. What do you want to grow up to be?" Barry snickered again.

A few minutes later, Will asked, "Do you think that snake in the mailbox was part of this?"

Barry shrugged. "I don't know when the gossip started. Could've been a prank, not a message."

"Nasty prank," was Tom's opinion. "I can't imagine how she felt when she opened that box and saw that snake. I'd be shocked, and I'm not afraid of snakes."

"Except the poisonous kind," Tom said knowingly.

"I have a brain. Unlike some people."

3

Barry thought the two of them were about to get into a pillow fight, so he spoke quickly. "We gotta find a way to help Lynn."

Two pairs of eyes met his. Then Will asked the all-important question.

"How can we do that?"

LYNN HEADED FOR her mother's bedroom a short time later. Time to mend fences somehow, although Nancy could remain in high dudgeon for a long time.

Except she feared that this time she hadn't made her mother angry, but instead had hurt her. She never wanted to do that. They might prickle each other, get tart, or indulge in small arguments, but this was different.

This time she'd told her mother to make herself scarce. Never mind that that hadn't been her intention. The road to hell and all that.

She knocked on Nancy's door. When her mother didn't answer, Lynn entered anyway. Her mom sat stiffly in the upholstered chair beside the bed.

"I'll leave in the morning," Nancy said, an edge in her voice.

"Mom, no! That's not at all what I meant!" She closed the door behind her.

"Well, I'm obviously discommoding your roomers."

"Not that much. I just noticed they were behaving differently and I felt bad about it."

Nancy finally looked at her. "Maybe I should pay rent. It would make me equal."

"Oh, God." Lynn sat on the edge of the bed and stared at the woman she'd loved her entire life. Her heart began to ache. "I went about this all wrong. I didn't mean to make you feel this way. I should have spoken to the boys."

"Water over the dam," was Nancy's only response.

Lynn sat quietly, wondering what she could do. "I was wrong. I apologize. Try to forget what I said."

Nancy sniffed.

Then something rose in Lynn, born in a bottomless pit of grief, propelled by all the stresses in her life now and her constant need to cope with a million things all by herself. Suddenly she was through coping.

She stood up. "I've got enough on my plate, Mom. I can't do this. I can't handle one more damn thing. You decide whether to accept my apology. I can't worry about this, too!"

Then she stormed from the room and had to stop herself from slamming the door.

She fled from it all to her attic aerie where nothing could touch her. Nothing. Her private hermitage where she left the world behind.

She was unaware that Jax, standing in his bedroom door, saw her run. Unaware that his face darkened and his hands clenched.

LATER, AFTER HAVING done countless push-ups, sit-ups, knee bends, twists and whatever else he could fit into that small room, Jax washed up in the empty group bathroom.

Then he cleaned the tub and sink. The boys weren't bad about it, but sometimes the spit and polish in him took over. Satisfied not even a drop of toothpaste remained on the sink or floor, that everything gleamed as much as such old fixtures could, he headed downstairs.

Nancy was in the kitchen, sipping tea. At least she'd emerged from her self-imposed isolation. He suspected she'd taken her anger out on Lynn, which was why Lynn had vanished to her apartment.

Other than giving her a brief acknowledgment, he started making coffee. He wasn't happy with Nancy just then. Not when she'd clearly upset Lynn that much.

Nancy spoke just as he turned from the pot and tried to decide whether to sit at the table or take a mug upstairs.

"I acted badly," Nancy said. "I acted like a child, going to my room to pout."

He leaned back against the counter, folding his arms. "I'm not the one who needs to hear that."

"But I can't climb those damn stairs to tell her."

"Then it'll have to wait, I guess."

"Could you…"

Jax shook his head. "This is between the two of you, and I'm not getting in the middle. Anyway, she needs to hear that from you, not me."

Nancy sighed and sipped tea. "I guess you're right." Then, "I suppose it's Lynn's turn to pout in her room."

"I very much doubt she's pouting."

"Then what's she doing, hiding away?"

This really wasn't his place, but he poured some coffee, then sat at the table. "I don't know Lynn very well."

Nancy looked at him. "I feel like I hardly know her myself anymore."

"What she's been through…well, it changes a person. Forever. She's been to hell and isn't quite all the way back. She's working on it, though."

"That's why she's keeping so busy on this house. Hiding."

Jax shook his head. "It may have started that way, but that's not it anymore. She loves what she's doing. She's doing it for *herself*. But it's a big job and, apart from the pleasure and sense of achievement she gets, she's got a lot of worries about it. Puzzle pieces to be balanced against money and time and priority. Every day has her head whirling about this project. I'm surprised she's not wiped out, honestly. It's a hell of a lot for one person to take on solo. But she's doing a great job of it."

"So maybe she's up there collapsed," Nancy remarked.

"Or just out of steam. Needing a break. I mean, not only is she handling massive renovations, but she has a houseful of people. The boys, me."

"And me," Nancy added.

"Bursting at the seams," he agreed. "Give her some time. She's not a woman to take anything lying down. She'll get back on her feet soon."

At two in the morning, Terri Albright looked up at the house where Jax was staying now. She'd heard he was already under suspicion for her little arson. What if she added to that suspicion? Except they'd probably arrest him and she wouldn't be able to get at him at all.

She ground her teeth, frustrated beyond words while wondering when she'd hear that third juror had keeled over. Too long. It had been too long since she'd left the poison in his stash of soft drinks.

She also didn't have an endless amount of time for leave. She'd have to report or go AWOL, which wouldn't help anything at all.

Hatred filled her, scorching her insides and never quitting. She didn't want to put off getting this Stone guy, although she supposed she could. Go back and get that last juror first.

But with each move, she made it more likely that the current investigation would grow broader and more intense. Making everything more difficult.

No, better to take care of this guy here. In a place where he should be hard to find so it might not be linked to the others. She'd had to access protected personnel information to find out this much.

So it might appear unrelated if she killed him here. It might look like there'd been a fight and he'd gotten the worst of it. As little as she knew about people around here, she knew there were some heavy drinkers and brawlers, especially out at the roadhouses.

If she could lure him to one of those… Or maybe she could get him somewhere else and dispose of him there.

Yeah, that was a possibility.

At last feeling she might be getting a handle on this problem, she turned and slunk away into the shadows.

Ted was going to be so proud of her when she finished. She knew he would.

Chapter Ten

Sunday morning dawned with storms. Heavy rumbles of thunder rolled across the city and surrounding ranches. The last leaves were torn from trees, leaving only slender-needled evergreens alone.

By 10:00 a.m. it looked as if winter's breath was finally blowing across the land. The world had turned gray and stark.

So far, Jax hadn't seen Lynn and supposed that she and her mother hadn't made up yet.

Dang! Those two women were close. Even he could see that. But he didn't think that Nancy was considering all that Lynn had been through.

She'd certainly been through a lot, but she'd picked herself up and had taken on a huge task with evident skill and with a heavy dose of determination. He admired her more with each passing day.

And wanted her more.

The car keys he now possessed sat on the small battered dresser, taunting him with his original plans, taunting him with his unwillingness to leave this town he'd hated so much in his youth.

He'd attended schools here, always feeling like a kid

outside the window of a candy store, a place he lacked the coinage to enter.

Always the outsider, with the ugliness in his home holding him prisoner. A prisoner of silence because he didn't want anyone to know what was happening. He was ashamed, and even more ashamed on his mother's behalf. She guarded the secret of their painful life as tightly as he did, and he sure as hell hadn't wanted her to get into any more trouble with Samuel.

Although trouble waited around every corner for her. And for him, too. A shameful existence, the shame compounded by Samuel's hellfire sermons directed at making both of them feel like sinners.

And at school he'd seen kids who didn't have problems like his. At least none that showed. The others knew how to exit the prisons of silence, if they were there. Knew how to reach out and make friends with kids.

All he'd had was Adam. Thank God for Adam. He had never known if Adam had suspected the state of Jax's homelife, but his friendship had been steadfast. His military career had proven Adam's quality time and again.

For Jax the military had been an escape. At first anyway. Then as he settled into the Marines, he'd discovered a world that matched his needs and a sense of mission that made him feel whole again. Pride had been discovered, as well as his ability to deal with the worst of situations. A whole new way of looking at himself and the world.

He sighed, looking at those keys, and wondered when Lynn and her mother would sort out all of this. He could understand both sides of this problem. Lynn, probably feeling overwhelmed, had tried to make one little thing right.

Instead, she'd apparently gone about it the wrong way.

But Nancy's response had been wrong, too. Instead of going to her room in a huff, she should have discussed the problem in more depth.

Even during his short time as a roomer here, he'd felt the reluctance of the students to barge into a kitchen that was almost always occupied. Maybe he himself was adding to their hesitancy.

But after all his years dealing with young people their age, he understood it. He recognized it. Young people on the cusp of becoming adults were often intimidated by the older adults they'd been taught to respect and to keep quiet around.

None of that kept them from antics or hijinks typical of their age. Not until they understood the seriousness of what was required of them, the knowledge of the importance of their duties. Only then did they begin to slip into the shoes of confident, capable adults.

Regardless, there had to have been a better way to deal with the situation. Maybe this time Lynn had misjudged her mother.

Jax certainly had. He'd thought Nancy feisty enough to withstand such a suggestion. Maybe there were several reasons she was getting therapy.

He shook his head, wondering why he was maundering his way through all of this. Was he bored or something? Or was he being drawn into all this drama? There seemed to be enough of it to go around.

All his new clothes needed a trip through Lynn's washer, so he donned his cammo, belted it and headed downstairs, thinking that he ought to head for Maude's diner to get breakfast. Maybe bring back breakfast to the house.

Except he had no idea whether the two women would emerge from their separate corners to eat.

This would have been amusing had he not come to care so much for Lynn's feelings.

As he emerged from his room, he heard the three young men talking in one of the other bedrooms. Making up his mind, he knocked on the door.

Barry opened it after a short pause. "Hey," he said.

"Hey," Jax replied. "Listen, I'm thinking of going to Maude's to pick up breakfast. Any of you interested?"

"In going to Maude's?" Barry asked.

"Either that, or I'll bring back for everyone."

Barry lifted his brows. "You have any idea how much we can eat?"

Jax answered wryly. "You better believe it. I command units full of guys your age."

That made Barry grin.

"So give me your orders or tag along. My treat, your choice."

The boys decided not to tag along. Calculus test in the morning. Jax was looking forward to taking his new car out for a spin and planned to double all their orders for fried potatoes, flapjacks and more, and even some lattes.

Step in the right direction, he thought.

Neither Lynn nor Nancy were in sight as he passed the kitchen, but he decided to bring breakfast home for them anyway. If they didn't want to eat, the boys would probably scarf theirs down as well.

And he was damn well going to make sure *all* of them ate in the kitchen. Make a point.

He arrived at Maude's before the after-church crowd had taken over, and while Mavis raised her brows at the size of his order, she and her mother set to work immediately. By the time Jax left, he had six bags full of food and two trays of lattes.

It might be enough. He almost laughed aloud.

Back at the house, he discovered Lynn in the kitchen. She looked worn-out. *Bad night*, he guessed. And no sign of Nancy.

Lynn's weary eyes widened as he brought in the bags and set them on the table.

"What?" she asked.

"We're having a family breakfast. The *whole* family, including Nancy. I gotta bring in the coffee, then ring the breakfast bell. Will you set the table for six?"

And damned if Nancy was going to beg off.

TEN MINUTES LATER he had the entire group around the table. The benefit of being accustomed to taking command. He put a certain tone in his voice, which he used as necessary, that no one argued with, not even Nancy.

Maude and Mavis had packed the insulated containers with family-sized portions, rather than individual, when he'd said he was feeding six, three of them college age. Easy.

He opened those containers now and placed them along the table with serving spoons.

It was a *lot* of food. Both Nancy and Lynn appeared astonished, but the boys just grinned. Good eats for all and plenty of it.

At first there was little conversation, but Jax waited patiently for someone to start the ball rolling after they'd all filled their plates. He'd done enough, brought them all together, and now he had to let one of them take the next step.

Will, with his red hair and freckles, spoke first. "This is great, Jax. Thanks!"

A chorus of agreement passed around the table. Still not enough to kick that conversational ball across the field.

"So what do you do, Jax?" Barry asked. "Apart from the obvious."

Jax smiled faintly. "Now that the war's wound down, I'm going to be in charge of our recruiting operations in Denver."

"Is that a step down?" Tom wanted to know.

"It's an honor, actually. Don't you know I'm the perfect representative of the Corps?"

That elicited some laughter from the boys, but as they quieted Barry said, "You're not kidding, are you?"

"No, I'm not. It really is an honor. I'll be one of the public faces of the Marines. Walk carefully, behave above reproach, etc. Plus, I'll wear the blues all the time."

Tom grinned. "I bet women love that."

"I don't exactly mind it myself, although cammo is more comfortable."

The conversation lagged for a bit, then Nancy said, "I want you young men to know that I didn't mean you to feel you had to stay out of the kitchen when I'm here. You have kitchen privileges, and rightly so. I guess I was getting in the way."

The three students hastened to assure her she had not, even though it had become patently obvious that they'd been avoiding the room.

"We just didn't want to intrude on you," Tom said.

"Well, you won't," Nancy replied firmly. "Not at all. You may have to sidestep occasionally if I'm doing something, but we'll all manage."

Lynn looked at her mother, a smile dawning. "Thanks, Mom."

"It's only right."

The conversation continued more easily then, the students talking about their courses, their majors, and even some of their hopes for the future. Meanwhile they demolished the flapjacks and potatoes, along with the remaining scrambled eggs.

Nancy joined the conversation. "I've always thought that the saddest part of this town is how little real opportunity it offers to young people. It's bleeding the youth away from here."

"There's plenty of life here, Mrs. West," Barry protested. "I'll be coming back after nursing school. I like it here that much."

"Good for you," Lynn said. "We need more nurses."

"*Everywhere* needs more nurses," Barry replied. "Lousy wages and miserable hours. But it's important work."

"Without enough respect," Lynn remarked.

After breakfast, the three boys kicked into high speed. Will said, "Just sit here and enjoy coffee while we clean up. Oh, wait, you like tea, don't you, Mrs. West?"

"Call me Nancy, please. Just put the electric kettle on if you don't mind. I can make my own tea." She smiled warmly.

Jax sat back to finish his own latte and watched the young men. And this, he thought, ought to ease at least one tension around here.

LYNN WAS ASTONISHED how much one breakfast together had achieved. Jax had been right—a *family* meal. She only wondered why she hadn't thought of it herself.

But then, she wasn't one to organize other people's lives. She gave her roomers all the freedom young adults deserved and didn't want to encroach or make them feel obligated.

But Jax had taken care of it, maybe because he was just a roomer, too. One of them. And maybe because he knew how to corral people and get them in line, turn them into a friendly group.

Whatever it was, some of her tension eased out of her. But this entire experience hadn't dimmed her attraction to Jax one bit. It had enhanced it. Another kind of tension.

The desire to feel his hands on her naked skin, to feel his mouth and tongue finding their way around her every curve and hollow, had made it hard to sleep last night.

Guilt and yearning had warred within her, along with her upset with Nancy. It had been a long night of arguing with herself. A very long night.

She knew she hadn't any reason to feel guilty. Matt was no longer with her, and she believed he wouldn't want her to remain alone. But feelings didn't yield to logic, and her feelings for Jax were growing stronger by the day even as her guilt persisted.

Damn, she really *liked* Jax. That was what made it so hard to resist his pull on her. Desire meant nothing without something more, at least for her.

But last night, in the privacy of her own thoughts, guilt aside, she had fantasized about making love with Jax. She didn't know what kind of lover he might be, but that didn't matter. It was her own fantasy, after all.

Her body had begun to respond as she imagined him kissing her, holding her against that hard body of his. Imagined him slowly undressing her and baring her to his gaze.

Felt his touches and caresses, all gentle as the smoky haze of passion enveloped them.

Then with a snap, she came out of the fantasy and faced reality again.

Damn, sometimes it was almost too much to bear.

This would be another day off, she decided. She needed to recover, although from what she didn't know.

THE KITCHEN HAD been completely cleaned and the students had headed back to their studies. Nancy sat at the table with a fresh cup of tea. Lynn sat beside her, the two of them murmuring away last night's rupture.

Jax was just deciding he needed to leave them alone when his cell phone rang. Lynn immediately looked at him.

Jax answered the unspoken question. "In the military, you can't go anywhere without leaving a contact information behind." He smiled to reassure her, then headed for the cold front porch as he answered.

The biting wind snatched at him with icy teeth. Cold tendrils crawled through his short hair. His cheeks started to stiffen almost immediately.

It was Sunday, yet Hugh Briggs was calling from his home.

"What's up?" he asked Briggs with the merest preamble.

"Another juror has died. Looks like poison, but they're not sure yet. Keep on your toes, Jax. This'll heat up the investigation, but you can't count on that."

"I know." Any thought that there wasn't a real threat was gone now. Any notion that no one would be able to find him here vanished on winter's breath. He'd been on alert, but maybe not high enough.

Briggs waited for his further response.

So much to consider now. "Maybe I should get along to Denver. I don't want anyone here to be at risk."

"So far these deaths have been carefully pinpointed. No one else has been hurt."

"Doesn't mean it can't happen." Jax ran his hand over his head. "Okay, it's time for me to start seriously thinking. Time to somehow become proactive."

"I don't know how," Briggs answered. "But you're the tactician."

"Right now I'm rooming with a houseful of people. That should give me some time."

Briggs answered after a few beats. "Yeah, it should. These other guys were living alone. It's not as easy to get to you."

"Maybe not. Thanks for the warning, Hugh."

"What else are friends for? Watch your six, man."

"You watch yours, too, Hugh. Don't forget you were the prosecutor."

JAX DISCONNECTED AND slipped his phone into his breast pocket. *Watch his six?* Right then he felt as if a full three-sixty-five might not be enough. Behind him was a houseful of people. Was he putting them at risk? How could anyone hope to take him out in a town this small without doing something so obvious that the killer might not be able to escape?

He'd want to get away, that was certain. There was still another juror besides Jax. And Hugh.

All the others had been at the same station. Hugh would be an easier target than Jax.

Might be easiest for this lunatic to kill the others first. The assassin only needed to wait for Jax to return to duty, even if it would be in Denver. And easier to escape in a large city.

The other juror was probably next.

Not that that made Jax feel one whit better.

He swore, considered packing up right then, and walked back into the house.

To see Lynn sitting alone in the kitchen. She looked as if she'd had a really rough night.

And she mattered a hell of a lot more than he did. He was essentially sure that the others in this house weren't at risk, but he should go anyway to add that last sliver of safety.

Only he couldn't leave her. Something stronger than his own survival had gripped him.

As the day meandered on, Lynn left the living room alone and sat on a folding chair in the dining room. Papers were spread out in front of her on the table she'd built with sawhorses and plywood. The room had become purely a work space, with tool chests lining one wall and bigger tools, like the circular saw and trowels, on top of them. Stacked drywall leaned against another wall along with a couple of buckets of joint compound and rolls of drywall tape. Not to mention a pretty large bucket of nails for the job.

Everything she needed for the moment.

She studied her lists of supplies for future projects and a sketch of what she wanted to do with the upstairs bath. Trying to figure out costs and quantities. Tapping a pen against her teeth from time to time.

Lost in safe thoughts. Thinking it was a shame that Adam was away having a good time on his honeymoon. A selfish thought, but he'd always been willing to help her with the large, heavy sheets of drywall. One person alone couldn't do the job on such large walls.

Not that she needed to do any more drywalling just yet.

She was trying to avoid thoughts of Jax. He'd come back inside from his phone call, his face expressionless, but still he had struck her as disturbed.

And the way he had looked at her. As if he were making a decision of some kind. As if she existed on the far side of a rushing river he couldn't hope to cross.

That wasn't true at all, but she didn't know what she could do about it. Nor was she even sure she should. Matt sometimes seemed to hover around her, a warm presence. But if he was, he could see everything. More guilt.

Rain began to fall outside, tapping gently on the porch roof, a muffled sound from here. It would be stronger in her attic and she'd always enjoyed the sound. With possible snow flurries later in the afternoon, her electric fireplace sounded really cozy.

Maybe she should just quit pretending. Maybe she should invite Jax to join her upstairs. TV, music, whatever. He might like some quiet escape, too. His bedroom wasn't exactly a great hangout.

"Lynn?"

She turned her head and saw Jax standing in the doorway.

"Busy?" he asked.

"Pretending to be. It's kind of a lazy Sunday afternoon, I guess. Anyway, I'm not on any clock but my own."

"You have a demanding clock from what I've seen around here. Your mother went to take a nap."

"She surprised me this morning." Then Lynn straightened and almost before she knew it, she said, "How'd you like to come upstairs? I have a big-screen TV and it's rumored there's some football on."

A smile flickered over his face. "An invitation I can't refuse."

"I didn't think so." Her spirits began to lift.

"Need me to bring anything up?"

"My huge secret is that I have game food up there. And coffee, beer and soda. In fact, I've got plenty of food up there. Just bring yourself."

"I certainly will."

Leaving all her plans and her lists as they were, she headed for her attic, wishing she'd worn something nicer than her usual work clothes. Of course, Jax was wearing his. Hah!

As she walked down the second-floor hall, she heard the boys talking together in Barry's room. A funny way to study for calculus, but what did she know?

She felt a flicker of suspicion when she realized they were talking far more quietly than usual. That snake? No, not these boys. Not *her* boys. They weren't in there conspiring. Even if they sounded like it.

THE ATTIC WAS just what she needed on this gray day. Warm light from lamps reflected off gleaming wood. The big-screen TV she rarely watched hung over her electric fireplace, and she clicked it on, then ran through the guide to find the games.

"Pro or college?" she asked Jax as he stood nearby.

"Is there any soccer? I've seen enough young men get hurt that I don't appreciate football anymore."

She looked at him with surprise, then got it. "Those long-term concussion effects?"

He nodded. "And more."

She scrolled down a few more channels, then found the soccer. "UEFA Champions League or Bundesliga?"

"Champions," he answered.

She clicked it on, then passed him the remote. "Surf all you want. Take a seat. Beer? Something else?"

She brought him a beer and a soda for herself, then sat in the other chair, putting her feet up on one of the ottomans. Maybe this setting was *too* cozy. "I need to get some recliners. Seriously. That dang TV is hard to watch from here."

"But not from the bed."

Everything seemed to still. The voices of the soccer commentators fell into the background. Their eyes locked and Lynn felt there wasn't any air left in the room.

Then Jax looked away, releasing her. "We used to play soccer a lot when we were overseas. Touch football didn't interest the locals much."

She looked at the can of diet soda in her hand, then popped the top, releasing the sound of fizz. "Why should you care what interested the locals?"

"We weren't there to make enemies, Lynn. Far from it. Get up a good soccer game and plenty of young locals wanted to join in. Make friends. Get to know each other."

She tried not to look at him for fear the room would become airless again. For fear the heat that had begun to fill her would worsen into a blaze. "I had no idea."

"It sure as hell wasn't meant to be a war of conquest. Alexander the Great was the last man to ever conquer any part of that land and we didn't try. A war against an insurgency. Against extremists. A war for freedom."

She nodded, interested in whatever he chose to say about it. About anything.

"Our reasons didn't matter when things heated up," he said after a few moments. "But enough of that."

Given his on-the-ground perspective, she could understand why he didn't want to talk about it. Matt never had, either. Some things were kept in a locked box, safe from the knowledge of the uninitiated. She'd seen some of the effects of that war on Adam. She hoped Jax didn't experience the same fallout. Not everyone did, Adam had told her.

The game on TV was moving fast. The ball hardly ever held still and those men were running back and forth at top speed.

Jax spoke. "A dive? Really? The other player didn't even touch him."

Evidently, the official agreed. No penalty.

Lynn pretended to watch with interest, but the truth was her gaze kept wandering from the screen to Jax. She could have simply stared at him for hours, drinking him in.

Oh, man, she had it bad. Once again she forced her attention to the screen.

A soccer game, however, had nothing on Jax. Her situation was growing more precarious with each passing minute. She shouldn't have invited him up here. He could have entertained himself.

And now she feared her haven would always remind her of him.

He turned his head toward her as the game drew to a close. "Lady, if you keep looking at me like that, I won't be responsible for the consequences."

"What?" she asked on a sharp intake of breath. She was horrified to have been so transparent.

He smiled, an almost lazy expression. "You're not

alone. And this is not wise. Not now. So I'll take myself downstairs and try to forget I want you like hell."

He rose, took his bottle to her sink and rinsed it before dropping it in the trash. He gave her another smile as he headed for the stairs. "See you later."

Oh, God. Lynn pressed her hands to her hot cheeks. It had been a gentle but embarrassing letdown.

I want you like hell.

Oh, man. Oh, man oh man oh man.

ONE FLOOR BELOW, the three students still filled Barry's room. They all had their laptops and were, indeed, trying to study for the calculus exam. Mostly.

"Why the hell did I sign up for this course?" Tom asked the world at large.

"Beats me," Will answered. "So you go to Ag school and then back to the family ranch? Are you going to teach integrals to the cattle?"

Tom joined the laughter. "We got some smart steers out there on the range."

"Smart enough to stay away from you," Will snickered.

"I hope so. Some of them still have their horns."

Barry stood up. "Break time. I'm gonna run down to the kitchen and grab some sodas."

Will and Tom, left by themselves, closed their laptops.

Will spoke. "We're not getting any good ideas about Lynn."

"Nope," Tom answered. "And I don't see what we could do to change the gossip. That's the problem."

Tom reached for some chips, dumped a handful into his plastic bowl, then passed the bag to Will, who took a double handful.

Barry returned with soda and handed the cans around. "So?" he asked as he sat on the edge of his bed.

The other two shook their heads. "No new ideas."

"We gotta do something. This ain't right."

The sound of crunching chips filled the room.

"That was some breakfast this morning," Will remarked.

Barry cocked a brow. "Did you feel rounded up?"

The other two snorted.

Tom asked, "What else do you expect from a Master Gunnery Sergeant? You wanna argue with him?" Then he added, "That's a mouthful of a title, isn't it?"

After a few more minutes, Barry started talking again. "It seems like gossip has a life of its own, right?"

Nods.

"And it soaks up new bits as it goes around. Like that game of telephone."

"Right," Tom answered.

"So how about we put a few more tidbits out there?"

"Like what?" Will asked.

"Well, if a military man gets involved with another military man's wife, there's some kind of charge. Maybe even the end of a career. Jax isn't stupid."

Tom and Will forgot the corn chips.

"You sure about that?" Will asked Barry.

"Positive. Remember my cousin Jim, the one in the Army? He told me about it once, how a colonel got into all kinds of trouble by sleeping with a sergeant's wife."

"Oops," said Tom.

"It's totally against the rules."

"Plus," said Will, raising a finger for attention, "say that Jax and Lynn were having a serious affair while Matt was still alive. Then why would it take two years for Jax to get here? Seems like he'd show up sooner than this."

"There's another thing we could plant as soon as we have the chance," Tom offered. "Put it about that this rumor was started by someone with a serious grudge against Lynn."

The other two looked at him.

"Isn't that obvious?" Will asked.

"I'm not sure people are thinking about it. They've just got a juicy story to enjoy. And by the time it got to Barry here, it even made sense."

"So who has the grudge?" Will wanted to know.

Barry stood up. "Luke Macy and Madge Kearney."

"Madge?" Tom said. "Why the hell Madge?"

"Didn't you hear?" Will asked. "She made a little scene at Maude's with Jax. Just a little thing, but people noticed, then brushed it aside. After they'd shared it, of course. Evidently she's had a thing for him since high school."

"My, my, my," murmured Barry, imitating his favorite TV detective. Then he set his can of soda aside, saying, "Calculus, guys. That exam is still tomorrow morning."

Two groans answered him.

LUKE AND MADGE rendezvoused again at a different roadhouse, this one farther from town. Neither of them wanted to appear to be an item for two reasons. First, they weren't. Second, they didn't want to be linked in any way to the mess they were busy creating.

"That rumor has sure taken hold," Luke said over a beer. "It's gotten even bigger."

"Yeah, but what about your part of this?" Madge

wished she'd brought an insulated bottle of daiquiris. She settled for a shot of bourbon, which she hated.

"I told you, a fire."

"What in the hell good will that do? And why burn down the house you want so much?"

"At least Lynn wouldn't own it. Anyway, my thinking is, if there's a second fire where Stone is staying, it might get him tossed in jail."

Madge's head lifted as she considered. "Yeah," she said quietly. "Yeah. That might be good."

"Anyway, it won't be a big fire," Luke continued, draining his beer and signaling for another. "Just a small one."

"What makes you think that'll make Lynn give up?"

"Well, if it doesn't, there are stronger persuasions. I'll bet she doesn't have a will."

Madge's eyes widened, then a slow grin spread across her face as a delicious shiver ran through her. "Oh, I like that."

"Thought you would."

Madge's smile grew almost dreamy. "Him in jail and her…well, whatever." She didn't want to say the words.

After a few minutes, sick of the bourbon in front of her, she announced, "Before you do anything, I want another crack at Jax."

"Soon, then," Luke answered. "Because I can't wait forever."

"And *I* can't get him if he's in jail."

Chapter Eleven

In the morning, Jax walked briskly to the Sheriff's Office, needing to stretch his legs rather than drive. His laundry was in the dryer at Lynn's, but the camos he was wearing again were also in desperate need of a wash. Later today. Lynn was generous with her machines.

Thanks to the motel fire, he didn't even have his regulation parka. Couldn't be out of uniform, though. Even though he shouldn't be wearing his camos while he was here and not traveling on business. Oh, well. Who was going to gig him?

A minor shakeup in his otherwise orderly world.

The gray sky overhead still promised snow or sleet, but yesterday's predicted flurries had never arrived.

By the time he entered the warmth of the Sheriff's Office, his earlobes were burning from the cold. The dispatcher, of indeterminate age with a smoke-roughened voice, sent him straight back to Dalton's office.

Dalton nodded him inside and waved him to a chair.

"What's up?" Dalton asked.

"The fire," Jax answered promptly. "What happened and am I still under suspicion?"

Gage Dalton lifted one eyebrow, probably the only one

he still could, since the other side of his face was badly scarred by fire. "I never said you were under suspicion."

Jax nearly snorted. "What else does it mean when I'm asked not to leave town? When you find me a place to room an hour after I meet you?"

A crooked smile crept across Dalton's face. "I didn't want any moving parts of the puzzle to slip away. There were a few others I asked to hang around. Truckers. They were *not* happy."

"I bet not. So?"

"So." Dalton leaned forward, picked up a pencil, and rapped the eraser end on his nearly buried desk. "I'm limited in what I can tell you."

"Understood."

"It was arson, definitely. A lousy arson. A man with your experience would know how to do a better job. A much better job."

Jax favored him with a short nod. "That place still went up like tinder."

"It *was* tinder. The fire marshal isn't saying much in detail yet. She has a lot more work to do. Suffice it to say she thinks a nuisance turned into a much bigger fire than intended. And resulted in an unintended homicide."

"I can see that. But it's a danger in setting any fire in an occupied structure."

"And a danger to those who have to put it out regardless. We've got two firemen with contact burns. Nothing major, though, and they're carrying on as if it's nothing."

Gage would certainly know that burns weren't *nothing*. So did Jax.

"Anyway," Gage said, changing the subject. "How are you making out at Lynn's? No desire to escape her mother and her roomers?"

"Lynn's a gracious landlord. Her mother is a trip, and her roomers are all nice guys. No complaints at all. Thanks for the referral." More than thanks, actually. Despite everything, he was enjoying himself more than he probably should have.

Except for this tug and pull of his attraction to Lynn. In a way it was uncomfortable. In a way it was a constant, good surprise. Years ago he'd decided to have only casual relationships with women. Women who knew the score. Anything deeper might cause a lot of pain if it didn't work. God knew, it never did.

Lynn was different. Honest, earnest, delightful. The fact that she'd already done the military wife thing meant she knew *that* score. Maybe she hadn't minded it. Maybe she had.

But given that she'd paid the ultimate price of it when Matt was killed, he seriously doubted she'd want to take that chance again. There was never a guarantee that he'd finish out his career in a safe job like Denver. Never. Security was sure as hell one thing he couldn't offer a woman.

Especially with an assassin on his tail.

Ridiculous to waste his time even thinking about it. But Lynn made it impossible to ignore.

Annoyed with himself, he stopped at Freitag's Mercantile to get a warmer jacket than the one he'd purchased only a few days ago. The weather was changing faster than he'd expected. Besides, he hadn't planned to linger this long.

While he was there, he purchased a large insulated bottle, then backtracked and rounded a corner to Maude's diner. It had begun to fill up with the retired crowd.

What was it that made older folks gather in places like this for breakfast?

He stopped at the counter and asked Mavis to fill the bottle with lattes. Maybe Lynn would join him.

As he turned away to leave with his coffee and shopping bag, he realized the room had grown silent and everyone was staring at him, differently than the first time he'd come here.

He paused a few seconds, scanning all the curious faces, then left. What the hell had that all been about? He hadn't received that kind of attention before. But he sure as hell couldn't ask them what was going on.

Odd. Useless to speculate. Meaningless since he'd be leaving soon.

Or so he told himself.

Hugh's warnings, however, clung to him. He'd been stalked before in much more dangerous situations, but if someone had their sights on him, he wasn't yet sure what he could do about it.

He needed a clue of some kind. A clue about who was after him. A clue whether he was here. A clue to what he intended.

His current living situation was a kind of protection. This killer didn't seem likely to want to take out a houseful of people. No, his mission required accuracy and secrecy, and Jax doubted it would be a bullet from a roof above. Unless this guy was some kind of fool, or very desperate.

So what then?

LYNN WANTED TO make herself scarce, but there was no place to do it. She couldn't play hermit in her attic—

that would seem too obvious. If she tried to work, she wouldn't be in isolation.

She listened to the forced air heat rumble to life and thought yet again that she needed a more powerful heater or blower or something. Enough to push sufficient hot air up to the attic vents beyond the trickle she currently received.

But that would be a professional job, just like most of the plumbing and all of the wiring. Expensive. She could probably afford it, but still had so many things left to repair and replace, she wasn't certain she ought to do it yet.

But with another winter moving in fast, she couldn't help but think about it.

When Jax returned, she was almost afraid to look at him.

He dropped a bag outside—she heard the rustle—then appeared in the kitchen carrying a large insulated bottle.

"Lattes," he said. "Want some?"

How could she refuse, even if she felt an urge to run. She'd revealed so much yesterday, she was uncomfortable with herself, with him.

"Where's Nancy?" he asked.

"She's in her room, I think."

Without a word, he headed down the hall and rapped on Nancy's door. Lynn heard her answer.

"Coffee klatch," Jax said. "Join us?"

"Well, for some tea…" Nancy answered on a light laugh.

"Great. I'll start the kettle for you."

A buffer, Lynn thought. He was creating a buffer. She didn't know whether to be more relieved or embarrassed. Maybe just as interesting was the way her mother had kept out of sight this morning. Perhaps Nancy hadn't re-covered from yesterday's hurt yet.

Lynn sighed. How had everything become so jum-bled?

Jax brought Nancy her teacup, saucer and box of tea bags. While the water boiled, he got two mugs and filled them from the insulated bottle, placing them on the table.

"There's more, Lynn, so enjoy."

He poured Nancy's hot water for her, then sat. "It's cold out there," he remarked. "Lynn? When I clear my clothes out of your dryer, would you mind if I wash my camos? They're on the edge of becoming ripe."

She had to chuckle. "I wouldn't know. You still smell of cold air. So you went to Maude's?"

"And Freitag's to get a parka. I didn't expect to be here long enough for the weather to turn like this. And to the sheriff's."

Lynn darted a look at him. "Everything okay?"

He nodded. "For me at least. No solution on the arson." Then he added drily, "*I*, however, would obviously know how to set a better fire."

Lynn nearly spewed coffee. "Oh, God," she said, reaching for a napkin from the stack in the middle of the table, then she started laughing.

"Exactly," Jax answered, smiling. "I thought that motel went up pretty good, but apparently the fire mar-shal doesn't think it was intended to. So some random firebug."

Nancy, dipping her tea bag in and out of the hot water, looked disturbed. "A firebug. They're dangerous."

"I agree," Jax replied. "Very."

Lynn relaxed at last. "I guess that takes you off the local speculation loop."

"I'm not so sure. When I can walk into a diner and make everyone fall silent, then find them staring at me, I must be suspected of something."

She looked at him. "But of what?"

He shrugged a shoulder. "What's the point of worrying about it? It was just strange."

"I should say so," Nancy said tartly. "And rude besides. Well, I haven't heard a word about you from my friends, except some remarks about what a fine man you've grown into."

"They need to know me better," Jax answered her. "I'm not flawless."

"Who is?" Lynn asked, thinking of her own plethora of flaws. Such as mooning over a guy who was bent on leaving and finally had to tell her this wasn't the right time. How humiliating. She couldn't remember having done such a ridiculous thing since high school.

Maybe you never grew up.

"Anyway," Jax continued, "I stopped by Freitag's to get a parka. I didn't expect the weather to change so fast and it got me thinking it might not be as mild in Denver as I'd planned on."

"It might not," Lynn told him. "Weather reports a big cold front is pushing in. Something about the polar current dropping down early this season." The weather. She was reduced to talking about the weather?

Nancy flashed her a look that said she needed to do better than that. She probably did or become the most boring conversationalist on earth.

Jax's phone chimed and he fished it out of his shirt pocket to read a text. "Adam," he said, sounding surprised. "He says he and Jazz are having a wonderful time in Cancún and wants to know if I've had enough of the cold yet. Right!"

He tapped a response, then tucked the phone away. "That's great news."

"I really like Adam," Lynn volunteered. "He's nice, and he's the most helpful neighbor imaginable. Have you met his dog, Sheba?"

"Just briefly the night before the wedding."

"She's a prize, too. I guess she and Jazz's niece, Iris, are the best of friends, so I imagine Iris is glad to be dog-sitting."

"I barely got to meet Lily, either. Just dinner the night before. She's new around here?"

Lynn nodded. "Maybe six years. She wanted to raise Iris in a safer place. With a firebug, maybe we're not."

Nancy tsked. "This place is like any other, just not on such a massive scale. I used to hear the old sheriff, Nate Tate, muttering about how this county was going to hell in a handbasket."

Lynn swallowed her coffee quickly as a laugh tried to overtake her. "Really?"

"Really. Conard County doesn't have to be huge to have problems."

"True. There seem to have been a few lately." She looked at Jax and realized he'd gone very still, his gaze distant. "Jax?"

He seemed to shake himself. "I'm sure there were always things happening, but most of them never reached the public eye."

Such as? Lynn wondered, but didn't feel comfortable asking. She sensed that in some ways, Jax was locked up tighter than a drum. And again she wondered what had made him that way.

ON HIS WAY back from the miserable, endless and, in ways, terrifying exam, Barry had a brainstorm. He diverted his route and trudged his way over to Edith Jasper's house.

Miss Jasper had been a fixture in the school system for years, and even though Barry hadn't been old enough to take any of her English classes, everyone knew about her and some even joked that she'd die in that classroom using her pointer on the blackboard. She was famous, though, for getting chalk all over her hands, then putting them on her hips, leaving streaks on her skirts. Or forgetting she held the eraser and tapping it to her side.

A figure of humor although one of respect.

Everyone knew Edith Jasper in a new way now, as the elderly woman who walked a harlequin Great Dane around town. The dog was nearly as big as Miss Jasper, but so well-behaved he never tugged on the old woman.

Even at the grand old age of twenty, Barry was still nervous about approaching a teacher. With trepidation, he knocked on her door.

The elderly woman, with a crown of white hair and wearing a baggy sweater, answered with her dog in the background. Barry didn't expect her to recognize him, but she did.

"Why, Barry Hutchins!" she exclaimed. "To what do I owe this honor?"

Barry managed a smile, despite the rat-a-tat of his heart. Was he doing the right thing? "I wanted to talk to you, Miss Jasper."

"Well, come in, then. Bring yourself out of the cold. I was about to make tea. Join me?"

Barry hated tea. "No, thank you," he answered as he

stepped inside. The house definitely smelled like dog, and said dog merely gave him a sappy grin before lying down.

"Well, I believe you won't refuse one of the scones I made this morning. From all my years of reading, I started to fancy the idea of a British high tea. It has replaced my supper." She waved to a chair that looked almost as old as she did. "Do sit down while I bring you a plate."

"Thank you, ma'am."

Despite the warm greeting, Barry felt like a trespasser here, and sat on the very edge of the chair. The next thing he knew, Edith Jasper handed him a napkin and a small plate with three scones on it. A few moments later she returned with her tea.

"Now, what can I do for you?" she asked.

"Well, it's kind of hard to explain."

Edith Jasper nodded. "Many things in life are. Start where you like and we'll sort it out."

Barry looked at the scones, a great way to stall, and besides, he didn't want to be rude. He bit into one. "These are wonderful!"

Miss Jasper smiled. "I've gotten pretty good at it. So what's troubling you, young man?"

Barry wiped his mouth with the napkin as his mother had taught him. "It's about Lynn Macy."

Edith frowned. "Has she come into some trouble?"

"Not exactly. But someone started a nasty rumor about her. I'm sure she hasn't heard it yet, but I was hoping you could help me stop it somehow before she does. You know everyone in town."

"The downside of having taught so many of them." Edith's eyes twinkled briefly. "What's the rumor?"

Barry hesitated, then jumped in. "That she was having an affair somewhere else when she said she was visiting her husband, Matt."

The corners of Edith's mouth turned down in a clear frown. "Now, who could be so cruel?"

"I don't know for sure. But then the rumor got worse."

Her brows, what was left of them, rose. "What could be worse?"

"That she was having an affair with Jackson Stone."

"Oh, now..." Edith fell silent for a minute. "That's quite beyond enough. Who could believe that claptrap?"

"I don't know if everyone believes it, but nearly everyone is talking about it."

Edith set her cup and saucer on the side table, beneath a fringed lamp that struggled to add a warm glow to the gray day. "I see. Bunch of fools. If that were true, then Jackson Stone would have arrived here long ago."

Having found a like mind, Barry's mood lightened. "That's what I think. Just that alone should make people question the story."

"People aren't logical, and even less so as winter begins to confine them indoors. Lacking sufficient entertainment, they make their own. Or lose their minds. Who knows, but it'll grow worse as the snow begins flying."

Barry nodded. "I need to find a way to stop it, but who's going to listen to me? I'm just a kid."

Edith's eyes sparkled. "Not a kid. A young man. Apparently with a good head on his shoulders. Let me think for a few minutes. More scones?"

Barry looked down at his plate and realized he'd devoured all three. "I don't want to eat your supper."

"There's no chance of that," Edith answered. "When I bake, I bake more than enough. Saves time for reading, walking Bailey and having friends over from time to time. I'm always ready for a drop-in."

She disappeared into her kitchen with his plate. Barry waited with a dry mouth, wondering if she'd be able to help, wishing he'd accepted the tea.

When she returned, she resumed her seat. "I suppose I could use my authority as teacher of so many of those people. Shame them into being quiet, shame them into feeling cruel. But that might take a while, and you're right, we don't want this claptrap getting back to Lynn."

Barry shook his head. "I'm worried about that. Me and the other students at Lynn's, we're all worried about that."

"The other students and I," she corrected him absently. Clearly, she was thinking.

Barry ate another scone. Well, two, while he waited.

At last Edith stirred. "Do you have any idea who might have started this malicious gossip?"

"Guesses," Barry answered, barely remembering to swallow the scone before he spoke. "Luke Macy. Madge Kearney. We can't think of anyone else with a grudge. I guess there might be some, though."

"Madge Kearney?"

"She made a play for Jackson Stone at the wedding, then again at Maude's when he and Lynn were there for lunch. People noticed, but it wasn't juicy, I guess. They moved on."

"Moved on, indeed. To a *real* scandal." Now Edith tapped her fingers lightly on the arm of her chair.

Barry put his empty plate on the side table so she wouldn't offer him more scones. He felt guilty about pigging out on them.

Edith spoke eventually. "I taught Madge and Jackson.

They were both in my senior English class. Luke, too, a few years behind them."

Barry nodded. "I guess, from the gossip, Madge feels she and Jax were an item back then."

Again Edith's brow rose. "Not a bit of it. Not even remotely. If Jackson knew she was on the same planet, he showed it in no way. Nor, frankly, did she in him. I guess that Marine uniform is a drawing card."

Barry had to grin. "Why wouldn't it be?"

Edith eyed him. "I always thought the other services could learn from that uniform. Regardless, this *is* a problem. Lynn doesn't deserve to have her reputation trashed."

"No," Barry agreed. "She's the nicest person. And she's working so hard on that house."

"Resurrecting a dinosaur," Edith said drily. "I was in there a few times when Matt's father was still alive. He'd let it go to rack and ruin. I hope to get a tour when she's finished."

"She ought to be proud to show it off."

But Edith had resumed thinking. "Madge Kearney. Now there's one whose reputation isn't the best. As for Luke Macy…someone should have taken him to task years ago. It's no wonder that Andy Macy left the house to Matt. Luke was, in the truest sense, a wastrel. Drinking. Fast women. Maybe some gambling. Spending whatever money that came into his hands as if it were water. He'd have lost any share in that house long ago."

"I didn't know."

Edith looked at him. "If anyone should be the subject of gossip, it's those two. Although perhaps they were, in years past. How would I know these things? I don't have my ear to every keyhole in town."

The image made Barry grin.

"But as to the present problem…" Edith sighed. "I don't want to slander anyone by claiming he or she planted this rumor. It's malicious. Terribly malicious. In any event, it very likely grew over the course of the telling. That makes many people responsible. Well, those who repeat it are responsible regardless."

Barry waited hopefully, even as he felt his hopes were being dashed. If no one could point a finger, then what?

Edith nodded slowly. "Very well, young man. Let me think about this. I doubt it will get much uglier in the next day or so, but we need to find a way to kill it. You keep thinking. I'll keep thinking. And perhaps I'll speak to some trustworthy friends."

Did she have any other kind? Barry wondered as he stepped again into the stinging cold.

And that damn calculus test. The other two guys had needed to run to following classes, but they'd be back soon and he could hardly wait to hear their moans and groans.

And if *they* had any ideas.

IT WASN'T EASY for Luke to hold back at Madge's request. He wanted nothing more than to scare Lynn, and while he was at it, he had to get rid of that Marine, who might prove to be too protective.

Why was Jax hanging around anyway? It was bound to make Madge madder than a hornet, wondering if he was developing a thing for Lynn.

Even Luke had the sense to see that angry as he was with Lynn, she was plenty desirable. She'd never returned that feeling, though, and he was enraged with her for being a constant thorn in his side.

Still, his ideas for how to deal with this didn't seem likely to achieve his goal. But as he'd said to Madge, he knew *other* ways to get rid of that infuriating sister-in-law of his. A perfect solution, as long as he could carry it off without coming under suspicion. No easy task in a town this size, especially when he had a motive.

He kicked a rock in the graveled parking lot of yet another roadhouse, wanting to drink himself into oblivion. Maybe he should. Forget it all for a while.

It had been consuming him for too long, and sometimes he needed a break. But that house was rightfully his, and the fury never entirely subsided.

Matt should have at least willed it to him. It was Luke's by birthright, after all. And Lynn? She could have made a new life elsewhere with all that insurance money.

He laughed bitterly when he thought of Madge's rumor taking on a life of its own. That might be enough to drive Lynn out of town. Maybe.

But Madge wasn't going to give up on that Stone guy. Not as long as he was here, and that had become his problem, too.

Why had he ever teamed up with her?

Of course, if he could frame Madge for whatever he did to Lynn…

He liked that idea. He liked it a whole lot. Whistling now, he headed inside for a few draft beers. He still had enough money for that.

THE FLURRIES STARTED to thicken by midmorning. Lynn took herself to the grocery to acquire some simple fare that would feed at least three people, and maybe the boys as well. That "family" breakfast had worked very well, and while kids that age might think they could survive on fast food and fat, they occasionally needed a dreaded vegetable or two.

For a fact, they *could* get decent food at the college cafeteria, but she guessed spending money on a balanced meal wasn't as attractive as spending money on hamburgers and pizza.

Maybe she should make her own pizza sometime. Better than that chain pizzeria on the edge of town, and Matt had always loved her pizza. But how many would she have to make for the crowd? She'd bet each of those boys could eat an entire pie.

The idea of making all the dough overwhelmed her. Which was kind of ridiculous, considering how much effort she spent on the house. On the other hand, she wasn't fond of bread dough. Such a mess with flour all over everything. She preferred plaster dust. A small laugh escaped her.

She scrapped the pizza idea before she reached the store. Beef stew, a great cold weather meal. Lots and lots of beef stew with some fresh French bread. She'd even sneak in a bunch of vegetables.

As she was about to enter the store, she ran into Madge Kearney. "Hello, Madge," she said, intending to pass by.

But Madge wasn't going to allow it. "Where's Jax?"

"I'm not sure." Which was true.

"Setting your cap for him?"

Lynn blinked. "No. Why would I?"

"Then why don't you let me see him?"

"You can always knock on the door."

"As if you'd tell him I'm there."

Lynn frowned, anger stirring in her. "What are you accusing me of? Keeping him prisoner? As if."

"He's mine," Madge said, glaring. "You keep your hands off him."

Lynn had had enough. "Listen, Madge, if he's yours he can find you. He's an adult and I'm sure he's found his way across more difficult terrain than this town. Maybe he doesn't *want* to find you."

"How dare you!"

"How dare I tell you that you're acting like a fool for all the world to see? Give it up, Madge. He's his own man and I don't want to hear another thing about this!"

Then she brushed by, ignoring whatever came out of Madge next. Dang! Even a trip to the grocery had become fraught.

TERRI ALBRIGHT WAS beginning to fear that she might lose it. She had one goal and one goal only, and it seemed to be slipping further away. Denver would come, she promised herself. Soon enough. Besides, waiting might cool down any heat behind her over the other deaths.

Still, as snow flurries started to swirl in the air around her remote camp, she wondered if she shouldn't just go on ahead to Denver. Damn weather. Even with the best sleeping bag she'd been able to find on her way out here, the nights were awful.

A small fire kept her fingers from freezing, but it wasn't enough. The coffee from the tin pot was the worst she had ever tasted, some kind of dried stuff. Food came out of a can, not very warm, or a packet of something dried. Water was another pain. She had to trudge a mile or more to reach a stream.

The cramps in her belly were a warning, too. Maybe she shouldn't have drunk any of that water before boiling it. She'd forgotten just once, and she hadn't brought any purification tablets with her.

From a desk job to this. Gloomily, she considered how ill prepared she was for this particular stage of her mission.

Denver sounded better by the hour. At least she'd be able to get a motel room.

Not here, however. A bitter laugh escaped her. The fire she'd set at the motel had put paid to that.

What the hell was Stone doing, hanging around for so long in that houseful of people making it more difficult for her to reach him? Getting it on with his landlady?

Oh, damn it all to hell, she thought as she tossed a few more twigs on the paltry fire.

And damn Jackson Stone. Oh, how she was going to enjoy killing him.

Chapter Twelve

The next afternoon, the flurries had grown to more than occasional whirling flakes. Beef stew simmered in a huge pot on the stove, filling the house with its delicious aroma.

Lynn sat at the kitchen table studiously ignoring her work area. Somehow she'd lost her momentum, and assured herself it would return. It always did.

But another thought began to plague her. Had she imagined some people at the grocery giving her sidelong looks?

She must have. In this town where she'd lived most of her life, the only time she had received looks like that was after Matt died. As if people didn't know how to approach her.

An odd thing about grief. Most people avoided it like the plague. It made them feel uneasy, maybe helpless. Maybe it reminded them of the icy breath of death whispering through their lives. That no one was immortal.

Everyone had to live with that eventually, some sooner than others. Or maybe folks just didn't want to be reminded of their own losses.

Whatever, the glances troubled her in retrospect. While she'd been in the store, she'd been too preoccupied to think about it. Now that she could, it proved to be a puzzle.

Whatever, she thought, dismissing it. There were no secrets in this town so eventually she'd find out, unless it had been her own imagination.

She heard her boys burst through the front door, laughing and talking together. She called out immediately.

"Fellows?"

A pause in the conversation, then all three came to the kitchen.

"Something wrong, Lynn?" Tom asked.

"Not a thing, except I expect you guys for dinner tonight. Beef stew. Hot, tasty and too much for the rest of us to eat by ourselves. You better come." She smiled as she said it.

Three grinning faces answered her. "You bet," Will answered. "Home-cooked. Yum."

Then they headed for the stairs, gabbing once again.

Each year she grew fond of her students, this year most especially Barry because he'd stayed here last year, too. She was going to miss him when he moved on to nursing school.

Tom, of course, would head back to the family ranch—unless something diverted him along the way. No, he'd be back to join his brothers and dad in managing a huge spread. Tom seemed by turns to be happy about it, then not quite so happy. She suspected that might have something to do with the ups and downs of life at home.

Her mother had vanished early this morning to join a friend on a trip to Casper. Expected back by dinnertime. As for Jax, she wondered where he'd gone.

None of her business, of course, but he'd been out for

hours and hadn't taken his car with him. As cold as it had grown, she'd wondered where he'd gone to ground.

Madge's place? Lynn could have snorted coffee. Jax couldn't have made it any plainer that he felt not the least interested in that woman.

I want you like hell.

That had sounded almost like a promise, and it hadn't been directed at Madge.

Hot desire began to zing through her. Yeah, she was getting it bad, and today she didn't mind at all.

Wrapped in a pleasant haze of need, she closed her eyes and listened to the stew slowly bubble.

JAX COULD NO longer persuade himself that the assassin would leave him alone in this small town. While he was at the rooming house, yes. But out here on the streets? There were a lot of ways that didn't involve bullets to kill someone. He knew quite a few himself.

The senselessness of all this didn't ease his mind any. Someone had a hell of a grudge, and while it wouldn't change Albright's situation at all, this could only be a very angry man. Angry beyond any common sense.

He had set out on a scouting mission, looking for anything that didn't seem right, looking for someone out of place. Someone too interested in him. Checking all the remote byways in the town, including alleys.

All the while he felt a tingling between his shoulder blades, a sense that something might strike him at any moment. He knew the feeling well. It had saved him more than once.

But it also didn't necessarily mean a thing. It would sure help if he didn't keep getting sideways looks from people he hardly knew, if ever he had. What the hell was bringing this kind of attention to him? Not that it was a lot, but it was enough to set his teeth on edge.

Unfortunately, after hours of pacing the streets, alert and scanning all the time, he concluded that he wasn't going to find a thing today. Not one damn thing.

This was a problem he wanted to take by the horns. Not let it ride as it seemed determined to do, despite making himself one big target today.

Unsatisfied, but unable to do any more unless something changed, he headed back to Lynn's house in snow flurries that were beginning to feel like the inside of a snow globe.

He was cold. It wasn't that he couldn't handle it or wasn't accustomed to it after the temperate climate of Afghanistan, but a couple of hot cups of coffee sounded really good. A luxury, one he was consistently grateful for. Like a hot shower.

Inside, the house was warm, and he shed his jacket, hanging it on one of a row of hooks near the front door. The aroma of wonderful food reached him. Since he didn't see Lynn working in the dining or living rooms, he headed for the kitchen.

She was sitting at the table, looking thoughtful and a little lost.

When she saw him, she smiled faintly. "How is it possible to feel alone in a house that's so full of nice people?"

Her words tugged his heart, but he didn't know how to answer her. He wished he had some wise or comforting words to offer.

"The coffee's getting old," she said with a wave of her hand. "Make more if you want."

He wanted and set about stacking the drip coffee maker for a fresh pot. "How are you doing?" he asked.

"I'm moody for no good reason."

He imagined she had any number of reasons, but didn't want to share them. He looked up as he heard a thud from upstairs.

"The boys are home," she said. "As if you can't tell. By the way, I'm making beef stew and everyone is invited."

"Sounds good, especially on a day like this." He rubbed his earlobes, warming them. "Thanks for the invite. You're sure I'm not imposing?"

"Of course I'm sure. I'm running a rooming house, not a hotel. If I didn't want the company for dinner, I'd have only cooked enough for Mom and me."

The coffee had finished and he asked Lynn if she wanted some.

"No thanks. I drank so much today that I ought to be jangling."

He sat across from her, studying her, seeing a very different side of the bright, driven, usually cheerful woman he'd come to know. "Where's Nancy?"

"Off to a shopping expedition in Casper. Man, how that woman shops."

"Must make her feel good."

Lynn rested her chin in her hand. "I guess. How was your day?"

"Wasted." But he didn't tell her why. "I'm used to being physically active. Walking around is relaxing." Not today, however, although his legs felt pleasantly stretched. "You're not working today?"

"I guess I need a break. Even the usual planning that's always rolling around in my head has fallen silent. But that's okay. I enjoyed making the stew. It's the kind of thing you wouldn't make for just yourself."

"If you did, you'd have to eat it for a week." He was glad to see Lynn perk up a bit as she smiled.

"I like stew, but not that much. I should probably put some in the freezer out in the mudroom and start cooking in advance to avoid the daily attempt to come up with something just for myself. Seems like too much trouble, though."

"The winter could do all the work for you."

She finally laughed, easing his concern for her. "I've used the porch that way a couple of times."

He drank his coffee, swallowing the heat gratefully. In no time at all, he was up for a second cup. Then he asked baldly, "Did something happen, Lynn?"

She looked up immediately. "No. Why?"

"Because while I've known you only a short time, you seem to be pretty upbeat. You don't look like it now."

She shook her head. "This happens from time to time. It'll pass. Probably at dinner tonight with everyone all around talking and, of course, praising my wonderful stew."

He chuckled. "I'm sure it's wonderful. I can smell it."

"There's no old shoe leather in it, that's for sure."

But then the faintly forlorn expression returned, and he thought he heard a faint sigh.

Damn, she was tugging at his heartstrings. He ached for her, a sensation he didn't often experience.

Helpless in a way he didn't like, he rose and rounded the table so he could sit beside her.

Then he wrapped an arm around her shoulders, offering the only comfort he could.

He was astonished when she turned toward him and leaned into him. His heart skipped a beat, then he wrapped his other arm around her, holding her snugly as if he could keep her troubles at bay.

He knew he couldn't offer her much beyond this, but his mind rambled over his idea of not being able to provide security. No, he couldn't. But if anyone knew life didn't offer any security, it was Lynn. The person she had most loved had been torn from her. It must feel so senseless.

With one hand, he rubbed her back gently, hoping it helped to remind her she wasn't alone. At least not right now.

Then she tilted her head back, looking straight at him. That did it.

LYNN WASN'T CERTAIN what she was doing, and she was past caring. When she tilted her head back to gaze at this remarkable man, one who was so gentle despite his calling in life, she knew she needed much more than a hug, much more than his hand stroking her back. Her entire body cried out for more. For the gift he could give her.

His head lowered. She knew what was coming and she didn't try to evade him. He hesitated just a moment, then she felt his warm mouth settle over hers, questing softly for her response.

God, he tasted and smelled good. Fresh air. Coffee.

Needy, she raised her arms and hugged him back, pressing into him as well as she could, given their awkward position on the bench. It didn't matter. The closeness mattered. The heat mattered. The *man* mattered.

Parting her lips, she invited him in. He accepted the invitation, and their tongues danced together, stoking the fire even more. A kiss, a wonderful kiss from a man who knew how to do it. The world spun away, no longer part of this private universe they were creating.

Just as she felt she needed to breathe, he raised his head, then began to trail butterfly kisses over her cheeks, to her earlobe, his heated breath sending a delighted shiver through her.

Now she wasn't hugging him, she was clinging to him, feeling his every hard muscle, loving his strength. Wanting to drag him upstairs to her attic and keep him there for hours on end.

Delightful fantasies skimmed through her mind, images of the two of them by firelight, away from everyone and everything. The scent of lovemaking commingling with the blaze in their bodies in the slightly chilly air that would keep them beneath the blankets. Laughter coming later. Private laughter, laughter to be shared only by the two of them.

The pulsing between her thighs, faint before, grew as strong as a bass drumbeat. Yes, they needed to go upstairs. Now.

Now.

Just as she made the decision, just as his lips started trailing along her neck, she heard the front door open and the rapid tattoo of feet on the stairs.

She jumped back like a startled deer. Jax still gave her a sleepy smile, but turned away, reaching across the table for his mug.

Lynn started to feel like a deflated balloon.

"Lynn?" her mother's voice called from the hallway.

"Lynn," called Barry from the stairs.

She saw Jax grin. "Oh, Lynn?"

And she started to laugh. A laugh that felt so good, reaching to every dusty part of her soul.

Nancy entered the kitchen, carrying several shopping bags. "I found the greatest outfit for you."

"Oh, God," Lynn groaned.

Barry peeked in. "You said dinner tonight, right? What time? I need to run to Freitag's. I found a hole in the sole of my running shoes."

"Six," she answered promptly.

"Thanks. Man, that smells good!" Then he was gone.

That left Nancy and her bags, which she placed on the end of the table. "You don't have to groan until you see it!" she announced sternly. "I think I'm getting the measure of your tastes. Or should I call them non-tastes."

"Oh, Mom…"

Nancy looked at Jax. "She'd be beautiful in anything, including those work clothes."

"She absolutely would," Jax agreed. A smile danced around his dark eyes.

"What is this?" Lynn asked. "A gang-up?"

"Well, you know," Nancy replied, "sometimes you have to go somewhere besides the lumberyard and hardware store. That stew smells good, by the way."

"Thanks," Lynn answered, dreading the moment the bags opened.

"I know you like denim," Nancy said with an exaggerated sigh. "But it *does* come in different shapes than jeans."

Nancy reached into the bags and pulled out a neatly folded set of denim. "See?" she asked triumphantly.

She shook out the fabric and displayed a denim pencil skirt with a cute embroidered jacket. "Now, you can't possibly object to this."

Nor did Lynn. She felt her mouth open in amazement.

"I knew she'd like it," Nancy told Jax. "There they

were, on a rack, practically labeled with her name. In fact, they shouted at me. So did a couple of shells to go beneath the jacket."

Then Nancy began to refold the items into the bags. "You can try them on in your hermitage, but I want you to do that at the very least."

Lynn nodded, still astonished. "Mom…"

"Don't thank me." Nancy smiled. "Just try them on. If you don't like them, I can donate them to someone who will. I'll put these bags near the foot of the stairs. I mean it about trying these on."

"Wow," said Lynn, watching her mother take the bags out. "Wow."

"I guess she tried really hard," Jax remarked.

"Evidently so." Lynn smiled then, feeling a whole lot better than she had earlier. She felt wrapped in love.

But she didn't dare glance at Jax. They had come so close. Now the moment was broken, possibly never to return.

DINNER WAS AS boisterous an affair as Lynn had hoped. Once again the young men cleaned up, leaving the kitchen spotless.

It would have been a good time to retire to a living room with coffee, except there was no living room. Not down here, and she was damned if she was going to head up to her attic with Jax, not with Nancy here. Boy, wouldn't Nancy make a field day of that.

Thus the three of them sat at the refectory table over cocoa. But of course, Nancy couldn't leave well enough alone.

"You really need to get this remodeling done, Lynn. Or hire someone so it will go faster. It's ridiculous to sit around this table all the time. We ought to be able to go into the living room."

At last, Lynn glanced at Jax. A smile danced around his eyes, creasing the corners, but he didn't let it reach his mouth. She was glad *he* was so amused by Nancy.

"I like doing the work," Lynn said for the umpteenth time. "And I'm sorry your room isn't comfortable enough."

Nancy raised her brows. "I didn't say that. Regardless, three people can't gather in my bedroom."

"And you can't climb the stairs to the attic where we *could* all gather. So here we are, like it or not. I need the dining room for a work space or I'd spend a bunch of time in an unheated garage that needs repairing as much as any other place. The living room has to be done for obvious reasons, and that's first on my current agenda."

Nancy sighed. "I know, I really do know. It's just that I worry about you. You can't even entertain, the way this house is now."

"My friends are familiar with the kitchen. Which is on my list after the upstairs bath. You won't have to endure this ugly avocado green forever."

Nancy tutted. "It *is* ugly and so out of fashion. But it *does* work after all. You made a wonderful stew for dinner in this room. And we seated six for dinner. Back to the old days, I guess."

Lynn was surprised. "Old days?"

"You couldn't possibly remember, but once upon a time, families ate in the kitchen along with hired help if there was any. Living rooms were reserved for Sundays and guests. Dining rooms? Well, if people had one, they were reserved, too, for holidays and perhaps Sunday dinners. The front-facing parts of the house, I guess you could say. And all the furniture was well protected. Meant to last more than a lifetime." Nancy shook her head. "Try to find that quality of furniture anymore."

"It would be hard," Jax agreed. "At least at a reasonable price."

Nancy tilted her head in acknowledgment. "Well," she said, rising to carry her cup to the sink, "I guess I'm worn-out from all that shopping. I'll go to bed now if you don't mind."

"Sleep well, Mom," Lynn said.

"Oh, I will. A couple of ibuprofens for these knees and I'll be out like a light. Good night, Jax."

"Good night, Nancy."

Which left the two of them alone once more in the kitchen.

Right back to where they'd been before Nancy had come home. Sort of.

Then Jax rose and reached for cups. "Why don't you head on up and relax? Maybe try on those clothes," he suggested. "I'll take care of these mugs and the saucepan."

"Thank you," she answered, but her feet felt leaden as she left the room.

Frankly, she didn't want to go alone. She wanted to feel his arms around her. His lips lightly tracing her face and neck. She wanted to feel that rush of desire again.

But it was not to be.

Instead, she steeled herself to try on the outfit her mother had given her. When at last she stood trying to see as best she could in her bathroom mirror, she decided she liked it. But where would she ever wear it?

STILL IN THE KITCHEN, Jax stood looking over the top of the café curtain at the night. He considered going out into the darkness to do another recon, then dismissed the idea. Not tonight, because he might have been obvious during his walk today. But at night the world provided a different view of dangers, of hiding places, of the shadows that could deceive.

Tomorrow night, he decided.

He just wished he'd been able to walk up those stairs with Lynn. Desire clamped his loins like a vise, aching and throbbing.

But it didn't take long for him to remind himself of all the reasons to avoid a deeper involvement.

There were sure as hell plenty of them.

OUTSIDE DURING THE wee hours, in the cold night, Terri Albright watched the rooming house, puzzling whether she could somehow take advantage of the situation as it stood. So far, no idea had occurred to her. How long was she going to have to wait, damn it? She had a limited amount of time because she was on leave and would have to return to duty, giving her no further chance to get at the guy.

Sure as hell Stone didn't appear to be in any hurry to head on to Denver. He'd have to leave soon, she promised herself, but the promise did nothing to ease her impatience.

God, this situation sucked!

Then she saw a dark figure approach the house slowly, looking around, mainly at the house.

What was he up to? His own game of vengeance? Against who? The woman who owned the place? At last he walked away.

For once her impatience eased. Maybe she needed to take some time to watch this guy, especially at night.

Most especially at night. He might turn out to be a useful tool.

Nodding to herself, she slipped deeper into the darkness, making up her mind to use that purple hair spray. A dog barked behind a fence, then fell silent after she passed. No one even looked out a window.

Terri loved dogs and wondered what kind of owner would leave that pooch out in this cold. None of her business, she reminded herself, as if she could do anything about it. She had more important matters to engage her.

Chapter Thirteen

Two days later, a phone call at 6:00 a.m. startled Barry Hutchins from sleep. Nobody called at this hour and he was annoyed.

"What?" he nearly snapped into his cell phone.

"Edith Jasper, young man."

At once Barry sat up, rubbing the sleep from his eyes.

Edith continued. "I realize that at your age anything before 9:00 a.m. is uncivilized, but for someone my age sleeping until six is a major achievement. When are you done with classes today?"

"Three," he answered groggily.

"Then get yourself over here for tea directly after. I'll expect you by three-thirty. I want you to meet some of my friends."

"Yes, ma'am," Barry answered, stifling a yawn. "I'll be there."

Then he wondered if he'd dreamed the call. He gave in to the yawn. No, it had happened. So off to the Jasper house this afternoon. A few of her scones sounded really good, whatever else was going on.

"I SCOPED OUT the house," Luke told Madge later that morning. Once again country music played in the background. This roadhouse opened early, not wanting to miss even the smallest business.

This time Madge got her daiquiris from a brilliant bartender who knew how to do something besides pull a beer or pour a shot—and disregarded the early hour. Luke was initially glad to see her drinking what she wanted instead of complaining about beer.

She didn't wait for Luke to explain what he meant. "Can you believe that damn Lynn Macy all but told me to stay away from Jackson Stone? What right does she have to say anything about it?"

"Good question," Luke said soothingly. "About the house…"

But Madge interrupted him again. "God, this is maddening. I saw him walking around town the day before yesterday. I wanted to talk to him, but that awful Edith Jasper got in my way. This town could do without her. Busybody."

Luke stared at her as she drained her daiquiri and signaled the bartender for another. Odd how he'd never noticed she was a lush. Not likely she'd ever be attractive to Jackson Stone if he noticed her drinking. The guy appeared to be a straight arrow. Damn him. But at least Madge's interest in him had led to her starting a useful rumor.

"Lynn needs this rumor to get back to her." With that, he finally gained Madge's attention.

"Why?"

"Because it will hurt her."

Madge smiled sourly. "You really want to hurt her, don't you."

"Believe it. That house is half mine—I don't care what the court said—and she's a bitch to not share it with me."

"I agree," she said, apparently not wanting to get into this whole house thing again. "But it's like nobody wants her to know about the rumor. Which is amazing in this town."

"I could tell her. Keep you out of it. Be all sympathetic. Maybe she'll even throw Stone out on his ear to let everyone know he wasn't her lover."

Madge pondered that. "I dunno," she said finally, draining her second daiquiri. "Where's he gonna go? I need time to reach him."

Luke sighed. "I don't have all the time in the world, Madge."

She scowled at him. "You've waited this long for that damn property. You can wait a week or two longer."

One thing Luke knew for sure. He wanted Lynn to suffer for her unkindness to him. Wanted her to pay. If she felt like she couldn't lift her head around here, that would be a start. Maybe she'd even decide she had to get rid of the house. Maybe. Then maybe she'd think about Luke and his position. Maybe she'd stop being so self-centered.

"I'll tell her," Luke said finally. "She won't throw Stone out. It'd be too obvious."

Madge regarded him dubiously and ordered her third drink. "Okay," she groused finally, "but you better be right about this. And honestly, I want to hurt that woman."

Well, at least they were together on this one point. Luke sighed and ordered a second beer himself.

And Madge moved on to her fourth drink.

"You'd better not drive," Luke said.

"I hold my liquor better than that."

"Lots of experience?" he suggested. She scowled at him. "Better watch it," he cautioned, "or the bartender will cut you off."

She waved her hand. "I'll just go somewhere else."

Luke began to wish he'd never teamed up with her. Constant objections, and all that drinking, which probably made her as porous as a sieve when it came to secrets.

He decided not to tell her about his idea. About how Lynn lived in her attic. He could arrange an accident up there easily enough.

Yeah, better not let Madge know or she'd drain a bunch of daiquiris and brag about it to the whole world, satisfying her ego by letting everyone know that *she* knew the truth.

"I'll talk to her," Luke said. "Soon. So find a way to get Stone's attention fast."

MEANWHILE, JACKSON STONE was having a very difficult time reining himself in when it came to Lynn. She'd become a constant torment in her own way.

Like the rounded contours of her butt when she bent over her worktable. By the way her breasts lifted the front of one of her long-sleeve shirts. He supposed he should be grateful she didn't pull on any snugger tops.

Then there was her pretty face, those soft lips he'd only begun to discover. His hands itched to touch her intimately.

Not to be. Not when he needed to find an assassin first. Not when he was heading to Denver soon. Not while he was still wearing a uniform. Military uniforms probably put her off these days. Small wonder.

He'd noted all the photos of Matt Macy upstairs, too. She probably wasn't completely over him. He understood that. There were things in his own life that he wasn't completely over, too.

But damn, the way she had turned into his embrace,

198 Conard County Protector

the way she had hugged him back, the way she had lifted her face for a kiss. All of that haunted him, kept rousing his desire.

Aw, hell.

Lynn seemed to be avoiding the work in the living room, so he wandered into the dining room, where she was poring over some drawings.

"Give up on the living room?" he asked lightly.

She turned to smile at him without straightening. Her forearms rested on the table, one hand holding a pencil. And her heart-shaped butt was raised like an invitation.

He drew a deep breath and steadied himself.

"No, I didn't quit. It's just that it struck me since I had the roof replaced there's not going to be any more water damage. So I can take a few days to concentrate on something else."

Now she straightened. "Question?"

"Sure."

"You've been using the second-floor bath. Should I leave the tub and add a shower? Or remove the tub?"

He tilted his head thoughtfully. "I'm a shower man myself, but don't women like a long soak in the tub?"

She shrugged. "I suppose some do. I don't. The water gets cold too fast, for one thing. The other is that after sitting in my own dirt and all the soap in a tub, I still want a shower to get clean."

He laughed. "But that tub you have must be worth a fortune."

"Maybe. Cast iron, claw-foot. With a jury-rigged shower. Although if I put a separate shower in…"

She trailed off, looking down at her drawing. "It would fit even with the tub. Nah. I'd better keep the tub, too."

"How come?"

She smiled faintly. "I presume people prefer to bathe small children in one."

"I didn't think of that."

"I almost didn't, either."

He then asked a personal question, treading where he might not be welcome. "Did you and Matt want children?"

She nodded and sighed. "Yeah. Two. It never happened, obviously. Never the right time for one reason or another. I guess in the end that's good. It would be hard to raise two children alone."

He paused, then tried to leaven the moment. "Why do I think Nancy would move in to help?"

That drew a bright laugh from her. "You're right. I wonder if the two of us would survive it."

"You two get along pretty well. You're just both opinionated."

"To say the least. What about you? Do you think of kids?"

"Once in a great while, but as you say, the time...or the person, isn't right." Nor did he have the least idea how to be a good father, a worry that often troubled him.

Then he decided he needed to share some of his past with her. It would probably appall her and push her away. Which would save him, too.

"Got some time to talk? Privately?"

She nodded.

"Nancy?"

"She's out with friends again. But let's go up to my attic. No one will disturb us there."

He wondered what the hell he was about to do. He *never* shared his childhood with anyone. The humiliation still hadn't completely faded away.

Nor had the sense that he should have done something much earlier than when he turned sixteen. The feeling that he should have killed the SOB to protect his mother. Guilt plagued him as much as shame.

Upstairs in her charming apartment, seated before her fireplace, its cheery flames causing shadows and orange light to dance around the space, he sought a way to begin. Speaking about this was such unknown territory that he wasn't sure how or where to begin.

"This would be a good time for a shot of whiskey," he remarked when they were seated with the coffee she made. He was glad of the space the individual chairs put between them. Made it harder for him to look directly at her, too. He wasn't sure he wanted to read her reactions.

"I'm sorry. Teetotaling house. Well, mostly, except for the beer up here. Do you want one?"

"No need to apologize. It would just be Dutch courage anyway."

She took a few minutes to make coffee in a small pot before saying, "I guess this isn't good."

He shook his head. "I've never told anyone else."

"It's safe with me."

He wouldn't be here if he'd thought otherwise. But where to begin? Samuel, of course. His fiery sermons that had left his wife and son feeling like sinful slugs destined for hell.

"My father," he began slowly, "was emotionally and physically abusive." He heard Lynn draw a sharp breath.

"Oh, God," she murmured.

"Yeah. I realize it happens to a lot of people. It also leaves an indelible mark. Anyway, I grew up with his Bible-thumping daily rants about how my mother and I were heading to hell if we didn't stop sinning. In my earlier years I didn't know what sins were, or which ones I was committing, but his description of hell terrified me."

He sipped coffee to wet a suddenly dry mouth. "I grew up believing I stood on the edge of a fiery abyss. Trying to behave in a way that wouldn't take me there, although I never knew what those sins were."

"That's awful beyond words," Lynn said quietly.

"It seemed natural to me at the time." He shrugged. "There was Adam, of course. We had good times together, but we never, ever, talked about what was going on at home. I was too ashamed. Maybe part of me assumed it was that way in every house. As I grew older, I knew it wasn't. I heard other kids talk."

"So you grew even more ashamed."

He didn't answer, but sat silently staring into the flames on the fireplace. He remembered how terrified he'd been of putting logs on the woodstove as a youngster, seeing those flames and embers as the gateway to hell.

"It was a secret," he said presently. "A family secret, and huge penalties were threatened if I talked outside the house."

He rubbed his eyes. "Anyway, I'm not sure how old I was when I woke up one night and came down the stairs to find my father beating my mother. Badly. I hadn't known, despite her bruises. She always explained them away and I finally quit asking. I guess she was trying to protect me."

"Probably," Lynn said quietly.

"After I saw that happen, I was no longer spared the physical punishment for every imagined sin or misdeed. I became terrified. And even though the thought crossed my mind, I didn't dare tell anyone else. I wasn't worried about myself so much, but I was terrified about what he'd have done to my mother."

He didn't look at Lynn. He didn't want to see her revulsion or, worse, her disappointment in him.

"Mom was never allowed out of the house, except once in a while when Adam's mother came over and brought him along. The bastard left her face alone, mostly. Same with me. I guess he didn't want anyone to see the bruises when I went to school."

"Oh, God," she breathed.

Jax shifted on his chair, facing perhaps the worst part of all. "It wasn't until I was sixteen that I…took it on. Stood up to him. I punched him out good. Really good. Threatened to kill him if he laid another hand on Mom. I must have had some kind of look in my eyes, because it stopped. It just stopped."

He sighed. "Too late. The damage was done. I should have killed him long before that. I'm sorry I didn't. Ashamed that I didn't do something sooner."

Then he fell silent, staring into the flames of hell.

LYNN ACHED FOR HIM, ached so hard that it hurt. With each breath the band around her chest grew tighter. Now she knew why he'd been such an introvert in school. Shame had kept him silent and withdrawn until it had become a way of life.

Thinking of all the hatred and pain he'd endured, all the suffering, facing it all alone without a living soul to turn to. Maybe even afraid to pray.

But to which god? she wondered. The god of vengeance or the god of love that he probably couldn't have imagined or believed in.

"Oh, Jax," she whispered.

"I survived," he said after a bit. "I survived and found out that Samuel's view was absolutely wrong. I found a different world, a better one in many ways. Well, except for war. There I walked into the very hell that Samuel had ranted about. But it was different because *men* make war."

She could understand that, glad only that he had made a distinction between men and God.

"Anyway, when you asked about kids, I thought about all of this. I wouldn't know how to be a good father. Not after Samuel."

Lynn hesitated, then offered, "It might be simpler than you think. Just don't do anything your father might have done."

At last he looked at her, his face stony. Then, slowly, he smiled faintly. "I guess that's one road map."

BARRY ARRIVED AT Miss Jasper's house just before three-thirty. He'd heard she was a stickler for promptness and he didn't want to irritate her.

She welcomed him into a house redolent of delicious baking and his mouth immediately began to water. "Your house smells wonderful, Miss Jasper."

Her elderly face crinkled in a smile. "I imagine you can't smell Bailey right now."

Barry laughed. "Absolutely not."

"Well, come in, come in. We're having a bit of a meeting in the living room, thanks to you. Just find a seat and I'll bring tea. Full tea, plenty of those baked goods."

Barry went to the living room on the left and froze on the threshold. What was he doing *here*?

He recognized Judge Wayne Carter and his father, lawyer Earl Carter. Reverend Molly Canton of Good

Shepherd Church. Librarian Emma Dalton who was married to the sheriff. Sarah Ironheart, who'd been a deputy here forever. A high-powered group.

A young college student was bound to feel intimidated.

But Miss Emma, as everyone called her, waved him to a seat beside her. "Don't be nervous, Barry. But since you brought this to our attention, you should be part of discussing solutions."

"Thank you, Miss Emma."

He had little to say except *thank you*, as Edith Jasper passed around plates and told everyone to help themselves to the pastries on one of those tall stands of stacked plates. Barry couldn't pass on the cinnamon buns, sticky or not.

Earl Carter, in his rumpled tweeds, began the conversation. A plump man in his sixties, he wore a gray combover proudly. "Unfortunately, we can't make a claim of slander against anyone, especially since we can't pinpoint the person who started this."

His son, the judge, spoke. He wore his usual jeans and cowboy boots with a blue flannel shirt. Barry had heard that he even wore those clothes under his judicial robe. "It wouldn't matter. The embroidery that's probably been added while this story has made the rounds would make it impossible to find the responsible parties anyway."

Reverend Molly Canton joined in. Her face was invitingly warm, her hair a rich chestnut streaked with gray. She wore her favored black skirt and a clerical shirt with collar. A dark gray sweater wrapped her. "I rarely give a fiery sermon, but I know how, and I'll give one. There's Saint Paul, of course. He *did* have something to say about gossip. Then there's the commandment *You shall not bear false witness against your neighbor.* Harmless rumors are one thing. Malicious gossip is entirely another."

"Malicious gossip can ruin lives," Sarah Ironheart agreed, neat in her deputy's uniform. "We've *got* to spike this one."

"Countergossip?" suggested Edith.

"Can you make it juicy enough?" wondered Sarah.

"That's the problem," agreed Miss Emma. "The entire problem. We need to move the town on to a new harmless scandal of some kind. I swear this is the spiciest rumor to ever spread around this county. No wonder it's on so many tongues."

Barry listened, then had an idea of his own. "I kinda know the girls who mentioned it to me. Well, I could identify them again anyway, I guess. And I could tell them they're totally wrong about Lynn. I mean, if Jax had been her lover all those times her husband was out of town, why would it take him over two years to get here? And why is he sleeping on a different floor of the house in his own room?"

He reached for another roll. "Besides, that house is almost never empty. If the guys suspected anything, they'd talk about it. As it is, they're upset by the gossip."

"That's a good argument," Edith said. "But will it spread far enough?" She looked at Barry.

"I can get the guys to help spread it. And our other friends. The thing is, don't most people feel important if they know a different story? One that really makes sense?"

Sarah Ironheart nodded. "It's true. People *do* like to know more than others. They won't be able to resist spreading it."

Barry felt pretty good then. He was the recipient of a

lot of smiles and nods. He also felt better about having allies besides the other roomers. That deserved another cinnamon roll.

"All right," said Edith, apparently the chairwoman of this gathering. "We'll spread the truth as a counter-measure. It may take a while for it to get very far, but once the ball is rolling, it should start rolling faster. And Molly will give a splendid sermon on Sunday." She shook her head slightly. "In my experience, most people would rather be nice than ugly, so that will help. I just hope we can stop this before it gets back to Lynn."

Barry hoped so, too. Lynn was far too nice to be treated this way.

But he had a feeling this was going to be like Sisyphus trying to roll that boulder uphill.

As Jax finished his second beer, emerging steadily from the past, he looked closely at Lynn. Beneath the layer of her sympathy for him, he saw heat building in her gaze. She wanted him. God.

He'd have been only too happy to oblige, but the memory of being stalked by an assassin reared up and silenced other thoughts. God, to drag Lynn into that. However remotely. She didn't deserve a large loss in her life. Not another one.

But the urge to move toward her steadily grew, until it had become nearly overwhelming.

Abruptly, she stirred. "Oh, dang. I can hear clatter-ing up through the heating duct. Mom must be cooking. I need to go help." She gave him a wan smile. "You can stay up here, if you want."

Given how raw he'd been feeling such a short time

ago, the invitation tempted him. But he shook his head. "Time to face the world again."

She rose. "I thought you were doing that."

He rose to follow her down the stairs, hoping the boys wouldn't see him emerge from the attic. Wouldn't that set their tongues wagging.

NANCY HAD INDEED begun cooking dinner. She smiled as Lynn and Jax joined her. "Steaks," she said. "I found some excellent ones from the butcher. Expensive, I know, but it's a treat. I have one each for the boys, too. I hope they like baked potatoes and broccoli."

Group dinners were going to become a tradition here, Lynn thought with mild amusement. Except for the fact that she wouldn't be able to keep it up once Nancy returned home. If Nancy ever did.

"You have that nice cast-iron grill to cook them on, too," Nancy continued. "I'm assuming, since it fits over two burners, that the whole thing heats well?"

"If you let it preheat long enough. I also have a smaller one if you need to add it."

"Good. We'll see."

Nancy nodded, then began to rub butter on the potatoes, wrapping each in a separate piece of foil. When she at last put them in the oven, she announced she was making tea and wondered if they'd like coffee. She didn't wait for an answer. "Of course you will." She set about making it, while heating water for herself.

"I like this induction boiler," she announced. "I wish you had an induction stove. So efficient and easy to clean."

Lynn watched her mother, wondering why she was

being so chatty about dinner. It was almost as if she were distracting herself. But from what?

Nancy at last joined them at the table, hot beverages all around. Jax remained silent, watching alertly. Evidently, he too felt something was going on.

At last satisfied, Nancy put her tea bag on a nearby saucer. Then she sighed.

"Mom? What's going on?"

"It shows?" Nancy shook her head. "I didn't want to tell you this."

"What's that? You've never kept secrets from me before."

Nancy looked down. "Because I've never had an embarrassing one before. I lost my job."

Lynn drew a sharp breath in shock. "But...but why?"

"Downsizing. Isn't that what they always call it? The legal business has fallen off because of the economy. Part-timers go first."

"Damn it," Lynn said. "Damn, that's awful! But then why are you buying steaks?"

Nancy shrugged. "Because, unlike your father, I know how to save money. Plus the firm cashed out my 401K. I still have time to decide whether to roll it over. Anyway, I'm financially set for years yet, especially since I've stopped paying rent on my apartment."

Lynn's jaw dropped. "You've given that up, too?"

Now Nancy grimaced. "It was financially wise."

Lynn braced herself, guessing what was coming. "Mom?"

Nancy averted her face. When she spoke, her voice sounded muffled, thick with embarrassment or sorrow. "Will you rent me a room? That one in the back that I'm using?"

Oh, God, Lynn thought. Her mother fussing around all the time? She loved Nancy, but this? Full-time? "Of course I will," she said, feeling bad about her reaction, knowing full well she'd never, under any circumstances, leave her mother homeless. Hell, she'd share her attic if Nancy could climb those stairs. "But no rent. You're my mom."

Nancy shook her head, sounding as if she sniffled a bit. "No, you're entitled to that. And I'd feel better about it, too." Then she shook herself. "Maybe it won't be for too long. I'll try to find my own place."

"Mom, don't even think about it. We'll manage."

Nancy at last offered her a watery smile. "I'm so ashamed. Humiliated to have to ask."

"God," Lynn said, "don't be. Things like this happen to a lot of folks. But you've got to stop buying steak for six people."

Nancy sniffled once, then gave a small laugh. "I promise." She looked at Jax. "I hope I didn't embarrass you, spilling all this in front of you."

"No, Nancy. I'm a lot harder to embarrass than this." Surprising Lynn, he reached across the table to cover Nancy's hand with his. Lynn was touched by the gesture.

Nancy drew a deep breath. "Earl Carter asked me for a date just yesterday. I suppose I should be happy about that. I haven't lost all my attractiveness."

"No, you haven't," Lynn protested. But her mind still ran over all the changes this would mean. "Well, as long as you can stand me stirring up dust and making a lot of noise, it'll be okay. And don't forget I'll get around to your bedroom eventually."

"I don't object," Nancy said. "I actually admire what you're doing. You'd never guess how much I wanted to

remodel that house we lived in when you were young.
Your dad never had two dimes to rub together, though,
and I doubt I could have done the work myself. Even if I
could have afforded the supplies. Anyway, I just worry
about *your* finances, not to mention your safety."

"I've been doing this for a while," Lynn reminded
her. "I'm careful. And Matt left me very well-set. Although," she added, trying to tease her mother, "when
I get finished here, I may do some remodeling in other
houses as a job."

"Oh, goodness!" Nancy answered. "Are you serious?"

Lynn had certainly thought about it. With all the
skills she was learning and all the pleasure she took in
the work, why not? But she merely smiled. Now Nancy
would have something else to nag her about. *That* thought
didn't exactly make her happy, but she didn't truly mind.

Her life had just majorly changed. Not good. But
maybe not so bad either.

LATER THAT INCREASINGLY cold night, Luke stood on the
sidewalk looking at the house that should have been his.
The bitterness never left him, gnawing away at his brain,
at his gut. Sometimes it was so strong that he thought it
would kill him.

He wished he'd never teamed up with Madge. Her
rumor idea had been good, but it was only temporary.
Sooner or later, the rumor mill would move on to something more interesting. Whether it did or didn't, though,
he was sure it wasn't going to harm Lynn in any way.
People knew her well—she'd grown up here. Her char-
acter would not yield to this kind of smear, not for long
anyway.

But his concern about Madge extended far beyond

her reluctance to do anything that might interfere with her ability to stalk that Stone guy. It was interfering with his own desires.

Worse, she was a lush. One big lush, and with four or five daiquiris in her, who knew what she would say? Would she repeat his unwise threat that there were other ways to get rid of Lynn?

Man, he should have kept that to himself, instead of trying to play the big, tough guy. Once again he'd shot his mouth off when he shouldn't have. He'd always done that too often, and despite being aware of it, he kept right on doing it, mainly because in the heat of the moment he couldn't zip his lips.

Now, on top of everything else, he had to worry about Madge.

Standing there, looking at his house, trying to figure out a decent plan, he kept coming back to a fire. A small one that wouldn't do too much damage but that might frighten Lynn.

Or better yet, might make her accept his help with some repairs. He had to be careful, however. His desire for that house had blown up big-time when he'd sued her. Everyone knew about it.

Maybe he hadn't been wrong when he'd suggested killing her. He wasn't sure he could do it, but damn, he wanted to.

Unfortunately, Madge knew all about it. Because he'd shot off his mouth.

Damn it all to hell. He might have to silence Madge as well. Or maybe silence Madge first so no direct line could be drawn between him and anything that happened to Lynn.

But first he needed people to see him as the sympathetic brother-in-law. The one who would put aside his grievances to help Lynn.

That would be a good thing. If he could ever get the bitch to stop slamming the door in his face.

His thoughts returned to the idea of a small fire. Yeah, maybe that was it after all. And damn Madge and her stupid idea that the Stone guy would ever want her. Only a blind fool would want that woman.

CROUCHED BEHIND A bush on the far side of the street, Terri Albright watched Luke Macy study the house. In her rare ventures to the bar, where if anyone asked, she could claim to be checking out the college, she'd heard about the lawsuit. About how he'd lost.

Her instincts said Luke was planning something. Maybe she could use him as a means of getting close to Jackson Stone.

Because Stone sure as hell didn't appear to be in a hurry to move on. No, he was settling in like a bug in a rug.

She swore silently. She had to get close enough to shove her KA-BAR into him. Or slash his throat. It shouldn't be this difficult. It shouldn't.

But it was.

She squatted there, wondering if there was some way to use Luke Macy as her tool. There had to be. After all, the guy was still apparently bitter about the house. Why else would he be standing there staring at it in the middle of the night?

She began to consider ways to get close to Luke, to manipulate him. To make him do something to get Stone alone. Just for long enough. Soon enough.

Ideas began to fester inside her.

Chapter Fourteen

In the morning, winter's cold breath blew through the streets, tearing the very last brown leaves from the trees. Gray, skeletal fingers reached toward a dark sky filled with heavy, drooping clouds. There'd been no more flurries, but the skies augured blizzards to come.

Halloween was right around the corner. Lynn didn't indulge in the increasingly popular decorations, but she asked her mother to go to the store for a ton of Halloween candy and a pumpkin.

Nancy brightened. "I can make pumpkin pie!"

Lynn smiled. "You do make the best piecrust."

"I tried to teach you," Nancy replied, ever the one to get in even the smallest of digs. "But you never liked any kind of cooking."

It was true, Lynn admitted to herself. She really didn't. Never had, never would. For her it was a necessity, unless an infrequent urge struck her.

She heard the rapid clomp of three boys racing down the stairs, one of them calling out, "See you later!"

Before she could answer, she heard the front door close behind them. Nancy was already pulling on her coat, undoubtedly with visions of a shopping expedition in her mind. Boy, did that woman love to shop, even at the grocery.

Jax had gone out earlier, saying something about a run.

Which left Lynn at sixes and sevens. She ought to be working, but the desire to do so had recently fled. She supposed it must have to do with all the recent changes and trying to adapt to them.

For some reason, with Halloween looming that weekend, she started to think about the upcoming holidays. Thanksgiving, Christmas, New Year. The boys would go home to their families, Jax would be off to his new posting and she and her mother would rattle around in this big old house.

So she started making a guest list of her friends, then asked herself what she was doing. This house wasn't ready for any kind of entertaining.

In past years, friends had asked her to join them when she was alone, but she always felt like an intruder amidst all those happy families. An outsider, even among good friends.

Odd. But then, she was odd.

Smiling wryly at herself, she looked around the kitchen, imagining how it would look repainted, resurfaced, with new appliances and a smaller table. Her mother was right about getting an induction stove. She truly liked her gas range, but one of those ceramic tops would be a whole lot easier to clean.

A Christmas tree, she decided. She hadn't put one up in quite a while, in fact not unless Matt would be home. When he wasn't, the sight of it never cheered her.

But now she had her mom here, and maybe the boys would enjoy it, too, before they skedaddled for the holidays. Maybe she and Nancy could wrap some empty boxes to put under it for some cheer. But man, wouldn't it look odd in that torn-up living room?

She laughed at herself, feeling a tad better. Holidays were always a tough time for her since her marriage, and tougher now that Matt was gone.

So she generally skipped them.

Perhaps not this year. Soon she should be able to find live poinsettias, too, to put around downstairs. Somewhere.

Okay, maybe lights to string up outside. Twinkling colors. She bet her boys would be glad to help her hang them. They were such good guys.

And green garlands with red bows along the porch railing.

Satisfied with her mental image, she tried to return her thoughts to work. They didn't want to go there. Not at all.

Too many changes too fast. Especially Nancy. Her mom was certainly going to change the dynamics around here. Lynn wondered how much she would still claim charge of. Her work, obviously, but what about the rest?

Only time would tell.

Gads!

Her mother returned surprisingly soon with several grocery bags. "The dentists around here are going to love me," she announced cheerfully.

She emptied the bags on the trestle table and Lynn was amazed. Bags of miniature candy bars, packets of M&M's. Gummies individually wrapped in small bags.

"Wow!" Lynn said.

"And these," Nancy announced, showing her a stack of decorated brown bags.

"You're going to bag them?" Lynn had never bothered.

"Oh, yes," Nancy said, pleased. "I'll do all the work, but it will make the children feel special."

"I know it will."

A knock at the front door dragged Lynn's attention away. "Be right back."

Lynn opened the door and found herself facing Luke Macy. God, no. Couldn't this guy take no for an answer?

"Hey, Lynn," he said with his smarmy smile. Then he frowned. "There's something I think you should know about. It's important."

"What? You're leaving town?"

He feigned sadness. "Seriously? No, there's a lot of gossip about you right now. I'm telling people it's not true, but..." He shrugged.

"So now you're my gallant defender?" She couldn't keep the sarcasm out of her voice. Nor did she invite him in from the cold, even though keeping the door open was freezing her.

"Hey, there's a difference between going for what's mine than letting you be slandered!"

"Slander?" She shook her head. "I suppose it all begins with you."

"Hardly." He put his hand to his heart. "I swear I didn't have anything to do with it. But they're saying you cheated on Matt all those times you claimed you were visiting him. And that you cheated on him with Stone."

Lynn felt as if he'd slapped her face. She wanted to slap his. Her breath stuck in her throat.

"That's a vicious lie," Nancy said sharply from behind her. "Vicious and malicious, and it's not one bit true. You get out of here, Luke Macy. Don't ever come back!"

He turned and walked away, shaking his head.

Lynn stood frozen and Nancy had to close the door.

Which she did with a bang. "Nobody would believe that tripe about you."

"But what if they do?" Sudden tears began to stream down Lynn's face. "Oh, Mom…"

Nancy gathered her close and stroked her hair. "It'll be all right, baby. You'll see. Just keep holding your head up."

LYNN SPENT THE next few hours sitting at the refectory table alternating between horror, pain and anger. And doubt. Luke could have made it all up. He was such a snake.

But she also doubted he *had* invented it. Was he bright enough to create a rumor that fit together so neatly? Or to be believed when everyone around here had his measure?

Someone smarter would have had to start it. But who?

Nancy put several miniature chocolate bars in front of her. "Chocolate always helps. Sorry I don't have a pint of ice cream. It's so soothing to sit and eat the whole thing with a spoon."

Lynn tried to smile but failed. She hurt too much.

"You'll see. People will come to their senses."

If it suited them, Lynn thought. But only if it suited them.

WHEN JAX RETURNED, his heightened senses alerted him to a change in the house. He hooked his jacket on a peg and went to the kitchen, finding Nancy and Lynn sitting at the table, Lynn looking sad enough to nearly break his heart.

He looked at Nancy. "What happened?"

Nancy snorted. "Dear old snake-in-the-grass Luke Macy came running by with an ugly bit of gossip about Lynn that he just couldn't wait to share."

Jax spied a nearly full coffeepot and poured himself some before joining the two women at the table. "What is it?"

Nancy answered. "Did you know you were having an affair with Lynn before Matt died?"

Jax's head jerked in shock. "Seriously?"

"So Luke said. It seems that every time Lynn left town to visit Matt, she was actually visiting you."

Rage rushed through Jax. "Really. During all those times I was probably on the other side of the planet. Besides, Lynn wouldn't dream of such a thing."

"Well, someone's cruel enough to deserve a piking."

Jax fell silent, unable to think of any way to stop the rumor. Except one. "I'll leave in the morning. Head on to Denver."

"Don't you dare," Nancy said sharply. "Don't give in to this. Besides, you don't want to inadvertently support the rumor right about the time you might have heard it. Leaving to protect Lynn. No, you stay right here. And I'll talk to all my friends, making it clear that not only is the rumor not true, but it's vicious and only a vicious person could have started it. They're not the kind to believe such a story anyway or they wouldn't be my friends."

Jax fell silent for a minute or more. "Madge Kearney caught up with me as I was cooling down after my run. I feel like an elk in that woman's sights. Could she be malicious enough to start this kind of talk?"

"It's possible," Nancy answered. "Anything's possible, but how drawing you into it would make it easier for her to lasso you I can't imagine. Or maybe someone added that bit later."

Lynn spoke, her voice a bit unsteady. "Does it matter

who started it? What am I gonna do? Sue?" Then she rose and went up to the safety and security of her attic apartment.

A SHORT WHILE LATER, Nancy prodded Jax. "Go on up to her. I would, except those stairs would cripple me. She doesn't need to be up there brooding by herself. God knows that girl has had all the brooding and sorrow she needs for a lifetime."

Jax nodded, agreeing. He didn't feel perfectly comfortable about invading Lynn's private space without an invitation, but Nancy was right. Lynn didn't need to be alone with this.

Before he left the kitchen, Nancy pressed a small bag into his hand. "Offer her this box of chocolates. I was saving it for her for later, but this seems like a good time. I'll take care of dinner, so she doesn't need to think about that."

"Thanks, Nancy."

She shrugged. "Unless I miss my guess, you have strong shoulders. Strong enough for her to cry on if she needs to." Her face darkened.

"I swear if I find out who started this…"

"Wait," she said. "Just a moment."

He heard her walk to her bedroom, then return quickly. She handed him a bottle of wine. "I know I'm not supposed to have this stuff here because of the students, but I keep this in my bedroom where they won't find it."

He smiled and started for the stairs. "I think Lynn will survive."

Jax had strong suspicions about Madge because he couldn't imagine who else might have a reason to start this rumor. But even though he'd grown up here, he was still a stranger and didn't know all that much about people here. He could be wrong.

Regardless, he was getting sick of Madge. He'd have loved to tear into her, but he wasn't the type. He hoped Lynn was, although he'd gathered from Madge's complaining a little while ago that Lynn had already told her to stuff it.

She's keeping me from seeing you.

Yeah, right.

At the door leading to Lynn's stairs, he knocked. He didn't wait for a response, but passed through and marched up those stairs. If there was anything he could do to make Lynn feel better, he was going to do it.

And screw the assassin who was on his tail. He'd given him opportunities and they hadn't been taken, even last night when he'd wandered streets and alleys while the rest of the household slept. The guy couldn't be here, must be waiting for Denver, a much larger city where a killing wouldn't stand out as much.

He *had* seen Luke staring up at the house, though. That man would bear watching.

He found Lynn curled up on her bed under a comforter in the relative dark. There was little enough light from the gray day to pour through the attic windows. He set the wine on the kitchen counter, along with the bag of chocolates, then turned on a few lights and the electric fireplace. The room filled with a warm glow.

He sat on the bed beside her and began to gently rub her shoulder through the comforter. He thought he felt a shiver run through her.

"It's too much, isn't it?" he said quietly. "Too much happening, a lot of it not so good. Although I must say your mom is a gem. Irritating, but a gem nonetheless."

He thought he heard a watery chuckle, then slowly, her damp face emerged from beneath the covers.

"I'm overreacting," she said shakily.

"I don't think so. Now you're going to feel uncomfortable every time you leave this house. That's not right."

She didn't deny it. Her eyes closed and she drew an unsteady breath. "No one who knows me will believe it."

"Nope. Not a one." He didn't mention those who didn't know her well, the ones who were doing the talking.

"But someone's talking. A lot of someones." She pushed herself up, wiping at her face. "I've dealt with worse. Like after Matt died. It wasn't only the grief, it was the folks who avoided me, like I had the plague or something."

"Probably because they didn't know what to say. Maybe because they didn't want to bury you in condolences that wouldn't help at all."

"They don't, do they? In fact, they feel empty. Automatic."

"Heartfelt, I'm sure. But I know what you're saying. They just don't matter at such a time, except maybe from a very few people."

He wanted to hug her, but wasn't sure she was ready to be touched. "Listen, your mom sent up some chocolates and wine for you."

She sat up straighter. "Wine? She knows the house rules."

"She's human and stashes it in her bedroom. Where no one will open it without her knowing, if they even find it."

She rolled her eyes, sniffling. "That's my mom. I promised the college I wouldn't have any spirits in the house. Well, except for my beer up here. And you're right, the boys never come up here. It'd be a dead giveaway if they took some of those bottles."

He chuckled. "None of them strikes me as the type to want to get into that kind of trouble. And while I've been here, none of them have come home smelling like beer or acting like they've had too much to drink."

"That's true," she admitted. "The college tries to make sure I don't get any troublemakers."

"There you go. Want a glass of wine? Or would you prefer chocolates?"

At last the smallest smile dawned on her face. "You don't have to babysit me, Jax."

"It may surprise you, but I *want* to be here with you. This isn't babysitting." Far from it. Wrong time, but her mere presence was fanning the flames of hunger in him.

After a moment, she threw back the comforter and padded over to the small counter where he'd left the bottle and the bag.

"A screw-top chardonnay," she remarked.

"What? You expect her to deal with a cork in that room?"

At last she laughed. "I was joking. I'm not some kind of wine snob."

"Good, because I don't know a damn thing about it. My education was deprived in some areas."

She sent him a sideways look. "This isn't an important one. Would you like a glass? No goblets up here."

"A glass would be perfect."

She poured for them both and handed him a glass. "I love chardonnay," she told him. "I guess Mom's tastes are similar."

They sat before the fire, feet up on hassocks. Jax felt

pleasantly warm, and the soft glow of lamps held the unpleasant day at bay.

"Why," Lynn asked, "do you think Luke came to tell me about the rumor?"

Jax shrugged. "He's the guy who sued you. I get the feeling he'll do anything to make you miserable."

"Yeah, probably." She shook her head. "Sometimes I think he's a bit unhinged."

"He's obviously nasty."

"He started that lawsuit only a couple of weeks after Matt was buried. I'll never forget how I felt when the papers were served. Thank God for Earl Carter. He stepped in and told me he'd take care of everything. He pretty much did, but it didn't make me feel any better."

Jax sipped his wine, deciding he liked it. "How could it? I'd have hated Luke."

"I think I still do."

And none of this was helping her get away from her sad, grim thoughts, which was what he'd come up here to do.

Then at the same instant, they looked at each other.

The heat of desire broke its bonds.

JAX ROSE SLOWLY, never taking his eyes from her, everything else forgotten.

Lynn too rose, facing him. "Jax?" she whispered.

"I don't think I can stop," he answered, his voice low. "Tell me to go now."

She gave a jerky shake of her head. "I've been wanting you almost since I saw you. I'm as bad as Madge."

"You couldn't possibly be. Besides, I feel the same about you, and don't mention that woman to me. She's infuriating and a liar. You're not. You're lovely, admirable and, oh, God, so beautiful."

"Me?"

"You need to look in a mirror." He stepped toward her, slowly closing the space between them. "Even in your work clothes. I can't stop staring at you. Do you know you have the most attractive tush?"

She gasped, then a laugh spilled out of her. "Don't make me laugh. It'll ruin the mood."

He reached her and pulled her into his arms. "Laughter *is* part of the mood. Laugh away, you won't stop me."

She drew a sharp breath and her eyes grew hazy and heavy lidded. "I don't want to stop you. Don't stop, Jax. Please don't stop."

As if he could. Pressing his mouth to hers, he once again tasted the honeyed space, drawing his tongue along her lips, feeling a shiver course through her. From there, temptation led him down the side of her throat, feeling silken skin with his lips and tongue.

"You smell so good," he murmured huskily.

"So do you," she whispered.

But he also detected the scent of rising passion just beginning. The scent itself was nearly maddening. Soon it would perfume the entire room.

His fingers plucked at the buttons on her shirt, opening them, eager to bare her to his gaze. His body engorged almost painfully, not wanting to wait. Too bad.

Then he felt her reach for the hem of his sweatshirt, sliding her hands beneath, touching him, touching his heated skin, fingers dancing in a way that drove him even higher if that was possible. Light touches, growing bolder.

He stripped the shirt from her at last, revealing a plain

white cotton bra. He dealt with it with a simple twist of his fingers and then she fell free.

Reaching out, he cradled her breasts. "So perfect," he murmured, brushing his thumbs over her hardening nipples.

"Jax, please," she moaned. "Please!"

Reluctantly, he released her long enough to rip his sweatshirt over his head, to unzip his jeans and kick them away. Then he knelt before her, kissing her just beneath her ribs, then over her belly as he pulled away her jeans and undies.

Kissing her at last at the apex of her thighs.

She trembled and he felt her on the verge of collapse. He rose to his feet and lifted her easily across his arms, carrying her to the bed.

She lay there naked, looking up at him with a drowsy smile, surely the most gorgeous woman he'd ever seen. A firm body from hard work, delicate feet with high arches. The stuff of his dreams.

LYNN, ACHING THOUGH she was, stared at the man who stood over her. Perfect in every respect, muscled for endurance, not for show. Hard, even around his waist, a surprising washboard belly. She hadn't guessed…

Not a spare ounce of weight on him. Not one. And as she took in his arousal, her every nerve cried out for the pressure of his body on hers, for him to fill her until she cried out.

But instead of giving her what she wanted right then, he bent over her, stroking her gently, igniting zings of electricity everywhere he caressed her.

Reaching out, she wanted to touch him as he touched her, wanted to memorize all of him with her hands until he was imprinted forever on her memory. Longing to savor every moment while still growing impatient for fulfillment.

When at last he lay down beside her, she was burning like a torch. The press of skin on skin filled her with pleasure. He radiated heat that wrapped around her, seeming to make her safe, safe enough to throw caution to the wind.

Then he took her around the waist and lifted her until she straddled him, his hardness pressed to her softer petals.

"Ride me," he said gutturally, lifting her by the hips and lowering her gently until he filled her. She threw back her head as tender tissue stretched to receive him. So good.

Then she leaned forward, hands on his broad shoulders, rocking slowly. Groans escaped them both.

She rode him to the stars, then at the same moment she shattered into a shower of sparks, he joined her.

LATER THEY RESTED beneath the covers in gentle embrace. Her head rested in the hollow of his shoulder, her arm stretched across his chest. One of her legs lay across his.

His arms wrapped around her, holding her close. The air around them held the perfume of their lovemaking but Lynn could still inhale his particular scent. The scent of man. The clinging scent of the outdoors. A wisp of soap.

The taste of wine as she raised her head briefly to kiss him.

When he spoke, it was a single word. "Wow."

"Double wow," she replied, feeling as if she could purr like a contented cat.

He laughed quietly, giving her a squeeze.

Lynn could have lain there nearly forever, enjoying this closeness, hoping for another experience like the one they had just had. She was, she realized, going to hate it when this man returned to duty.

But Jax's mind had begun to stray. He'd been lax about this assassin. What if he was pulling Lynn into danger beside him?

The idea of leaving her had been difficult for some time, but now he hated the thought.

But the danger. Oh, man, the danger. He ought to pull on his clothes right now and leave her safely in her world while he dragged himself away from it.

But now that might seriously wound her.

Soon, he promised himself, but not right this instant.

A few minutes later, his cell phone rang. He stiffened immediately.

"Do you have to answer?" she asked drowsily.

"Yeah." He tried to lighten his tone. "A Marine is never off duty, even while on leave."

She sighed, but didn't protest when he rose to tug the damn thing out of his jeans on the floor. Then he closed himself in her small bathroom.

Damn, it was Briggs again, but the call had already ended. He returned it immediately.

"Stone," he said.

"News," Briggs answered. "The investigative team suspects Albright's sister, Terri Albright. A Marine. She's on leave right now."

Jax swore. "Well, that might explain a lot. I've been on the lookout for a man."

"That would be the first thought, given the violence. Nobody's sure yet, but the circle is closing."

A woman, Jax thought after he disconnected. A

woman. He knew women in the Corps, efficient and deadly. Good fighters. Certain stereotypes lingered, he thought with disgust. Including in him. He never would have thought this assassin could be a woman. But why not, given what he had seen of women in battle?

He wore his own blinders.

Damn it to hell. He'd been looking at the wrong people. He could have let Terri Albright walk up to him in broad daylight and shove a knife under his ribs.

Stupid. Stupid, stupid, stupid.

MADGE WAS ON her fourth daiquiri in the middle of the afternoon. Luke sat across the table at the roadhouse, fuming. God, he should never have hooked up with her.

"I put a snake in her mailbox," Madge said, her voice slightly slurred.

"Why the hell did you do that?"

"I wanted to scare her. But Stone was there and got to play the hero. I didn't expect that."

"What good would scaring her do?"

"Make me feel better," Madge answered. "Plus, I wanted her to wonder if somebody was out to get her."

"Guess that didn't work."

Madge shrugged. "The rumor is working better."

"Yeah? Well, I told her about it and all I got was a door slammed in my face. What's more, there's push-back now."

Madge looked at him. "Pushback?"

"Seems some people aren't going to let it continue. They're making it die down already."

"Hell," said Madge and waved to the bartender for another drink. "Doesn't matter. You'll think of something." She gave him a sloppy grin. "It's your turn now."

Like kids playing a game. Only this was no game. Luke eyed Madge with disgust. How had she ever gotten married so many times? He guessed some guys hadn't been able to see anything but her ample breasts and generous cleavage.

Instead of bringing another daiquiri, the bartender came over holding a cup. "Sorry, Miss, but I'm cutting you off. Too much, too fast."

"You can't do that!" Madge's voice rose.

"I can. Next drink is coffee." He put a full mug on the table in front of her.

"This is an insult!"

The bartender shrugged and walked away.

Luke struggled to suppress a grin.

"I'll just go somewhere else," she announced loudly. "You treat a lady like this? This bar sucks."

Luke watched her yank her jacket on and storm toward the door. Her unsteadiness was visible. He hoped, savagely, that she'd wrap her car around a tree. Or a signpost. At this point he didn't care if she died or spent the rest of her life in a wheelchair.

Then he returned to thoughts about how to get even with Lynn. Damn her to hell. Would it have been so hard for her to just *share* with him? He was entitled.

He was sipping his way through his second draft beer when an attractive young woman with nearly black hair streaked with purple walked through the door. She was wearing jeans and a jacket, but that did nothing to detract from her. She wandered up to the bar, unzipping her jacket to display a nice rack beneath a tight turtleneck.

Luke waited a minute, saw men look, but none moved toward her. She sat on an empty stool, no one nearby.

Then Luke approached the bar. "Buy you a drink?" he asked with his most winning smile.

She looked at him from dark eyes, hesitating. He liked that hesitation. Not a bar rat. Then slowly, she smiled. "Sure, why not?"

Before long he learned her name was Terri and that she was scoping out the area with an eye to attending the community college. A very open young girl, not in the least trying to keep secrets from a stranger. Naive. Oh, yeah!

After a bit, feeling he'd created a trustworthy impression and some decent rapport, he offered to show her around, waxing eloquent about his knowledge of the area. Even offering to introduce her to some other students who could talk with her about the college.

She seemed so appreciative. Well, she might be an amusement to distract him while he plotted. He sure needed something to use to put a brief hold on his fury. It was starting to wear him out.

Terri smiled at him, looking as if he were the best thing since sliced bread.

That was fine by him. And it appeared he was done with Madge. Even better.

"I needed to meet someone like you," she said quietly, and let him buy her another beer.

Chapter Fifteen

A woman. Jax was still mad at himself. Stereotyping. Damn, he ought to know better. But kicking his own butt wasn't going to improve anything. Now he had a better idea what to watch for. Just be glad that Hugh Briggs had given him the heads-up. Maybe Briggs had suspected that Jax would fall for an assumption. Maybe Briggs had initially fallen for it, too.

Not that it made Jax feel any better about himself.

When he looked at Lynn, he was reminded of all the amazing things a woman could do if she put her mind to it. How could he have ignored that fact, even though it was about someone else?

But self-castigation wasn't going to get him anywhere.

Nancy invited him to join her and Lynn for dinner. The woman was still working on her matchmaking. He'd have been amused if the truth weren't getting so close to Nancy's wish.

When he looked at Lynn now, all he could see was her gentle face, all he could do was remember that wonderful time they'd shared just this afternoon. A time he wanted to repeat soon, but instead he had to figure out how to deal with a killer. One who might not care if someone else got in the way.

But in the process of stepping back, he might wound Lynn, who wouldn't expect a distance between them now. Nor should she.

God, the horns of this dilemma had pierced him to the core.

After a savory dinner of roast pork and stuffing, after he had helped clean up, he announced he needed to go out for a walk.

"Gotta keep those muscles stretched," he said. Lynn appeared disappointed, maybe even a little hurt. But why should she? At this time of evening, she couldn't expect them to trot upstairs. Not with Nancy still up and very much aware, judging by the faint smugness on her face, of what might be happening.

The three students blew in along with the frigid air, carrying pizza boxes that had to be stone-cold by now, considering the pizzeria was on the edge of town.

Jax shrugged inwardly. What kid didn't like cold pizza, as long as it hadn't sprouted icicles?

So once again he trod the night-darkened streets of Conard City. Tonight, for some reason, the streetlights, turning into lanterns as he approached the downtown area, didn't seem to be driving back the shadows very well. In fact, they added to them.

At night, though, he could see the increased number of hiding places, especially in the alleys. But what made him think this woman would hide? The best strategy of all would be for her to appear in the open, as if she belonged here.

Early holiday shopping had begun, drawing many residents out on this cold evening. Freitag's was bright with light and full of people. The little toy store he'd never seen as a child also contained quite a few people. The bakery was open, catering to shoppers who might need a warm drink or a hot bowl of soup.

Inside it, he saw about a dozen people at tables. At one table he spied Luke Macy with a black-haired young woman with outrageous purple stripes in her hair. She was smiling and he was laughing.

Damn, Jax hated that man. But there he was, catting around as apparently he always had. Her expression suggested she was fascinated. He hoped she figured out that jerk before she got hurt.

But nothing seemed out of place. Not one thing. No one acted suspiciously. No one looked at him oddly or too intently. No battle-honed instinct warned him.

Damn, he just ought to get on to Denver, promising Lynn he'd return soon. He'd be able to. Recruiting had fallen off markedly after a twenty-year war. A generational war, some called it, because sons and daughters had followed their fathers and mothers right into it.

Because many young people couldn't remember a time without a war.

Besides, the number of recruits sought by the military had fallen off, too.

Starting to feel grumpy, seriously annoyed with himself, he slowly walked back to Lynn's place.

Denver, he thought again. It would be easiest to kill him in the bigger, more anonymous crowds. They would provide the best cover. The best escape routes. His death could easily be passed off as an unfortunate mugging.

A return to Denver would be the best way to protect Lynn from the ugliness that stalked him. And he was far more worried about Lynn than himself.

LYNN SHARED A cup of tea with her mother after Jax left. Tea and sympathy, she thought, though she wasn't asking for the sympathy.

She had other things on her mind, things she didn't want to share with Nancy.

She didn't know whether to be disappointed or worried that Jax had left for a walk. She'd felt the tension in him since that phone call and wondered if he'd been called back to duty. That had happened once with Matt, when his unit received orders to depart. He'd had to race back to join them.

It could happen.

But what if he was regretting their lovemaking? What if he considered it just a fling he needed to escape? She hadn't gotten that feeling, not the way they had hugged and laughed afterward. Not the way he had squeezed her with a tight hug before he dressed. He hadn't acted like a man who wanted to get away.

But what if he'd been disappointed in her? What if he'd wanted something she hadn't provided? What if she was a lousy lover? Matt had never complained about any such thing, but Matt had loved her. Jax did not.

She looked down into her teacup while Nancy talked about a card game she had planned for the next evening with her friends. She resisted the urge to press her hands to her warm cheeks. God, what if her mother saw her blush?

Suddenly a word that Nancy spoke caught her attention. "Did you say *poker*?"

"What's wrong with that?" Nancy asked her. "You think we should play Old Maid?"

Unhappy or not, Lynn had to laugh at that. "Just tell me you're not gambling for real."

Nancy shrugged. "None of us is wealthy enough to play for real money. Chips only, dear. Give me some credit."

Lynn answered drily. "As long as it's not a credit on my bank."

It was Nancy's turn to laugh. "What a thought!"

"I never know what you might do, Mom."

"Good. I wouldn't want to be too predictable."

But Nancy was in so many ways. She loved to shop. She loved to gather with her friends. She loved to needle her daughter. Lynn hadn't gathered with her friends in a few weeks now. She missed them.

But not as much as she was missing Jax, and he'd only been gone for a few hours. Not long at all. Dang, was she going to feel truly awful when he left to return to duty.

She ought to be worrying about that. Instead she worried about the tension she'd sensed in him since that phone call.

JAX TURNED AROUND and returned to the bakery instead of heading straight back to Lynn's place. Melinda still had some baked goods left for her evening crowd, so he bought some cheese Danish for the women back at the house.

While he stood paying, he felt a niggle at the back of his neck. He was being stared at.

He turned quickly but saw no one looking at him. He scanned the room again as he left with his white bag of delights, but everyone appeared involved in their own conversations.

Heading down the streets, he was reluctant to dismiss that feeling. Even animals knew when they were being watched, and war honed that instinct in humans.

But wherever the feeling had come from, it was gone as he walked away from the bakery. Casual interest on someone's part? Maybe. But whatever had caused it, given that an assassin was after him, he took it as a warning.

And a reminder to get out of this small town as quickly as he could unless he discovered a valid clue. But first he had to find a way to ease himself away from Lynn. A way that wouldn't leave her feeling wronged or used.

Damn it all to hell. He should never have given in to his desire for her. Should never have put her in the position to feel wounded.

Maybe it was time for a brain transplant.

LUKE ENJOYED HIMSELF hugely with Terri. She hung on his every word, laughed at even his worst jokes, and the expression in her dark eyes… Well, he figured she was seriously drawn to him.

Over the last couple of years, he'd forgotten how good it could feel to win a woman's undivided attention.

After they'd filled themselves with the bakery's delights, Luke suggested Mahoney's bar, right around the corner.

Terri looked hesitant. Luke liked that in her. Not at all easy. A little hard-to-get only made the chase better.

But at last she nodded. "I can't stay too late," she told him. "I'm staying with a friend out on one of the ranches. I don't want her to worry."

"I'd even be glad to take you home."

She shook her head. "I have my own car. But thanks."

Well, strike one. No hanky-panky in the back seat of his car. Maybe tomorrow night.

Mahoney's was crowded. It always was. The jukebox

played, voices grew louder as the alcohol flowed, but Luke didn't mind. The noise would make a cocoon for them to talk without being overheard. Although why he should worry about being overheard he didn't know. Or didn't think about.

After a couple of beers, while Terri sipped slowly on her first one, he found himself talking. About the house, about Lynn, about his anger and frustration.

He had found a sympathetic audience, so he didn't hold back. He went so far as to say he wanted to get even with Lynn.

Terri was all sympathy. "I wish I could help," she said when he finished his rant.

"Maybe you can," he said heedlessly forgetting that some things were better kept to himself.

"Just let me know," she replied with the sweetest smile.

Luke was pleased. She understood why he was so angry, and she wanted to help him in some way. Good. He might have found a better ally than Madge.

By the time they parted, they'd made a date for the next afternoon. His head swimming with desire and beer, Luke ambled home. He felt as if he were walking on air.

TERRI RETURNED TO her miserable camp about a mile out of town, beneath trees that lined the side of a dirt road. Almost nobody drove along there, she'd found, so her small camp stove wouldn't be noticed, especially since she'd pulled back farther into the woods.

But it was getting outrageously cold and she was outrageously tired of instant coffee. At least it was hot. She warmed her hands over the propane burner, then put the small pot on to boil water. Her gloves didn't feel thick enough, her hands lost the flame's heat too quickly.

Meeting Luke Macy had worked out better than she had hoped when she saw him standing in front of that house. Now she had the entrée she'd needed in the one-horse town. Potential college student, friend of Luke Macy. She didn't have to lurk any longer.

The more important thing was now she could walk around town on the arm of that lousy con artist who presented himself as the Big Man-about-town. She'd have to giggle like a disgusting infatuated kid. People would look and hardly notice, including that hateful Stone. She'd have cover to get close to him, but her time was getting short. Too short.

She might just have to kill Stone *and* his new girlfriend. Both of them. Leaving a bigger trail than she wanted to.

When at last she crawled into her sleeping bag, using her jacket for a pillow, she stared up into the night, indulging dark thoughts of her own, thoughts darker than the midnight above.

Figure it out, she told herself. *You're smart enough.*

Chapter Sixteen

When Jax returned to Lynn's place with his bag of pastries, Lynn had vanished and only Nancy sat in the kitchen, drinking her inevitable tea. He placed the white bag on the table, saying, "Danish for you two." Then he looked around. "Lynn?"

"She went up to her hermitage. Why don't you go on up?" she added suggestively.

This time, Jax was far from amused. "That's enough, Nancy. I wasn't invited."

For an instant she appeared taken aback. "I was only thinking about her being alone. She hasn't been too happy of late. Anyway, I wish to hell she'd get a house phone or something so I could call her and tell her you brought home these nice Danish. She loves them."

Well, Jax allowed, Lynn had seemed a little down. And she was only going to get more down when he had to tell her a lie, that he'd been called early to Denver. He never lied.

God, how was he going to manage that? If it felt like his skin was being ripped off, how would she feel? Not that bad, he hoped. He hoped like hell he hadn't taken this too far for her sake.

But he couldn't tell her the truth. He couldn't make her worry about him. She'd had enough of that with Matt.

He made coffee to drive away the chill and plopped down at the table with Nancy. She got a plate and put the Danish on it. They both looked at it, but neither reached for any.

"Melinda makes the best Danish," she remarked.

"I haven't had any before."

Inanities, both of them acutely aware of Lynn upstairs. Hiding? Fearing what he might say? Trying to pretend it didn't matter?

Or kissing him off first, to spare herself humiliation.

After a while, Nancy made herself some more tea. Eventually she spoke.

"I know Lynn finds me irritating," she said. "She's grown up and I'm still acting like her mother."

"You *are* her mother."

She shook her head. "I don't quite mean it that way. We clash a lot, mostly because I keep wanting things to be different for her and she doesn't want the same things. I need to learn to bite my tongue. I doubt I ever will."

"She loves you, too."

"I don't doubt it, but she's never tried to tell me how to live or how to dress. She's never been a girlie-girl, if you get what I mean. No interest in clothes or makeup or all that other stuff. A tomboy of sorts. A special person."

"Very special."

Nancy smiled faintly. "She's also very strong, as well as strongheaded. We've been clashing since she was ten years old over one thing or another. A decent father might have understood better, but she never had that."

Looking down into her cooling tea, she sighed. "I never wanted her to restore this house. An overwhelming task requiring so many skills, but look how well she's done, how much she's had to learn to do all this. I definitely didn't want her to take roomers. I thought of college students as wild, partying young men. Well, look at this group. I was wrong once again."

Jax nodded, listening with interest. Nancy was opening up in a way he never would have suspected. He also thought Lynn needed to hear this more than he did.

He looked up at the ceiling.

Nancy saw his gaze and nodded, as if she understood he was thinking of Lynn upstairs by herself. "She needs the space up there right now. If we're going to live together, I need to learn to give her space. Living apart achieved that for a while, but no more living apart, at least until I can manage a place of my own."

Jax nodded and went to get another cup of coffee before returning to the table.

Nancy sighed again. "She's been so wounded in important ways. Losing her father, losing Matt. Especially Matt. Yet she just keeps plowing ahead. She's remarkable."

"She's got a spine of steel," Jax agreed. Down, but apparently never out for the count. She just kept right on putting her life back together.

He'd known a lot of people who weren't capable of that. He never wanted to be someone who made her rebuild herself all over again. Another good reason to hightail it out of here, before feelings grew too strong.

A little while later they heard Lynn's light footsteps in the hallway overhead. She appeared just a minute later, her hair damp, her clothes fresh.

"Man," she said as she joined them. "That shower felt good. I hope I left some hot water for the boys."

"They can take cold showers," Nancy said. "Might do them some good."

Lynn grinned. "Now, Mother..." Then she saw the plate on the table. "Ooh, is that Danish?"

"Jax brought it home," Nancy said. "Grab some coffee and dive in. I know you love it."

Jax was so relieved to see Lynn smiling that some of his tension seeped away. For tonight at least. She grabbed a napkin and tucked into a large piece of the Danish.

"Heaven," she said as she slipped a bit into her mouth. "Thanks."

"Speaking with your mouth full?" Nancy teased.

Lynn swallowed. "Not fair, asking me a question when I can't answer."

Jax laughed. "You two make quite a pair."

Sitting there, he realized that the bonds of this small family were strong, and that he'd been invited into the tightly knit group created by mother and daughter. A special place. Something he'd never known, except in the brotherhood of the Corps. And that wasn't the same. Not like this.

"I think I'll get back to work tomorrow before the fundraiser for the motel," Lynn announced. "Well, I've sort of been working, but that's more like daydreaming about later projects. The point is, if I don't get that living room done, nobody will have any place to congregate except in this kitchen. I don't know about you, Mom, but I'm getting awfully tired of it."

"And I'm sick of this ugly green," Nancy remarked tartly. "If I could, I'd pay someone to come in and blow it up."

Lynn giggled. "That'd ruin all my plans."

Nancy arched a brow. "No, it'd just mean you don't have to do the demolition."

Even Jax laughed at the image, although he felt far from laughing about anything.

"Or," said Nancy, "I could just get a gallon of paint and cover it all up."

"Dang, Mom," Lynn said. "This room would be unusable."

"Well, of course. And then you'd have to get to it sooner."

"Sheesh, organizing my life much?"

Nancy smiled. "Just trying to be helpful."

NANCY WENT TO her room a half hour later, saying she wanted to watch the late-night comedy shows. "I love them. When you get to my age, you don't seem to need as much sleep. Staying up late and getting up early. Sort of like my father used to do."

"While dozing in his chair on and off," Lynn teased.

"Well, yes. And if I doze off, you won't hear me complain."

Feeling suddenly shy, Lynn looked at Jax. In the instant their eyes connected, a powerful electricity surged between them. Jax's eyes blazed. Her own felt heavy lidded. Her heart skittered.

"Upstairs?" he asked quietly.

She nodded and headed that way with him right behind her. As they passed through the second-floor hallway, sounds of a video game emerged from one of the boys' rooms.

Imagining their fun leavened her heart. Then her feet grew lighter as well. She and Jax took the stairs to her attic like kids at a full run.

By the time she reached the top, she was laughing and he was grinning.

He spoke. "We aren't eager or anything."

"I can't wait," she answered truthfully, breathing more heavily. Familiar with each other now, they stripped before one another's gaze. Lynn enjoyed unwrapping herself all the while watching him do the same, as if he were a Christmas present. Maybe he was, early or not.

A wonderful-looking man. She wouldn't have changed a single thing about him. He drew her to him, pressing their bodies close together.

"You're beautiful," he said, his voice husky.

"I'm too ropy from all that work."

He pulled his head back a bit. "Ropy? You need to look at yourself in a mirror sometime. What you are is gorgeous and perfectly proportioned."

A giggle rose in her. "You're just saying that."

He lifted her from her feet and placed her on the bed. "You're perfect."

He lowered himself beside her and began to run his hands over her. "Perfect," he murmured again.

He sure didn't take long to arouse her, she thought hazily. His hands seemed to be painting her with fire. The kisses he dropped lightly over her neck and breasts made her sizzle. She heard herself call his name.

But he was far from done teasing her. He drew one of her engorged nipples into his mouth, and with each suck he plucked a cord that ran all the way to her center, causing her to throb. She dampened, readying for his possession.

"Jax…"

"I want to take my time," he whispered, "learn every inch of you."

She grabbed his shoulders, pulling hard. "Screw that," she said. "Next time. This time…"

He slid his hand between her legs, rubbing gently. "Easy, easy…"

But she didn't want to wait. Each moment felt as if it were stolen, a gift, one she didn't want to waste. Her body demanded him with the force of the tidal wave he unleashed in her, a wave that rolled over her, then pulled her into a rip current she couldn't escape.

"Jax…"

He gave in to her demand at last, settling himself over her, finding his way inside her.

She gasped with sheer pleasure, feeling that she was somehow coming home, even as his steady movements and his mouth on her breast lashed her higher into the wilds of passion.

For this short time, he belonged to her. He *was* hers.

With a shudder, she exploded into hot embers in his arms. She felt him jerk, then follow her into a place beyond the stars.

AFTERWARD, STILL DAMP, they cuddled beneath the comforter, wrapped in each other's arms as if they had melded into one.

Neither spoke, as if they both knew they had been thieves of time, stealing these minutes out of the maw of reality.

A sudden hammering on the downstairs door jerked them out of heaven and dropped them with a thud back into the present.

"Lynn!" yelled Tom. "Lynn, there's a fire!"

Lynn opened her eyes and saw the flicker of firelight

in the front attic windows. "Oh, my God..." She was out of the bed like a shot, cramming herself into clothes.

Jax jumped up as if he were on fire himself. He started yanking on his clothes.

Lynn headed down the stairs as fast as she could go, with Jax right behind her.

The boys already clutched Nancy and her jacket and were scuttling her to the back door with them.

Seeing the hot red glow through the front window, Lynn and Jax grabbed their jackets from the hall peg and hurried after them, bursting through the door into the backyard.

"I called the fire department," Will said just as the sound of sirens filled the night air.

"I need to see," Lynn said, heading around the side of the house to the front. She couldn't possibly stand there and just wonder. "I *have* to see!"

"Be careful," Jax said, taking her arm. "Steady. You don't want to break a leg out here."

She didn't care. Was all her love and work going up in smoke? A dream, once shared with Matt, now hers alone, but still a dream to take the old run-down house and make it bright and beautiful once again. Dying in a blaze.

She rounded the corner to the front and saw that her porch roof was on fire. She froze, but Jax pulled her back to the sidewalk across the street.

All she could do was stare. Just stare helplessly.

Flames licked their way along the roof of the front porch, blackening the porch ceiling beneath, trying to leap up the side of the house above it. Her heart began to crumble even as the sirens drew closer. The coda to her life as she'd rebuilt it?

JAX SAW THAT once her shock began to pass, fury began to tighten her face. He got it. He definitely got it. All he could do was draw her into his arms and hold her as the fire seemed to grow like a ravening beast.

But before it could spread much beyond the porch roof, the fire department arrived and began to douse it with water. A few of the firefighters retrieved Nancy and the boys safely from the backyard and insisted they all move to the far side of the street.

She couldn't take her eyes off the mess, hardly noticing her mother and her roomers.

"My roof," she murmured. "The heat will peel the paint. The gingerbread will have to be scraped and painted again. The new roof... All that work..."

At last she began to cry.

And Jax began to think of vengeance. He thought of Luke. He also knew he couldn't leave Lynn as soon as he'd planned. To hell with whether he got knifed in the back.

PASTOR MOLLY CANTON ARRIVED, edging her way through the growing crowd of onlookers. The fire was out, the flames gone, but the firemen still had to pull out their axes and open the roof, open the walls to make sure there were no remaining hot spots. More damage. More destruction.

Molly, dressed haphazardly in jeans, Wellingtons and a bright red parka, approached Lynn and gave her a tight hug. "We've got the church hall set up for you. All of you. You'll be warm tonight, or as many nights as you need."

Her feelings dulled, Lynn barely managed a nod, clinging to Jax's arm. "How could anyone..."

Then she stiffened and straightened. "Boys," she said to her roomers, "please take my mother to the church."

"What about you?" Barry asked.

"In a bit," she answered tightly. "In a bit."

"They're ready for you," Molly said to the students. "I'll stay here for now. In case Lynn needs anything."

But all Lynn could do was stare at the destruction. As if trying to believe it. As if mentally and emotionally trying to grasp the catastrophe.

Jax stood with her, wishing he had more to offer than a hug. Then he urged her to follow the others to the church. "You can face it in the morning," he said firmly. "In the morning light. It's not going away."

Neither was he.

GOOD SHEPHERD CHURCH boasted a large basement hall for gatherings. Old fieldstone walls encased it, covered these days with banners for various organizations. Guarded by a wooden cross with golden rays surrounding it. Stacked chairs lined the sides, six cots had been prepared with sheets, pillows and brightly colored quilts.

A group of women had come out of nowhere and had started making hot soup, coffee and toast. Nancy marched into the group and joined them in preparing the food. "Keeping busy," she said. "Before I find someone to kill."

The firefighters had been invited down for hot soup and coffee. They paraded through in their turnout gear, jackets hanging open now, helmets gone. The students each sat on the edge of a cot, looking so out of place, as if they didn't know what to do.

Lynn couldn't stop pacing. Jax watched her, seething with an anger he couldn't show. Wanting to wrap her up in comfort and safety, a safety he couldn't promise.

"I'll fix it," he heard her mutter as she strode by him, rubbing her upper arms, wrapping herself tightly in them. "I'll fix it all."

It was the same grit that had carried her through the loss of Matt, the remodeling of his family's house and a lawsuit by her brother-in-law. Jax wanted to be there to help with every step of her recovery. But first he had to deal with an assassin. To make her safe from that. To make himself safe enough for her to be around.

TERRI ALBRIGHT WAS in a hellish mood, burning with anger. Yeah, she'd wanted to give Luke a bit of help with his house problem to keep suckering him along, but she hadn't wanted anything like this. Maybe she should have believed him when he'd said if he couldn't have that damn house then neither could Lynn. A male reaction. The same kind of reaction that made men grow violent over a divorce. But this made the whole situation more dangerous, hanging around a guy who would probably become the primary suspected arsonist.

Damn, she'd planned to go with him to the fundraiser in the afternoon, the one planned to rebuild that outdated motel. She was sick of hearing how it was a landmark. That fleabag?

But she figured that in a crowd, clinging to Luke as if he were God's gift, she'd look innocent enough, much as acting like that sickened her. She was no insecure teenager to hang on a guy the way she pretended to hang on Luke. But he made her part of the local scene. He gave her a chance to watch Stone and possibly separate him from the herd as night fell.

Now this. She had to work it to her advantage somehow. Maybe it would be enough to make Stone move on to Denver, now that he wouldn't have anywhere to stay. He hadn't been in that house long enough to develop any kind of enduring relationship with the Macy woman.

No reason for him to hang out in this two-bit town that laughably called itself a city.

She still wanted to bash Luke's face in. The guy was a damn fool. He'd done thousands of dollars of damage to a house he wanted to claim as his own. Did he somehow think this fire would make Lynn Macy give up the house? Did he really just want to ruin what he couldn't have? He'd said so, but was he really that twisted?

Well, maybe he was. What did Terri care if she could turn it to her own ends?

Maybe, she thought as the morning began to arrive with a pale gray light, the fire would provide enough of a distraction to keep anyone else from paying attention to Stone's disappearance.

Because she *could* make him disappear. There was a lot of empty land around this town, land where a body could get lost forever.

She pulled her open sleeping bag tighter around her shoulders as she sat staring at the slowly brightening sky. Then she lit her camp stove and boiled water for instant coffee, for hydrating that dried-out crap that some called food.

After this, she was going to have a big, juicy steak. For now, she considered her waning time for this mission, and decided that if Stone didn't leave fast, she *had* to do him here.

And maybe give Luke some payback.

NOBODY SLEPT IN the church hall that night. Everyone was too wound up. Soup simmered on the stove, the bevy of women who had showed up to cook had taken their departure. The firemen had vanished.

Then came the police, along with Melinda, who owned the bakery. With helpers, she arrived with sweet rolls and breads fresh from her ovens. A few others trickled in, among them Edith Jasper, this time without her dog, Bailey. Earl Carter arrived shortly after her and focused his attention on Nancy West.

Well, that was blossoming, Jax thought. He hoped it would help make Lynn happy despite the night's tragedy.

Sheriff Gage Dalton stepped up to Jax. "It seems fire follows you."

"Unfortunately." He met Gage's dark eyes. "You think it's linked with the motel?"

"We've surely got us an arsonist. And no, I don't think it's you. But this fire doesn't need the fire marshal to tell me it's no accident. Notice anything unusual around the house?"

"Just Luke Macy, and I gather he's not unusual."

Dalton chuckled. "Oh, he's unusual all right. But not just as an annoying visitor to Lynn. So nothing?"

"I've been…watching for something out of place," Jax said reluctantly.

One of Gage's brows lifted. "Trouble on your tail?"

"Maybe so. But it's directed at *me*."

"How bad?"

Jax shrugged. "Nothing I can't handle."

Gage nodded slowly. "If you remember anything, or need my help, let me know."

Jax agreed, then looked around at the other deputies who were taking statements from Nancy and the boys. It didn't require much time. None of the house's residents had been aware of anything until the fire.

As the day outside the basement windows brightened, Lynn came over to Jax, who had paced nearly as much as she had. Anger still burned in him, but for now his concern for her triumphed. One blow too many for this brave young woman?

"I'm going back to the house," she said tautly. "I have to see the damage."

"I'm sure it's extensive." His answer was cautious. Just then her face was so stiff he couldn't read her.

"Oh, I'm sure, too," she answered almost bitterly. "I want to blame Luke, but why would he try to burn down the house he wants?"

Good question, Jax thought. Just as they were approaching the basement stairs, Madge appeared. Her jacket was open, just enough to display her ample cleavage.

She simpered beautifully when she saw Jax. "I guess you'll be needing to find somewhere to stay, Jax. I have an extra bedroom…"

Lynn cut her off. "You're making a fool of yourself, Madge. Leave the man alone."

Then she shouldered past Madge and started climbing. Jax smothered a grin and followed right after her as if Madge didn't exist. He took some small pleasure in the moment.

The walk to the house didn't take very long. A couple of blocks. Lynn ate up the distance, her strides long, maybe driven by fear of what she would find, or perhaps by fury. Or perhaps by a determination to see the full dimension of the destruction she faced.

They came around the corner and Lynn stopped so suddenly that Jax nearly bumped into her. "What?" he asked.

She pointed and breathed, "Oh, my God."

He looked down the street and astonishment flooded him. A small lumber truck filled the street in front of her house, fully loaded. A dumpster occupied her front yard and men on ladders were tearing away the porch roof.

"I can't afford this," she whispered.

He studied the scene and felt an unusual warmth grow in old, cold places inside him. "Somehow I don't think you'll have to."

She looked sharply at him, then continued her march down the street. One of the men supervising from the sidewalk greeted her with a smile from beneath an orange hard hat. Tall and lanky with a weathered face, he wore jeans and a shearling jacket. Worn work boots encased his feet.

"It'll take a few days, Lynn, but we'll get this fixed for you."

"But Len, how do I pay for all this?"

"You don't," he answered with a shake of his head. "You're one of my best customers, to begin with. Then a funny thing happened. A bunch of guys showed up and volunteered. Can't do much about how this is making you feel, but we can fix the property damage."

Jax saw a tear run down Lynn's face. "Oh, Len..."

He waved a hand. "We all know how you feel. Just glad we can help. Now you go back to the church, eat something and stay warm. You'll be surprised by the end of the day."

"I don't know what to say," Lynn said as she and Jazz walked back to Good Shepherd.

"How about that sometimes people can be wonderful?"

"They can, can't they."

"I've seen the worst in people, but I've also seen the best. And the best is pretty amazing." Which was true. When you saw a man give his life to save a buddy... Well, people didn't get much better than that.

LYNN WAS STILL overwhelmed by the time they reached the church basement. Now Maude and her daughter, Mavis, had showed up with plenty of hot food.

"Soup ain't enough." Maude sniffed as she thrust foam containers at the two of them. "Now sit down and get something warm inside you."

Chairs had been stacked along one wall, ready for meetings, and the boys had pulled a few off the stacks. Nancy sat on one of them, conversing with Barry.

She looked up at Lynn. "It'll be okay," she offered quietly.

Lynn swallowed hard. "Apparently so. Len Danvers is already out there with a crew, ripping out the mess. How did your knees survive the excitement?"

Nancy smiled. "These boys of yours practically carried me all the way here. Remarkable young men."

All three looked uncomfortable at the praise.

"You *are* remarkable," Lynn told them. "All of you. And thanks for the warning last night."

"Lucky we were still playing video games," Tom answered. He elbowed Will. "Except this sleepyhead kept dozing off."

"Did not."

"No, you just lost a thousand points without clicking a button," Barry retorted. He and Tom both snickered, while Will looked embarrassed.

"Eat," Maude demanded, hands on her ample hips.

"All of you. I didn't carry all this damn food over here to have it ignored."

"Yes, ma'am," Barry answered meekly.

Maude snorted. "You won't sell me that attitude, boy."

Barry clearly tried to smother a grin.

Nancy had opened her box and picked delicately at the mound of home fries. "How are you going to pay Len for the work?" she asked bluntly, heedless of who might hear.

"Apparently I don't have to." Amazement touched Lynn's face once again.

Nancy nodded with satisfaction. "That's the kind of neighbors I remember. I guess this town hasn't changed all that much in nearly twenty years."

Lynn nodded, reaching at last for the omelet in her box. "I have a lot of good neighbors. It's overwhelming."

She had finished half her omelet when Luke Macy showed up. Lynn felt Jax stiffen beside her and heard her mother mutter something.

"Lynn," he called from across the basement, hurrying toward her. "I just heard. My God!" He dragged another chair over so he could sit facing her. "I am so sorry!"

"Sorry for what?" she snapped. "That *your* house is damaged?"

"No, no," he said hastily, reaching for her hands. She jerked them back and would have spilled the remains of her breakfast if Jax hadn't snapped out a hand to grab the container and pull it away.

"Lynn, please," Luke said, looking wounded. "I just wanted to offer my sympathy. I want to help with the repairs."

Lynn had had enough. "Leave me alone, Luke Macy.

And if you ever set foot in my yard again, you'll be trespassing. Do I make myself clear?"

"But Lynn…"

Edith Jasper, who'd been over at the food table talking with Maude, spoke up loudly. "You, Luke. Yes, I'm talking to you. When a lady tells you to get lost, you'd better get lost. You wouldn't know anything about that ugly rumor that started running around last week, would you? Because it's got your fingerprints all over it."

"I never—"

"You heard the lady," Jax said, rising, towering over Luke. His voice was steely, his posture subtly threatening.

Luke looked up at him and decided to skedaddle. Without another word, he strode away and up the stairs.

"I can't believe the nerve!" Nancy exclaimed.

"Me neither," Tom said. "Don't you worry, Lynn. We see him in the yard, we'll send him on his way, won't we, guys?"

The other two nodded.

"What's the rest of this rumor?" Lynn asked quietly. Another problem, another thing to worry about.

"Pay it no mind," Edith Jasper said. "We're taking care of it. Aren't we, Maude?"

"Damn straight," said the heavyset woman. "Sorry, I got to get back to my diner. I'll be back with lunch, just before the fundraiser for the La-Z-Rest. What's this town coming to?"

With a shake of her head, she pulled on her coat and departed with her daughter, Mavis, on her heels.

TERRI ALBRIGHT WANTED to throttle Luke Macy. Right on the spot and damn the witnesses. They were meeting in Mahoney's bar and she'd insisted on a back booth. They were supposed to be acting like lovebirds, but at that moment she could barely control her face.

"What do you mean you're not taking me to the fundraiser?" she asked quietly.

Luke looked startled. "What do you care about a stupid fundraiser?"

She struggled to smile adoringly. "You said you'd help me meet people. There'll be lots of people there."

"None I want to see."

She leaned forward, trying to appear girlish and disappointed. She hoped he couldn't read murder anywhere in her expression. "You promised," she pouted.

"We can do other things."

"I don't want to do other things. Just for a little while. Please?" Now she was wheedling and hated the sound of her own voice.

He signaled for another beer. "Okay, what the hell. But I want you to spend the night."

More fury rose in her. This sleaze expected her to pay with her body for a small favor? He was lucky his beer didn't wind up in his face.

"We'll see," she said coyly, glad she didn't have to try to blush. As if she could.

"There's no *we'll see* about it," he said flatly. "You're playing me."

That was so close to the truth that Terri was astonished. The fool actually had enough sense to realize that? She couldn't afford to lose him yet. Her mind swiftly calculated her next move.

She summoned a hurt expression. "I am not," she answered. "How could you even think that of me? Maybe I don't want to go with you *anywhere* now."

That took him aback. "I didn't mean… Oh, okay. We'll go to this damn thing. No strings. But not for long."

"Thank you," she cooed.

And wished for a hot shower to wash him off.

Chapter Seventeen

After the lads and Jax had folded up the cots and leaned them against the wall and had helped open the lengths of folding tables that nearly filled the basement, the fundraiser began.

First came the men and women bearing delectable cakes, pies and cookies for sale. A ton of food. There were even crafts, hand-stitched quilts, knitted sweaters and scarves, and some very pretty handmade jewelry. Beautifully embroidered linens took up a large space on one table. Pastor Canton had offered a door prize of fifty dollars.

Local businesses had leaped in to help as well, making every kind of donation from winter clothing to groceries.

In fact, the long tables were loaded with donations, all proceeds to go to rebuilding the motel and helping its hapless owners.

Quite a well-organized little do, Jax thought. He was surprised by the number of people who turned up, people more than willing to purchase a glass of hot cider on a cold day, glad to pay for a ticket for a free meal, or to purchase so many of the other donated goods.

Purses and wallets opened easily among people he

was sure didn't have much extra money to spare. All for a good cause.

Like Len Danvers busy working on Lynn's porch.

Jax hadn't noticed anything like this when he'd lived here as a kid. In his isolation, it had all passed by him, escaping his awareness.

God, he'd been bent.

Lynn's mood appeared to have improved, although he couldn't tell if it was a front. If it was, she was doing a great job of it, constantly moving and smiling and helping where she could.

Then Luke Macy arrived with that girl on his arm, the one with the black bob and purple streaks. That hair was memorable. He watched with interest as Luke guided her around the tables, as she cooed over things and managed to get him to buy her a few trinkets from the woman selling handmade jewelry.

It seemed to Jax that Luke withdrew his wallet reluctantly. Tightwad.

But as the couple left after only a short visit, he noted something in the woman's movements.

It niggled at him. Something upright in her posture when she escaped Luke's arm for a minute. Something in the way she moved. Uneasiness prickled him even as he reminded himself he'd probably seen her before around town.

He couldn't escape the feeling there was something more.

But damn it all if he knew what it was.

As IF BY MAGIC, all the donations disappeared in around four hours and the raffle prize was awarded. Quite a few folks lingered for a while, chatting as they drank coffee or cider, some even eating their recent purchases. Molly Canton moved among them, smiling pleasantly, thanking them all for coming.

Eventually, though, the inevitable cleanup began. Some people remained behind to help. Lynn, the students and Jax pitched in as well. Edith supervised, declaring that her age made her well suited to management. A lot of laughs answered her as good-humored people worked.

Then the basement became a shelter again. Tables gone except for two with chairs around them. Cots once again ready to hold refugees such as Lynn and Nancy.

"It went well," Lynn remarked to Jax as at last they sat at one of those tables with fresh coffee and a large walnut coffee cake between them. "Unfortunately, I don't know how much it will help the Blent family, the ones who own the motel."

He blew gently on his coffee, then sipped. "Every bit helps. Even if they had insurance, there are still the deductibles."

"I didn't think of that." She sighed, pushing a stray auburn lock behind her ear. "I suppose now I'll have to think about deductibles, too. And I guess I'd better call *my* agent. Len's a dear soul, but he shouldn't have to bear that cost alone."

"I think Len's more interested in getting things squared away as fast as possible for you, to allow you to go home again."

She smiled faintly. "He probably is."

Nancy joined them. Someone had even rustled up some tea bags for her. "Isn't this cozy?" she remarked lightly. "A few curtains, a couple of easy chairs, some low lighting instead of that miserable overhead fluorescent tubing? It would be perfect."

Lynn nearly choked on her coffee. "Mom!"

Nancy laughed. "Knew that would get you. It's been an awful day in so many ways, but a good one, too, if you know what I mean. We had hundreds of people go through here this afternoon, and from what Molly says, many more dropped donations in the bucket just inside the church door. It's always nice to see so many people pull together."

"It's a good feeling," Lynn agreed. But inwardly, she was still reeling. Her house was a mess, but that could be repaired one way or the other. It was the fire that bothered her more than anything else. Arson. Who the hell would hate her so much?

The only person she could think of was Luke. But he wanted the house, too. Why would he set a fire?

There was the motel fire, too. Maybe just an arsonist running around town? That was truly scary. Any of her neighbors and friends could become the next targets. And what kind of person got a thrill from setting fires, especially fires that could kill people?

She didn't want to ever know someone like that. But it *could* be someone she knew, even if only distantly.

Through all the riot of emotions that had swarmed through her today, this was the first time she felt the icy trickle of fear.

What next? Who next? Herself again?

Desperate to escape this new anxiety, she rose. "I'm going to look at what Len accomplished today."

Jax stood immediately. "I'm going with you."

She was so grateful for his company and felt weak for wanting it. She could take care of herself. She always had.

But something was different this time.

Malice.

TERRI WANTED TO ditch Luke, wanted badly to *throw* him into a ditch. Everything about him disgusted her, but his utter lack of loyalty, his utter lack of honor—these were intolerable. Luke was a man without purpose except his own gratification.

He was a weak, selfish, childish man who used charm to oil his way through his petty cons. But that charm was only skin-deep. The man inside was a cesspool filled with snakes. And they weren't even deadly snakes. The rub of it was that she'd need him at least a little longer.

But he'd given her what she wanted. Recognized now by any who gave a damn, she was *Luke's new girl*, able to walk around town as freely as anyone. And today's trip to the fundraiser had given her an added bit of intelligence. Stone was joined at the hip with that Macy woman. She doubted she'd be able to separate them long enough to get him alone.

She might have to kill them both. But this time the idea didn't daunt her. Instead, it excited her.

A new plan began to take shape in her head.

LUKE WAS ANGRY with Terri. She'd expected him to pay for her every drink, her every meal and now that ridiculous costume jewelry at the fundraiser.

And that business about wanting to go to the fundraiser to meet people? She'd hardly talked to a soul.

But she *had* clung to his arm and hung on his every word. He was mad that she'd refused to come home with him, but, he reminded himself, her reluctance would make the conquest all the sweeter.

After a third beer, wondering where the hell the girl had gone, he had soothed himself. Having her hang on

him like that, look up at him with adoring eyes for all
the world to see...

Well, that swelled his ego pleasantly. He'd never
minded when someone had made him feel important,
look important.

Because somewhere deep inside, Luke knew he'd
never been important.

But he was important now. To Terri. And to Lynn,
whether she knew it or not. He was going to enjoy seeing
that house burned to the ground. No one would have it
then, and destroying all her ridiculous hard work would
only make it better.

He wished that damn Marine would leave, though. It
would make his life so much simpler.

LYNN AND JAX walked toward her house. The evening
wind had taken on a sharp bite as daylight began to fail.

Astonishing Lynn, Jax reached for her hand and held
it. All she wanted, she realized, was to be back in bed
with him in her attic. Under the covers or in front of
her electric fireplace, sharing some wine, maybe some
cheese. Talking. Getting to know one another better.
Finding heaven in each other's arms.

No. It couldn't happen, and not only because of the
fire. He wore a uniform. He could be called into danger
at any moment, maybe never to return. Going to be a
recruiter right now didn't make him safe in the future.

And Matt had taught her the dimensions of real loss.

Seeking to corral her thoughts, she said, "You got that
phone call yesterday. Or was it the day before? Everything's running together."

"A hell of a lot has been happening."

"No kidding." She hesitated, plunging in even though

she felt she had no right. "You tensed. You have to go back on duty soon, don't you."

It wasn't a question. Nor did he offer her a denial. "Yes," he said. "It's only to Denver. I'll come back to visit."

To *visit*? Oh, she wanted much more than that, but had no right to ask.

Then, as she sometimes did, she felt Matt with her, a warm presence that occasionally seemed to be watching over her. She felt a glimmer of reassurance. *It will be all right.*

The front of her house was illuminated by floodlights, probably driving the neighbors crazy. Len was there, however, loading up his truck to leave.

"Sorry we can't take the Dumpster away yet," he said to Lynn. "There's still some more demolition to do. We got the building permit and I persuaded the inspector to come out and look this over."

"Thank you," she answered, staring up at the front of her house. A tarp covered the porch roof, sealing out the elements. "Big job," she said quietly.

"Not that big," Len said bracingly. "Some roof joists need replacing, of course all the roofing. A few slats of siding, but the good news is the inspector found no damage inside the house wall. Some of the gingerbread on the porch took it on the chin, though."

"Oh, God."

Len laughed. "I remember your misery at having to paint all that stuff. Trust me, we'll make it as good as new."

Lynn faced him. "Keep good records, Len. Of the damage and of the work you're doing. I'll get on the insurance company tomorrow."

Len touched the brim of his hard hat. "Photos, photos and more photos. I think I've taken more than the fire marshal. Anyway, a little more checking out in the morning, then I think you and your roomers can move back in, as long as you're willing to use the back door."

"That would be wonderful!"

"The church basement ain't no place to live." Then he looked at Jax. "You keep an eye on her."

"I intend to," Jax replied.

As she and Jazz strode back to Good Shepherd, a new feeling filled Lynn. Snow began to fall lightly, sparkling in the glow of streetlights and lamplight from within houses.

"Christmas will be here soon," Lynn remarked.

"Time flies."

"Yeah. But I was just remembering how, when I was younger, the sight of the first snow flurries filled me with such excitement. Such a sense of wonder."

Then she turned her head to look at him. "As horrible as this day has been in so many ways, I'm feeling a touch of that wonder now."

He squeezed her hand. "I may be feeling a touch of wonder, too," he answered.

A remarkable statement from him, Lynn thought. From a man who had probably known very little wonder in his life.

BACK AT THE church basement, Lynn and Jax found her three roomers and Nancy involved in a cutthroat game of Scrabble.

"She's beating us," Will said, looking up. "All those seven-letter words!"

"At my age, young man, I have a head full of more

words than you." Her eyes twinkled. "Especially since I was a legal assistant."

"No fair," Tom muttered, but the other two guys laughed.

Barry looked up from reaching in the bag for more tiles to ask Lynn, "How's the house?"

"Len said there'll be another inspection in the morning, but we may be able to move back in."

"Oh, gawd," Will said. "Back to homework. I like it better here."

Tom and Barry laughed.

Smiling again, Lynn made her way to the coffeepot and returned to the table where the huge coffee cake had amazingly lost half its volume.

"Maude brought sandwiches," Nancy said. "In that refrigerator. Salads, too."

Lynn looked at Jax and saw him smiling. The day still held warmth and wonders despite everything.

Chapter Eighteen

As soon as Terri heard that Lynn Macy was moving back into her house, she got ready to put her plan into action. Luke wasn't going to like it, but that was fine by her. In fact, she relished the coming event, the look that would appear on his face.

Jackson Stone liked to walk at night. Nearly every night. He'd given her the sense that he was alert, looking for something. Maybe he'd heard about the two other jurors? But why would someone have warned him all the way out here?

It didn't matter. He was probably just that way after too much combat. And the deaths would never be traced to her. Never. She'd been careful. But still, he'd been hyperaware. If he thought someone was looking to kill him, he'd never suspect Luke's current bimbo with the purple sprayed hair. Which was the whole point of her playacting.

But she needed a way to distract him, to turn his hero instincts against him. And she knew just how to do it.

Luke was born to be her foil.

THE FOIL HIMSELF had begun to feel irritated, ego notwithstanding. Luke made up his mind that he was going to force the issue with that young woman. As a college student, she had nothing to offer him except a roll in the hay. No money, no steady job to support him and apparently no inclination to be domestic.

Imagine her wheedling that stupid jewelry out of him. Imagine that he had actually paid for it. Imagine her refusing his mild suggestion that she come to his place, just a suggestion.

Yeah, tonight or tomorrow night he was going to push it with her or drop her. See how she liked that kettle of fish.

Satisfied with his decision, he ordered another beer and was glad she wasn't there giving him doe eyes. He was beginning to distrust those doe eyes, flattering or not.

THE AFTERNOON OF their return to the house, the boys departed to resume their normal schedules. Nancy took up her station in the kitchen with the teakettle near at hand. Jax made a pot of coffee.

And Lynn wandered around the house, especially the front, looking for interior damage. She could find none. Thank God.

Len showed up to tell her they had the county's go-ahead and that he'd ordered matching shingles for the roof and some siding for replacements.

"As for the gingerbread…"

Lynn groaned. "Can't do it?"

"Oh, we can do it. A guy who does woodworking said it would be fun, so he's heating up his lathe and I've given him some sturdy oak to work with. I've even got some new beadboard for the porch ceiling. It's gonna be like nothing ever happened."

"Oh, Len." Lynn started to choke up. "I have a call in to the insurance company."

Len waved a hand. "They'll take forever. I'm not worried about it. This work gets done before winter sets in. Final word."

He refused a cup of coffee and left smiling, as if very pleased with himself.

"I can't believe this," Lynn said to her mother and Jax. "I just can't believe this."

"Enjoy it," Nancy suggested. "You've got some good people taking care of you."

"I certainly do."

Jax watched as more good people showed up—Lynn's friends, including Lily Robbins, who'd been maid of honor at his buddy's wedding, and her daughter, Iris, who struck him as a pistol. Casseroles arrived along with the friends and neighbors until Nancy began fussing about where she was supposed to put them all.

Lynn laughed for the first time since the fire. "Manage it, Mom. Or I could invite everyone to sit at the refectory table in the kitchen for a supper."

"Might not be a bad idea," Nancy muttered as she limped around the kitchen, moving covered dishes. "Those boys of yours better have good appetites."

Lynn studied her mother. "Mom?"

"What?"

"How's your arthritis? You're limping."

"I didn't have my medication at the church. It'll start working soon."

"But maybe you should sit down."

Nancy shook her head firmly. "Haven't you heard? My physical therapist says it all the time. *Motion is lotion.* In other words, use it."

"Or lose it," Jax remarked.

"Exactly, young man. You Marines get it."

"Knee replacement?" Lynn suggested gently.

Nancy snorted. "The problem will have to get a lot worse before I'll endure that. Now quit worrying. Just help me figure out where to put all these casseroles. Sinful to waste food."

Many of the casseroles made their way into the upright freezer Lynn had on her mud porch. "I almost never use it," she remarked.

"It'll get a workout now. Nobody's going to cook for at least a week. And we're going to have this beautiful eggplant parmesan for dinner tonight. Although those young lads probably won't want any." Nancy put her hands on her hips. "I've noticed the mere word *eggplant* makes youngsters run for the hills."

"More for me," Jax remarked. He was enjoying all this fussing and bustling, enjoyed seeing so many people concerned about Lynn. She was far from alone in this town.

Tomorrow, he decided. He'd leave tomorrow. She'd be safe among all these people, and if he did have a killer on his tail, he'd drag that tail to the big city with him.

NANCY RETIRED EARLY, and Lynn looked at Jax with clear longing. "Join me upstairs?"

"Wild horses couldn't keep me away." Especially now with coming sorrow riding his shoulders. Tomorrow he was going to leave this woman. To ensure her safety. To give her space to decide that she really didn't want him in her life after all.

Because he was sure she didn't. The uniform. The uncertain life. His own mixed-up past that sometimes still made him doubt his own judgment.

This was purely sexual need on her part, he told himself as he mounted the stairs behind her. An itch being scratched. As kind and nice as she was, she was also human enough to want a man's touches. She'd never dream she might hurt him.

And he was human enough to give in to his own desires. But he had to get out to protect her from a possible killer and most certainly from a growing need that might leave her feeling bereft all over again.

Upstairs, she moved around, turning on a few lamps, starting her electric fireplace. Instantly, the room became as cozy as he was sure she had intended.

The coziness drew them together. No hesitation. Knowledge of each other's desires was strong enough to throw away any reluctance, imagined or otherwise.

He undressed her slowly with hands that almost trembled. He trailed his lips across each new bit of skin he bared, finally latching his mouth to her erect nipple and drawing a groan from her. Before he could do more, she jumped into the bed and pulled the covers up.

"Hurry up, Marine," she teased. "This gal won't wait forever."

He grinned and shed his own clothes faster than if an alert had sounded. Moments later he was under the covers with her, giving her the opportunity to explore him with her hands and mouth. To bewitch him as his loins throbbed so hard it was almost painful.

At last he rolled over, catching her wrists, his mouth finding its way to her throat. "You're driving me to the edge of insanity."

"You aren't the only one," she whispered. "Oh, Jax, fill me. Please fill me."

He slid into her warm depths, welcomed by her heated embrace. He'd never wanted anything more.

He never would.

LATER, LYING IN bliss beneath the comforter, the attic grown warm around them, they hugged tightly. But reality intruded. It always did.

"When are you leaving?" she asked a long time later, running a fingertip along his upper arm. Causing another shudder of desire to rocket through him.

He didn't want to answer, didn't want this time ruined. "Jax?"

"Tomorrow," he said finally. "I have to find a place to stay and time is limited." The truth. He hoped she didn't keep pressing because he rarely lied and didn't want to start with her.

But she murmured one more question. "Will you come back sometimes?"

His heart squeezed until he didn't know if he could force a word out. "I said I would. Just as soon as I can." *If* he could. If he didn't get himself killed.

That was the truth. Sometimes an omission was necessary.

LUKE STARED AT Terri as if she'd lost her mind. "A walk? At two in the morning? It's cold out there," he said.

She'd expected some stubbornness. She knew, however, from scoping out the situation that Stone liked his middle-of-the-night walks. She needed this opportunity and she'd figured out how to use it. How to use Luke.

"I like to look at the stars," she said, making herself pout. Although the pout wasn't all pretense. If he interfered with her...

"Oh, hell," he said.

They were leaving the bar, Luke pleasantly full of beer, Terri as clearheaded as she'd been in her entire life. "Just a short one," she said softly, running a finger along his cheek. "Then we can go warm up. At your place?"

She watched the change happen. He looked less annoyed now, and far more hopeful. "My place," he repeated. "Okay, then. A walk. But I still think you're nuts."

She managed a giggle. "Nuts is what you want."

JAX SLIPPED OUT of the warm bed, his every cell reluctant to leave Lynn. "I'm going to take a walk," he said, dropping a kiss on her lips. "Just a short one."

"I can come with you."

He gazed at her, allowing himself these few stolen moments. He understood that she didn't want him out of her sight. Well, he didn't want to be, either.

"You know I like my walks. Well, my jogs."

She nodded slowly.

"Keep the bed warm for me," he said gently. "You probably won't like it when I slip like a Popsicle back under those covers, though."

That drew a laugh from her, a sound he liked to hear. "Early morning with the roof," he said as he dressed. "I know you won't be able to keep out of it."

Again she laughed. "You know me too well. But I want to come anyway." She started to throw back the covers.

Then he spoke difficult words, words that sliced them both. "No. I don't want you to come."

The sudden hurt on her face nearly killed him. Now

he'd done the last thing on earth he ever wanted to do: he'd wounded her.

But, he thought as he descended the stairs, he needed to make a target of himself this one last time. The need to clear this up was driving him harder with each passing day. The closer he drew to Lynn, the more he wanted this killer stopped.

His own skin had begun to matter a lot more to him than it ever had. Because of Lynn. Because for the first time in a long, long time, he wanted to see the sun rise on a new day. Because for the first time in forever, he wanted to build a future.

The night had grown downright cold. People would be staying indoors. Yeah, the hour helped, but even in this small town, people were out at odd hours. Staggering home too full of booze. Walking dogs.

But this was all part of the plan he'd been seeding. Nearly empty streets made an attack easier. Following the same damn path every night made him easy to find. He'd learned long ago that developing habits could be dangerous. This time it might also be helpful.

He'd been out only fifteen minutes when he heard footsteps behind him. His neck prickled but then he heard a man's voice, a woman's quiet laugh.

A couple. The killer after him wouldn't be part of a couple.

He kept walking, sensing that at least one of them was watching him. He supposed he was a matter of slight interest at that hour. But the back of his neck wouldn't stop prickling.

Let it be, he told himself. *Wait for the moment—if it comes.*

Then he heard a scuffle behind him.

TERRI'S MOMENT HAD COME. She knew how Stone would react. The fun part, aside from killing Stone, was what she was about to do to Luke.

The smile that appeared on her face was unpleasant. Ugly even.

"I don't want to go home with you," she said loudly enough to be heard.

"But you said…"

Stone's steps ahead of them had slowed.

"No, you heard what you wanted to," Terri said, her voice rising. "Leave me alone!"

"Terri…"

"Get your hands off me, you pervert!"

STONE TURNED. THE woman was pummeling the guy. What the hell? He started back.

Terri shoved Luke hard, catching one of his feet with one of her own, causing him to stagger and grab her for balance, just as she wanted.

Stone was coming. *Ever the hero*, she thought, both satisfied and bitter. She shoved her hand into the pocket of her parka, finding the unsheathed KA-BAR. Just a few seconds and Stone would be there.

"What are you doing with a knife?" she cried at Luke, stepping back, pretending to struggle against Luke's grip. She pulled out the knife, letting it flash just briefly in the dim light.

"My God," she screamed. "What's that knife? Help!"

At this point it didn't matter if neighbors started to pull on robes to come onto their porches. She needed only a few seconds now.

"Terri," Luke shouted. "Please…"

JAX SAW THE knife glisten. He couldn't tell which of them held it, but it must be the guy or the woman wouldn't scream like that.

He shouted, "Stop it now!"

The woman shoved Luke again just as Jax reached her, his eyes fixed on the knife.

Then he knew.

TERRI TURNED, READY to stab Stone just under the ribs, to drag the knife down and gut him. He was so close the outcome was inevitable.

But just as she thrust the blade toward him, only a foot away, he grabbed her forearm as quickly as a striking cobra, wrenching it until she lost her grip on the KA-BAR.

"You must be Theresa Albright," he said as he whirled her around and seized both her wrists behind her back. His tone was like ice. Or like the steel she'd just dropped.

When she heard her name, she knew it was over. Her brother would never be avenged.

Chapter Nineteen

In the very wee hours, the Sheriff's Office swirled with activity.

Terri Albright had been escorted to a holding cell just upstairs. Luke Macy sat in a chair, still shaking from his close call with that lying woman.

Jax had given his statement more than once. The only truly upsetting part was that he'd had to call Lynn and tell her he wouldn't be back until sometime later in the morning. Twenty minutes later she'd appeared in the office, her gaze wide and worried. She took one of the chairs lined up in front of the windows and waited.

Jax wanted to go to her and reassure her, but he wasn't yet free to. Two trips to the interrogation room would probably be followed by yet another, and he'd been warned not to speak to anyone. He tried to make a helpless gesture with his hands, hoping she'd get the message that he wasn't avoiding her. She didn't respond in any way.

His earlier fury gave way to a heart-sinking sensation. How would he ever explain to her why he'd withheld so much information? Would she even care at this point?

He doubted it. He turned back to the officer whose desk he sat beside. Lynn shouldn't even be here.

Gage Dalton emerged from the back offices and waved him to come. Jax rose and followed him down the hallway, this time to the sheriff's own office.

Gage waved him to a seat. "Let's go through this again. This woman was out to kill everyone who helped get her brother convicted of war crimes, right?"

"Exactly."

"And you were informed of this by the JAG attorney who prosecuted the case?"

"Yes."

Gage sighed and tossed a pencil on his desk. "No one else knew about this."

"No."

"Why didn't you tell me about this?"

"Because there wasn't a damn thing you or anyone else could do. Hugh had no idea at first if that was what was really happening. Then investigators decided that *might* be the case. It wasn't until just lately that they figured out the killer was Albright's sister Terri. Hell, I wasn't even looking for a woman."

Gage gave a crooked smile. "We're all guilty of that mistake too often."

"*I* sure was."

Gage rocked his creaky chair slowly. "The fire at the motel? Was that her?"

Jax shrugged. "You'll have to ask her."

"She's a clam. Already demanded a lawyer. I guess she took that thing about name, rank and serial number to heart."

Jax leaned forward. "She didn't take the right things to heart."

"Apparently not." Gage sighed again. "I wager that blithering fool Luke Macy was responsible for the fire on Lynn's roof. He'll probably sing for us. As much as he knows anyway. I hope this rattled some sense into that man."

Jax's answer was dry. "I bet that's the first time he's ever had a woman draw a knife on him."

A chuckle escaped Gage. "Probably more than one wished they had. We have the number for Hugh Briggs, so we'll call him in the morning and get the full scoop from that end. At least as much as the investigators will share. In the meantime, scoot. From the look of her, I think you have some fence-mending to do with Lynn."

More than a little, Jax thought as he made his way to her through the outer office. More than a little.

He halted in front of her. "Take you home, lady?"

A minute passed before she finally stood. "Yes."

When they finally reached her house, the first light of dawn filtered through foggy air. She took a long look at him.

"You," she said, "aren't even safe off the battlefield."

Then she marched to the attic without offering him an invitation.

Nancy, wrapped in a flowered robe, appeared in the doorway of the kitchen. "Coffee, soldier? You're going to need it."

He followed her briskly, telling himself he had survived worse.

But it sure as hell didn't feel like it.

LYNN REAPPEARED AT midmorning, dressed for work. Without a word, she marched into the living room and picked up her pry bar. A minute later she was banging on walls, her thuds a counterpoint to the hammering from her porch.

"Lynn."

She stopped banging as if she sensed Jax in the doorway. "You said you were going to Denver, that you needed to find a place to live. Why are you still here?"

"Because I don't want to go."

Her arm paused midswing. "Yeah. Sure. You've been lying to me the whole time you've been here. You didn't trust me. Seems like you should have left at the beginning."

Every muscle in his body tightened at her rejection and accusation. Words, however, were far from adequate to mend this rupture. He must have taken leave of his senses, because she was right. "I didn't know at first. Then I didn't want to worry you."

"Then you should have just marched on."

He hesitated, then laid himself on the line. "I couldn't leave you."

A flimsy excuse, however true. It sounded weak to him even now. When her face remained unyielding, he turned, saying over his shoulder, "I'll be gone in an hour."

The loss of Lynn was going to stand right at the top of all his losses. A wound that might scar over but would ever be part of him.

Hell. He should have done something different. *Anything* different. He'd failed her. And himself.

LYNN TURNED BACK to the wall, beating it with the crowbar, not caring if she did additional damage. But tears began to run down her face, leaving damp trails through plaster dust.

He was leaving. For good. For the best, she argued with herself, but didn't believe it.

Tears began to turn into sobs. A man in uniform. She should have known better.

But...

She leaned against the wall as memories of her time with Jax flooded her. He was a rock-solid man, a decent man, one who had helped bring her fully back to life.

Of course he'd wanted to protect her. He'd spent his life trying to protect both his ideals and the people who depended on him. It was the kind of man he was.

She needed to accept that. Accept him. What had she wanted? Some kind of imagined perfection?

She dropped the crowbar and dashed the tears from her face. Then she marched upstairs, finding him in his room, packing his duffel.

"Where do you think you're going?" she asked.

"Denver. As you ordered."

"Oh, damn, Jax."

He straightened and faced her. "Isn't that what you want? To get this lying Marine out of your life? To return to the safety you've created for yourself?"

She winced. He was right, she *had* been trying to build a cocoon for herself. "Some safety with Luke trying to burn my house down."

One corner of his hard mouth twitched upward. "Well, apart from that jackass."

"I think he's going to be out of my hair for a while now."

Jax nodded. "He was in full confession mode, wasn't he? Wanting to disassociate himself from Theresa Albright. But that's another story for another day. All I can tell you is that when I first arrived here, I had no idea someone was after me. And when I got the first hint, it was just a hint. Nothing actionable. I also figured that if someone wanted to kill me, it'd be much easier in Denver."

She nodded and took a step toward him.

"But I was a fool," he said. "A damn fool. Every time I thought of hitting the road, I had a bazillion reasons not to leave you. *You*, Lynn. I never felt about anyone the way I felt about you."

She sighed, her heart aching and soaring all at the same time, and stepped closer. "I'm sorry I got so mad at you."

"It was understandable in the circumstances. And you're right, I can't make you safe."

"No one can. Jax…" She scoured her face with her shirtsleeve, turning damp plaster into a paste. She laughed weakly. "I'm a sight."

He crossed the two steps between them and took her into his arms. "You're a wonderful sight, Lynn. Always wonderful." He bent his head and kissed her deeply.

She was melting, she realized. Melting into him. Could she live without him? No. The realization hit her hard.

"But you have to leave," she whispered reluctantly.

"Not today, if you don't want. Not for a few more days. And I'll come back, I swear. If you want me to."

She burrowed into him. "Jax, please, don't ever leave me for good."

"I couldn't," he answered huskily. "I couldn't. I love you too much."

Her heart leaped, soaring for the heavens as she allowed her own feelings to burst through. "I love you, too. Forever."

"Start planning the wedding," he said softly. Then he swept her up in his arms and carried her up to her attic.

Downstairs, Nancy smiled knowingly and started another pot of tea.

"High time," she said to the tea bag. "High time."

* * * * *

COMING SOON!

We really hope you enjoyed reading this book.
If you're looking for more romance, be sure to
head to the shops when new books are
available on

Thursday 1st September

To see which titles are coming soon, please visit

millsandboon.co.uk/nextmonth

LET'S TALK
Romance

For exclusive extracts, competitions
and special offers, find us online:

- facebook.com/millsandboon
- @MillsandBoon
- @MillsandBoonUK

Get in touch on 01413 063232

For all the latest titles coming soon, visit
millsandboon.co.uk/nextmonth

MILLS & BOON
A ROMANCE FOR EVERY READER

- **FREE** delivery direct to your door
- **EXCLUSIVE** offers every month
- **SAVE** up to 25% on pre-paid subscriptions

SUBSCRIBE AND SAVE

millsandboon.co.uk/Subscribe

JOIN US ON SOCIAL MEDIA!

Stay up to date with our latest releases, author news and gossip, special offers and discounts, and all the behind-the-scenes action from Mills & Boon...

 @millsandboon

 @millsandboonuk

 facebook.com/millsandboon

 @millsandboonuk

It might just be true love...

GET YOUR ROMANCE FIX!

Get the latest romance news,
exclusive author interviews, story
extracts and much more!

MILLS & BOON
Desire

Indulge in secrets and scandal, intense drama and plenty of sizzling hot action with powerful and passionate heroes who have it all: wealth, status, good looks…everything but the right woman.

MILLS & BOON
True Love
Romance from the Heart

Celebrate true love with tender stories of heartfelt romance, from the rush of falling in love to the joy a new baby can bring, and a focus on the emotional heart of a relationship.